continued . . .

Armed and Glamorous

"Whether readers are fashion divas or hopelessly fashion challenged, there's a lot to like about being *Armed and Glamorous*." —BookPleasures.com

"Fans will relish *Armed and Glamorous*, a cozy starring a fashionable trench coat, essential killer heels, and designer whipping pearls." —*Midwest Book Review*

Grave Apparel

"A truly intriguing mystery." —Armchair Reader

"A fine whodunit . . . a humorous cozy."
  —The Best Reviews

"Fun and enjoyable. . . . Lacey's a likeable, sassy, and savvy heroine, and the Washington, D.C., setting is a plus." —The Romance Readers Connection

"Wonderful." —Gumshoe

Raiders of the Lost Corset

"A hilarious crime caper. . . . Readers will find themselves laughing out loud. . . . Ellen Byerrum has a hit series on her hands with her latest tale."
  —The Best Reviews

"I love this series. Lacey is such a wonderful character. . . . The plot has many twists and turns to keep you turning the pages to discover the truth. I highly recommend this book and series." —Spinetingler Magazine

"Wow. A simplistic word but one that describes this book perfectly. I loved it! I could not put it down! . . . Lacey is a scream and she's not nearly as wild and funny as some of her friends. . . . I loved everything about the book from the characters to the plot to the fast-paced and witty writing." —Roundtable Reviews

Hostile Makeover
Also a Lifetime Movie

"Byerrum pulls another superlative Crime of Fashion out of her vintage cloche." —Chick Lit Books

"The read is as smooth as fine-grade cashmere."
— *Publishers Weekly*

"Totally delightful . . . a fun and witty read."
—Fresh Fiction

Designer Knockoff

"Byerrum intersperses the book with witty excerpts from Lacey's 'Fashion Bites' columns, such as 'When Bad Clothes Happen to Good People' and 'Thank Heavens It's Not Code Taupe.' . . . quirky . . . interesting plot twists." — *The Sun* (Bremerton, WA)

"Clever wordplay, snappy patter, and intriguing clues make this politics-meets-high-fashion whodunit a cut above the ordinary." —*Romantic Times*

"A very talented writer with an offbeat sense of humor." —The Best Reviews

Killer Hair
Also a Lifetime Movie

"[A] rippling debut. Peppered with girlfriends you'd love to have, smoldering romance you can't resist, and Beltway insider insights you've got to read, *Killer Hair* adds a crazy twist to the concept of 'capital murder.' "
—Sarah Strohmeyer, Agatha Award–winning author of *Kindred Spirits* and the Bubbles Yablonsky novels

"Ellen Byerrum tailors her debut mystery with a sharp murder plot, entertaining fashion commentary, and gutsy characters."
—Nancy J. Cohen, author of the Bad Hair Day mysteries

"A load of stylish fun." —Scripps Howard News Service

"Lacey slays and sashays thru Washington politics, scandal, and Fourth Estate slime, while uncovering whodunit and dunit and dunit again."
—Chloe Green, author of the Dallas O'Connor Fashion mysteries

"*Killer Hair* is a shear delight."
—national bestselling author Elaine Viets

**Other Crime of Fashion Mysteries
by Ellen Byerrum**

Killer Hair
Designer Knockoff
Hostile Makeover
Raiders of the Lost Corset
Grave Apparel
Armed and Glamorous
Shot Through Velvet
Death on Heels

Veiled Revenge

A CRIME OF FASHION MYSTERY

Ellen Byerrum

AN OBSIDIAN MYSTERY

OBSIDIAN
Published by the Penguin Group
Penguin Group (USA) Inc., 375 Hudson Street,
New York, New York 10014, USA
Penguin Group (Canada), 90 Eglinton Avenue East, Suite 700, Toronto,
Ontario M4P 2Y3, Canada (a division of Pearson Penguin Canada Inc.)
Penguin Books Ltd., 80 Strand, London WC2R 0RL, England
Penguin Ireland, 25 St. Stephen's Green, Dublin 2,
Ireland (a division of Penguin Books Ltd.)
Penguin Group (Australia), 707 Collins Street, Melbourne, Victoria 3008,
Australia (a division of Pearson Australia Group Pty. Ltd.)
Penguin Books India Pvt. Ltd., 11 Community Centre, Panchsheel Park,
New Delhi–110 017, India
Penguin Group (NZ), 67 Apollo Drive, Rosedale, Auckland 0632,
New Zealand (a division of Pearson New Zealand Ltd.)
Penguin Books (South Africa), Rosebank Office Park, 181 Jan Smuts Avenue,
Parktown North 2193, South Africa
Penguin China, B7 Jiaming Center, 27 East Third Ring Road North,
Chaoyang District, Beijing 100020, China

Penguin Books Ltd., Registered Offices:
80 Strand, London WC2R 0RL, England

First published by Obsidian, an imprint of New American Library,
a division of Penguin Group (USA) Inc.

First Printing, February 2013
10 9 8 7 6 5 4 3 2 1

PUBLISHER'S NOTE
This is a work of fiction. Names, characters, places, and incidents either are the
product of the author's imagination or are used fictitiously, and any resemblance
to actual persons, living or dead, business establishments, events, or locales is
entirely coincidental.
   The publisher does not have any control over and does not assume any responsibility for author or third-party Web sites or their content.

ACKNOWLEDGMENTS

The process of writing a book, from the first words to the bookstore shelf, involves so much more than just the author. Every book is a journey, and with every book I've written, I've encountered people who have been generous with their time, knowledge, and expertise. I am forever grateful for the moments they have shared that have spun my imagination into scenes, characters, plotlines, and stories.

While I was researching *Veiled Revenge*, I was blessed with a fabulous behind-the-scenes peek into the "nation's attic," the costume collections at the Smithsonian National Museum of American History, as well as personal stories behind some of the amazing clothes worn by Americans since this country's birth. It was a little piece of Heaven for me. I am indebted to Museum Specialist Carol Kregloh, Associate Curator Katherine Dirks, and Curator Nancy Davis, Division of Home & Community Life, Smithsonian Institution National Museum of American History. I am in awe of the work they perform to save, collect, and exhibit precious clothes that give us a view of what people were wearing and how they lived at various times in our history. If there are sartorial or other errors in this book, you know who to blame: Me.

As usual there are the friends who cheer me on and soothe my doubts. They are my sounding board and I would be lost without them. Many thanks go to Lloyd Rose, Jay Farrell, and Rosemary Stevens.

Not to forget, there are always others who share the writer's adventures in publishing. I am grateful to my encouraging agent, Paige Wheeler, and I would also like to thank my editor at New American Library, Sandy Harding.

Finally, when you're writing a book, you need someone who has your back, and rubs it too. That person is my husband, Bob Williams, who keeps my spirits up, critiques and edits my work, and offers me unfailing support. He has my thanks and gratitude and love. I've got his back too.

chapter 1

"Mock the shawl and flirt with disaster," the fortune-teller said, her hand raised in warning. "Some say it has unearthly powers. Some even say it's haunted. You who scoff at this ancient garment, mind you don't lose your way, your money, or even your life!"

The members of Stella Lake's bachelorette party laughed. But beneath the laughter, fashion reporter Lacey Smithsonian detected a hint of wonder. *Could Marie possibly be serious?*

With her cascading black ringlets and her Ruben-esque figure swathed in swirls of gold skirts and flounced-out sleeves, Marie Largesse looked the part of the Gypsy soothsayer. The bachelorette party kept her busy fore-telling happy love lives for the bridesmaids and guests, but her haunted Russian shawl stole the show.

Marie held the embroidered garment just out of touching distance, stroking it gently with her bejeweled fingers and tracing the flowers with her purple-painted nails. The rose tattoos on her hands almost looked like a living extension of the shawl.

"But it's so gorgeous! It totally begs to be touched." Bride-to-be Stella reached longingly for the shawl, then she pulled back her hand. "Wait, if it's spook-infested, I'm not so sure, Marie. I'm afraid of haunted things."

"It's wise to be careful, because the shawl is very pow-erful. However, I'm pretty sure you can hold it safely,

Stella. If you're really in love." Marie smiled and draped the shawl over Stella's shoulders with a gentle pat. "Legend says the shawl has few powers of wickedness over true lovers. Why, this capricious piece of cloth may even choose to bring you good luck."

The lavishly decorated shawl nearly enveloped Stella's fire-engine-red bandage dress, but it couldn't hide her cantilevered cleavage and fresh hairdo. Her romantic streak was reflected in her Cupid curls brushing against her collarbone, newly highlighted in light pink—not shocking scarlet, as she had threatened. Topping Stella's look was a new pink rhinestone tiara, chosen by Lacey for the party.

Marie's shawl was glorious indeed, black as a bayou night, with roses of many hues, red and pink, purple and blue, tucked into a profusion of leaves stitched in the colors of every season, from spring green to verdant summer, to the golds and reds of fall and the browns and grays of winter. The bachelorettes clapped, and Stella sighed with relief at Marie's reassurances.

"Are you sure, Marie? Absolutely, positively? 'Cause the path to true love has been pretty rocky for me and Nigel. I already broke my leg for love. I can't take any chances on irritating a haunted Russian shawl. And when you say 'few powers of wickedness,' like, exactly *what* powers? And *how* few?"

Marie fluttered her fingers. "You'll be fine. Try not to worry, Stella. Worry brings its own kind of negative vibrations."

"Not worry? Worrying is in my DNA."

Everyone laughed. Stella enjoyed being the center of attention. After all, it was her wedding shower. Still, she shrugged off the elaborate wrap and carefully handed it back to Marie. She stepped away from the shawl and drew a deep breath.

When she wasn't fretting over her wedding, Stella was the manager of Stylettos Salon in Washington, D.C.'s trendy Dupont Circle neighborhood, and Lacey's least predictable best friend. With her wedding only a week away, Stella was becoming more and more superstitious. And more of a trial to her maid of honor, Lacey Smithsonian.

"If it's really okay for me to borrow the shawl, Marie, that takes care of something old and something borrowed. My gown is new, so now I'm just looking for something blue. I'm thinking maybe a blue margarita. I could use one right now."

"Something blue will come your way—have no doubt," Marie said. "Blue that matches the eyes of your children, when they come."

"Blue-eyed babies? *Moi?* Wow." Stella's own sparkling eyes were light brown, almost hazel. "Blue eyes would be something! Just like Nigel's mom. Wow, thanks, Marie!" Her worries over for the moment, Stella shimmied away to the party's sound track, which was playing Cyndi Lauper's eternally popular "Girls Just Want to Have Fun."

"Marie makes a good Gypsy fortune-teller, doesn't she?" Lacey said to her other best friend, attorney Brooke Barton. "This fortune-teller thing was my idea, wasn't it? Wow, am I good. Sometimes."

Ms. Smithsonian was congratulating herself on putting together a bachelorette party for Stella that did *not* involve a drunken walk of shame through Georgetown with all the bridesmaids and friends wearing ridiculous sashes and tiaras, or being mooned by hunky male strippers, or indulging in lewd food items while someone sold honeymoon sex toys in neon colors. *Stella can save all that for the honeymoon.*

"It was genius to have Marie here telling fortunes," Brooke agreed. "Everyone's positively transfixed by her. Great idea, Lacey. Stella owes you for this."

Michelle, Stylettos' striking African-American assistant manager, giggled at her fortune as Marie peered into her palm. "You telling me I'm going to hook up with a white boy? Another one? No way! Couldn't he be sort of, you know, sweet and milk chocolate?"

"I still have my doubts about how psychic she really is," Brooke said, "but Marie puts on a good show."

Lacey looked quizzically at her friend, Brooke Barton, Esquire, lawyer by day and wacky conspiracy theorist by night. Tonight Brooke was looking less than usual like a well-starched Washington attorney. Her long pale blond hair caressed her bare shoulders, and her smoky eye shadow and mascara kicked up her comely lawyer-next-door looks a notch or two.

All the pretty bridesmaids were looking their best tonight. *Most of us, anyway.* Lacey had erased the faint shadows of overwork beneath her blue-green eyes with concealer and a dusting of blush on her high cheekbones. She caught a glimpse of herself in a mirror, over the console table covered with champagne bottles and crystal flutes. She pushed her hair away from her face. It would be weeks before she needed to have the blond highlights in her honey brown hair refreshed. By Stella, of course. After the honeymoon. She turned back to Brooke with a lifted eyebrow.

"Seriously, Brooke? You believe in little green men, things that go bump in the night, and the Loch Ness monster, but you don't believe Marie is psychic?"

Brooke snorted. "Call me skeptical."

"I have called you many things, Counselor, most of them good, but skeptical is not one of them. Besides, Marie is exceedingly psychic with things like, um, the weather," Lacey replied. Marie's bones did seem to have a direct hotline to storms, rain, and wind. She was as good as or better than any meteorologist in town. "And I do worry when she faints."

"Certainly she faints more than anyone I've ever known." Brooke furrowed her brow in concentration. "In fact, I've never known anyone who faints. Have you? So nineteenth century."

Marie Largesse fell into a stupor when her psychic circuits were "overloaded," purportedly with visions of horror, death, and doom. Or so she said. No one was quite sure what Marie experienced when she fainted, not even Marie. But death and dismay generally followed those spells.

"I wonder what Marie sees when she drops into the astral netherworld." Brooke pondered, one hand on her chin.

"Doesn't matter. She can never remember." Lacey was just as curious about the netherworld of Brooke's complicated mind. "But it can't be good."

"So if Edgar Cayce was the Sleeping Prophet, then Marie Largesse is the Fainting Psychic? I've heard of fainting goats, but a fainting psychic is just weird." Brooke reached for a mushroom puff pastry on a silver tray passed by a server in a white blouse, black slacks, and pink cummerbund, matching the party's color scheme.

"Your words, not mine. Anyway, Marie predicted beautiful spring weather for today and tomorrow," Lacey pointed out, "and just look!"

"I'll take it," Brooke agreed. "I'm so ready for spring."

"And I'm crossing my fingers that tonight is all about harmless bachelorette party fun. No disasters. No fainting allowed."

"Yes, it's harmless all right." Brooke sniffed. "Reading palms and cards? 'You will meet a tall, dark stranger'? The kind of thing any charlatan fortune-teller could pull off."

"If you're so dubious, test Marie. Go ahead. Mock the shawl."

"No need to be hasty, Lacey. I'm wide open to the possibilities. Of the shawl, that is. Especially if Gregor Kepelov, that emissary from the dark side of Mother Russia, gave it to her. Besides, it's Marie's powers I doubt, not the shawl." Brooke drained her champagne flute. "Maybe there is something to the shawl bringing good luck. After all, Stella got lucky, landing Nigel, surviving that fall off the rocks, getting perfect wedding weather, and ordering us all to wear *pink* for the wedding." She sighed. "I saw some lovely gray bridesmaid dresses when I was shopping. I love that smoky color! Why couldn't she go with gray?"

"Freeze right there, Brooke. It's not like I'm the biggest fan of all things pink and rosy. But gray? Definitely not gray. It's a spring wedding. It should have spring colors! Why dress like a tropical depression anyway? Is it in the wardrobe handbook for young attorneys?"

"Yes, it is. Gray is lucky for lawyers. Pink is lucky for—*defendants*. And talk about luck! How did Stella and Nigel manage to snag a Park Service permit for a wedding on the Mall amidst those pink cherry blossoms she's so fond of?"

"And on such short notice too."

Brooke scanned the tables for more appetizers. "Her future father-in-law, the British ambassador, probably had something to do with it."

"Former ambassador," Lacey corrected her. "Possibly, but Stella told me some other wedding party had a permit for two years and suddenly canceled. Probably a sad tale there."

"Dame Fortune has smiled on Stella. And I have to say this venue for the bachelorette bash is working out. Nice job."

"Thanks. I was afraid it could end up seriously—" Lacey hunted for a word.

"Tacky?" Brooke selected from a passing tray another pink champagne cocktail, named by the bartenders the "Stellarrific Rose" for the evening, in Stella's honor. She lifted her glass in a salute to Lacey.

"Not *tacky* exactly." Lacey saluted her in turn. "But it *is* a bachelorette party, so mortification is always a danger. I caved in and bought her the tiara. It was the one thing she really wanted for tonight. I'm surprised our feisty stylist agreed to stay in town for her bachelorette party and not indulge in the stupider rites of waning singlehood, like a drunken road trip to the beach or something."

"I'd have filed a restraining order," Brooke said.

There was a squeal of laughter from one of the bridesmaids. Lacey looked up. Everything was going well.

The party was gathered on a Sunday evening in April in a side room of a brand-new restaurant named Rosebud's, on U Street, in a very happening and rapidly gentrifying Washington, D.C., neighborhood. It was once a rough part of town, but only occasionally dangerous these days, and generally not until after two in the morning. Lacey and Brooke were cohosting the event, but Lacey had made all the key decisions. Rosebud's was already a hit, but having just opened, its private party rooms were still affordable. This Sunday was the only night they could reserve this close to Stella's wedding; next Saturday would be the big day.

"It even has pink rosebud drapes," Lacey noted. "This place is as tasteful as we could manage, keeping in mind the bride's extravagant preferences."

"If only she'd change her mind about the pink bridesmaid dresses."

"A woman who's been planning a cherry blossom wedding since the third grade is unlikely to be swayed from pink bridesmaid dresses." Lacey laughed. "Just be thankful she's letting us choose our own dresses, and not the Bustiers of Doom she would have cinched us in."

"You're the big fashion maven—couldn't you suggest something else?"

"When has Stella ever listened to me?"

"Always! She reads everything you write! Every third word out of her mouth is a quote from your Crimes of Fashion, and your Fashion Bites."

"Fashion certainly *does* bite. But Brooke, my words somersault around her head. Stella's interpretation of my advice stands my hair on end."

"Good thing she's such a great stylist. She can fix that." Brooke tugged on a lock of Lacey's hair for emphasis.

Life is funny, Lacey reflected. There was a time when

Brooke and Stella couldn't stand each other. They had eventually bonded over gunpowder, tequila, and danger, and now Brooke was a bridesmaid in reluctant pink in Stella's wedding. Lacey was the reluctant, but determined, maid of honor.

"Do you suppose she'd mind if I show up in a nice *taupe* dress?" There was a hint of a whine in Brooke's voice. "Maybe with a pale pink belt?"

"Mind? She'd only kill you. She's already fretting over every single pink petal that buds, blossoms, and falls."

"Stella would file suit against Mother Nature to stop the cherry blossoms from fading." Brooke shook her head. "I guess there had better be pink buds for her wedding. And pink bridesmaids in pink dresses."

"Brooke, we have to suck it up on the pink dress question."

"I'm a lawyer. I'm not good at sucking it up. Sucking *up*, yes. A completely different thing."

"You have bought your dress, haven't you?"

Brooke contemplated her champagne glass. "Umm, I've been really busy."

"You have one week, Brooke. One week." Lacey sipped her own champagne. "Go pink. Or die."

Around them, the crowd seemed to be in high spirits. Even the stringy-haired cocktail waitress looked enthusiastic. She was sallow-skinned with a prominent and crooked nose, but the effect was softened by a lyrical voice and a vaguely foreign accent. The name on her badge was Tilda. She leaned down to collect glasses at the table where Marie sat, and she reached out to stroke the shawl.

"Do be careful, hon," Marie said, putting her hand on Tilda's. "It's very old. And it has a spirit of its own."

"How fascinating. It must be very valuable to you." The waitress smiled.

"I could never put a price on it."

"My grandmother had such a shawl. Not nearly so grand as this one. Such intricate needlework." Tilda touched one pink rose, then another. "But her shawl is most beautiful in my memory."

"Why, of course it is. You're not from around here, are you? Are you Russian?"

"A little, on my grandmother's side. A lovely memory, her shawl. But now—" Tilda patted the garment gently and then straightened up. "Work to do. Thank you for letting me touch it. So beautiful." She picked up empty glasses and set them on her tray. Marie winked at Lacey.

"My shawl has another admirer."

Lacey regarded the efficient Tilda, who was heading back to the kitchen. "Not everyone is superstitious, Marie."

"No, but she was respectful. That's important when it comes to matters of the spirit." Marie yawned, one tattooed hand fluttering gracefully over her mouth.

"Don't wear yourself out, Marie," Stella cooed, back with another Stellarific Rose. "Fortune-telling is hard work, doll."

"No worries, sugar. I have a new girl opening the shop in the morning." The Little Shop of Horus was Marie's occult bookstore, psychic reading studio, and candle shop in Old Town Alexandria. "She's got good vibes and all that. And compatible tattoos."

"Compatible tattoos?"

"All butterflies and roses. No death's heads or ugliness to invite evil," Marie said. "So Gregor's picking me up tonight, and I plan to sleep *late*, sugar."

"I totally can't wait to tell Nigel you said we're going to have a blue-eyed baby. Someday. But maybe I shouldn't scare him before the wedding? Guys don't like their brides suddenly babbling away about babies, you know."

"Oh, Marie! Read me! Please." Rosalie, one of the bridesmaids, stuck out her hand. Marie smiled and took her open hand in her larger ones. She closed her eyes and concentrated.

Stella gave Lacey a hug. "I so owe you, Lace. The Stellarrific pink champagne cocktails? Awesome. Totally awesome. And I love the tiara you got me!" She touched the faux jewels on the top of her head. "Pink stones! I am totally wearing this with my veil. It's so *not* cheap-looking."

It wasn't cheap either: pink Swarovski crystals. "You're welcome. And thank you for not making us shake our booty from here to Georgetown or Rehoboth."

"I'm not sure I'm up for partying all night anymore either," Stella stage-whispered. "Maybe I'm getting old. But don't tell anyone or I'll wreak havoc on your hair."

"It's called maturity, Stella." Brooke broke into the conversation.

"Ma-*churr*-ity? Criminy, that makes me sound ancient!" Stella was in her mid-thirties, but she had stopped telling anyone her age. "And I gotta watch the dark circles under my eyes, not to mention these awful lines starting. Need to be beautiful for my beau." Stella tottered to the nearest table and eased herself into a chair. "Walking on these babies is killing me." She showed off sky-high red patent leather stilettos that would have felled a lesser woman.

It was a major feat for Stella to wear heels at all after suffering a broken leg a few months before. These days her waifish high-heeled gait had a slight tilt to it.

"Those things ought to come with a surgeon general's warning," Lacey said.

"You're telling me. But there is no way I'm going to knuckle under to doctor's orders on this. I'm going to wear cute footwear for my wedding, if it kills me. And they're not even as high as I'd like. Nosebleed high, that's what I wanted."

"What did you decide on for the wedding?"

"Either these red stilettos, or those super-adorable Victorian lace-up boots we found. The heel is a little lower and they support the ankle. They came in white leather, but I could have them dyed pink."

"Pink. I vote for the pink boots," Lacey said.

"*Not* the red stilettos?" Brooke teased. "I don't know, Stella. Sounds to me like low-heeled boots are just a couple of steps away from Birkenstocks."

"Bite your tongue, Brookie," Stella said and struggled to her feet. "Now, I gotta get some more of those ham-thingy appetizers. They are majorly delish."

"Sit, Cinderella. I'll get you a plate." Brooke moved off in search of the ham thingies. They were definitely the more-you-drink-the-better-they-taste type of appetizer.

Stella sipped her pink champagne. "Can you believe it, Lacey? I'm getting married. To *Nigel*."

"Last I heard. You sound unsure. Shopping for a different groom to match the shoes? Something pinker?"

"Oh, no. I'm sure. Nigel's the one. We are getting married. Pretty sure. Unless somebody drops dead between now and Saturday."

"No dead bodies! Don't even think it."

"I'm kidding," Stella said. "Like I said, I'm waltzing down the aisle. In the pink. Things actually seem to be working out for me, for once. But it's always something, isn't it? Like *her*. I can't believe she had the nerve to show up."

"Who?" Lacey scanned the room.

"Rosalie—the buttinsky having her palm read. My cousin."

Stella indicated the frizzy-haired bridesmaid huddling with Marie. Rosalie's hair was a creature with a mind of its own. Medusa-like, it had started the evening curly and then exploded into a ball of baling wire, courtesy of the D.C. humidity. Despite her hair, Rosalie appeared to be having a great time.

"You invited her, didn't you?"

"Well, kinda, sorta. My mother forced her on me. I mean, I have plenty of bridesmaids without her. Bridesmaids I actually *like*. But she's *family*."

Lacey took a closer look at Stella's cousin. Underneath Rosalie's wild curly hair were brown eyes, blotchy skin, and flat cheekbones. It was a plain face that might have been improved with a bit of subtle makeup. She wore a sleeveless green sheath that made her skin look a little olive. It was a little too tight, and a little too long, and her black shoes were too heavy for a light spring dress. Obviously Stella hadn't had a chance to make over her cousin—yet.

The stylist grimaced as she explained, "Rosalie's a bookkeeper for an auto supply store near Princeton—not the good side of Princeton either—but she's not exactly a typical Jersey girl. Look at her! Dull, dull, dull."

Lacey thought a rosy-hued bridesmaid dress, no matter how dreadful it might be, would perk up the woman's looks and make Rosalie a little rosier. "She'll probably clean up nicely."

"Optimist," Stella said.

Marie finished telling her fortune and Rosalie gazed at Stella with a mix of admiration and envy. And possibly fear.

"So, Rosalie, what's the outlook, fortune-wise?" Stella asked.

"I'm going to meet a great guy," Rosalie said. "Where and when and who, that's all a little fuzzy. But she said it'll be raining."

"If Marie says rain, bring your umbrella." Lacey smiled and put her hand out to shake. "Hi, I'm Lacey."

Rosalie squeezed her hand, starstruck. "I know! I read the papers. Lacey Smithsonian. You and Stella have such exciting lives."

"Busy, at any rate," Lacey said. "Have you picked out your dress yet?"

Rosalie's hair bobbed as she nodded enthusiastically. "It's really pink. I hope you like it. I'm so excited! I've never been a bridesmaid before."

Stella grabbed a hank of Rosalie's hair. "And you never will be again if we don't do something with that hair! I made an appointment for you tomorrow at Stylettos, before you head back to Jersey. And you can get a blowout Saturday morning before the wedding. Okay?"

"Wait a minute, Stel." Rosalie looked wary. "Remember the last time?"

Fellow bridesmaid Michelle picked up her cue. "Stella says you'd like something new and sleek. I'll take good care of you." The assistant manager of Stylettos, Michelle was charming and soft-spoken, where Stella was opinionated and loud.

Rosalie squinted at her. Michelle was a striking woman with milk chocolate skin and an amazing updo, a French twist that swirled into a crown of curls. Though Lacey hadn't seen Michelle's dress, she knew that any shade of pink she chose would complement her skin tone.

"I don't remember saying anything like that, but if Stella—" Rosalie grabbed her hair into a ponytail with a look of terror. "You're not going to cut, are you? It took me two years to grow it out from last time." She shot an accusatory glare Stella's way. "I was practically bald."

Stella shrugged and waved her drink. "So we learned something. Really short hair doesn't work for you. And you got even, didn't you, Rosalie? You wouldn't believe it, Lacey. She attacked my car. Disabled it completely."

"Oh, please," Rosalie said. "It was just the plug wires. Easy-peasy. It's not like I put a potato in the exhaust pipe or anything."

Weddings always bring out the best in people. Lacey didn't know quite what to say, but Michelle stepped in again. She eyed Rosalie's hair with interest. "It just needs a trim, just an inch or two. And if we straighten it a little, you won't even know it was cut."

"Straighten it?" Rosalie's eyes were wide.

"Trust me, I am the expert straightener. And it will last."

Rosalie took a gulp of her drink. "If you're sure. And you have to promise you won't scalp me."

"I promise. You can trust me, even if you can't trust Stella." Michelle smiled.

"That was a joke, Rosalie," Stella said. "Hey, would I steer you wrong?"

"Yes, you would and you have," Rosalie replied, backing away from her cousin.

"Michelle is a terrific stylist and she really understands naturally curly hair," Lacey said.

Rosalie shook her head. "Hair and makeup, hair and makeup! It's always come so easily for Stella. But when she does *my* hair and *my* makeup, she makes me look weird. Like a clown."

Stella sighed. "You're just not used to looking different."

"Maybe I don't like looking *crazy*. Hey, speaking of crazy, I need a drink." Rosalie headed to the bar. Stella covered her face with her hands.

"Honestly, I don't how I'm going to make it through this wedding. And to top things off, Lady Gwendolyn made me invite . . . my *mother* to all the festivities."

"You can't not invite your mother, Stella. My advice, play nice."

"Ha, easy for you to say. You have a great mom. Mine, not so much."

Lacey rolled her eyes. She had yet to meet the notorious Retta Lake, but she was looking forward to it. She'd already met Lady Gwendolyn Griffin, Stella's soon-to-be mother-in-law, who'd submitted like a lamb to a radical hair and makeup makeover under Stella's supervision.

"My mother doesn't even really believe I'm getting married," Stella said. "Retta's all negativity. Who'd want her around? Anyway, Lady G guilted me into it. She may look all House of Windsor and *Downton Abbey*, but she can badger with the best of them. And my mother's coming a week early. Her idea, believe me. And Rosalie's only here to be gossip central for the relatives back home. This party will be all over her Facebook before midnight." Stella tossed a sour look toward her younger cousin. "And I'm going to have to do something about *that*!"

"That?" Lacey squinted at Rosalie.

"That mop of hair. And did you hear her? It's not like

she's ever *grateful* or anything. Plus, the salon's going to be short-staffed on account of the wedding anyway. I'm totally doing her a favor."

"Sometimes it's hard to take charity, Stella. Even from your cousin. At any rate, Michelle will have it under control. More pink champagne?" Lacey inquired. "No one wants to see a glum bride. You aren't having, um, cold feet, are you?"

"In these hot shoes?" Stella lunged for another pink cocktail. "No, no doubts about Nigel, or the cherry blossoms, or anything like that. But there is something. Something that could wreck everything. Besides my mother and my cousin showing up to ruin my big day."

Alarms were going off in Lacey's brain. "I'm your maid of honor. You can tell me anything." *I really don't want to hear this, do I?*

"I meant to tell you. But it's too awful, Lace. I'm too ashamed to tell *you*."

chapter 2

"Spill," Lacey insisted. "I don't want any surprises."

Stella was constitutionally unable to keep a secret. "I think I might hate my dress," she said in a conspiratorial whisper. "Totally hate it. In fact, I don't love it at all."

"But you look great," Lacey protested. After all, the stylist was decked out in classic Haute Stella.

"Not *this* dress!" She pointed to her bandage-tight red dress. "This dress rocks. It's gonna rock Nigel later tonight, if you know what I mean. No, no, no, I'm talking about my wedding gown."

Not the giant white puffball! Lacey knew if a woman didn't feel right in what she wore on one of the most important days of her life, it could poison the entire event.

"You don't like your wedding dress? But it's . . . pretty." Lacey pictured the layers of white organza and the lightly beaded bodice, highlighted with a sprinkling of faux pearls and sparkling rhinestones. She'd been astounded that Stella had been able to find a dress on such short notice. The wedding was rushed, with barely three months to plan the whole thing.

The hunt for the Great White Whale of Dresses had come down to the giant ball gown style or the mermaid silhouette. To Lacey's surprise, the ball gown had won, and it was a sale gown that needed only minimal alterations. It was white, it was poufy, and the strapless bodice pushed up Stella's Girls to a seductive-but-not-trashy level.

"Yeah, it's *okay*. But it's like the dress that everyone's wearing this year, and last year and next year. It's like the expected dress. The typical dress. The just-say-yes-to-the-dress dress. And I'm so not the typical say-yes-to-the-dress bride."

Lacey found it hard to argue. "I know you wanted something like a pink leather bustier or a miniskirt with a graduated train, that mullet skirt look—something." She had to shut off the vision. "But it would have to be custom made and there isn't time."

"It's not that. I'm not even sure I wanted it to look so Las Vegas showgirly and all. It's just that *my* dress, my wedding dress for that, hopefully, once-in-a-lifetime occasion—well, it's just not *special*." Stella looked heartbroken. "I know I'm someone people think would probably get married in, you know, a Dragon Lady red leather mini with, like, lightning bolts up the side or something, Lace, but I've been thinking about my wedding day since I was a little girl, wearing a bride's costume on Halloween. Little fake pearls and tiara and veil and everything."

"You really had a bride costume? Not a little Goth princess outfit?" *Where did that Stella go?*

Stella downed her champagne cocktail. "Oh, I had one of those too. But the point is, I've always dreamed of this day and I want it to be out of the ordinary. Fabulous, stupendous. Extra-special, *special*."

"But, Stella, you'll *make* it special." Lacey groped for something positive to say. "You have, um, pink-highlighted hair. Besides, you get to wear Marie's haunted shawl. Something borrowed, something old? And that is definitely one of a kind."

Stella lowered her voice. "And that's another thing. You know I adore Marie, but what if that spooky Russian thing really is dangerous?"

Lacey gave herself a mental head slap. "But Stel, you

heard Marie. The shawl can't hurt people in love. Like you and—"

"I know, I know, and I am totally in love with Nigel Percival Griffin."

"Wait a minute. Percival?"

"But what if the shawl doesn't believe me? I mean, Nigel and me, we've had bad luck. Seems like ever since we met."

"You've had your share. But I believe it simply has to be over and done with."

"Do you, Lace? Really and truly?"

"Law of averages, Stella. You're due for good luck. And besides, Marie hasn't fainted, has she?"

They turned in unison toward the voluptuous psychic, busily spinning dreams out of thin air. "Not yet, anyway."

"That's her?" a man with a British accent was saying. "Not really? In the red stilettos? With the pink hair? You're having me on, mate."

"She's the one, Bryan. As of Saturday, I'm off the market." Another British accent. This one belonged to Nigel Griffin, Stella Lake's fiancé.

Lacey was exiting the ladies' blushing-pink lavatory at Rosebud's when she heard voices coming from the end of the bar, near the hallway to the restrooms. She stopped to listen because it sounded interesting—a reporter's habit. She could see a slice of the speakers in a strategically placed mirror at the end of the hall, but they couldn't see her. The two were leaning on the bar, drinking beer like old buddies.

Nigel Griffin was tall and thin, good-looking in an un-athletic English way. His large teeth were straight, having had the advantage of braces during his teen years at an American prep school in D.C. He was slightly rumpled, as usual, in khakis and a blue oxford-cloth button-down shirt. Lacey had only a partial view of the other man, who wore gray slacks and a navy jacket.

"What I mean is, how can you look at *that* when my sister Adele is still carrying a torch for you?" the stranger called Bryan was saying.

"Adele is lovely, she just doesn't do it for me." Nigel lifted his beer.

"But Adele—"

"Mate, Adele is *driven*. Sure, she's pretty on the outside, but on the inside your sister is Margaret Freaking Thatcher. She'd invade the Falklands on a dare."

"True enough. That's Adele. I simply can't believe that pint-sized hairdresser .turns your crank. And who was that immense, weird, black-haired Gypsy woman? Nearly smothered me with a black shawl."

"Don't exaggerate, Bryan. It's just Marie. Psychic. Great friend of Stella's."

"She passed me in the hall and practically bowled me over. The thing got tangled in my tie clip. Took a minute to get free." He gave a short laugh. "So the massive psychic is chums with the tiny impish pink-haired bride? Certainly fits."

Lacey could feel steam coming out of her ears. *What the hell is Nigel Griffin doing here anyway, and who's this sexist slob he's boozing with?*

"As the Bard says: 'Love looks not with the eyes but with the mind,'" Nigel said.

"And the 'course of true love never did run smooth,'" Bryan Whoever-he-was replied.

At least he's semiliterate, even if he is a creep, Lacey thought.

"God knows it hasn't run smooth so far," Nigel said. "So I guess we've got the true love part in the bag."

"Maybe it isn't supposed to work out," Bryan said. "All for the best, what?"

"Are you my best man, or not?"

Really scraping the bottom of the best-man barrel there, Nigel. Lacey was due back at the party, but this sounded too important to miss.

"Nigel, she works in a hair salon. Common as clay," Bryan continued. "My sister at least has some class. Even with the Thatcher DNA. And money too."

Lacey had two issues with this buddy-buddy scene. First, Nigel Griffin wasn't supposed to be spying on his bride-to-be and her bachelorettes. Grooms were *never* welcome at bachelorette parties. And second, if this "Bryan" had such a snotty attitude toward Nigel's choice of bride, what was he doing being Nigel's best man? The best man's job was to support the groom. And Lacey's job was to support the bride. She emerged from the hallway, shoulders back, eyes blazing.

"Nigel Griffin! What are you doing here?"

Griffin's eyes went wide. "Shhh, Smithsonian." He put his finger to his lips. "No need to make a fuss. And don't tell Stella! Just wanted to see one of those famous American bridal rituals I've heard so much about."

She stood with her hands on her hips. "You're spying."

Bryan turned his pale gray gaze on Lacey. He was tall and thin and so blond he seemed to be bloodless. "This one's more promising. Who are you?"

"No, no, no, mate." Nigel shook his head and his finger. "You do not want to mess with Smithsonian. She can be very hard on a person. Especially low-class persons like yourself."

"Let me be the judge of that, old man."

"Bryan, trust me. You do not want Smithsonian to show you her famous scissors trick. Or whack you with a sword cane. Possibly rope you like a calf."

"Better and better." Bryan had an unsavory grin. "I like a nice bit of rope work myself."

"Very well, let her go all American cowgirl on you and shoot you like the dog you are." Nigel pantomimed shooting a gun. "What else, Smithsonian? I forget. Such a long list of lethal attributes."

"Too many to keep track of, Nigel. Hard to choose just one." Lacey eyed their pitcher of beer on the bar. She'd never actually thrown a drink on anyone. It was tempting. She'd always wanted to. *But who gets the first pitcher?*

"Come on, old chap. Introduce me properly," Bryan said.

"Remember, you insisted." Nigel raised his hands in defeat. "Allow me to introduce Lacey Smithsonian, lethal fashion reporter for a local rag, *The Eye Street Observer.*"

Bryan put out his hand. Lacey just stared at it.

"Not quite lethal, but close enough," she said. "I am the maid of honor. Stella is my friend, and I don't appreciate your comments."

"And Smithsonian doesn't think I'm half good enough for Stella," Nigel added.

"Not on your best day, Nigel," she agreed.

"Sorry. Culpeper's the name. Bryan Culpeper." He smoothly scooped up his glass of beer off the bar with his unshaken right hand. "Sometimes my mouth outruns my brain. I apologize if I offended you."

"'If'?" Lacey wasn't an expert on the class distinctions of English accents, but Bryan's sounded to her on the posher end of the scale.

"This miserable wreck is my best man," Nigel said warily. He edged an inch or two farther away from Lacey.

"Your best? Are you sure?" Lacey asked. "You could do better. For Heaven's sake, Nigel, even Kepelov would be a better best man. At least he likes Stella."

"Kepelov? Ha. Chap can be a little scary." Nigel squirmed. "Bryan and I are mates. I used to date his sister."

"We're practically in-laws," Bryan clarified. "Now, what about you? I could get to like a sweet thing like you."

Lacey shoved Bryan's beer-holding hand right up into his chin, spilling Sam Adams all over his face and his starched white shirt and tie. He leapt backward against the bar, dripping and cursing. The blasé bartender threw him a towel as he sputtered unintelligible British curses.

"My goodness," Lacey said, delighted with herself. "What a mess you've made! For your information, I'm not a sweet thing, I'm in charge of the bachelorettes, and you're not welcome at our party."

She turned on the cowering Nigel Griffin. "I recommend that you leave. Now. Before I rat you out to the bride. And take your *worst* man here with you."

She exited, head held high. *That was for Stella.* Lacey couldn't help smirking to herself. *Not bad*, she thought. *Not bad at all.*

"I warned you, mate," she heard Nigel say to the still-dripping Bryan as she strode away. "You got off easy."

chapter 3

"What took you so long, Lacey? I could have given you a shampoo, cut, and blow-dry in the time you've been gone," Stella complained.

Lacey was still steaming. She was debating whether to tell Stella about the intruders at the bar when a pair of arms swept them both up in a hug.

"Mis amigas! What's up with you two? You're like two little schoolgirls passing notes in the corner. Is this the bachelorette party or what? Because I am an honorary bachelorette!"

"Miguel!" Stella squealed and lunged into a hug. There were air kisses all around. "You came! I was afraid you wouldn't make it! And hey, you cut your hair and you didn't let me do it?" Stella smoothed back his sleek short hair with an expert touch.

"It's a long train ride down from Manhattan, sweetie. It was wearing me out. High maintenance."

Miguel had chopped off the long glossy black ponytail Lacey remembered, but his short combed-back style was just as flattering and more rakish. Tall and thin, Miguel was effortlessly stylish. Women couldn't help looking his way and into his liquid brown eyes, before they figured out he was gay, but that didn't stop the fairer sex from loving him. Originally from D.C., he was working as an image stylist in Manhattan. Among his clientele were fashion photographers, celebrities, and the occa-

sional star diva who needed a jolt of fabulous. Miguel
could bring the fabulous.

The first time Lacey met Miguel Flores, he was
bruised and battered from surviving a violent armed
robbery at Bentley's Boutique in Chevy Chase, Maryland. He was the victim of a real-life crime of fashion,
and his story was one in which Lacey had mixed high
style and true crime on her fashion beat. Miguel was also
an old friend of Stella's and instantly became Lacey's
friend too. He and Stella once ganged up on Lacey while
shoe shopping, the result of which was a pair of shoes
sitting in Lacey's closet that cost over six hundred dollars. *On sale.* Miguel's fashion advice was seldom easy on
the wallet.

"We must dish, my darlings," Miguel said. "I want
good gossip. And good golly, Miss Molly, look at you,
Stella! Pink frosting on the bride as well as the wedding
cake?" He tousled her pink-tipped curls.

"Do you just love it?"

"Only on you, dear."

High-pitched laughter distracted Stella and her curls
swiveled.

"Hold that thought, Miguel. I want more flattery, but
first I have to go save poor Marie from my idiot cousin."
Stella tottered on her sky-high heels. "Even I can tell
Rosalie's fortune! She's a bookkeeper, for pity's sake.
Fifty years of adding and subtracting, that's her future."
Stella pointed her stilettos toward Rosalie.

"Let me look at *you*, darling. My, we're very *Philadel-
phia Story* today, aren't we?" Miguel lifted an eyebrow
and a glass of pink champagne in a toast to Lacey and
her outfit.

She had chosen a late-1930s garden party dress. The
evening was a bit chilly, but the dress and the teasing air
of spring had called to her. It was pale yellow voile over
a cream-colored slip. The original belt was long gone, but
Lacey substituted a green ribbon at the waist. The style

was all in the details—the covered buttons, the lace cuffs, and the small decorative lace pockets high on the bust.

"I love it," Lacey admitted. "But I don't exactly blend in."

"Blend in with these giggling girls? Why on earth would you want to? Could they disarm a killer and use his own sword cane against him? Please. I'll take you on my side anytime, Lacey."

Most of the bachelorettes wore skinny strapless summer dresses. They were pushing the spring season, which in the Nation's Capital was unpredictable at best. Lacey couldn't blame them. Once the buds appeared on the trees and light green leaves peeked out, spring fever couldn't be held back. Even Brooke was in her sober, lawyerly version of spring-induced giddy finery. Lacey made a mental note to ask Brooke where on earth she'd found a strapless gray pinstripe dress. *Was it from Brooks Brothers' Taking the Office to the Picnic Collection*?

"Whatever works, Miguel. Swords, scissors, or my devastating wit. As for clothes, I have a fatal attraction to things that are pretty. But tell me about you. What are you up to?"

"Boring. First you. I hear you and the hunky Vic Donovan are hot and heavy these days."

"You've been talking to Stella," Lacey said. "The Twitter Tease of Washington Gossip?"

"Stella tells me *everything*. I don't even have to ask. It's more efficient that way," Miguel said. "But I realize I can't believe half of what she says. Now, is it true you and Donovan are *muy serioso*?"

Lacey couldn't keep herself from smiling at the very mention of Vic's name. "Could be halfway true. *Un poquito serioso*."

"Stella said more than halfway. Of course there hasn't been much room for idle chitchat, in between discussing the wedding dress and her hair and Nigel the Wonder Man. Tell me, Lacey, is he really George Clooney, Hugh

Grant, and Paul McCartney rolled into one? Can he be cloned? I can't wait to see this marvel."

Lacey thought about the scene at the bar. "Well, maybe the Hugh Grant part—"

"Don't tell me Nigel's not all he's cracked up to be. I knew it!"

"He's certainly cracked." She tried to be fair. "Oh, Nigel's cute in that British romantic lead kind of way, the guy who stumbles and bumbles around before figuring out what he's doing in the final reel. Some people actually think Nigel's a babe. He's just not my type."

"Back to your devastatingly hot private eye. How serious is it? White-lace-and-promises serious, nervous-breakdown-over-the-flowers-and-the-dress serious?"

"Yes, I'm still going out with Vic."

"But you're not talking." He poked her in the ribs. "Spill, Smithsonian, I'm sure it's juicy."

Lacey had a secret, and Miguel might be one of the first people she'd want to tell, but she wasn't interested in divulging it anytime soon.

"My lips are sealed. This is Stella's night, Miguel. It's all about her, not me. But you can tell me all about *your* love life."

He lifted his shoulders and let them drop. "They come and they go. But I'm open to suggestion. And I am such a pretty boy." His smile revealed white and even teeth.

"Pretty is as pretty does. Perhaps you're too pretty, Miguel."

"Too pretty? Impossible! And speaking of *too pretty*, look who the cat just dragged in." There was a new arrival at the doorway.

"Is that Leonardo? The hairstylist?" Lacey couldn't remember the last time she'd seen that celebrated diva. He and Stylettos had parted ways with a vengeance.

"Leonardo I'm-too-cool-to-have-a-last-name?" Miguel said. "He's under the mistaken impression that he's an *artiste*. But why not cut to the quick? Let's call him a *barber*."

Since he'd left Stylettos—where he was a major pain in Stella's backside—Leonardo had shuttled back and forth among salons all over the District, insulting clients and attacking their hair, declaring his genius, and generally playing the diva.

"He wasn't invited," Lacey said.

"You surprise me. And that *hair*," Miguel said. "What was he thinking? He looks like a part-time Swedish dominatrix. At a Roman bathhouse."

The first time Lacey saw him, Leo had a sweep of auburn hair. Now he sported a platinum blond Caesar cut and a stroke of blue eyeliner. But the expression on his face was the same bored arrogance. Lacey wondered if it was possible to be born with a supercilious look on your face. Leonardo strode into the center of the pink party room.

"Stand back!" Miguel intoned loudly. "Man making a scene." A few of the bachelorettes giggled. The intruder stood stock-still and glared.

"Back in D.C., Miguel? What's the matter, Big Apple take a bite out of you?" Leonardo said.

"Dear Leo the Cowardly Lion," Miguel drawled, "haven't you learned by now not to judge others by your own failures?"

Leonardo stepped closer to Miguel, glowering. They were almost nose to nose when Stella inserted herself into the breach. She looked like a tiny pink badger between the two tall men.

Though she be but little, yet she be fierce, Lacey quoted silently to herself.

"Miguel is here for my wedding—he's my stylist and my consultant," Stella said. "He gave up a special gig just to be here for me. More than I can say you ever did for me, Leo."

Miguel gave her shoulder a squeeze. "There you have it. It's all about Stella tonight, not you. Shoo, fly."

"You're not on the invite list, Leo," Stella added.

"It's Leonardo. And my sweet deluded Stella, I can see

you do need *someone's* help. Mine, for instance," Leonardo said, focusing on her curls. "But isn't Miguel's taste a little rococo for you? You could have called me, you know. Though even I can't perform miracles." He gestured toward her hair. "Pink highlights? Really? What a tragedy."

"Leo, take your bitch act on the road, why don't you?" Miguel stepped into his face. "You're so last week."

"You wish."

"No, I don't."

"Scram, Leo!" Stella's expression was murderous.

"Don't be silly. I just got here. Anything good to drink?" Leonardo spun on his heel and headed to the buffet table for a pink cocktail.

"I swear, he's worse than a barnacle on the butt of a boat. I'm going to scrape him off." Stella started after him, but Miguel held her back.

"He hates not being queen bee, so to speak," Miguel said. "Don't worry, Stella my sweet, I won't let him ruin your party. He'll just make a fool of himself. He'll be over in this town. As if he weren't already. And think of the gossip we'll score."

The way Miguel talked about their gate-crasher made Lacey wonder. "Miguel, did you and Leonardo ever — you know?"

"Have a fling? Let me think." He pretended to search his memory. "I am popular, you know, and Leonardo wasn't always such an exhibitionist. He was even rather delicious once. I'm embarrassed to say this: Yes. We flinged. And flanged. And I flung him out. There, it's out. I don't know what I was thinking." Miguel briefly covered his face in mock shame.

"Did he have a hard time letting go?"

"I practically had to pry his fingers off. Like a zombie. He's dead to me."

Leonardo helped himself to a Stellarrific cocktail, then twirled, as graceful as a ballet dancer, and bowed toward Stella. "Congratulations, dear Stella. Our bride-to-be."

"Are you high?" Stella demanded, clenching her fists. "You are not invited! Go away!"

His smirk soured just a bit, but he recovered. "I was crushed, so I crashed. We're such good friends, you and I. We have such a long history, and yet you neglected to invite me. Invitation lost in the mail, no doubt. And yet you invited Twinkle Toes here." He cast a sneer toward Miguel. "Plus, I thought with your tendency toward the obvious you might hire some awesome male strippers. With all those ripped abs and porn star moves. They *are* all gay, you know. Once they see me, anyway. So I'm here for the show."

"Strippers?" Rosalie's eyes went wide. The bedraggled bridesmaid stood off to the side, listening intently.

"We're going for a little class here, Leo," Stella said. "So that excludes you."

"So adorable, Stella." He directed his attention to Lacey. "And the empress of the fashion crime. Still dressing from Grandma's ragbag, I see. What's on the menu tonight, Smithsonian? Mayhem, or murder?"

"Take your pick, Leo. If you remember, last time we met, you were a suspect."

"The name is Leonardo, and I suspect everyone." He stroked his hair, smoothing the blond fringe on his forehead. He reached for Lacey's hair. "Still, I'd like to get my hands on those tresses of yours. Get them out of Stella's clichéd clutches."

Lacey smacked his hand away.

"Keep your mitts off Lacey's mane," Stella growled. "Marie's telling fortunes, Leo. Want to risk it? Or should I tell you what's going to happen if you don't leave?"

"Fortunes? Really? I love fortune-telling!"

"Watch out, Leonardo," Lacey warned. "Marie's shawl has magical powers."

"Magic?"

"Now you've done it," Miguel said. "He's such a sucker for show biz. He'll never leave on his own."

Leonardo pushed his way through the bachelorettes

to Marie, who was taking a break. "Pretty shawl!" he cooed. "Is it really magic? Let me see."

The psychic held the wrap close, protectively. "Careful, Mr. Whoever You Are. This shawl was given to me by my fiancé, Gregor Kepelov." Marie backed away from him. Bachelorettes started forming a protective barrier around her.

"I only want to touch," Leo purred. "Tell me about its powers."

Marie couldn't seem to resist talking about the shawl, even to this annoying interloper. "This very special shawl, one of a kind in all the world, came from an ancestor of Gregor. Her name was Irina Katya Kepelova. She worked at the mill where they wove the fabric. But Irina wanted a shawl grander and more intricate than any produced in their sweatshop."

She had everyone's attention now. Lacey had heard only bits and pieces of the shawl's history. Marie wrapped the shawl slowly around her shoulders. She snapped out one draped arm, like a dancer, to show off its glory. The bachelorettes gasped and giggled.

"Irina selected the finest, softest wool she could find and she embroidered each blossom and every leaf. But if you look closer, there are other pictures here, very tiny, in between the flowers and the leaves. You might mistake them for a misshapen blossom. But Irina made no mistakes. Everything she stitched, the people and cities, the mountains and mythical creatures, this perfect little house and this church, all tell the tragic and triumphant story of the Kepelov family."

"Stella says it's cursed," Rosalie said.

"No such thing as a curse," Leonardo sneered. "Magic is altogether different."

"This shawl is haunted," Marie said. "Inhabited by the spirits of all the Kepelova women who have passed on. They left their marks on the shawl in needle and thread. And their blood and tears. I believe they also left a little of their spirits."

Great story. Lacey slipped out her tiny digital camera and snapped a couple of frames. She contemplated how she could use it in a Crime of Fashion story. *First you have a beautiful, one-of-a-kind Russian shawl. The hook is its history, and the hook has a twist: The shawl is haunted.* She wondered if she should save it for Halloween. But Halloween seemed very far away, and she always needed a new story to feed her unique twist on a fashion beat.

"This shawl and my Gregor's far-flung family have survived every recent upheaval in Russian history." Marie was enjoying her tale, adding a little verbal embroidery of her own. "Every one of those tragedies has left its mark in the shawl, recorded by the Kepelova women. Perhaps the shawl has protected them from disaster."

Leonardo reached out to the shawl. "Let me touch it and make a wish. If it's so magical, let's all make a wish."

"Leo, go home," Stella said. "That's my wish. You're making a fool of yourself."

"The name, my dear, is Leonardo!" He snatched the shawl from Marie's hands and danced away, swinging it over his shoulder like a cape. "Make another wish!"

"The shawl does not grant tawdry wishes! Do not mock the shawl," Marie cried, "or you'll be sorry."

"Me? Mock the shawl? I mock everything," he replied.

Dancing with the extravagant shawl like an imaginary partner, Leonardo snapped it in the air as he imitated a flashy tango, five steps forward, a sharp spin and a snap of his head. He seemed to be having the time of his life, embarrassing Stella at her own bachelorette party. He flung the shawl back around his shoulders and rubbed it against his neck lasciviously, as if he were doing a striptease.

"Is this where he takes his clothes off?" Rosalie's frizzy hair was bobbing with excitement. "And Stella said no male strippers! Woo-hoo! This totally rocks!"

"There are no male strippers!" Lacey tried to take the

shawl from the spinning Leonardo. Stella was hopping mad. Marie and Brooke seemed rooted in place in horror.

"Amen, sister," said Michelle. "This here is a party, not an orgy."

"Stop it right now! No one's taking their clothes off here," Stella said. She made a grab for Leonardo, but he twirled out of reach. "And Leo's the last man on earth I want to see in the buff."

"Trust me, darlings, there's nothing special to see." Miguel tried to tackle Leonardo as he dodged away. "Take it from someone who knows."

But as quickly as he began, the prancing Leonardo jerked to a halt. His face contorted in anger as he threw the shawl down. "Ow! It bit me. That damn thing bit me." He rubbed his neck furiously.

"You mocked the shawl." Marie shook one beringed finger at Leonardo.

The bachelorettes and servers stood agape while Lacey lifted the garment carefully off the floor. She saw nothing amiss, not even a loose thread, not a drop of blood. She folded it gently and handed it back to Marie.

"It's a fraud!" Leonardo shouted, still furiously massaging his wounded neck. "There's nothing magical to that dreary old thing and it bites. Now tell me my fortune."

"You don't deserve any fortune from me." Marie backed away from him, clutching her shawl to her breast. "You've made your own fortune."

Leonardo glared around the party room at the stunned guests. His little act had fallen flat, and his Caesar haircut made him look like a deranged dictator at bay. His nostrils flared. He released his neck and grabbed Marie's hand.

"I want to know my future!"

Marie gazed into Leonardo's face. Her mouth and eyes opened very wide.

Then she fainted.

chapter 4

"So she fainted." Vic Donovan nuzzled Lacey's hair and whispered into her ear. "Tell me more."

"Bad things happen when Marie faints. You know that." Lacey was trying not to be superstitious, but Marie's spells had a history of preceding some dark episode. "It's best to treat it as a storm warning. Admit it—she is good with the weather."

"The connection is not scientifically proven."

"Still . . ."

"Okay, I give up," Vic said. "Storm is coming. Give me the blow-by-blow. Nothing bad happened after that?"

"So far. Though Leonardo's lunatic scene definitely put a damper on the party. And Stella's already on pins and needles."

"Stella's always on pins and needles." Vic hushed her with a kiss. "And what about you and me? I haven't seen nearly enough of you since we got back from Sagebrush."

"You're seeing me now." She kissed him back, reclining on her blue velvet sofa, shoes off. She was exhausted, though keyed up after the party. "But I've been so busy writing that accursed book with Mac and Tony. And you've been busy catching up on work. And there are all the endless last-minute wedding details, and I'm Stella's maid of honor, and now tonight of all nights Marie has to *faint*—"

Lacey wanted to chill out. Tomorrow was a workday and the wedding hovered over her like an unburst rain cloud.

"Shhh. Sweetheart, Stella will be the Queen of the May, with you or without you."

Lacey counted on her fingers. "It's only April. Stella hates her wedding dress, her mother is coming, Marie faints, and Brooke will somehow concoct a conspiracy out of the whole thing."

"Stella will be the Queen of April and Marie will faint. It's what they do. But what I want to know is, when can we go buy an engagement ring together?" He kissed her fingers.

"Oh. Well, maybe I can pencil that into my busy schedule. After Saturday. Stella's wedding day."

"I suppose you want something big and gaudy?"

"Never gaudy. More like big and tasteful." She grinned and pantomimed wearing a giant rock on her ring finger. He laughed as she fluttered her fingers at him. "But, Vic, honey, we don't have to do anything right away. Do we?"

Lacey's biological wedding clock was not ticking as urgently as Stella's. Lacey wanted to savor her semi-secret engagement for a little while, without putting out a press release for the public or her entire circle of friends and family. Mac and Tony knew, and a very few others, but she'd sworn her editor and coworker to secrecy, at least for the time being.

Everything that had happened in Sagebrush, Colorado, was a mere handful of days in the past, but it all seemed far away and dreamlike now. She recalled a whispered "I love you" in the midst of flying bullets. And Vic's proposal? So incredible, it was as if she'd dreamed that too. The memory was delicious, but she wasn't willing to share it yet. Her ring finger was still bare.

Following an exhausting flight from Denver and a taxi ride back to her apartment building, she had stepped into the dusky night and taken a deep breath. The Virginia air was perfumed with honeysuckle and magnolia, the night sultry and sweet with the intoxicating aroma of spring. After that wild ride in Sagebrush, Lacey had never been so happy to get back in one piece to Alexandria. She was home.

She leaned back in Vic's arms and closed her eyes.

"Sweetheart, people don't have secret engagements in the twenty-first century," Vic whispered.

"They can if they want to."

Although the look on Vic's face was troubled, it didn't change the handsome features she loved to gaze upon. Lacey played with the dark curl that fell over his forehead.

"Do you really want to keep it a secret, Lacey?"

"Just for now, until Stella's wedding is over. It would be rude to intrude on her big moment. She might murder me."

Vic sighed. "Women."

"Don't forget you're marrying one." She kissed him again. "Thank you, dear."

"Doesn't mean we can't go shopping for that ring. Consider it a secret mission, for a secret decoder ring. We could leave town, maybe head up to Annapolis or down to Richmond. We could go in disguise."

"When? I have work! The bride-to-be requires constant handholding and reassurance. And—"

"And what?"

"Well, I can't get Marie's fainting spell out of my mind."

"Sweetheart, you're borrowing trouble."

She felt his breath on her neck, followed by more kisses. "Why would I borrow trouble? When so much of it lands at my feet for free?"

Lacey couldn't shake vivid images of what had happened at the party only hours before. Stella's doubts about her dress, Nigel's surprise spying mission, his obnoxious "best" man, Leo's nasty turn as a psychotic party crasher. And Marie's fainting spell to top off the festivities. She'd witnessed Leonardo recoiling in fear from the sight of the hefty Marie slumped over the table as if she were dead. Lacey and Brooke had run to Marie and lifted her head, making sure she could breathe, checking her pulse.

"You've done it now, you freaking diva!" Stella had wailed at Leonardo. "You pissed off the haunted shawl! At *my* bridal shower! It's a well-known fact Marie only faints when something terrible is about to happen. And this time it's going to happen to *you*, Leo."

Leonardo withered before Stella's rage. "That is just so—just—" he sputtered. He scratched his neck where he claimed the shawl had "bit" him and grimaced in pain. "I don't believe a word of it. It's all just a load of bull—" He backed away from Stella and her gathering bachelorettes, who formed a protective wall around their fallen fortune-teller.

"You've caused enough trouble, sugarplum," Miguel broke in. "You are out of here."

Leonardo tried to sneer. "Ooh, Miguel, I love it when you act all butch."

"I'm not acting. I'll crush you like the bug you are." Miguel took a firm hold on Leonardo's arm, propelled him bodily out the door, and slammed it behind him.

In a few minutes Marie revived, with no apparent ill effects and no memory of what had made her faint. The party limped along until the pink champagne ran out and Gregor Kepelov arrived to retrieve his Gypsy psychic. But the fête had lost its fire.

Lacey shook her head and tried to clear her thoughts. It was dark and quiet in her apartment, alone with Vic, but her thoughts were abuzz. Vic stroked her face.

"Where'd you go just now?" he asked gently. "Back to the party? Or should I say the scene of the crime?"

"Yes, except there's no crime. Just an indelible stain

on my party-organizing street cred." She groaned loudly. "Parties are stressful."

"Well then, darlin', let me help you with that." His kisses did their part. "Let me soothe away your pain, party girl."

Lacey forgot all about the botched bachelorette bash. At least for a while.

chapter 5

"He's dead! No joke, Lacey. Leonardo is dead! Like, *totally* dead! I'm telling you, Lace, Leo is *el muerto*."

The Monday-morning crowd in the lobby of *The Eye Street Observer* turned to stare at Stella Lake, as much for her outfit as for her outburst. Her shocking-pink sleeveless spandex top dipped far below daylight standards of decency in the Nation's Capital. Her short magenta skirt was just this side of street legal, and everything was so tight that Lacey wondered how Stella could even breathe. She wore towering pink sandals and carried a small purse in the shape of a pink corset. She was dressed very perkily for a messenger of doom.

"Dead!" Stella repeated it as she clung to Miguel's arm. He gently disentangled himself from her so he could hug Lacey hello, smoothing his pale blue polo shirt, which he wore outside his black jeans rather than tucked in. Although he was wearing his darkest shades, it was possibly the most casual Lacey had ever seen him. *Casual, or grief-stricken?* Lacey wondered. As cool as his demeanor might be, Miguel looked shaken, not stirred.

Lacey shushed Stella, but *not* attracting attention was a lot to ask of her distressed friend. Of course Lacey wanted to know everything, but there were too many news-seeking ears in this place. She dragged Stella and Miguel into a distant corner of the lobby.

"Miguel, he's not really dead, is he?" Lacey asked. "He couldn't be."

"Unfortunately, *está muerto* is correct," Miguel said softly.

Harlan Wiedemeyer, *The Eye*'s death-and-dismemberment reporter, was about to enter one of the elevators, but upon hearing the word *dead*, he spun on his heel. Harlan's eyes lit up with a newshound's prurient interest in a good headline, or a good doughnut. He bounced over to them like a child's beach ball, and he rather resembled one.

"What? Some poor bastard died? Smithsonian, *who, what, when, where*, and most of all, *how*? And what's the connection with our resident queen of fashion fatalities?"

"Harlan, hush." Lacey glared at him. "This has nothing to do with me."

"Your denial is music to my ears," Wiedemeyer said. "Good stories always start with a denial—you know that."

"Don't butt in," she practically hissed.

"Really? Smithsonian, how would I cover all the poor bastards of this world if I didn't butt in? How would any of us cover the news without a natural curiosity about the morbid and grotesque?" His chubby cheeks bobbed in a cheery smile. He brushed doughnut crumbs off his jacket. "Now, who was the poor bastard?"

Wiedemeyer reached for his notebook, but Lacey stopped him with The Look. Although Harlan Wiedemeyer sometimes became involved with workaday police reports, his special beat for *The Eye* was the weird, the strange, and the bizarre in everyday lives. His stories might involve unusual deaths and disasters, unexplained exploding toads or falling frogs, mysterious creatures from the deep, or a fatal two-ton spill of pinto beans. And if anything involved Lacey Smithsonian, Wiedemeyer wanted to be in on it. She had a history of being in the neighborhood of unusual deaths.

Lacey the Murder Magnet, that's me.

"Leonardo died," Stella broke in, needing a booster shot of attention. "He was, like, alive and annoying last night. And now he's dead."

"Leonardo? Leonardo who? Not the actor? The *Titanic* guy? Never liked that movie myself, but my Felicity, oh, my God, does she love that scene where—"

"No, no, no. Leonardo the hairstylist," Stella wailed. "Here in the District. We used to work together at Stylettos, my salon, or actually, he usually worked against me. But I knew him for a long time, once upon a time. We were sort of friends. Once."

"And this poor bastard's last name?"

Miguel sniffed. "Just Leonardo. One name, like Cher, Madonna, Liberace, Caligula, Stalin—"

"Leonardo was once known as Leonard Karpinski," Lacey put in. "Now go, Harlan. Do your own digging, into your own stories." She pointed Wiedemeyer to the elevator, gave him a little shove, and waited until the elevator doors closed. She turned grimly back to Stella. "What happened?"

"The *shawl* happened."

"It wasn't the shawl."

"Weren't you paying attention? Leo mocked the shawl. Marie fainted. And now he's dead. Like Grim Reaper dead. Ipso facto, the shawl did it."

Ipso facto? Stella's been hanging around with Brooke. Lacey looked to Miguel for help. Miguel took off his shades. His eyes were slightly red, as if he'd been crying.

"He was found dead only this morning. I heard it on the gay gossip drums, and Stella heard it through the salon grapevine. And yes, I have explained to her that it is not *our fault* that he's dead. *Yes*, it's tragic. *Yes*, he probably brought it on himself. And *no*, no one knows exactly what happened. Stella's acting like a bad hairstyle I can't do a thing with. And we really must deal with last-minute wedding details today, like the *reception*. I'm terribly sorry, but we have no time for this *Leonardo el Muerto*

Misterioso business. I'm counting on you, Lacey, to help me chill her out."

"Smithsonian! I want this story." Wiedemeyer popped back out of the elevator and into their little huddle. Death had lured him back, like the scent of a Krispy Kreme doughnut, and he had ears like a bat, or at least like his hero, the late lamented Bat Boy from *Weekly World News*. "It's confusing, but interesting. I smell a story here."

Lacey took Wiedemeyer by his shoulders and physically steered him backward in an awkward two-step. "I'm warning you, Harlan."

He calmly took a Krispy Kreme doughnut from a white bag tucked under his arm. "Have a doughnut. Everything, Smithsonian. I want all the facts, or else I will sic our intrepid police reporter on you. And you know Trujillo's a chronic byline thief."

"And you're not? Go work the story then! Call the cop house, see if they'll give you a cause of death for one Leonard Karpinski. And let me know what you get."

Wiedemeyer bit into the doughnut's fluffy glazed perfection and smiled blissfully. He gracefully waltzed backward with his doughnut into the open elevator, surprisingly light on his feet for a man of his beach-ball build.

"I mean it, Smithsonian. I want all the gory details—" The elevator doors shut, but she could faintly hear his last words "—on this dead bastard!"

Too many people were still staring slack-jawed at Lacey's trio in the lobby.

"Let's get out of here. Now," Lacey said. "Buy me coffee, you two, and fill me in."

She buttoned the navy linen bolero jacket over her early-1940s navy and yellow dress. It had seemed appropriate to this breezy spring day—before the day carried chilling news of the death of someone she knew, though didn't necessarily like. In any case, someone too young to die. The late stylist known as Leonardo had been only in his early thirties.

Their brief walk across Farragut Square from *The Eye*'s offices to the coffee shop was a reminder of how glorious spring could be in the District of Columbia. Red and yellow tulips and a few late daffodils bloomed in small flower beds in the greening square. The trees were leafing out into their summer glory. The warm air fairly cuddled Lacey's cheeks. Unfortunately, each soft breeze now reminded her of how brief life could be. Moments later, after dodging a gaggle of gray-suited lobbyists marching toward K Street, they settled with coffee and sweets into a wooden booth at Firehook Bakery.

"Here, have a butterfly," Miguel said, offering Lacey a pretty iced cookie to go with her coffee. "Stella already grabbed the tulip."

"Do you know what happened? Aside from the shawl mocking, I mean," Lacey said.

"Only that he's dead as a doornail." Stella bit thoughtfully into her cookie. "Leo was not a nice person. Always thought he was the queen bee of every hive he ever buzzed into. But jeez, last night I just wanted him to leave. Not *die*."

"Do you know how he died? It could have been natural causes, couldn't it?"

Surely that's possible, Lacey thought. *Even though he was still young. Stress, anxiety, a faulty heart valve? Something like that?*

"Anything is possible," Miguel said. "Leonardo was found outside his apartment building this morning. Facedown in that little postage-stamp-sized yard they have, behind some bushes. Like a fallen lawn gnome."

"Maybe he was mugged," Stella suggested.

"Could be," he mused, "but muggers don't usually kill you. Unless it was some doped-up meth head. Speaking from my experience as a *muggee* and armed robbery survivor, you just hand over the Gucci watch, the Ralph Lauren wallet, the Bentley leather jacket, and you both walk away. After the first few times, it's like a business transaction. 'Hi, I'll be your mugger today! Let me tell you about our specials!'"

"You have lived in some seriously bad neighborhoods," Stella said.

"But colorful."

"Maybe Leo had a weak heart," Lacey said.

"If he had a heart," Stella interjected.

"He had one," Miguel said. "Rusty, not often used, but easily bruised."

"No way!" Stella said in disgust. "He was mean as a crocodile. Like you wouldn't believe what he would do to clients he was pissed at. Chop, chop, chop! There were tears, I tell you. Many tears. Lots of cleanup and Kleenex."

"Tell me about it." Miguel stirred his coffee furiously. "Leonardo could nonchalantly say the most horrible things to you, about you, about everyone he knew. He was so nasty. At the same time, he'd be devastated if anyone did the same to him. Even though he deserved it."

Fling or no fling, it sounded to Lacey like Miguel and Leonardo had had a serious relationship. Once. One that had gone seriously bad.

"You reap what you sow, and sadly, Leo's been reaped." Stella munched on a cookie and sighed. "I'm not even sure where he was working lately. He jumped around a lot since he quit Stylettos."

"You can't insult everyone you meet," Miguel said. "What goes around comes around and bites you in the butt. Leonardo always had dreams of glory, his own salon, his name in lights. Not going to happen now."

Lacey's cell phone tinkled with the sound of cathedral bells. "Hello, Brooke."

Stella brightened instantly. "Brookie? Say hello for me!"

"Stella says hello."

"Did you hear that Leonardo character who crashed our party was found dead this morning?" Brooke was breathless with excitement.

Stella and Miguel jammed their heads against Lacey's

to overhear this conversation. Lacey put the phone on speaker and set it in the middle of the table. After the mid-morning rush, Firehook was nearly empty, the gray-suited lobbyists gone, and the trio in a back booth was well out of earshot of stragglers.

"It's the topic of the hour, Brooke. I'm here with Stella and Miguel."

"Good! We'll conference," Brooke said.

"How did you hear?" Lacey asked. It was mere curiosity; Brooke always knew when these things happened. She was connected.

"WTOP radio online: 'Prominent District Hairstylist Found Dead,'" Brooke read.

"He wasn't *that* prominent," Stella said.

"Does it say anything else?" Lacey asked. "Anything helpful, like cause of death?"

"No. Nothing obvious, apparently. 'Manner of death withheld pending autopsy.' Presumably he wasn't shot, stabbed, beaten, or run down by a car. Nothing like that. It says that when he was found this morning, neighbors first believed he was drunk or homeless, or both."

"A homeless guy in that eight-hundred-dollar jacket Leo was wearing last night?" Miguel impatiently drummed his fingers on the table.

"Where did he live?" Lacey asked.

"Off Fourteenth Street, near the little theatres," Miguel said. "He bought a place there before all the gentrification. When you could still find a parking place."

"Before Whole Foods," Stella added. "I remember. He had a party when he moved in."

"Well, team," Brooke said, "what are we going to do about this?"

"We are going to mind our own business," Lacey said. "We have a wedding to make happen." *We are not* CSI District of Columbia.

"Maybe we should send flowers." Stella played moodily with the remains of her cookie. "When we find out where the funeral is. Oh, my God, you don't suppose it'll be on Saturday? On my wedding day? He wouldn't dare do that to me."

"It would be so like him, the little attention whore," Miguel added.

"Surely not," Brooke said.

"Enough of Leonardo." Miguel put his hands on the table. "Stellarrific and I have got to get back on the wedding. People to see, places to go, menus to verify."

"Oh, all right," Brooke said. "Go. Do your wedding thing, Stella. Meanwhile, I'll try to find out the cause of death."

"Leo mocked the shawl," Stella said. "That's the cause of death."

Lacey put her finger to her mouth to shush Stella, but it was too late.

"The shawl!" Brooke breathed the word reverently. "Holy Roman Empire. I'd forgotten about that ridiculous business with the shawl."

"Brooke." Lacey picked up the phone and took it off speaker. "There is nothing to the shawl. Leo was being a jerk last night. His death today is just a tragic coincidence."

"A coincidence? Please," Brooke said. "There are no coincidences. What was it exactly that Marie told everyone about the shawl?"

"You were there. You don't need any help from me and Stella."

"I'll call Marie. She and her shawl might even need a lawyer."

Lacey rubbed her forehead. "Shawls don't kill people. People kill people."

"And they'll have to pry my cold dead fingers off my shawl? Whatever. I would think your Spidey senses would be tingling over this, my dear fashion sleuth. Your ExtraFashionary Perception *is* tingling, isn't it? You're just not *telling* me you're tingling."

"No, Brooke, I am not tingling, jingling, or ringling. But I must return to the office and finish a regular, good-for-everyday-use fashion column," Lacey said.

Brooke laughed. She was clearly thrilled by the thought of a Killer Shawl carrying an ancient curse.

"How long do you think it will take her to call Damon?" Stella whispered.

Lacey covered the phone with her hand. "She's probably texting him as we speak."

"That's just what we need." Miguel groaned. "Leonardo was killed by aliens. Or the CIA. Or Elvis in his blue suede shoes."

Lacey blew out the deep breath she was holding. Damon, the mad genius behind the popular Conspiracy Clearinghouse Web site—also known as DeadFed dot com—was Brooke's boyfriend and soul mate. Together they sought to uncover the mysteries of the universe, most of them apparently dark conspiracies controlled by criminal masterminds. She could imagine Damon's Web headline: Haunted Russian Shawl Stalks Washington! Leaves Corpses in Wake! CIA Stonewalls!

Lacey shook her head to clear it. In a town where Congress made laws no one read, where hidden secret bunkers really existed, where every sixth person was said to be a spy, it was easy to believe that a conspiracy lurked behind every cherry blossom. And her friend Brooke Barton was always quick to jump into the nearest bizarre conspiracy theory with both feet. Brooke, Lacey reflected, was a lot like Harlan Wiedemeyer. The difference was that Harlan simply thought Bigfoot and exploding toads were *fun*. Brooke believed they were a matter of *national security*.

"Well, if you're not interested in getting to the bottom of this, there's *someone* I can talk to," Brooke said.

"No, Brooke, wait! Not Damon. Not DeadFed."

Brooke laughed and clicked off.

"Lacey, are you listening to me?" Stella demanded. "This is only the beginning."

"We can't know that. This has nothing to do with the shawl," Lacey said.

"Don't forget, Marie fainted. *Fainted*. That's bad,

Lace. Very bad. That shawl is haunted and we were all there to witness the mocking. It's not through with us. I got a bad feeling, a very, very bad feeling."

"What you have, Stella darling, is a bad case of bridal jitters," Miguel said.

"That's right," Lacey added. "Shawls do not kill people. And clothes are not haunted."

Or are they?

chapter 6

The question of whether clothes really could be cursed lodged in Lacey's head like a virus and followed her back to the office. Maybe "haunted clothing" could at least inspire an idea for a Fashion Bite. She was on deadline and she was willing to take any idea the world handed her, even a crazy ghost of an idea.

First, Lacey called Marie Largesse, the fainting psychic. The new girl at the shop said Marie hadn't come in yet, and Marie wasn't answering her home phone or her cell. And Marie had said she was going to be sleeping late.

The newsroom was quiet in the late morning. Reporters were out covering the Hill or interviewing sources over the phone. Or they were busy with pre-story procrastination: surfing the Web, reading e-mail, playing computer solitaire, drinking coffee, gathering their thoughts. They weren't paying any attention to the fashion reporter in the room. It was as if Lacey worked in a different universe. And luckily the writers most interested in keeping an eye on her weren't around. She didn't even see Wiedemeyer, or her editor, Mac Jones, or her sometimes-rival, Tony Trujillo.

Just the way I like it.

Lacey found very little literature about "ghostly garments" or "haunted clothes" or "cursed couture" on the Web. She tried every promising search string. A few pieces of fiction turned up, including a story called "Furisode," by Lafcadio Hearn, about a haunted kimono in Japan that sickened and killed everyone who wore it. There were several blog posts too, but none that explained why or how a particular item was allegedly haunted. A tantalizing story about a haunted wedding gown in a museum, supposedly observed moving its sleeves, eventually was attributed to people walking on loose floorboards near the display case, which caused the mannequin wearing the gown to wobble.

Brooke would be so disappointed.

There was one more place to try. Lacey had a source in the massive costume collection in the Nation's Attic: the Smithsonian's National Museum of American History. She'd been lucky enough to snag a recent interview with the woman and a behind-the-scenes tour to view some of the historic wedding dresses and other garments that had been donated through the years. Yet she had learned so much more. Every item told a story, and the Smithsonian Institution had documented thousands of those stories.

There were more than thirty thousand items in the collection, including every kind of garment that could be worn on the human body, underwear to outerwear, from shoes and hats to jewelry and costume jewelry, along with makeup, combs, and brushes. The oldest item was a dress dating from the late seventeenth century. But not everything related to clothing was in the costume collection.

The First Ladies' gowns constituted their own collection, and the famous (and allegedly cursed) Hope Diamond resided in the Department of Mineral Sciences at the Smithsonian Museum of Natural History.

If *The* Smithsonian had no knowledge of suspected "hauntings" associated with its immense collection of historic apparel and wearables, one Lacey Smithsonian was pretty sure no one else did either. It was time to test that theory.

Lacey left a voice mail with her source, a charming

woman named Noël, who had not only a deep knowledge but also an abiding love for the collection. Noël
called her back shortly, but had no stories to offer about
demon-possessed or ghost-inhabited clothing. Not exactly.

"Some of our interns report feeling depressed whenever they handle clothes that belonged to Clover Adams," Noël told her.

Clover Adams might bring anyone down, Lacey
thought. Clover was celebrated as a dazzling nineteenth-
century Washington hostess; her devoted husband was
Henry Adams, the grandson and great-grandson of pres-
idents. Clover Adams fell into a deep depression after
her father's death, and in 1885 she killed herself with
potassium cyanide. Many Washingtonians (and many
tourists) knew her name by way of the famous hooded
statue that guarded her grave at Rock Creek Cemetery.
Neither explicitly male nor female, the ambiguous and
haunting monument had been commissioned from the
sculptor Augustus Saint-Gaudens by her mourning husband, who, legend had it, never again spoke his wife's
name. The sculptor had given it the grandiose title *The
Mystery of the Hereafter and the Peace of God that Pass-
eth Understanding*. But everyone knew the gloomy figure simply as *Grief.*

I'd be moved by Clover's legacy too, Lacey thought.
Had her depression somehow found its way into her
clothing? Did Clover's dresses contain her gloomy aura?
Or were the interns depressed simply because Clover's
story was so melancholy?

"And although it isn't exactly haunted," Noël continued, "we do have in the collection a wedding dress that's
known as the Bad Karma Dress. Did I show you that
one?"

Lacey remembered the gown well, with its layers of
ethereal lace that ruffled their way up to the waist, the
graceful bodice and delicate sleeves. That particular con-

fection of white lace was designed by Christian Dior and made for a bride who died soon after her wedding. However, in such a large collection there had to be at least a few items associated with heartbreak.

Every Smithsonian costume exhibit was the culmination of years of planning. Special mannequins were made to fit the clothes and evoke their period and mood. Displaying the gowns and dresses and shoes and hats at the museum was a way of keeping their stories and their owners alive. With regret, Lacey realized the public would never see more than the smallest fraction of this glorious collection. And while the collection also had men's clothing, Lacey had focused on the women's.

The fabulous dresses were carefully stored behind the doors of endless rows of plain beige cabinets. Dresses that were sturdy enough were hung, while more delicate items were protected by muslin or acid-free paper and laid flat in long drawers. Lacey had glimpsed only a few of the highlights of the gowns hidden there, but she'd been hypnotized by the depth and wonder of it all, as Noël and her assistant pulled dress after amazing dress from the Smithsonian closets, each owned by women, famous or unknown, throughout American history, and lovingly preserved for posterity.

The Smithsonian clothing collections were personal, even intimate, but according to Noël, they were *not* haunted. Clothes, it seemed, did not have the kind of magnetism for ghosts that creaky old houses and woods and lonely bridges possessed. But clothes had something better than ghosts. In Lacey's opinion, they had *magic*.

Lacey was initiated into the magic spell of clothing when as a teenager she had first visited her great-aunt Mimi and her wonderful trunk, where Mimi kept all the unfinished clothes and patterns and fabric for outfits she planned to make one day, but never did. Mimi's trunk was a veritable pirate's treasure chest of styles of the late 1930s and 1940s, full of enchanting apparel made to fit and flatter real women. All of those artifacts held magic for Lacey, even if others couldn't feel it.

Unfortunately, Lacey was finding the magic elusive in her research into "haunted clothes." Marie's shawl and Leonardo's death kept crowding her thoughts.

She didn't feel remotely recovered from the Sagebrush adventure, Stella's impending wedding was sucking up all her energy, and now there was the untimely death of Leonardo. On top of everything else, it was spring! Lacey craned her neck to look out a corner of her window and gaze dreamily at the flowers blossoming in Farragut Square.

I should have taken the whole week off.

She'd compromised with her editor to work Monday, Tuesday, and part of Wednesday, and then take the rest of the week off to deal with any unexpected wedding details that might crop up, Stella's-wedding-wise.

Lacey had the vacation time stored up, but with the newspaper industry in the shape it was in, she was afraid that if she took too much time, her job would vanish. Her fashion beat would be parceled out to the guy who took classified ads and an underpaid intern who didn't know a pleat from a pedal pusher. Besides, Mac Jones always whined when she asked for time off.

"You're gonna give up some future weekends to make up for this favor, right?" Mac had said.

"Right. I'm owed the time, Mac. It's not a *favor.*" But Newspaper Guild contract or not, Lacey wasn't eager to push too hard for her rights. Mac grudgingly granted her request, as long as she'd finish a column or a Fashion Bite or two ahead of deadline. And there was also the "true crime" book that Mac and Tony (and very reluctantly, Lacey) were cobbling together from the paper's Sagebrush reportage. Lacey had to steal the time for that late at night.

And have I mentioned it is spring! She wanted to luxuriate in it, bathe in it. She wanted to walk around the Tidal Basin and enjoy the lush cherry blossoms with her secret fiancé, Vic. Stella wasn't the only one in love with those pink and white petals.

Leonardo's sudden and unexplained death and a strange shawl of Russian origin were just too many layers of additional stress. She needed answers before she could calm down enough to write a story for her own beat. Short of calling the police department and asking questions she knew they wouldn't answer, Lacey sought out the next best thing to being there: Tony Trujillo, *The Eye*'s police reporter. Sure, Tony was a byline hog, but what reporter wasn't? He was a pal—and a born gossip.

Tony wasn't at his desk. Lacey circled back to her own cubicle and found him snooping around the food editor's domain. Felicity Pickles, grand dame of *The Eye*'s food section and Harlan Wiedemeyer's heartthrob, had not yet graced the office with her presence and the delicacy of the day. Felicity had trained the reporters and editors to behave like circus seals, begging for tasty nibbles from her test kitchen every day. On those infrequent days when Felicity didn't feed the masses, there was sorrow in the land, and Tony looked sorrowful.

"She's not here." Lacey pointed out the obvious.

"I can see that," Tony growled. "And the candy machine in the break room is broken. Doesn't anyone have anything to eat around here?"

"O cruel fate. Don't look so downhearted, Tony. It's almost lunchtime," Lacey said. "Working on anything interesting?"

"*Nada*. The usual."

That could mean anything or nothing. "What, no homicide or strange crime in the city?"

"Day is young." Tony flashed his killer smile. "What's up in the world of hats, hose, and haberdashery?"

"Same old, same old. Navy and white are in for spring, because they're *always* in for spring. This year with a dash of yellow. Yellow is the new black. Actually it's not. But somebody is bound to say it is. Might as well be me."

"Then I guess you're at the head of the pack."

She took a deep breath. "Hey, Trujillo, I heard a body was found this morning."

"Like many a morning. Tell me more." Tony made himself comfortable in Felicity's chair and propped his booted feet on the wastebasket. He sported a new pair of snakeskin cowboy boots he'd bought on their recent shopping expedition in Steamboat Springs, Colorado. He balanced his coffee cup on his knee. "You got a fashion clue? Know the victim, or just interested in my beat? There are days your beat seems to wield more weird murder wattage per square mile than mine, you know."

Lacey hesitated. Her week was jammed, including a final fitting scheduled for her maid of honor dress. She didn't know what to do about Stella "hating" her wedding dress, but she comforted herself with the knowledge that a dress was not a life-or-death decision, no matter what the bride said. Even so, Lacey still had to ride shotgun on Brooke or she would show up in something better suited to a courtroom proceeding or a funeral than a wedding. And she had promised Stella to help check out the reception venue and fret over the pinkness of the cherry blossom petals with her.

Tony sipped his coffee and waited, probably hoping a cart full of cookies would soon materialize, along with Felicity. "You were saying?"

She decided to spill. There might be a news story surrounding Leo's death, but whatever it was, it had nothing to do with her. Tony was welcome to it.

"Remember Leonardo, the temperamental diva stylist who used to work with Stella?" He looked blank. "He was a suspect in the Angela Woods murder."

"Rings a bell. That Karpinski guy? Arrogant and unpleasant? What about him?"

"He's the dead body. Can you check it out?"

Tony sat up straighter. "Sounds like you already have. What do you know?"

"Nothing. Except—he crashed Stella's bachelorette party last night. And he's dead this morning."

Tony grinned and put his snakeskin boots on the floor. "Brenda Starr, you've done it again. Wherever you go, bodies follow. Or is that *fall*?"

"Hilarious, Trujillo. Leonardo's demise had nothing to do with the party."

"You say that *now*. I'll make some calls and— Hey, wait a minute! You threw a Girls Gone Wild bachelorette bash and didn't tip me off?"

"Tony!" She snorted. "Are you a bachelorette?"

"No, but I know a few. Oh, that's right, I forgot. Smithsonian isn't known for her party-giving flair. And on a Sunday night? But I'm sure it was *killer*. Maybe the dead guy ate something lethal at your party."

"You want lethal? You're asking for it, Trujillo."

"Of course I am. How did he die?"

"I'm asking *you*. Call your sources. I'm not the police reporter."

"I'm glad we got that straight. For once," Tony said. "Sometimes I wonder."

"Can you find out for me without whining?"

"I can, if you tell me one thing." Tony looked around. He picked up her left hand. Lacey pulled it back. Tony dropped his voice. The sports guys were glued to their TV and the annoying junior police reporter wasn't around. "When are you going to announce the big engagement? Remember, Lois Lane, you said yes to Superman, and don't forget there are witnesses. So where's the ring?"

She grabbed him by the lapels of his leather jacket. "Shut up, Tony. That is classified information."

But Tony had seen and heard Vic's proposal, while everyone was dodging bullets in a cabin in the wilderness back in Colorado.

"Is it a secret, or have you changed your mind?"

Yeah, every woman dreams of that romantic moment,

under attack and surrounded by her nosy coworkers.
When Vic proposed, she was thinking only about him.
And the bullets.

"Nobody changed their minds." Lacey turned away
from Trujillo. "I just have too many things on my list
right now."

"And that translates to nothing on your finger?"

"Listen, boot boy, I am dealing with Stella's wedding!"

"And she's supposed to be the crazy one." He had the
nerve to snicker.

"Well, it's catching, so back off."

Tony just laughed. "Are you stuck on what to wear to
a wedding? How not to outshine the bride?"

"I like it. Let me write that down."

"Hey, Smithsonian. Don't run away from love. I hear
it's great stuff. Me, I can take it or leave it."

She graced him with a smile. "You ought to take it,
Tony. With the right bachelorette."

"I might do that someday. Without the bullet holes."
He winked at her and she laughed.

Trujillo had a history with women. They generally
melted when they met him. It was easy to do when he was
so easy on the eyes and so charming. His olive skin, dark
eyes, and flashing grin were surefire attention-getters in
D.C. If that weren't enough, Tony Trujillo was a real guy's
guy and seemed comfortable in his own skin, his leather
jackets, and his cowboy boots, a sexy contrast to the nervous buttoned-down lawyers and lobbyists of the Nation's Capital. But once women got to know him, it was a
different story.

He was a flirt and a heartbreaker. Like many men in
Washington, Tony had a fatal flaw: No matter how fabulous the woman at his side might be, he was always looking for the *next* incredible woman to walk through the
door. He once told Lacey it was impossible for him "to
settle on just one female when there are so *many* women,

so pretty, so smart, and well, just so impressive. How could I possibly settle for just one?" Lacey liked Tony, but they were friends and nothing more. She felt sorry for the women he went out with.

"Leonardo," Lacey reminded him. "Cause of death unknown. Take it away, Trujillo. Let me know what you find out."

He nodded and leaned over Felicity's empty desk one last time, looking for crumbs. *Nada*. He sighed and headed back to his corner of the newsroom.

Lacey attacked her deadline Fashion Bite one more time when Brooke called.

"If this is about your bridesmaid dress, Brooke, think pink. Like that blouse you've been wearing to perk up your gray suits."

"It's rose, not pink. Damon likes it."

"Rose, then," Lacey said. "A rose by any other name would look just as pink to Stella."

"But a whole dress, Lacey? It could damage my credibility as a legal eagle."

"Be brave, girlfriend. Pink, or bear the Wrath of the Bridezilla."

While she was on the phone Tony shot her an e-mail, which she read while Brooke nattered on about the legal implications of pink versus gray. Leonardo's death hadn't been ruled on yet by the medical examiner. There would definitely be an autopsy. The late Leonardo's housemate said the deceased texted him from a bar that he was distraught over "some fortune-teller's prediction."

"All I know is the D.C. cops are trying to find this fortune-teller," Tony's e-mail concluded. "Off the record, one cop told me it looked like some kind of poison. Probably because there was no apparent trauma, or maybe that was an early guess by the medical examiner. What do you know about all this?"

Not nearly enough, Lacey thought. But poison? Leonardo hadn't eaten anything at the party. He'd slugged

down some pink champagne, but they all drank that and
no one else died. Tony's tidbit should have set her mind
to rest, but it had the opposite effect.

"I haven't found out anything about Leonardo yet.
The cops aren't talking, or else I haven't found the right
cop yet, and Marie hasn't answered my calls either,"
Brooke was complaining in her ear.

Lacey made her excuses and hung up without men-
tioning Tony's info. Poison? Brooke would find out soon
enough from her own police sources, and then she would
call Damon Newhouse, who would soon create a storm
of cyber-nonsense about the "haunted Russian shawl"
over at DeadFed dot com, delighting his credulous readers and infuriating a skeptical Lacey Smithsonian. She
wondered exactly what Leonardo's housemate had told
the police about the "fortune-teller." Had they located
Marie, and if so, what was she telling them?

*What exactly is the shawl supposed to have done, and
who has it harmed, if anyone?* Lacey asked herself. *Where
did this curse nonsense get started? Maybe if I can find
Marie she can clear the whole thing up.*

It felt like hours since Stella had burst into the lobby
with her news. Lacey filed a news brief on the opening of
a new clothing store, then turned off her computer and
grabbed her bag, intent on consulting the psychic. She
could warn Marie that in the matter of the shawl, discre-
tion was the better part of valor.

Lacey momentarily wished she had driven to work
today, but the roads into the District were always such a
mess: According to headline news in her own paper, the
city was rated second in the country for gut-wrenching
traffic. Now she'd have to take the Metro to Alexandria,
then back again, before this day was over.

She almost made a clean escape from the office, but
her desk phone rang and she made the mistake of answering it.

"What's the deal with this ghost shawl?" the voice demanded without preliminaries.

"Damon." Brooke was even quicker on the trigger than Lacey expected. "I'm fine, and how are you?"

"I understand this shawl, or whatever it is, has mystical powers and it's Russian in origin, is that right? Is it some sort of secret Soviet-era assassination weapon? A high-tech weaponized babushka of death?"

Lacey rubbed her forehead, trying to avert the headache she was sure to have. "*The X-Files* went off the air—have you heard? Are they still in reruns in your head? Or are you listening to the *other* voices in your head?"

"Don't change the subject, Smithsonian. You are Spook Central right now, you and your baldheaded ex-KGB buddy, Kepelov. Don't tell me you don't know. You know what's going on, and DeadFed needs to know. The world needs to know."

She exhaled loudly and tried to breathe in some fresh air. "I don't have time for you, Damon. Or your insane ramblings. I'm on deadline."

"We're all on deadline, Lacey. All of us, all the time. We're on a deadline to disaster."

Lacey knew why reporters were hated in so many quarters of the Capital City. Because of reporters like Damon. Reporters who only reported what they already believed and who twisted every fact to fit their beliefs.

"Don't you have any blue aliens or cannibal congressmen to report on?"

"That's a good one." He laughed. "And they're supposed to be green, not blue. The aliens, not the congressmen. Sorry, fresh out of alien cannibal congressmen. I'd kill to write that story though."

"And I'm fresh out of Soviet weaponized shawls. Bye." Lacey hung up and raced for the door. Her cell phone rang. She checked the number: Damon again. She turned it off. She wanted to get to the bottom of this haunted shawl nonsense before Damon Newhouse turned it into this week's "alien autopsy" story. Not only that, he often linked her articles in *The Eye* to his site, making it seem like she was his partner and collaborator, part and parcel of his whacked-out world.

The problem with Damon is not just that he's crazy. Who cares if he's crazy? It's that so many crazy people believe him.

FASHION BITES

The Magical Properties of Clothes

Do you believe in the magic of what you wear? That your clothes have a meaning, a story to tell, or even a life of their own? Or do you scoff at the very idea that your clothes can speak for you, or speak to you?

What about that dress that always seems to bring you luck? Is it an illusion, or is there really something magical about it? Do you bring it out again and again to revive that blissful mojo? Or what about the suit you wore when disaster struck? Is it really cursed or just a reminder of bad times? Whichever it is, do you avoid it like the plague?

Of course you do—we all do. Even if we don't admit it. We all invest what we wear with memories, meaning, and personality.

Clothing preferences start in the nursery. Children often have clothes they cling to—the shoes they won't take off, the dress they wear until it's in tatters. Perhaps they refuse to wear any color but red or periwinkle. They grab hold of what they love, what makes them feel good, with joy and abandon. And stubbornness. But they know what they want. That's one of the privileges of childhood. Your personal style hasn't been drilled out of you yet by people telling you what you should want to wear.

Our clothes become personal symbols to us. You might have a dress you wore when trouble struck. You wore it again: more bad luck. Someone lost a love, or a loved one lost his or her life. You will never wear it again, and no one would blame you, because the very sight of it brings back sad memories.

Is there a summer frock somewhere in your closet that you can't bear to part with? It's long out of style, the sleeves too puffy, the skirt too full, and it's too optimistically pink (or green, or yellow). But it's the dress you wore when you first fell in love. And you'd like someone to someday rediscover the dress that drew Cupid's arrow. That dress will never get thrown away.

Women are drawn to style, and men are drawn to a woman with style. It may be the way her silver hoop earrings catch the light with just a hint of the Gypsy. It reminds him of something he can't quite recall. Ask him years later if he remembers those exact earrings and he won't—but he'll remember you.

He remembers the red dress you wore on your first date. Not the style or the cut or the length, but the color. The lure of the red dress, celebrated in so many songs, may be only a biological imperative, but guys are crazy about the lady in red. Is the magic in the red dress—or in you?

Another man might fixate on that long-lost girl in that perfect miniskirt he can't quite forget. Or the aquamarine sweater that matched her eyes. Even if her eyes weren't really quite aquamarine. He may dwell fondly on the black tights and plaid skirt that a certain girl wore in high school. He may even remember her cowboy boots and her silver spurs as they jingle-jangle-jingled.

Our clothes help us create our own aura, our own style, our own magic. Some days our clothes just do their jobs and we do ours, no magic involved. But think about this the next time you're dressing for a big event, a first date, a special party, a wedding: Is the magic in the clothes we wear, or is the magic in us? And does that magic linger in what we wear, even after we've put the clothes aside?

Of course it does. That old black magic might just be a Little Black Dress.

chapter 7

The purple AMC Gremlin was parked illegally in front of *The Eye*'s offices, next to the flower seller hawking fresh violet-hued irises.

There could only be one bright, shiny, freshly washed grape Gremlin like that in the entire Washington, D.C., area. Some people called Marie Largesse's mid-1970s psychedelic survivor of a vehicle *ugly*, but Lacey thought it had an undeniable air of goofy cuteness. In many ways, a Gremlin seemed like the perfect car for an ex–New Orleans fortune-teller—her mechanical *familiar*, so to speak.

Lacey was heading to the Metro to travel to that very car's owner when she spied the purple Gremlin parked in front of *The Eye*. A tourist aimed his camera at the ancient purple car juxtaposed with the violet flowers. The Gremlin was empty, and Marie was supposedly sleeping late today. *Who's got the Gremlin?*

Someone grasped her arm. Before she even turned around she knew who it was by the heavy feel of his hand.

"Hello, Kepelov," Lacey said. "Nice day for irises."

"All this time we are friends, Smithsonian, and you never call me Gregor?" His other hand held a large bouquet of the violet blooms, which with a slight bow he presented for Lacey's approval. "Do you think my Marie will like them?"

"Yes, Kepelov. Gregor. Marie will love them."

"And me?"

"She already loves you. Why, I have no idea."

Gregor Kepelov laughed and Lacey squinted at him in the April sunshine. He seemed slightly different somehow.

"The mustache. It's gone," she said.

"You noticed! No one else notices."

He'd shaved off his bushy blond mustache and he wasn't wearing his usual Moscow-meets-Montana cowboy attire. Instead he was in crisp gray slacks and a blue shirt that brought out the cool blue of his eyes. Kepelov's face always struck her as just a little bit off normal and his stare somehow too intense. He made her uncomfortable. Lacey could easily imagine him as the KGB spy and assassin he used to be. And might still be.

"What brings you to Eye Street?" she asked. "Surely not the blossoms."

"These? A happy coincidence. I come on a little errand. To see you."

"Funny, I was just on my way over to see Marie."

"She said you would be coming." Kepelov thumped his shaved head with an index finger. "Psychic, you know. But Metro is slow and I am fast. Allow me?"

Fast? In the Gremlin? "Marie had a feeling?"

"You are surprised? She also had a little visit from police. To discuss the death of a certain Mr. Leonardo."

"Aha. You want to drive me across the river in that thing? Will it float?" She had never actually been inside Marie's gaudy little car. He shrugged.

"My car is in — garage. For upgrades," he said vaguely. Kepelov wasn't exactly the purple Gremlin type; he was more the invisible gray surveillance vehicle type. He opened the passenger door for her. "But Gremlin is classic American drag race car. Little car, big engine. Decent mileage too."

"Pretty conspicuously purple, isn't it? For a spy?"

"Me, a spy? What spy? Lacey Smithsonian, you have wonderful sense of humor." He climbed into the driver's seat while she buckled up. "True, I was with KGB, but long ago. KGB is no more, and Gregor Kepelov makes a new life in America. Because inside? I am a *cowboy*." Kepelov thumped his chest.

"You're a cowboy and I'm the Queen of Sheba."

"Besides, who would suspect any driver of this fine purple vehicle of being a spy?" He gave her his unlikely lopsided grin and pulled the Gremlin into Eye Street traffic, heading for the Potomac River and Alexandria, Virginia.

What spy? Everyone knew Washington, D.C., was Spy Central. According to the District's Spy Museum, the city was awash in intelligence agents, either for other nations or for America. Kepelov might not be on any particular intelligence service's payroll, but he was certainly a freelance operative, a "soldier of fortune."

Lacey had first encountered him in the guise of a seeker of lost treasure, a sometime associate and sometime enemy of Nigel Griffin, Stella's betrothed. Kepelov had made connections in the local security industry, and he'd even taught a session of the private investigation course Lacey had taken a few months before.

Kepelov's main interest, besides Marie, seemed to be hunting for purloined jewels and lost artifacts. He favored anything with a Romanov provenance that he could sell to collectors for big money. Lacey was never quite sure whose side he was on, except his own. And, she hoped, Marie's.

"How fortunate I caught you heading for subway," he said as he threaded the little Gremlin between two big black Lincoln Town Cars, practically the Official Vehicle of Washington, D.C.

"Why exactly did you come to get me? I was already heading that way."

"For a few minutes of pleasure of your company, Smithsonian. My Marie needs your assistance. She values your opinion, you know. You have experience dealing with police here, and she is perhaps a little too—honest."

"She told the police about the shawl, didn't she?" Lacey had been afraid of that. "She told them a haunted shawl killed Leonardo because he mocked it?"

"That is how she sees it, so that is how she tells it." He shook his head. "My business? I tell nothing to nobody. My darling Marie, her business is tell *everything* to *everybody*."

"I'm guessing—and hoping—the police figured she's crazy."

"That would be lucky break."

"Unless they think she's crazy like a fox, and knows more than she's telling."

"Everyone always knows more than they tell. You know that. I know that. But a shawl killing a person? Would look stupid on police report. The cops might suspect Marie is using the shawl for distraction." Kepelov pulled into traffic in front of a speeding bus and Lacey gasped.

"Be careful! These D.C. bus drivers are insane," she said. "They kill someone every month."

"I learn to drive in Moscow with lunatic KGB instructors. Kill people every *day*."

Lacey held on to the seat belt as her stomach lurched. "Okay. You want to protect Marie. But why does she believe this wild tale about the shawl, Gregor? Did you fill her head with the idea that the thing is haunted, or cursed or possessed or whatever it is?"

"Not me. To me it is an old family heirloom, very pretty, very historic, but just a shawl. It was Olga."

"Olga? Who's Olga?"

"My sister."

Kepelov shot across two lanes of traffic to make a right turn onto Fifteenth Street. Lacey gasped again. He paid no attention. *Probably KGB driving instructors never gasp.*

"Are you following someone? Or fleeing someone? Are we being pursued?"

"No. Not yet. Is how I always drive. Why do you ask?"

He roared down the street, as loud as a Gremlin can roar and far faster than she thought it was capable of speeding.

"Because you're driving like a maniac."

"Thank you. Back home in Russia is great compliment. Only maniacs get anywhere in Moscow traffic. Force of habit."

Lacey tried to swallow her fear of meeting imminent death on the streets of D.C. "You have a sister? Olga?"

"It happens. Even in best of families. You have a sister too, no?" He checked the rearview mirror as if they were being followed.

Leave my sister out of this. "So your sister, Olga, told Marie the shawl was haunted?"

"I'm afraid so. Olga is, like you say in America, piece of work."

Says the Russian piece of work! "I can hardly wait to meet her," Lacey said. A car honked and a driver flipped the bird at them, whereupon Kepelov hit the accelerator and wove through traffic. "If I live that long."

He surprised her by laughing. "You amuse me, Lacey Smithsonian."

"My pleasure. You don't think the shawl is haunted, do you, Gregor?"

"Before today, I would say no. But today? With the death of this Leonardo?" He shrugged.

"Tell me about the shawl." Lacey had heard a little about it from Marie, but not from Kepelov. Things often were lost in translation.

"You probably know all this. It is old family heirloom, of my very old family. One of a kind. It tells the story of the Kepelovs in tiny pictures, tales told by thread and needle. Deaths, disasters, triumphs, all our little ups and downs. Quite the conversation piece. Always draws a crowd."

"Why do people think it is haunted?"

"You must understand one thing, Lacey Smithsonian. *Everything* in Russia is haunted!" He turned his head and the Gremlin jerked. "Russian winters are very long. People need something to do. They write stories. They tell stories. Long stories. Ghost stories. *Long* ghost stories. They embroider a shawl like they embroider a story. In my family, the two go together. The old grandmothers, the *babushkas*, they sit together long winter nights, they sew, they embroider, they tell stories. The shawl has been in many hands through many generations. A bride dies, a husband runs away, a child falls down a well, the story is embroidered into the shawl. Suddenly the shawl itself is haunted! So typical. So Russian."

Even in fear of death in a speeding purple Gremlin crossing the Potomac River, Lacey pushed for a little more background. *How reporters really die*, she thought. *Asking one too many questions.*

"But there must be a specific story, a kernel of truth that started the legend?"

"Irina Katya Kepelova. It started with her. She was the great-great-great-great-whichever-great-grandmother it was who first took it into her head she wanted a shawl like no other. The family was very poor back then, so a new shawl was all she had to give to her daughter for her wedding trousseau. She embroiders it in secret. She explains to the daughter on her wedding day how she sews it with little flowers, usual sort of thing. But also how she puts in a tiny house to represent her house, where her daughter was born. The river through their village. The church where the daughter is wed. She adds a wedding veil for a good marriage, a crown for prosperity, a firebird for good luck, rings and crosses and icons. So small you almost cannot see them. Very Russian stuff. She leaves lots of room for the daughter and her daughter's daughter's daughters to add their own history to the shawl."

"Pretty nice wedding gift."

"Perhaps a little too nice. Irina Katya Kepelova had a greedy niece, so greedy she would steal a hot stove. Old Russian saying. The niece gets her hands on it and *bingo bango*, she dies of fever, wrapped in the shawl. The shawl returns to Irina Katya's daughter. With death in it. Maybe a curse. After that, most people are not so eager to steal the shawl. But some want it more, because now it has some kind of power, some kind of magic. Goes on and on like that. Generations of crazy stuff."

"What do you believe?"

"Me? I believe you should live in a warm place where winters are not so long." He laughed. "But after so many years, so many people saying this thing is cursed, is haunted, is full of ghosts— " He let the thought drop.

Kepelov circled off the Fourteenth Street Bridge on the Virginia side of the river and careened south down the George Washington Parkway toward Alexandria.

"Is there another reason you want me to speak with Marie?"

"Marie and Stella believe you have the, what do they call it, the EFP."

He has to be laughing at me, she thought. "Ha. Talk about people making up crazy stories."

"ExtraFashionary Perception, they call it," Kepelov said. "Clothes talk to you, Smithsonian. Or you know how to look and listen. Whichever. They believe it and so I believe it too. All I ask is look and listen. If you find the shawl has no mystical powers and you convince Marie of that, all is good." He paused for a breath. "And if it is truly possessed, well— That is maybe even more interesting."

"Because it might be worth something?" Lacey didn't trust him.

His smile was always a little startling. "It's always about the price, yes? But have no fear. I would never take the shawl away from Marie. It is a present, an heirloom. From a man to his betrothed."

"I suppose the legend would make it more valuable?"

"To a Russian? Of course. But the old Soviets, my old buddies, ex-KGB, for example? They would be more interested in what it could do. If it can do anything."

"And pay a high price."

"Why pay, when you can terrorize and steal? Intimidation and theft work so well."

It was no secret that the KGB and the Soviet military had delved deeply into fringe science and paranormal research in the post–World War II era. Millions of rubles were spent on psychics and weapons of the mind in an effort to outmaneuver the Americans in the arms race, the missile race, the space race, in *any* race.

"Is that why you were attracted to Marie? Because she's a psychic?" If that's the case, he might have looked for one who didn't faint in the presence of danger.

"Always the skeptic, Smithsonian. I respect that. But I love my big beautiful Marie. She is my bounty and my treasure. Okay, maybe someday her psychic powers lead us to other treasures, together. A little bonus. But I would love her just as much without all the astral *this* and the paranormal *that*. She has a great big heart. You know that. Who would not love Marie?"

A catering van cut right in front of them, and Kepelov pounded the Gremlin's horn like the pounding in Lacey's heart. It made no difference to the truck driver. The Russian was not about to be shamed by a big slow American van, so he floored the Gremlin and swerved in front of a Prius on the right. He passed the van and cut in front of him, with his own triumphant third-finger wave.

"Asshole," Kepelov yelled out the window.

"You having fun?" Lacey yelled at Kepelov.

"If not fun, why do it? I came to America to have fun!"

"Good. As long as *one* of us is having fun." Lacey held her breath and shut her eyes.

"In the old Soviet days in Russia, someone like Marie would be at the mercy of KGB. Like a bug under a microscope. You have no idea what kinds of things KGB would do to people to find out secrets of the mind."

"I'd like to know some of those secrets too," Lacey said.

"I would be disappointed if you did not. Like I always

tell you, Lacey Smithsonian, you would make excellent spy. Except for your impulse to be a good reporter and tell all the world the news." He chuckled.

"The Soviets?"

"Psychics were in great demand. Far more than you know. Did you know Boris Yeltsin was object of psychic attacks from KGB and others when he stood against the coup attempt?"

Psychic attacks? She tried to picture what that would look like. *Brain waves radiating from their heads?* "Did it work?"

Kepelov made a face. "Yeltsin was so nuts on a stick already, who can say? KGB and friends did not want Russian government to be reformed by Yeltsin, so they used whatever they had. But to protect Yeltsin from psychic attacks, his people brought their own psychics. To form protective mind shield around him."

"Spy versus spy, the paranormal version." Lacey tried not to laugh. "At least it meant full employment for starving psychics."

"No psychic ever starved for long in Russia. No charlatan either. You are skeptical, you scoff. I scoff too. Even the U.S. had secret psychic programs. Not nearly so successful as Soviets."

"No, of course not."

He laughed again. "KGB even studied a Russian psychic who could stop the heart of a frog, stone dead, using just her mind. Stone-cold dead. What do you think of that?"

"Kill a frog? I think that's no way for a girl to find her prince."

chapter 8

"But, Marie, why would you tell the police the shawl killed Leonardo?"

Lacey was seated in Marie's bungalow, in a funky purple velvet Art Deco chair dating from the 1920s. To avoid sinking into it, Lacey kept her hands on the stout wooden arms. Marie's house was packed with over-stuffed furniture. The small Craftsman bungalow was in the Del Ray section of Alexandria, not far from the Braddock Road Metro. It was the first time Lacey had been inside and she was fascinated by Marie's place. There was so much extravagant décor to look at, it was hard for her to stay on topic.

"Well, cher, it's what I believe is the truth. And the police knocked on the door while my head was full of sleep. I was too groggy to just make something up. The news was so shocking, I could hardly believe it, but when they said Leonardo was dead, I just *knew*." Marie rubbed her eyes and smiled sadly at Lacey. "It was the shawl. It had to be."

Marie was one of those rare women whose luminous clear skin and dark eyes were expressive enough without makeup. Though she was a large woman, her body looked bountiful and curvy, but never fat. *Voluptuous* was the word people usually used for her. Lacey didn't quite know how Marie managed that, but she envied her.

However, she'd told the D.C. cops Leonardo was mur-

dered by the shawl! It was all Lacey could do to keep
from groaning. But it was impossible to be irritated at
Marie. She looked so unhappy and vulnerable. Her dark
hair tumbled over a gauzy blue dress with silver sequins
sparkling across the bodice and sleeves. The sparkly
frock covered most of Marie's tattoos, including the eyes
of Horus on her shoulders. *Probably from Fortune Tell-
ers R Us Dot Com.*

The fortune-teller's feet were bare and her nails
painted a deep purple, her favorite color. Yet, beneath
her consciously exotic look, Marie was a canny business-
woman and her outfit suited her business. It wouldn't do
for a professional psychic to be caught wearing torn
jeans and baggy sweats. Or a lawyerly gray suit.

"Do you remember what made you faint?" Lacey
asked. "Or did you see anything before that?"

"Oh, I never remember. You know that, Lacey, cher."

She tried another tack. "How did the police get your
name?"

"Something about the bachelorette party at Rosebud's, I think. They said Leonardo called his housemate
from some bar afterward. He was drunk and babbling
about how he wasn't invited, and he mentioned Stella
and the 'fortune-teller.' The police probably got my
name from the restaurant. I handed out lots of my cards
too. You don't have to be psychic to find me."

"We know you have nothing to hide, my darling," Kepelov said loyally. "You were plying your trade."

Marie nodded in agreement. "I only told Leonardo
not to mock the shawl. He was so rude and just making
an awful scene. It wasn't like I predicted he'd meet up
with the Grim Reaper. But then there was the—incident."

"When you fainted," Lacey filled in. "Even if the shawl
had some dark power or evil intent, Marie, surely a human
being would have to, let's say, do its bidding for it to have
its way? I mean, it doesn't have teeth and claws, right?"

"Right." Marie nodded, her eyes large. "I just put on
a fresh pot of coffee. You want some?"

"Sure, why not?" Lacey had already had her dose of caffeine for the day, but if it helped clarify things, it might be worth a jittery day and a sleepless night.

Kepelov brought a tray laden with mugs of coffee, cream, and sugar. He handed Marie hers with a murmured endearment that Lacey didn't catch. Lacey hesitated just a second too long when Kepelov handed her a mug. He frowned playfully.

"What, you are afraid of my coffee? Smithsonian, I am wounded! I do not slip you a Mickey in the coffee today, I promise. Only that one time! Are we friends or are we not friends?"

That one time. He was teasing her about their first encounter, in the cellar of a farmhouse in the French countryside, in Normandy. Lacey had been searching for a lost corset full of Romanov treasure, and Kepelov and Nigel Griffin were hot on the same trail, though they thought they were searching for something quite different. Kepelov reached the cellar first. Some sort of secret Soviet knockout drops on Kepelov's handkerchief, and Lacey was out like a light. Neither of them won that round.

"Gregor, darlin', maybe Lacey just doesn't like this chicory coffee from New Orleans," Marie said soothingly. "If you don't feel like coffee, cher, Gregor could whip you up some Earl Grey? Hot chocolate? Brandy?"

Lacey shook her head to cast all thoughts of that day in the cellar from her mind. She took a sip. Just chicory coffee, and tasty at that.

"Good coffee. Kepelov, *Gregor*, I had no idea you were so domesticated. You seem to be adept at whipping up all kinds of concoctions."

"I have a variety of useful skills in the kitchen and elsewhere." Gregor and Marie exchanged a smile and he rubbed her shoulder.

"Gregor is a man of many talents," Marie said with a low, intimate laugh. "If you know what I mean."

We are so not going there.

"So, Lacey Smithsonian, how is it that the late Mr. Leonardo met his untimely death?" Kepelov asked.

Lacey shook her head again. "The police and the medical examiner aren't releasing any information. But off the record, I hear one of the cops said something about poison."

Kepelov sipped his coffee contentedly. "Poison? Very interesting. Very flexible medium, poison. So many kinds, so many ways. Could have been administered anytime, anywhere. Not necessarily at the party." He focused on Marie. "How are you feeling, my dear? Not faint?"

"I'm fine, Gregor, sugar. Fit as a fine fiddle."

"What do you really think of the shawl, Marie?" Lacey set her mug on the small star-covered bench that served as a coffee table. "Is it haunted or possessed, or just possessed of a creepy past?"

"That lovely thing, creepy? I should say not. And I would say, in my professional opinion, it is *not* haunted, so much as it is *extraordinary*. When I touch it, I feel all the love that went into it. It pulses with the life and energy of all the women who worked on it, and wore it, and added to its history. When it's around my shoulders, it holds me with love. That's what I feel. But it does have this—dark legend attached to it."

"Where's the shawl now?" Lacey asked. "I didn't have a good chance to examine it last night. Would you mind if I take another look, Marie?"

"Sure thing, cher. Be right back." Marie disappeared into her bedroom. They heard closet doors slamming, then drawers opening and closing. She returned empty-handed and nervous. "I don't understand it. I'm sure I put it in the closet last night. Gregor, I can't find it. It's not anywhere I ever keep it. The shawl is gone."

The three commenced an exhaustive search of Marie's bungalow. The house was small and it didn't take long. They looked everywhere: in the two small bedrooms with tiny closets, the cozy living room and dining

room, the kitchen and one bath, the half-finished base-
ment with laundry facilities, and the trunk of Marie's
purple Gremlin. But no shawl.

"You have no idea where it could be? Or who could
have taken it?" Marie and Kepelov shook their heads.
"No one else has been here today? Except the police?
And you didn't show it to the police this morning?"

"They didn't ask to see it," Marie said. "They thought
the whole thing was silly. Cher, I can see you think I
should know. I think so too, but I have blind spots, so to
speak, in my—in my third eye." Marie rubbed the middle
of her forehead. "Lacey, I cannot foretell my own fortune! I cannot see the things in the future that are closest
to me. It's awful for me sometimes, to feel so helpless—"
Her eyes filled with tears. "Oh, Gregor, cher, I'm so sorry.
I'm devastated."

Gregor hugged Marie tight. He lifted her face and
kissed her lips and forehead. "Not to worry, my darling.
We will continue our search. And you remember the legend of the Kepelov shawl? It always comes home."

A knock on the front door startled them. Kepelov
peered out a side window before he went to the door.
Lacey half expected to see the D.C. police arrive for another round of questioning. But it was a woman who
marched into the room. A woman with a dour look on
her face.

"Ah, Lacey Smithsonian," Kepelov said, shutting the
door, "allow me to present my sister. Olga Kepelova."

chapter 9

There was nothing soft about Olga Kepelova. Even her brother, the rough and tough Gregor Kepelov, seemed to shrink back from her. Olga took in the room with a glance and a nod. It must have passed muster.

"Why, Olga, what a pleasant surprise," Marie said. "You should have told us you were coming. I would have made beignets."

"Is not necessary, Marie. I am family, apt to show up anytime," Olga announced icily. "Social visit only."

Olga's direct stare made it clear she took no prisoners. She looked a bit older than her brother and just as tall. Her dark brown hair was severely blunt cut at her chin. Straight eyebrows framed those penetrating eyes, pale blue like her brother's. Her plain brown shirt and slacks begged for anonymity, but it was hard to look away from her. She was somehow riveting. She stuck out her hand for Lacey to shake. Her handshake was firm, but cool.

"I am pleased to meet you," she said carefully, in an accent that was thicker than her brother's.

"It's a pleasure," Lacey responded. "Gregor never mentioned having a sister."

Olga managed a stiff smile. "That is so like him."

"You didn't tell us you were coming," Kepelov said.

"What, you don't like surprises?" she asked.

"No," he said. "But you know that."

"That is what makes it so enjoyable for me." Olga smiled at him.

"Are there more of the Kepelov clan?" Lacey was curious.

"There is another brother. We do not speak of him." Olga lifted her head and sniffed the air. "I smell coffee. I would like a cup."

"Where are my manners?" Marie, who had been watching Olga as if hypnotized by a snake, scrambled to the kitchen to retrieve the coffee herself this time, leaving Gregor behind, also hypnotized.

"I take it black as night," Olga called after her. "No sugar."

"I'll keep that in mind, sugar," Marie said from the kitchen.

"Lacey Smithsonian." Olga turned back to her. "Why do I know that name?"

"I'm a fashion reporter. For *The Eye Street Observer*, in the District."

"I never read about fashion. So frivolous." The woman wrinkled her forehead and touched its furrows. "Ah, now I remember. You are the one."

The one. It was the one thing people said to her that most drove Lacey crazy. *The one* WHAT? *What did she hear about me? And did she hear it from* The Eye, *or* DeadFed?

"The one?"

"Gregor has mentioned you, and the famous Romanov corset. What a lucky find."

"You could call it lucky," Lacey agreed.

"But it was more than luck, was it not?" Olga stared at her.

Lacey lifted one eyebrow. "Perhaps it was fate."

The tiny corset, ripped by bullets and spilling its hidden treasure of diamonds, had been worn by one of the Romanov princesses during their terror-filled execution in 1917. It was a spectacular discovery, not to mention a fabulous news scoop for Lacey and her paper, but the

U.S. government had swooped in and gathered up the corset and the diamonds, for the treasure's own "protection." Whose protection, Lacey wasn't sure. The American and Russian governments were still hammering out a complicated deal for the corset's eventual return to the mother country, but not without a few perks for the United States, including a guarantee of the first museum tour. Everything would, of course, take years. But then, the corset had been lost for nearly a century, so it had all the time in the world.

"Are you looking for diamonds today?" Olga asked.

"Just answers. About the shawl."

Marie bustled out of the kitchen with a cup of her hot chicory brew and handed it to Gregor's sister, who turned around twice before deciding to sit down in a yellow velvet Art Deco chair. She sat down carefully, as if the chair might bite her bottom. Lacey imagined that Marie's cozy living room, with its plush furniture, might have been the most feminine space Olga had ever occupied.

She would no doubt be more comfortable, Lacey thought, *in a plain white room with stainless-steel tables and dentist chairs. With a naked lightbulb suspended from the bare white ceiling.*

"My dear Olga, to what do we owe this unexpected pleasure?" Kepelov said, with a trace of sarcasm.

"A sister cannot see a brother and his bride-to-be?" She snorted. "Very well, I came to see the shawl."

"Why?" He squinted at her.

"Why not? To see what condition it is in. To see if it needs cleaning. To repair any pulled threads. To make sure everything is in order for the wedding." She turned to Lacey. "Family heirloom, you know. I am the eldest Kepelova daughter, it is my responsibility."

"Oh, Olga! I'm afraid—well—" Marie groped for words. "I can't find it. It's missing. We've just this minute discovered it's not here. That is, we've misplaced it. Somehow. Somewhere."

"Misplaced it? You have lost the family's shawl?

What happened?" Olga carefully set the coffee mug down and stared at each one in turn.

Pretending to be a fly on the wall, Lacey sipped from her lavender Little Shop of Horus mug and settled into her velvet chair. Gregor Kepelov took a breath and seemed about to try to finesse the situation, but Marie spoke very fast, not in her normally leisurely Louisiana drawl. She had taken the shawl to a party the night before, she told Olga, and now it was missing. And a man at the party who had "mocked" the shawl and its legend was now dead.

Marie would make a terrible spy, Lacey thought. There was no guile about her, which was part of her charm. Gregor Kepelov added nothing. He waited for Olga's reaction, and Lacey, fascinated, took it all in.

"Perhaps Gregor shouldn't have mentioned to so many people all those ridiculous stories about the shawl," Olga suggested.

"Who talks the most in this family?" Gregor asked. "You!"

"Are you saying the stories aren't true?" Lacey inquired.

"I am not saying these stories are not true." Olga was nonchalant. "Strange things happen, coincidences happen. Who can say what is true? And it is all only old family lore, you understand, from many years ago. But this legend makes it more interesting. More valuable to steal. Such an old and sentimental garment should be guarded most carefully."

"Why didn't you take over the shawl, Olga? You said you're the eldest daughter," Lacey said.

The woman grimaced. "Who would want the burden of it? I am not married, nor am I likely to be. I have no one to leave it to."

"I feel terrible." Marie was on the verge of tears.

Lacey tried to be the practical one. "If you brought it home, Marie, and no one has been in the house until now, then it must be here somewhere."

"I don't know—I can't remember."

Olga gave a small shrug and turned her formidable gaze on her brother. "I told you not to give the shawl to your fiancée until the day you are married. I told you it was not safe, that this is the history of the shawl. But do you listen to me? No." She turned to Lacey. "That is part of the tradition. The bride gets the shawl on her wedding day. Not before. Never before."

It was the first time Lacey fully realized the seriousness of Gregor Kepelov's feelings for Marie. Until now she'd still been concerned he might be simply playing Marie for a fool. Lacey started to trust him a little more. But if he knew this shawl might be dangerous, why give it to the woman he loves? Why let Stella borrow it for the wedding, to serve as her "something old, something borrowed"?

"I do not believe in the Kepelov family superstition," Gregor said evenly, meeting Olga's stare. "My Marie has a gift. Her gift is stronger than the foolish legend of the shawl. And she will wear my name when we marry. Who more than her deserves to wear my family's history? I take responsibility for its loss."

Olga didn't bat an eyelash, but Lacey could tell her brother had scored his point.

"'The foolish legend,' as you say. Neither do I believe it," she said. "In principle anyway. But . . ." She changed the subject. "Marie. Are you certain you had the shawl with you last night, when you came home?"

"Well, I—" Marie began. "I fainted, and after that happens, I'm always a little foggy, in sort of a gray zone. I'm not all there for a little while."

"You must learn not to faint," Olga commanded. "The mind plays tricks. You may have left it somewhere. Gregor, do you remember if she had it?"

"I was more concerned for Marie than for an old piece of history," he said.

Brother and sister shared a look. Lacey knew that look well. The look of a wiser elder sister, exasperated with a younger, scatterbrained sibling. It was slightly less obvious than an eye roll.

"I'm positive I had it," Marie said. "Pretty positive."

"Do you think someone at the party would take it?" Olga pressed.

"After the story that Marie told about it, everyone was convinced it was haunted and dangerous," Lacey said. "I doubt anyone would be brave enough. Marie, maybe you left it at the restaurant."

"I don't know." Marie sounded completely adrift.

"But someone could have taken it from here, from this house?" Olga inquired patiently.

"I suppose that's possible. Maybe I should call the police." Marie reached for the phone.

"Police? What have the police to do with it?" Olga said it as if calling the police were the most insane idea anyone could have. "It is a family matter. Gregor, did you insure the shawl?"

"No." Gregor put his hand over Marie's. "And we've had enough to do with police for today, my dear, don't you think?"

"Yes, sugar. I do believe you're right."

"Marie. *Exactly* what happened at the party?" Olga said.

There were purple bags under Marie's eyes. She settled into the turquoise sofa. Lacey was afraid she might faint.

"Olga. Can you not see she is exhausted?" Gregor said.

"It's okay, honey pie. There's no need for secrets." Marie started to recap the events at the bachelorette party and the many fortunes she had told while wearing the shawl. "And then this rude man, this Leonardo, a hairstylist who used to work with Stella, he crashed the party."

Olga looked confused. "What is 'crashed'? He drove through the window? In his car?"

"No, no. 'Crashed the party' just means he barged in without being invited," Marie continued. "No one wanted him there. And then Leonardo saw me telling fortunes and made fun of the shawl. He yanked it out of my hands, threw it around his shoulders, and *danced* with it. Why, poor Stella—that's our pretty little bride-to-be—was fit to be tied."

Olga concentrated on Marie's story, scowling. "He *danced* with the shawl? How? Like a waltz?"

"It was sort of a tango," Lacey offered. "Then he rubbed his neck with it. Back and forth, like a towel."

Marie nodded, her black curls bouncing. "And he had the nerve to complain the shawl scratched him. He must be sensitive to wool, or maybe the gold thread, I don't know. And now he's dead."

"Served the crasher right," Olga declared.

Leonardo was rash and rude, Lacey thought. *But death is rather a harsh punishment for party crashing and making an ass of himself.*

"No doubt another story to add to the legend," Kepelov said.

"You said you fainted." Olga pressed Marie for more details.

"Yes, but before that, Leonardo insisted I tell his fortune," Marie said. "I refused. I was highly irritated and didn't want my feelings to cloud my judgment. But he grabbed my hand and then—everything went black." She sipped her coffee. "Actually, it went more purple. I never go completely *black*. And today, you'll have to forgive me, after I faint, it's as if I have a hangover. I'm just not at my best."

"I see." Olga turned to Lacey. "Did she tell your fortune too?"

"No."

"Why not?"

"The party wasn't about me. Marie's fortune-telling was for Stella's guests. I was the hostess."

"The hostess?" For the first time Olga seemed amused. "You must tell me your secrets to hosting such interesting parties. And perhaps we shouldn't worry."

"Not worry? What do you mean, Olga?" Marie asked.

"According to legend, the shawl always comes back. Fate has a way of catching up with us, whether we are ready for it or not."

Lacey wasn't sure fate was after her, but the chimes of her cell phone rang. They might as well have been wedding bells. "Sorry. I have to go. The bride-to-be is calling me. Olga, lovely to meet you. Gregor, thanks for the lift, but I'll just grab a cab."

"Smithsonian," Kepelov said. "Not necessary. Purple Gremlin and I will be happy to take you wherever you need to go."

"You're too kind, really, Kepelov. But, ah, Marie needs you here."

Marie blinked in concern and took Lacey's hands in hers. "Cher, traffic's going to be something else today! Watch out for those crazy drivers. It's dangerous out there."

"I wouldn't worry. I already survived Gregor driving your purple Gremlin."

Kepelov jingled his car keys. Lacey speed-dialed for a taxi.

chapter 10

Skipping town without leaving a forwarding address is not an option, she reflected as her bright orange Yellow Cab lurched through Washington traffic. There would be no rest for the wicked, or for the weary maid of honor, whose responsibilities included ensuring that Stella's nuptials would come off without a hitch.

Lacey had been summoned to the site of the wedding reception, the Arts Club of Washington, to meet Stella and Miguel Flores.

The event had theoretically been completely planned and scheduled, except for the details—wherein dwelt the devil.

The vows were to be exchanged on the west lawn of the Thomas Jefferson Memorial, by the Tidal Basin. That stunning outdoor wedding site would accomplish two of Stella's key goals: a uniquely Washington setting and maximum cherry blossom coverage. It was also surprisingly affordable, a mere fifty dollars for the permit. Lack of parking around the Mall was a challenge, but wedding guests would be shuttled to and from the ceremony via a tour bus. All they had to do was pray for perfect April weather and follow the innumerable Park Service rules, designed to leave the grounds the way they found them. And presumably Stella and Nigel would live happily (married) ever after.

The Park Service permit gave the wedding party only

two hours, max. Therefore it was impractical, if not impossible, to also host the reception on the National Mall. The reception would have to take place elsewhere. And though Stella had planned her wedding in her head for years, with and without an eligible man in mind, she had surprisingly little money saved for the big event.

"I was totally thinking, like, potluck in a park," she had told Lacey. "Barefoot. With, like, balloons and someone playing guitar? And maybe we could all blow bubbles? But once I got engaged for real, everything got so complicated. And so expensive."

Enter Lady Gwendolyn Griffin and her husband, Nigel's parents, vastly relieved that their wayward offspring was finally settling down. They offered to pick up the entire tab for the reception—at the Arts Club of Washington. A prestigious private club in Foggy Bottom dedicated to the arts, it was an unusual but classy choice for a wedding reception, and the Griffins were longtime members, who knew which strings to pull at the last minute. It was neither too intimate nor too grand, a little off-center for Washington but elegant nonetheless, and it was fully equipped for receptions, with both dining room and garden facilities. Lacey had been there for a few events on her fashion beat, and she seconded it as a great choice. And Nigel's mother never flinched at the price tag.

In addition, Gwendolyn had arranged for an Episcopal priest to conduct the ceremony. Stella's parents, a Christian mother and a Jewish father, had rejected organized religion, except when it came to occasions that required presents. Stella generally followed their example. She said she had no problem with the priest as long as she would be legally hitched to Nigel. Forever.

"I will be eternally grateful to Lady G," Stella had told Lacey when the reservation was finalized. "Who would have figured me and her would turn out to be such good pals?"

Who indeed?

Lacey's cab ride was the most relaxing part of her day so far. She leaned back and replayed Stella's riff on Lady G in her head.

"She's waited her whole life for Nigel to meet someone like me. Who am I to rob Lady G of the wedding reception of her dreams? And mine too! If we can still do balloons."

"Balloons. I'm writing it down," Lacey had said.

Lacey rather doubted that the wife of the former British ambassador had always been on the lookout for a daughter-in-law with a punk-rock attitude, a spiky personality, interesting tattoos and piercings, and a New Jersey accent. Lacey, as well as Stella, had been afraid at first that Stella might be a bit too exotic for an ambassador's wife. But Gwendolyn wanted grandchildren, which Stella might supply, and she had a taste for adventure, which Stella was sure to supply. She and Lady G took to each other like a firecracker to a match.

"You know she's even got guests coming from England? They'll be the ones in the funny hats. Like it's going to be the Kentucky Derby."

And we're off to the races. "I love funny hats. On other people."

"Me too. Nigel's cousins will be wearing 'fascinators,' those teeny tiny hats, you know like bands with feathers sticking up like a Martian's antennae? It's the latest wedding thing in England, like at the royal wedding? It's going to be totally rad."

"And Nigel's mother? She won't be wearing her tweed riding togs to the wedding, will she?" Lacey inquired.

Lady Gwendolyn Griffin had a wardrobe of browns and beiges in tweed, supported by endless pairs of sensible shoes suitable for shooting parties at their country estate in England. Stella had been trying to polish Lady Gwendolyn's Agatha-Christie-in-the-parlor look, with mixed results.

"Oh, no. Lady G promised," Stella said. "We went shopping together. She asked for my advice. Can you believe it? She's going to wear violet like we talked about."

"Like Eleanor Roosevelt." Lacey and Stella had seen pictures of Mrs. Roosevelt's inaugural gown. It was violet velvet and would, they decided, suit Gwendolyn Griffin about as well as it suited Eleanor.

"And it will totally complement the bridesmaids' pink dresses. And the copper highlights I gave her. With better hair and trimmed eyebrows. Lady G totally took my advice about everything. Except the hat. It might be a little over the top for D.C."

"It's going to be a really big hat, isn't it?"

"She's *English*. She doesn't care about the dress or the hair, but the big hat? De rigueur. And who am I to deny my future ma-in-law? So be prepared, the hat is gonna be gigantic, like something out of *My Fair Lady*. I want lots of pictures."

"And your mother?"

"She'd never wear a hat. That's for sure. I got no idea what she's wearing, she's holding out on me. Says it's going to be a *surprise*. I begged her to wear something that goes with my color scheme. She'll probably turn up in a burlap sack. With a lump of kryptonite slung around her neck. You can write her up as a crime of fashion."

"When Lady Gwendolyn showed you around the Arts Club, what did you think? Will it fit your barefoot-in-the-park vision?"

"I haven't seen it yet!" Stella had said. "Lady G's buying, so who needs to see it? And I'm not going barefoot. I want my heels sky-high, you know that."

Why maids of honor murder their brides.

Lacey's taxi finally rumbled to a halt in front of the Arts Club on Eye Street, just a few blocks west of her office, and tumbled her out of her reverie.

The neighborhood known as Foggy Bottom, one of

the District's oldest, was anchored by such weighty institutions as George Washington University, the State Department, the Kennedy Center, the Watergate, and the World Bank. The Arts Club faced James Monroe Park, a small but welcome green space separating Eye Street from Pennsylvania Avenue. The White House was only five blocks away.

Before she could even pay her driver, Miguel Flores, stylist extraordinaire, was opening her door and dragging her out. He looked so comically frazzled, all she could do was laugh.

"Lacey, Lacey, O best beloved maid of honor! Thank goodness you're here! Oh, my God! Where have you been? I possess *mucho Miguelismo*, as you well know, Lacey, but I cannot handle this Stella Bridezilla all alone! And the storm clouds are gathering!"

"What storm clouds?" Lacey gazed up at the beautiful azure April sky. Miguel's panic attack was not going to keep her from appreciating the Arts Club, that handsome redbrick Colonial-era building with its glossy black shutters, the historic mansion where President James Monroe had once lived.

Henry Adams had also resided there, she recalled, before he married the tragic Clover Adams. *Why does Clover Adams keep coming to mind? Bad omen?* she wondered, as Miguel chattered on nonstop.

"You were saying?" Lacey asked.

"The mothers-in-law! The mothers-in-law are coming!" Miguel shuddered dramatically, as only Miguel could.

"You haven't even met them yet."

"But I've heard tales." He rushed Lacey through the front door of the Arts Club beneath the arched and leaded windows. "Many tales. Dark tales. Tales Told in Tweed."

Inside the club, the air was cool and still, the polished wood floors gleaming. In the back was a secluded walled garden, a lovely surprise invisible to passersby admiring the edifice from the street. The Arts Club was neither too large nor too small, she thought. If Goldilocks had been looking for the perfect reception space, this one would be just right. And it couldn't be more Washingtonian. What could possibly go wrong in this charming setting?

"Oh, Lace, there you are! What took you so long?" Stella chirped. Although still on edge from the news of Leonardo's death, she was now clearly in full wedding-commando mode. Her eyes were sparkling, emphasized by glittery gold liner. "So what do you think of these digs? Is this great or what?"

"I love this place, Stella. The question is do you love it?"

"It's incredible. What's not to love?"

Miguel smiled for the first time, relieved that Stella was loving the venue. "It's very D.C., with a classy traditional vibe, but artsy and a little ironic. We should definitely rock it. Thank God you're good with it!"

"What, you didn't think I'd love it?" Stella demanded. "What did you think I'd want?"

"I don't know, I thought you might want to rent the Black Cat," he said.

Before Stella met Nigel, Lacey might also have picked that scruffy Fourteenth Street indie punk-rock music club as Stella's perfect wedding reception venue. But then, Lacey hadn't known about Stella's cherry blossom obsession either.

"The Black Cat? Miguel, a year ago, before Nigel, I would have totally rocked the Black Cat. For the whole wedding. In, like, a full-on Goth leather bustier minidress. But things have changed. And to tell the truth, I'm so knocked out by Lady G's generosity. I mean *no one* ever did anything like this for me. In my whole life. Never. It's so elegant, and Nigel and I could never afford this on our own. And yeah, I love it. I do. It's beautiful."

Whatever happened to the little black-leather punk goddess I used to know?

Stella was a chameleon, which was part of her charm.

Since Lacey had known her, she'd assumed at least a dozen very different looks and a rainbow of hair colors. But if after the wedding Stella morphed into someone else again, would Nigel still be there for her? Lacey looked at Miguel for reassurance. He put his arms around both women's shoulders.

"It'll be fabulous," he said. "There will be many touches of pure Stella, not Lady G, not Arts Club. And even more important, touches of pure Miguel."

"Hey, Lacey, I'm still Stella. Only better, now that I got Nigel. And I'm getting a mother-in-law I don't hate. I even sort of adore her. She's kind of cool. How awesome is that?"

"And, my dear, I'm heading up the cake committee as well as overseeing the décor," Miguel added.

"I thought it was going to be cheesecake," Lacey said.

"The *groom's* cake is going to be cheesecake," Miguel clarified.

"Didn't you know? I'm having a castle cake!" Stella said. "You were out of town doing your Sagebrush thingy when that got decided."

"A castle? As in knights-of-old castle?" Lacey raised one eyebrow dubiously.

"Can you believe it?" Stella's gesture would make the cake at least five feet tall.

"And I know someone who can take it over the top, with lovely fondant icing," Miguel said. "Even though we have decided on the cake at an unforgivably late date."

"Sorry!" Stella said. "Lace, it's going to have lots of flowers and vines and a little bride and groom on the top."

"On top of the castle?" Lacey repeated. She was trying to visualize all this—cake.

"Duh. My prince has come!" Stella laughed. "I'm having a castle cake and eating it too."

"It's not an easy deal to put it all together, and Bruce, my lovely baker, was semi-furious," Miguel said. "But I am something of a magician. And Bruce adores a challenge."

"Miguel's ex." Stella winked.

"One of my best exes. Bruce is a complete sweetheart. Exes with benefits."

"This cake is going to be one-of-a-kind," Stella said.

Lacey didn't have the heart to tell Stella that the idea wasn't *that* original. Food maven Felicity Pickles was also in the throes of planning her wedding, to Harlan Wiedemeyer. Every cake known to mankind was passing through *The Eye*'s newsroom (and stomachs) in the course of Felicity's exhaustive cake quest. She had already brought in pictures of a castle cake, Cinderella's pumpkin coach cake, a cake made from a tower of Krispy Kreme doughnuts, and many more.

"There's going to be a chocolate layer, and a white layer, and a marble spice layer," Stella went on, a dreamy expression on her face. "And cherry blossoms . . ."

Lacey was about to scream "Enough!" when the front door opened and Lady Gwendolyn Griffin marched in. As made over by her soon-to-be daughter-in-law, Gwendolyn now sported a sleek chin-length bob, trimmed eyebrows, and a dollop of makeup. Even so, there was still much of starch and tweed about her, including her brown tweed skirt, which she paired with a beige sweater and marble-sized pearls. And it couldn't be denied—her teeth might have been featured in the Big Book of British Smiles. They might have made the centerfold.

"Stella, my dear. Miguel, elegant as usual. And Lacey, so good to see you," Lady Gwendolyn said. "What do you think of this place? Charming, what?"

Stella gave her a big hug. "It's way beyond charming. I so owe you, Lady G."

Directly behind Gwendolyn another woman entered the hall, a woman Stella did not hug. She was of medium height and rail-thin, with gray hair and no makeup, but there was a nervous energy about her. She looked like an aging hippie. Stella had promised she would.

"Hi, everyone," the woman said as she moved into the room with quick, nervous steps. She put her hand out to

Gwendolyn and a mass of bracelets rattled. Her words tumbled out in a thick New Jersey accent. "I'm Retta, Retta Lake Sloan, Stella's mother, call me Retta, short for Loretta. You must be Nigel's mom. Who would have thought, my little Stella with all you high-class Brits, I swear it sounds like a marriage made on *Masterpiece Theatre.*"

"Pleased to meet you," Gwendolyn said, stepping back a bit, her smile frozen.

The two future in-laws couldn't have been more different. Lady Gwendolyn looked like a poster for high tea in the library with the vicar, while Retta had seemingly just stalked out of the muddy meadow at Woodstock, by way of Newark, circa 1969. She wore orange print leggings, an immense caftan-style top in green and blue and gold, Birkenstock sandals, and what appeared to be a ten-pound art necklace fashioned out of concrete, copper pipe, and broken glass. Retta's hair was a mass of unruly steel-colored curls she had never tamed or allowed a stylist to touch—not even her daughter.

"O.M.G., it's worse than I imagined!" Stella whispered to Lacey. "Her hair! And that necklace! Jeez, you'd think she was Dumpster diving again."

Stella had mentioned that her mother was a jewelry designer who made one-of-a-kind found art pieces, "like she was living off the land on a commune or something. Instead of living off Stepfather Number Three. Or Four. I forget." Retta's necklaces, Stella said, sold for a pretty penny, up to several thousand dollars, a much prettier penny than Lacey would be willing to pay. They weren't the kind of thing one of Washington's "Powerful Women in Pearls" or a woman like Lady Gwendolyn Griffin would buy. Retta Sloan's jewelry told the world her customer was a free spirit. Or, as Stella said, "some kind of chump."

"And who are you?" Retta said to Miguel. "Not the groom, I bet."

He drew himself up to his full height. "Miguel Flores.

I'm helping my *best friend* Stella with some of the wedding details."

"So where's the groom? I thought he was supposed to be here."

"Mom, back off," Stella warned.

Retta's gaze flicked over Lacey's vintage ensemble. "And what are you supposed to be, a lawyer? Is there a pre-nup I don't know about?"

"Lacey's a fashion reporter," Stella said. "And my very best BFF, Mom."

"No kidding. Is that supposed to be fashion?"

"Like you'd know fashion, Ma."

"I'm Lacey Smithsonian. I write for *The Eye Street Observer*. And my outfit is vintage." She offered her hand, wishing she were on another planet.

"No kidding. At least you recycle. You still look like a lawyer to me. Everyone here in Washington looks like a lawyer, except Stella. And I should know, I've paid enough divorce lawyers." Her laugh was a high-pitched bray.

Stella rolled her eyes. Lacey told herself not to be insulted and just enjoy the ride. "It's just the way she is," Stella whispered. "I toldja she would be a trip."

"You're having the reception here?" Retta glared at the hardwood floors and antique furniture. "I get the getting married outside in the grass kind of thing, but I don't know, Stella, this just reeks of dead white men. Ancient history."

"Lady Gwendolyn recommended it." Stella's expression said it all: Her mother was driving her crazy and the drive had just begun. "I love it. Lacey loves it. Miguel loves it. We all love it. You don't have to love it."

Retta rubbed her necklace as if it would protect her from the opulence. "Whatever. It's perfectly fine, Stella, it just doesn't feel like you. I expected something a little less, you know, cocktails-at-the-yacht-club. Something a little more you."

"Really? Like what's more me, Ma?"

"I always figured you'd get hitched on the back of a

motorcycle, or on the beach, or in some smoky nightclub or art gallery. Something more out there, you know? I never expected this peppermint pink preppy party you're planning."

"Actually," Miguel said, "there is to be no *peppermint* pink. It will be a medley of rose and cherry blossom shades. Pink is so retro now it's actually *out there*."

"I just assumed my girl would tie the knot in something new, modern. With an urban vibe, a stimulating color scheme, like say, gray and avocado."

"What? The color of mold in a garage?" Stella snapped. Gwendolyn put a restraining hand on Stella's arm. "It's my wedding, not my funeral! All my life I wanted cherry blossoms for my wedding."

"Cherry blossoms." Retta shook her head and the iron-gray curls bobbed wildly. "Maybe I should have let my baby girl have that pink bedroom she always wanted, but with all the pink-blue gender stereotyping, it just felt so wrong. Pink is so—so fifties—so girly."

Poor Stella, Lacey thought. *Meeting her mother explains a lot.*

"You don't have to come, Ma."

Retta seemed stricken. "Not attend my own daughter's wedding! What kind of mother would I be? I am your mother, you know. And I didn't say it was *terrible*, Bugsy. I just said it was, you know, unexpected."

"Bugsy?" Miguel whispered.

Stella looked mortified. "Don't call me that."

"Bugsy's a cute name," Retta insisted. "It's what I called you when you were a baby! What're you putting on airs for? For the BBC crowd?" She nodded toward Lady Gwendolyn Griffin, who stood by impassively.

"You know my name is Stella, don't you, Mom? Do I have to write it down for you?"

Lady Gwendolyn decided to take things in hand. "A tour is in order, don't you think?" She waved imperiously to the Arts Club representative and started walking. The others naturally fell in line behind her.

The Arts Club events coordinator, an attractive young man named Chet who seemed to have eyes only for Miguel, toured the group around the facility, showing them the bridal ready room upstairs, describing the accommodations on the mansion's main floor, and suggesting how magical the patio would become with the addition of flowers, candlelight, and coordinated linens.

Years of British Embassy experience in marshaling major events and formal afternoon teas in unlikely places had forged a spine of steel in Lady Gwendolyn. She could just as easily command a single program coordinator or a staff of a hundred. She was more than equal to any social setting that required cloth napkins and crystal goblets.

There were some last-minute adjustments to be made in the arrangements, such as a *yes* on the crab cakes and baked Brie, a *no* on the quesadillas, but Lady Gwendolyn Griffin did not beg for small favors, she simply made *statements*. She smiled with those huge teeth and assumed that her word would be taken as law. Perhaps lulled by her dulcet British accent, Chet nodded his assent to everything she said. Stella nodded too, through her expression of glazed irritation at her mother. Retta appeared to be having an out-of-body experience.

Miguel and Lacey both approved of Gwendolyn's instinctive command of the situation, if not her attire. *May the sun never set on Lady G's empire.*

Miguel winked at Chet, and Chet winked back.

"It shall all be done just as you say, madam," Chet said.

"What, no pasta?" Retta asked. "Everybody loves pasta."

"No pasta," Stella said firmly. "Nigel doesn't like it. It's full of carbs. Yes to bacon, no to pasta. Like Lady G was saying."

"Any other concerns, Stella?" Gwendolyn inquired.

"I thought it would be nice to have a pink tent out on the patio, just in case of rain?" Stella knocked on wood.

Easy to do, there was old wood everywhere. "And maybe pink helium balloons? But if it's impossible —"

"Darling Stella. If you want a pink tent full of pink balloons, my dear, then there shall be a pink tent full of pink balloons. Matter of fact, pink has always been my favorite color in a tent," Gwendolyn said. She snapped her fingers at Chet, who nodded.

Retta checked her watch for the twentieth time. "Looks like everything's all taken care of, so you don't need me anymore. Do you?"

"We haven't met Nigel yet," Miguel pointed out. "Remember? The groom."

"Mom can meet him later," Stella said. "You gotta run, right, Mom?"

"As long as the groom's not *imaginary*," her mother brayed.

"You'll see Nigel at the wedding," Stella said. "Why spoil the surprise?"

"Can't wait, Bugsy," Retta said, already halfway to the front door. "I'll go check out the snooty art galleries in Georgetown."

"Check out some hair salons on your way," Stella called after her. "Doesn't even have to be my salon. Try a rinse. A blow-dry. Some color. Any color, I don't care. And conditioner. Send me the bill! And don't call me Bugsy!"

But Retta was already out the door and out of earshot.

chapter 11

Stella's shoulders sagged. Miguel put his arms around her, chuckling. "Oh, hon, your mother is something else."

"You promised she'd be a trip," Lacey said. She took over the hug from Miguel. "Don't worry about it, Stel. Everybody has family members who aren't exactly—*exactly*—what we want them to be."

"About the wedding pictures: Does she have to be in them?" Stella was on the verge of tears.

"Now, Stella—" Gwendolyn began. "She is your mother."

"I'm sorry, Lady G, she's like a permanent wave I can't do anything about. I'm so embarrassed." Stella hung her head. Gwendolyn lifted Stella's chin with a gentle finger.

"Stella, my dear. Never apologize for other people. Never. Even your own mother. As hard as that may be. She is not your fault and no one here will ever blame her on *you*. And, after all, every truly great party needs an eccentric or two."

"Retta's on beyond eccentric! Eccentric is a dotty old aunt who pinches your cheeks. Eccentric is Miss Havisham, and she dressed better than my mom. I mean, eccentric is—"

Gwendolyn stopped her with a gesture of her regal hand. "My dear, she could be barking mad, indeed she may well be, but on your wedding day everyone will find her amusing. And when she's simply too much for you, just send her to *me*."

Stella threw her arms around Lady G and hugged her tight.

Gwendolyn took Stella's hand and led the wedding planning party out into the secluded garden at the back of the club. She directed Stella to a bench beneath a cherry tree and admired a cherub.

"That's better. I do love a garden. Now, dear, Nigel tells me there was some unpleasantness last night after your little soiree, the bachelorette affair. Someone died, I believe?" Gwendolyn was terribly interested. Too interested. This was clearly a woman who loved a mystery.

"The death didn't actually happen at the party, so don't worry, Lady G, you didn't miss anything grisly," Stella said.

"His body was found this morning," Miguel said. "In front of his building."

"That's all we know," Stella said. "So far."

Lady Gwendolyn seemed torn. She obviously didn't want anything to overshadow the nuptials, but she was a voracious mystery reader, the bloodier, the better. Gwendolyn Griffin was of the opinion that America was a seething cauldron of gore. And now a dead body had landed practically on her daughter-in-law-to-be's doorstep? It was simply too mysterious, not to mention too delicious, not to explore.

"Do we know how he died?" she asked.

Stella shook her head, but gave Gwendolyn the barest sketch of the "haunted Russian shawl" and the supposed curse. "Leonardo mocked the shawl, and now he's dead."

"My dear, I simply do not believe in invoking the paranormal in a mystery, unless it's absolutely necessary. Is foul play indicated? Or was he hit by a bus?"

"It wasn't a bus," Lacey said. "The medical examiner is conducting an autopsy, but that takes a while. Particularly in the District of Columbia. But I have some inside information."

"Aha! So we do know something." Gwendolyn turned her powerful gaze on Lacey.

"According to my coworker at the paper—and this is all just hearsay—Leonardo might have been poisoned."

"Poisoned!" Stella yelped. "Lacey! You didn't tell me that. That doesn't sound good."

"I didn't believe poison was an appropriate subject for discussion while we were talking about the appetizers."

"But that's just weird," Miguel said. "Leonardo didn't eat anything at the party."

"He grabbed a drink," Stella said. "Uninvited, I might add."

"No one else died. Or even had a tummy ache. Leo was the only pain at the party," Miguel added.

Gwendolyn lowered her voice. "Indeed. And what does that tell us? It tells us that this Leonardo person was *murdered*."

"Or killed himself," Miguel said. "It could happen. Or maybe it was an overdose of something that acted like poison."

"It tells me he should never have crashed my party," Stella said gloomily.

"Darling," Miguel said, "I imagine Leo regrets it too. Wherever he is."

"Poor man. And might there possibly be a funeral for him this week, do you suppose?" Lady Gwendolyn adored funerals. "A funeral and a wedding in the same week? What a coincidence! Circle of life, what?" It would certainly make her visit to the Nation's Capital even more unforgettable. "I mean, there are respects to be paid, after all. Not that I knew the deceased, of course, but I'm sure he had many fine qualities." Lacey, Stella, and Miguel were silent. "No? Really? Not a one?" She smiled her carnivorous smile. "Even better."

On Gwendolyn's first visit, Stella had endeared herself to her future mother-in-law by taking her to the funeral of a murder victim who had been dyed dark blue through and through. Lacey's sense of decency was affronted by the blue-on-blue open-casket service, but it was the highlight of Gwendolyn's American experience. Except of course for her son's unlikely engagement to Stella Lake. Her store of cocktail conversation had been replenished for years to come.

"A funeral? To steal the spotlight from *my* wedding?" Stella fumed. "Even dead, Leo's a scene-stealer!"

But Gwendolyn had already shifted from wedding plans to funeral plans. "I do have a nice black dress in my suitcase. It's best to be prepared. I must buy a new journal to record this experience. And a new fountain pen. So many adjectives, so little time."

"I'll ask Kevin. That's his roommate," Miguel said.

"How lovely. Thank you, Miguel. And look who's here. My bonny boy, the groom-to-be."

Strolling through the doorway of the garden in his everyday uniform of khaki slacks and blue oxford-cloth shirt, Nigel Percival Griffin made his belated entrance. Stella leapt up at the sight of him. Standing tall in her heels, she ran her hands through his shaggy light brown locks. She frowned, not at the love of her life, but at his *hair*.

"Nigel, pumpkin, sweetie, cupcake, you need a trim before the wedding. And use that conditioner I got you! You want to look your best for our big day."

He smiled sheepishly. All it took was a "Sorry, luv" for Stella to melt. "I've got all my future days to look my best for the woman I love. Mother, keeping the troops in good order, are we? You're looking well."

Nigel kissed Lady Gwendolyn's cheek.

"As are you, Nigel. But you're late."

"What did I miss?"

"Everything," she said. "As usual."

"Splendid." Nigel was in high spirits. "You didn't need me to help decide about the napkins and salad forks, now, did you? I'm sure you ladies have everything well under control, in your capable little hands. It's a great thing being the groom. I only have to show up. Not be late, not fall down, not forget my lines. Line, that is: 'I do.'"

"You don't think we'd leave anything really important up to you, do you, Nigel?" Gwendolyn asked. "Well, then."

Miguel tapped Lacey on the shoulder, feeling left out. "Oh, I'm sorry," Lacey said. "Nigel Griffin, this is Miguel Flores, our wedding stylist. Extraordinaire."

"And dashing man-about-town," Miguel added. "Lovely to meet you, Nigel. Stella's told me everything."

"That's my Stella. How do you do." Nigel remembered his manners and shook hands, one arm still slung around Stella's shoulder. "Surely not everything?"

"I think he'll do, Stella. He's cute." Miguel winked at Lacey. She gave him an eye roll in response.

"Smithsonian, looking smashing as always." Nigel didn't quite meet her gaze. She'd caught him spying on the bachelorettes.

"You never know where I'll pop up," Lacey said. "Maid of honor, keeping an eye on everything. By the way, where's the best man?"

"Oh, um—"

"That's right, the famous Bryan!" Stella said. "I haven't even met him yet, so I guess we'll all be surprised. I can't wait, he's like Nigel's oldest pal. Mate, I mean. No wait, *I'm* Nigel's mate. Or will be soon! But I'm sure I'll totally love Bryan."

Nigel looked like he wanted to climb over the garden wall. "Good old Bryan. Um, he had some, um, business," he said.

"Speaking of business, I must be leaving." Gwendolyn stood up and tugged at her beige sweater. *It can't really be tweed*, Lacey thought, but it looked like tweed. "I have to go amuse your father. Dinner with old friends."

"Wonderful," Nigel said, vastly relieved. "See you later! Give my regards to the old man. Nice place for a reception, this garden, so quiet out here off the street. Good job, Mother."

They moved through the cool calm of the Arts Club and back outside, where the sun beat brightly down on Eye Street. Nigel hailed a cab for Gwendolyn and bade her good-bye. But before she ducked into the backseat, she caught Lacey and Stella with her determined gaze.

"If any of you hear a word concerning the suspicious demise of our Mr. Leonardo, do please let me know. And if by chance there should be a funeral—"

"Don't be so gruesome, Gwendolyn," Nigel said. "We'll have none of the Lady Sherlock or Dame Agatha routine this week. We've got a proper wedding to attend to."

"My dear Nigel, I know you call me the Gorgon behind my back," Lady Gwendolyn said, as coolly as if she were addressing Parliament. "However, if you want people to think that *your* wedding guests, even uninvited ones, can be allowed to simply drop dead during *any* of the formal nuptial events without the proper public display of sympathy from the family, that's up to you. But I know my duty and I shall do it."

"Let them drop dead if they like, I say. Dear me, I'll never make a proper ambassador at this rate, will I, Mother?"

Stella stepped into the fray between mother and son. "If there's a service, Lady G, I'll let you know. Promise."

Gwendolyn beamed at her soon-to-be daughter-in-law. "That's my girl."

She gave the driver of the Yellow Cab (actually yellow this time) the address, Nigel slammed the door, and the cab sped off. "Really, Stella, you must not humor the Gorgon. The old man will have a conniption if she runs off to some funeral."

"Don't look at me, doll." Stella kissed Nigel's cheek. "I don't want a thing to do with Leonardo's murder. But whatever Lady G wants, Lady G gets."

"Murder? Nobody's said it was murder!" Nigel looked around, worried. "Did they?"

"Could be suicide," Miguel suggested. "Leonardo was not a happy person. Everyone knew that."

"Suicide. Good. Better at any rate than murder most foul. Don't want to get the Gorgon overly excited. Well, then, that's settled," Nigel said, though nothing was settled at all.

"You're right. Everything's settled. We're getting married! Unless something else happens, God forbid. And as long as the shawl is safely tucked away." Stella kissed him hard, right there on the sidewalk on Eye Street. Public display of affection was not a common sight in the District of Columbia. Passersby stared. "But you really should have been here." Stella scolded him gently. "You missed *my* mother. I needed your support."

"That is a shame," Nigel said. "After all you've told me, I feel as though I know her already."

Miguel whispered in Lacey's ear. "Come on, Lacey, you can't deny Nigel's accent is *adorable*. And he somehow escaped the genetic disaster of his mother's smile." He raised his voice to take his leave. "Alas, boys and girls, I have a cake to oversee, and a cake baker to pinch. Nigel, a pleasure. Stella! The dress! We'll talk! Lacey, I'll call you later, and let me know if anything juicy happens."

"What about Leonardo? Do you think there'll be a funeral?" Stella asked.

"I don't know about a *funeral*." Miguel slipped on his shades. "You know Leo. He always said when he died he wanted an extravagantly wild cocktail party thrown in his honor. He told me once, 'Cremate me and put me in an urn, next to the champagne bucket. I want to be the centerpiece.' Alas, he was serious." Lacey felt her eyebrows lifting. Both of them. "I was there! Leonardo probably said the same thing to everyone he ever slept with. That's half the D.C. gay population. *Someone* will probably throw him a last cocktail party. Not me. However, I wouldn't miss it if it happens."

"That cannot happen!" Lacey said. "And if it does, Gwendolyn Griffin must not hear about it. Especially if she thinks he was murdered! She'd insist on going, and then she'd tell everyone in England that's how we do funerals in the Colonies. Cremation and cocktails at five."

"You started it! You took her to the funeral of a dead blue guy." Miguel was finding this much more amusing than she was.

"Stella did that."

"At least you provided the dead blue guy."

"I did not, Miguel! Fate did that. Stella and Lady Gwendolyn took it from there."

"So who gave us a dead Leonardo? Fate? Or the haunted shawl?"

That's a good question, Lacey thought.

chapter 12

Miguel was gone. Stella and Nigel were still locked together in front of the Arts Club in a steamy Hollywood-quality embrace.

Just where is that famous British reserve? Lacey wondered.

"It's all right. Pay no attention to me," she said to no one in particular. "I'll just be on my way."

Yet she stood still. Lacey felt something, almost a tingling, as if she were being watched. The energy in the April air seemed to change, becoming charged with electricity—and it wasn't the lovebirds kissing on the sidewalk. Something felt odd, out of place, foreboding. Terrible.

At the edge of her vision she noticed a black limousine approaching, westbound on Eye Street. That couldn't be it. Black limousines were nothing out of the ordinary in Washington, D.C. Far from it. The city was lousy with limousines, black, gray, and dark blue, mostly Lincoln Town Cars. Like this one. Lacey stared at it and nearly turned away.

It crossed Twentieth Street, surged forward, jumped the curb, and rocketed down the sidewalk, picking up speed, deliberately heading straight for them. Pedestrians were diving out of the way in every direction.

Lacey heard someone screaming, but it sounded very far away. She knew without looking that Stella and Nigel had stopped kissing. They were right behind her. The car was hurtling at them faster and faster, yet time seemed to stop. In only a few seconds it would hit all of them. Lacey felt frozen to the sidewalk. There was no time to think. She had to move.

She squeaked out a scream as Nigel shoved her out of the car's path and she landed in the flower garden in front of the Arts Club. Stella and Nigel both landed roughly on top of her and the crumpled boxwood hedge that had cushioned her landing. The boxwood was softer than the concrete sidewalk, but just barely. The trio just missed the large stone bearing a bronze plaque commemorating the mansion as the historic Monroe House.

Everyone jumped at the boom that immediately followed. When Lacey lifted her head to look, she saw the limo had crashed into the poles holding up the canvas awning at the Hotel Lombardy, next door to the Arts Club. The awning was sagging over the crumpled hood of the car and steam was pouring from the engine. Miraculously, no one on the sidewalk seemed to have been hit.

Lacey was alive but muddy, scratched up, in shock, and very angry. She knew she would be bruised and stiff tomorrow. She was also vaguely aware that Nigel had probably saved her life. It was unsettling. She uttered a thank-you, but she wasn't sure he heard. He was helping Stella to her feet and brushing leaves and mud from their clothes. The aroma of broken boxwood leaves was overpowering. Lacey felt oddly exhilarated just to be alive.

"What the hell?" was the first thing out of her mouth when she recovered the last of her wits.

A great deal of foul language spewed forth from the happy couple as they tried to stand up. "Who is that freaking crazy maniac?" Stella screamed. "I'm going to freaking kill him!"

"Bloody hell! Bloody bastard!" That was Nigel. "Bloody, bloody, bloody hell!"

The driver's door creaked open and someone struggled out. The doorman from the hotel attempted to help, but the driver pushed him away furiously and sprinted around the corner, turning north on Twenty-first Street.

"Hey, what's going on? Are you okay?" someone shouted, but the driver disappeared, never breaking stride. It happened so fast that Lacey saw little more of the driver than a black-clad blur wearing a long scarf, huge sunglasses, and an orange and brown Rasta hat, the kind that often covered dreadlocks. Any of those accessories could be purchased on the run at a dozen or more street vendor carts in the District.

No one on the street ran after the driver or raised a hand to stop him, but a dozen passersby with briefcases immediately raised their cell phones to snap grainy photos. *That's so Washington*, Lacey thought. "*Who me? Intervene? I just want pictures to put on Facebook!*" No one would be able to identify the driver of the limousine at that rate, not the stunned eyewitnesses or their cell-phone pics.

Lacey struggled to her knees and staggered to her feet. Her hands were scraped and her knees were bloody and stinging. She shook leaves and dirt off her skirt, inspecting it for rips and tears. Scraping her palms was one thing, ripping a great vintage dress was something else entirely. She was shaking, however, her dress seemed to be dirty but intact.

"Stella, are you okay?" she asked. Stella was tightly wrapped in Nigel's arms, the two of them leaning against the building. Lacey heard sirens approaching from more than one direction. "How is your leg?"

"It hurts. But it's not broken," Stella managed to say. Her eyes filled with tears as she rubbed her recently healed leg. "I think. Thank God."

"She's fine, isn't that right, luv?" Nigel's eyes blazed with anger. "You're all right, aren't you? Talk to me, Stella."

She gazed into his eyes. "I don't know. Oh, my God,

we nearly got killed! Right here, right now!" Stella was crying. She tentatively tried putting weight on her foot. She breathed hard. "I can walk. Good thing I landed on Lacey. But just let me hold on to you, Nigel. I feel so shaky."

"That's right, luv, lean on me. Take it easy. Damned crazy drunk driver. Smithsonian, you in one piece?"

"A drunk?!" Lacey blurted out. "Driving a limo, in the middle of the day in Foggy Bottom?"

This was no accident. The car's trajectory was deliberate. The Rasta-capped driver who fled around the corner was lithe and quick. Missing the target and running into the awning poles, *that* was an accident; but this was an attempted murder.

Someone just tried to kill me. Or us.

She was so buzzed from all the coffee she'd drunk at Marie's and the encounter with the rogue limo that she felt dizzy and nauseous. She sat down on the sidewalk and managed to call Vic and leave a garbled message, just as two D.C. Metropolitan Police cars screamed up Eye Street to block traffic with their lights and sirens.

Stella was on both her feet now, and she grabbed Nigel by both hands. "This is crazy, Nigel. It's the shawl. It's after us. Like everything else, and it's not going to stop till we're dead. Now I know for sure we can't go through with this. Maybe your mother can get her deposit back for the reception."

"Stella! You're talking crazy. Did you hit your head?" Nigel asked. "Let me see."

"No." She jerked her head away. "You don't get it! We have bad luck! Bad things keep happening to us!"

"That's life, you know. Like the song. Riding high in April, shot down—"

"It's not life. It's us. We're cursed, you and me." Stella started to cry again. "I don't know why. Maybe we, like, burned down a building in a previous life. I know I love you and you saved me, Nigel. Again. And I want you to know that no matter what the shawl says, I do love you."

"I love you too, luv. Don't talk nonsense about the freaking shawl."

"I'm not talking nonsense. And that's why I can't marry you, Nigel."

He looked puzzled, as if he hadn't heard her right. "Sorry? Maybe I hit *my* head."

"I can't marry you, Nigel. If I do, we'll die. Tell him, Lacey."

"Stella—" Lacey began.

"Don't talk rubbish," Nigel pleaded. "Either of you."

"I'm not. We can't get married. We'll die." Stella collapsed into Nigel's arms, sobbing.

Nigel looked desperately to Lacey. "Do something, Smithsonian. She's out of her mind."

Lacey didn't have time to try to help. An officer tapped her shoulder.

"Miss, I'd like to talk with you."

Missed my deadline, Lacey thought as she checked her watch. *Mac will not be pleased.*

It was after five. It had taken all of Lacey's remaining working brain cells to discuss the "accident" with the cop. The pungent smell of boxwood wafted from her hands and clothes. Boxwood after a rain smelled like cat pee, though where Lacey had last smelled cat urine she wasn't sure. She'd never owned a cat. She longed to wash the smell and the dirt and blood off her scraped palms and knees and wondered idly how long before gangrene set in. The exhilaration of *not* being hit had worn off. Exhaustion set in.

She had described over and over to the police what she had seen and experienced, but not the peculiar vibration in the air just before the black limo attack. She suspected D.C. police officers were unsympathetic to reports of "peculiar vibrations." Lacey's description of the car's driver was sketchy, and the patrolman wasn't terribly impressed by her account of the Rasta hat, sunglasses, and scarf.

After giving their own statements to the young, bored, African-American cop, Stella and Nigel picked up the thread of their argument over whether there should or should not be a wedding. Stella finally marched off into the little park across the street, and Nigel followed. Lacey lacked the energy to referee. On her cell she found a couple of missed calls from Mac and called the office.

"Where the hell have you been, Smithsonian? It's after deadline," Mac barked without preamble. "You coming in?"

"Mac. I was nearly run over on Eye Street. Black limo." She paused. "Missed me, in case you wondered."

Mac was silent for a moment. Then, "Anything broken?"

"Only my spirit. I finished my Fashion Bite. It's in the queue."

There was another pause as Mac checked his editing queue online. She heard movement in the background. "Okay, got it. Magic clothes? Fine, whatever. You'll be in tomorrow?"

"Barring disaster. And black limos." Lacey crossed her fingers for luck.

Mac grunted and said, "Stay safe. And alive." He hung up.

The police finally finished their investigation, and she and Stella were able to clean their scrapes in the ladies' room of the Arts Club. The soap stung, but Lacey persevered. Looking in the mirror, she noticed a scratch on one cheek and wondered if it would be gone by the wedding day. If there was a wedding. Stella was all cried out and talked out. She had nothing more to say. *A first,* Lacey thought to herself. They hugged and parted at the front door.

"Call me later," Lacey said, leaving her friend in Nigel's hands. Stella just nodded.

After the day she'd had, Lacey was afraid if she got on the Metro someone would try to push her onto the tracks. She headed toward Dupont Circle, feeling the soreness starting in her knees, but instead of slowing down, she walked faster. She told herself she wasn't having a post-traumatic meltdown. *I'm not in shock, I'm just hungry!* She realized she hadn't eaten since half a cookie at the coffee shop that morning and too much coffee at Marie's. That was why her hands were shaking, she told herself.

Suddenly she was starved, ravenous. She needed to eat something. She needed Vic. It would be good to have Vic be with her and be in love with her. Very good indeed. Although he was still in meetings with clients and probably had his phone on silent, she called again to leave another message, telling him where to find her, if he should come looking for her.

"If you give me a ride home after dinner," she added, "you might just get lucky."

Trio Restaurant at the corner of Seventeenth and Q Streets, east of Dupont Circle, was a classic D.C. hangout. It was always crowded, a good place to go for dinner before heading to the nearby theatres, or after the theatre for a drink. Lacey had already had enough people and more than enough drama for one day, but the busy restaurant seemed comforting to her, despite the noisy crowd. Or maybe because of it.

By the time Vic arrived, she had started on her turkey potpie. She gazed up at him.

"Sorry, I was starving."

He hovered over her booth, searching her eyes. His green eyes looked troubled, but the rest of him looked delicious. "You do know it's impossible to park in this neighborhood, don't you?"

"Yeah, I know." Lacey smiled. "It's pretty hard to drive down the sidewalks too."

"Are you all right?" She nodded and he leaned down and kissed her. He lightly touched the scratch on her face, as gently as he could. "Scoot over. I want to sit next to you. And tell me everything."

chapter 13

"Would you recognize the driver if you saw him again?" Vic asked the next morning. He was calmer than he'd been last night when Lacey related the tale about the runaway black limo. Much calmer. Deadly calm.

They stood across the Tidal Basin from the Jefferson Memorial to watch the dawn light playing through the white columns. The sun rose over the eastern horizon behind the Jefferson, illuminating the cherry trees in full bloom around the Tidal Basin and casting long shadows. There was a blizzard of white and pink blossoms. Overhead the sky was streaked pink and lavender, behind bars of dark silver-blue clouds, as if to complement the blossoms. A bright bubble of orange foretold the coming of the day. The scene was as pretty as a postcard, which it might soon be. Artists and photographers were waiting there with their easels, tripods, and cameras for the perfect Washington cherry blossom image.

"Well? The driver? The one who tried to kill you?" he repeated.

"Ah, you had to go and ruin the moment." Lacey sipped her mocha latte. She wanted to savor this time before work with Vic. She didn't want to think about yesterday.

"It really would have ruined the moment if that idiot had hit any of you."

"True." She nuzzled the face she loved.

Vic looked particularly handsome in the early morning light. He hadn't shaved yet and the sun glinted off his sunglasses. He was delightfully clad in just-right, just-tight-enough jeans, black shirt, and black leather jacket.

Lacey's eyes were still puffy from sleep, though also hidden by sunglasses. She'd barely had time to wash her face and swipe some mascara on her lashes. Vic didn't seem to mind her face bare of makeup—he even seemed to like it, and he'd often told her that she "didn't need that stuff."

Well, he's a man, what does he know?

She had dabbed on extra war paint in his Jeep and felt ready to face the day. Lacey was dressed more casually than usual, navy slacks to cover up the scabs over her knees, a bright green knit top, and a vintage navy check jacket, with her favorite red cardinal pin that had belonged to Aunt Mimi. The air was crisp, so she had grabbed a blue-and-green-paisley shawl and a pair of green gloves for warmth.

He had surprised her with coffee, muffins, and a trip to see the cherry blossoms early in the morning, before the hordes of tourists descended and made it difficult to even walk along the path. Lacey was loath to leave her warm bed, and her knees and elbows were stiff and sore from her fling with the boxwood in front of the Arts Club. Nevertheless, she thought it was a wonderfully romantic gesture on Vic's part, a reprise of one of their first (unofficial) dates the previous year. And she was slowly waking up, with the rising sun.

Lacey loved the cherry blossoms in the early morning in the early spring. The delicate blossoms appeared—as Stella knew—for only a brief window in time each year. A windstorm or a heavy rain could blow them all away overnight. This year, however, they simply had to last until Saturday for the wedding. If not Stella's wedding, then someone else's. Cherry blossom time in Washington was zero hour for so many weddings.

"To answer your question, no. I couldn't identify him,

or her. He was wearing that Rasta hat and those giant sunglasses and the scarf. The thing that bothers me is—I don't know if that black limo was meant for me, for one of us, or all of us. Or for someone else on the same stretch of sidewalk. But it was deliberate."

"I'd prefer to think the hit was meant for Nigel, but none of that matters if you and Stella were collateral damage."

Lacey kissed him. "I love that you care."

"I'm not kidding, Lacey. And Stella's hairstylist buddy who died? Leonardo? That and this non-accident are beginning *not* to be a coincidence. As if there was any such thing as a coincidence."

"Leonardo was poisoned. Maybe. And we were nearly killed by a car. What's the connection?"

"I don't know. It's weird." He held her close. "Poison is the kind of thing a woman would be more likely to use. Don't look at me like that, Lacey. I'm not ruling out a man. Statistically, however, death by poison says the killer is a woman, a speeding car says a man. Though again, I'm not ruling out anything. Could have been a woman behind the wheel wearing that Rasta hat."

"Maybe it's one of each. In cahoots. Or, how about a Russian shawl, on the rampage?" Lacey offered half seriously. "That's what Stella thinks."

"There's a peculiar kind of insanity that attacks brides, I've heard," Vic said.

"If she *is* a bride this morning. Yesterday she called off the wedding."

Vic leaned in closer and put an arm around her shoulder. "I don't want to talk about her wedding. I'd rather talk about *our* wedding. Of course, I'll be turning the reins over to *you* on that." She looked at him in alarm. "But I'll hold off on that subject for a little while longer. I have something for you."

"Pepper spray? Stun gun? A new Taser, perhaps?"

He reached into an inner pocket of his leather jacket and pulled out a small, beautifully wrapped package, silver foil with a blue ribbon. "Happy birthday, sweetheart."

"I thought breakfast at the Tidal Basin was my present!"

In fact, Lacey had almost forgotten she was another year older. She had been trying not to publicize the happy event. Ever since she arrived in D.C., she had always tried to walk around the Tidal Basin on her birthday and see the cherry blossoms, as a gift to herself. She hadn't known how she'd manage to sneak that treat in this year. She was so busy trying to get work squared away and deal with Stella's wedding.

"How did you know it was my birthday?"

"It's one of those keen investigative skills of mine. Aren't you going to open it?"

The ribbon and paper gave way and Lacey gasped at the Movado box. She opened it and found a delicate gold watch with an elegant black face.

"Oh, Vic. It's beautiful. But it's too much! I don't know what to say. Other than it's way more impressive than my workaday Timex." She kissed him. "Thank you."

"Do you like it?"

"I love it." She held it up to the light.

"I wanted to give you *time*, Lacey. As hard as it is for me. You told me time was what you wanted."

Time. She hugged him hard, whispering, "That's the best thing you could possibly have given me."

"Maybe not. With all this craziness going on." He took off his sunglasses. "I know how goosey you are about proposals and weddings. It's taking all I've got not to press you for a date. I want to marry you while we still have time, you know?"

She kissed him and held tight. "I do too. I'm not running away from you, Vic. I just have to get through this week before I can think about anything else."

"Fair enough. Would you like to try it on?"

"Yes." She laughed and stuck out her wrist. He opened the watch and buckled the strap. She admired it.

"No pressure about the ring. Well, not a lot of pressure." He pulled something out of an inner pocket and put it in her hand. "This is from Nadine."

She opened her hand. "A Saint Christopher medal? From your mother?" It was on a thin gold chain.

"She figures if anyone needs safe traveling, it's you."

"That's very sweet." She fastened it around her neck. "I'm relieved it wasn't a handgun."

"That'll be her wedding present."

"Did you tell her about our secret engagement?"

"No, it's a secret, but you know how suspicious Nadine is. She knows something's up. Darn it all, Lacey, you've danced in and out of danger ever since I came back to Virginia. And before then, you danced in and out of my life."

Lacey leaned her head on his shoulder. "At least I have a dance partner."

"Meet me for lunch. I have another surprise for you."

Chapter 14

Giggling.

There was the sound of high-pitched giggling in the newsroom. It wasn't the raucous roar of cynical reporters, laughing at grim news or bad jokes or a politician's foot stuck in his mouth. It was younger, more delicate, more joyous. It was definitely giggling. An alien sound at *The Eye Street Observer*.

Children? Lacey was trying to locate the unusual sound when two small faces with fetching brown almond-shaped eyes peeked around her cubicle wall. They were a harmonious blend of their deceased Chinese-American mother and a long-missing African-American father: Mac's soon-to-be adopted daughters.

"Aha. I thought I heard something funny in the office today!" Lacey beamed at them. "Hi, girls! Is this Take Your Kids to Work Day?"

"Nope," Jasmine said. She was the older sister—twelve going on twenty-nine—and the more mature sister, who had taken care of ten-year-old Lily Rose in those sad last days when they lost their mother. Before they met Mac and his wife, Kim. "That's later this month. We're on spring break. This is Take Your Dad to Work Day."

"Mom is taking us shopping for dresses! For Miss Stella's wedding," Lily Rose said, as she jumped into the extra chair in Lacey's cubicle. Jasmine leaned on the arm of Lacey's chair.

It was surprising to her how readily the girls had taken to the idea that Mac and Kim would be their parents. But perhaps not such a surprise: With the girls' mixed heritage, they seemed a perfect match for Mac, a mixture of black and white, and his Asian-American wife, Kim. The little girls had turned Mac from a grizzly bear into a lamb at home. It had little effect on his newsroom behavior.

Lacey and Mac both had played a part in rescuing the girls from a hellish life. Lacey had teared up the first time the girls called Mac and Kim "Mom and Dad."

"Really?" Lacey said, tousling both heads at once. "Do you know what kind of dresses you want?"

"Something dressy enough for a wedding," Jasmine said. "Weddings are special days. We have to look perfect, you know!"

"They're going to be pink! 'Cause it's my favorite color and not Jasmine's," Lily Rose declared. "We're special honorary assistant junior bridesmaids."

"We're wearing pink because it's Stella's favorite color, not because it's *yours*." Jasmine gave her little sister a big-sister Look. "She was supposed to be just a flower girl," she stage-whispered to Lacey, "but I got her promoted."

"I'm too old to be a flower girl," Lily Rose protested.

"If you sit too long in that chair, you'll have to be a reporter," Lacey said.

"I'm ready," Lily Rose declared. "I wanna be a reporter! Like Miss Lacey!"

"Good, I could use some help. What do you want to write about?"

Lily Rose's eyes grew larger. "You mean I have to *write* things? Like in school?"

"That's the deal. That's what reporters do."

"I'd rather be a junior bridesmaid." She jumped out of the seat.

"Dad says you're writing a book with him and Tony Trujillo," Jasmine said with interest. "True crime. Good guys and bad guys way out West and the good guys win."

The book again. Mac and their publisher Claudia's
harebrained scheme was that *The Eye Street Observer*
could make quick money on a true-crime book, cobbled
together out of their own reporting of the Sagebrush adventure they'd all been a part of, the pursuit and take-
down of a killer and his accomplices in Colorado. Mac
and Claudia had the idea that they (meaning Mac, Tony,
and Lacey) could crank out a book in no time, slap a
lurid cover on it, and sell the same reportage a second
time. It was a dreadful idea, Lacey thought, which also
involved a lot of extra work.

"We're *allegedly* writing a book together," Lacey said.

"He says you're going to just *crank it out*." Jasmine
mimed cranking a meat grinder.

"I love it when people think writing is like cranking
out sausage."

"He writes every night," Jasmine said. "He is *seriously*
cranking it out."

"Won't that be cool?" Lily Rose chimed in. "A book
with our dad's name on it! And yours too, Miss Lacey!
Cool, huh?"

"Cool." Lacey put her forehead down on her desk.

"Do you have a headache, Miss Lacey?"

"Yes, his name is Mac. But he's a great dad, so I forgive him." *Almost*.

Her editor had been bugging her for more copy for
the book, the erroneously titled *Terror at Timberline*. The
events did involve a certain amount of terror, but they
did *not* happen anywhere near timberline, even though
Sagebrush, Colorado, always felt to Lacey like the very
ends of the earth. Mac was editing and merging the stories she had written in Sagebrush, but he was constantly
asking for more description, more dialogue, more con-
text, and her *feelings*. That was especially weird to Lacey.
Editors, in her experience, generally didn't give a hoot in
Hell about reporters' feelings. Apparently that was the
difference between newspaper journalism and a quick-
and-dirty true-crime book.

Crank it out like sausage and crank up the emotion.
The very thought made her cranky.

"I have an important question! Can we wear our
boots to the wedding?" Jasmine asked. "I am rocking
these cowboy boots." She put out one foot and admired
it. "You wrote in the paper that boots and dresses are
totally completely fashionable together right now."

"You read my stories?"

"I read them too!" Lily Rose piped up.

"Can we wear them? To Miss Stella's wedding?" Jasmine pressed. The boots were precious to her, Lacey suspected, not only because she'd never had anything so
cool, but because Mac had bought them for the girls far
away, way out west in Colorado. In fact he had gone to
some trouble to purchase those new boots, dragging
Lacey along for shopping advice, and personally packing
them all the way back to Washington. Today the girls
were clad in jean skirts, cotton tops, and those brand-new
cowboy boots. Pink boots and blue boots.

Lacey hesitated. Stella's wedding might not happen;
then again, with Stella, *anything* might happen. "I'm
pretty sure Stella wouldn't have a problem with your
boots. I think she'd really dig it if you wore them."

Lily Rose jumped up and down. She had energy to
spare. "Chill out, Lily Rose," Jasmine warned.

"Hey, you guys," a new voice said. They all peered
around Lacey's cubicle to see Kim Jones striding through
the newsroom. Mac was with her. "I wondered where
you were."

Lacey was always amazed that Mac, the grouchy slob,
had managed to find such a well-dressed and attractive
wife. The petite Kim Jones was wearing immaculately
tailored navy slacks with a crisp white shirt, and a cleverly tied navy, pink, and white scarf. It might have been
dull on someone else, but she made it look fresh.

"We found Miss Lacey," Lily Rose said. The girls both
smiled at their new mom. The adoption would be a formality, Lacey knew. They'd already become a family.

"We had important fashion details to discuss," Lacey remarked. "For the wedding."

"Not cowboy boots?" Kim was mock-dismayed.

"Lacey said Stella would be cool with it," Jasmine said.

"That means we get to wear them," Lily Rose added, threatening to jump up and down again. "Please?"

Kim lifted her shoulders and shared a look with Mac. He just shook his head. "Don't ask me, I'm not the expert." Mac scooted over to Felicity's desk to hunt for today's food item. But she hadn't come in yet and there were no treats. "Those boots cost a lot of money. It doesn't hurt for people to see them."

"See who else is wearing cowboy boots." Jasmine pointed at Mac's feet. He was wearing his new pair of black boots. Kim grinned.

"What? They're comfortable," Mac said. "Let's let 'em wear the boots."

"If you're sure, Lacey," Kim said. "They seem stuck on wearing those boots."

"I'll wear mine to that wedding too," Mac said.

"No, you won't," Kim murmured. "Just the girls."

"All you have to do now is find pink dresses," Lacey said. The girls giggled happily as they hugged their good-byes. A pang of guilt washed over her. She didn't want Kim to spend a lot of money on pink dresses that might not be used, if the wedding didn't happen. Then she slapped herself mentally.

They're little girls—pink dresses will never go to waste.

Kim smiled as she gathered her girls. Jasmine was almost as tall now as her mom.

"Ladies, we have a big day ahead of us," Kim said.

Mac ushered them out of the newsroom toward the elevators. Lacey watched them leave and reached for her cell phone.

"Stella, it's Lacey. How are you doing?"

"I'm alive, Lace, but my heart is broken." Lacey caught her in mid-sniffle. "More than that would have been broken if that car had hit us, I know. Nigel is my hero, Lacey, but he can't be my husband. Not ever!"

Lacey was glad Stella couldn't see the face she was making at her friend's dramatics. "Aside from that, how's the wedding planning going?"

Stella choked on a sob. "There is no wedding."

I'm ignoring all of this. She will change her mind. "Jasmine and Lily Rose were just here. They wanted to know if they can wear their pink and blue cowboy boots with their pink dresses. I told them they could."

There was a pause. "Oh! Cowboy boots, yeah, I saw them, they're totally cute. I don't want to disappoint the girls, but— oh, my God, Lace!"

"It's still off, then?"

"Oh, Lacey, it has to be. I don't want it to be over. On the other hand, I don't want to die. And not just me. Nigel too! And you! I almost forgot about you. We were all in the crosshairs of that black limo. And the shawl."

"That crazy Russian shawl has got nothing to do with anything," Lacey said firmly.

"Yeah, Smithsonian." A deep voice boomed behind her. "Tell me all about this crazy Russian shawl. And what *exactly* has it got *nothing* to do with?"

Lacey was so focused on Stella, she hadn't noticed the huge shadow looming over her desk, blotting out the sun. That shadow could only mean trouble. "Stella, I have to go now. Don't do anything rash. I mean it. Call me!" She clicked off.

An impatient cough rumbled. Lacey spun around in her desk chair. "Detective Lamont. What a nice surprise."

"I'll just bet." Broadway Lamont was a very large and imposing African-American homicide detective. Lacey had made his acquaintance in the course of several murder investigations, and although they had become sort of friends, he still scared the breath out of her.

Lamont never spontaneously visited *The Eye Street Observer*. When he showed up, there was always some sticky situation to be handled. Or one of Felicity's sticky buns to be munched. Lamont had a peculiar affection for Felicity. But she and her buns were nowhere to be seen, so Lacey had Lamont all to herself today. *Lucky me.*

She peered up at Lamont as he glowered down at her. He was not quite as big as a bull moose, but certainly more intimidating. Despite his musical name, he was not an entertainer. He once told Lacey, "My name may be Broadway, but I don't sing and I don't dance. I just want answers, and I want them fast."

"What's on your mind, Broadway?" she asked.

He grabbed a random chair, twirled it around, and sat down. He pulled her chair in, close to his face. "I am hurt, Smithsonian. Deeply hurt. Wounded, in fact."

"Um, sorry?"

"Wounded," he repeated. "You didn't think to call me? A friend of Lacey Smithsonian's drops dead and she doesn't think to call me, her best friend in the D.C. police department?"

That wasn't saying much. "If you're talking about Leonardo, he wasn't exactly my friend."

"Don't quibble. You knew the late Leonard Karpinski. Hairstylist. Plied his trade under the name of Leonardo. 'Leonardo,' what would you call that, Smithsonian? A *nom de hair*?" He chuckled at his own wit. "Yeah, *that* Leonardo."

"Oh. *That* Leonardo. I take it the Metropolitan police department is calling this a homicide?"

"No ruling yet. Let's just call it suspicious," he said. "Mighty suspicious."

Lacey craned her neck around the big detective, hoping Felicity Pickles had appeared, even though she suspected the food editor's secret plan was to fatten them all up and lead them to her gingerbread house in the woods.

Although Lacey had a rocky history with Ms. Pickles, they had settled into a sort of friendship. Not that they actually *liked* each other, but detente made life easier in the newsroom. And there was the little detail of Lacey connecting Felicity with her fiancé, Harlan Wiedemeyer. Lacey wondered if it would have been wiser to set her up with Detective Lamont. The big detective was clearly sweet on Felicity and her tarts. He had a notorious sweet tooth and a preference for the full-figured lasses of the world, especially lasses like Felicity, who were happy to feed his sweet tooth.

Lamont followed Lacey's gaze. Nothing. No Felicity.

Come on, Felicity! Where are those tarts of yours when I really need one?

"What can I tell you, Broadway? I didn't find the body. I didn't know he died until this morning."

His wicked grin lit up his face. "I'm told you witnessed the deceased making a damn fool of himself Sunday night before his untimely demise. Why don't you start with that crazy haunted shawl?"

It was too early in the morning to be needled. She stared at her empty coffee cup. "There is no such thing as a haunted Russian shawl."

"Really? Did I say it was *Russian*? Seems you do have some personal knowledge of this thing. Well, we've got one screwy Marie Largesse, who's swearing that a shawl killed Leonard Karpinski."

"So you're working this case?"

"I am not the lead investigator, thank the homicide gods, but I have been shanghaied into assisting in this investigation."

"Why you?"

"Homicide moves in mysterious ways," Lamont boomed. "Because that pretty-but-screwy fortune-teller of yours started flapping her jaw about haunted Russian shawls, cursed shawls, indeed, killer shawls. Maybe because I got a history with a certain screwy fashion reporter named Smithsonian. And just maybe because the screwy victim was a suspect in another hairstylist murder last year, also involving said screwy fashion reporter."

"Coincidence?" She toyed with her empty FASHION *BITES* coffee mug.

"As soon as the words *cursed shawl* were out of the Gypsy woman's mouth, Detective Hopkins, lead detective on the case, thought of me. With a smirk on his face, I might add. Crimes of fashion, even when they are fatal, are beneath him. He finally requested my assistance to sort out the various loonies on this one."

"Like me?"

"Who else? Rest assured, I am working on payback." He grabbed the mug from her hand. "Hey, where are your manners, Smithsonian?"

"Excuse me? My manners?"

"You going to offer me some wretched newsroom coffee, or what?"

"Didn't want to cause another suspicious death so early in the day."

"Do I look like a little sludge could hurt me?"

Broadway Lamont looked to Lacey like a runaway black limo wouldn't even crease his hair. Lacey grabbed her cup. "This way to the sludge shop." He followed her to the newsroom pantry and sniffed the noxious brew with relish.

"How about I make a fresh pot?" she said.

"Going all gourmet on me? Sounds like a guilty conscience, Smithsonian."

"I just don't want to go and kill a homicide detective by mistake," she muttered.

"Knowing you, it wouldn't be a mistake," he said with a chuckle.

The new batch almost smelled good. "You said Leonardo's death was officially suspicious?"

"Homicide, or suicide, or death by misadventure, all suspicious to me. All I know, Smithsonian, is Mr. Karpinski is dead, and in a manner we refer to technically as *freaky*. Poison. Not something you see much on the mean streets of D.C."

"What kind of poison?"

"Not sure yet. Lab test results won't be in for a couple

of weeks. But the medical examiner says it could be nicotine, and not from smoking."

"Nicotine? How?"

"Homemade. It's easy—gardeners use it for a pesticide. Apparently he was vomiting, had difficulty breathing, sweating, all the symptoms. According to the bartender at the dive where he went after your little soiree."

"Where was he poisoned?"

"If we knew where, we'd be closer to knowing who, wouldn't we? We're retracing his path for his last twenty-four hours. In those hours, he attended a bachelorette party. And your name came up. His path crossed yours. Nice job, Smithsonian. How do you do it?"

"Just lucky, I guess. It doesn't mean he was poisoned there."

He laughed. "Two words: *Killer Shawl.*"

Lacey narrowed her eyes at the mention of the shawl. "Leonardo didn't receive an invitation."

"Gate-crasher?"

"That's right." She poured the coffee "I forgot, how do you like it?"

"Black like me." He smacked his lips over the freshly brewed java. "So tell me—this psychic voodoo woman, Marie Largesse. Is she a few bricks shy of a load?"

"Marie is not stupid or crazy. She's a good person. She does, however, see things differently from you and me. You could say she's fanciful."

Lacey led Lamont back to her cubicle with their coffee cups. He filled up a chair, she perched on her desk.

"Fanciful," he snorted, propping his feet on her trash basket. "If that means all big eyes and purple fingernails and talk of hauntings and curses, then yeah, I guess she's fanciful. Cute, though. Delightfully full-figured."

"You questioned Marie yourself? I hope you were gentle with her."

"Hopkins brought her down to the station last night.

I sat in on it. All very cool and professional, he's a kid-gloves kind of detective. Unlike yours truly."

"You don't suspect Marie?" Lacey said. "She wouldn't hurt a fly. Even a nasty fly like Leonardo."

"You know me, Smithsonian." He peered at her over his cup. "I suspect everyone. Including you."

"I'm flattered. Listen, Leonardo wasn't invited to the party. No one knew he was coming, except maybe him, so no one could have planned to kill him there. He was an unpleasant surprise."

"Maybe someone got tipped off, knew he'd show up, planned a surprise of their own."

"Like who?"

"His spurned ex-lover Miguel Flores? Another friend of yours?"

"Miguel? He was the spurner, not the spurned."

"Cuts both ways. I figure eventually we'll find whoever tapped Leonard K with a lethal dose of something, maybe nicotine. But just out of curiosity, who do *you* think decided they were never getting another bad haircut from Leonardo?" Lamont drank the brew. "Not bad coffee, by the way."

Could be worse. "I don't know who'd want to kill Leo, other than his clients. He could be a real jerk."

"You telling me you haven't been cogitating over this, coming up with your own list of bad guys? And a dozen ways to get yourself into trouble?"

"Cogitating? Not me. Haven't given it a thought."

"Since when?"

"Since someone tried to run me over yesterday. And the bride and groom too."

"Wait a minute!" Lamont put down his coffee cup. "Someone tried to mow the three of you down? What, like pins in a bowling alley? Just hours after this Leonardo dies? And you didn't think this was of interest either?" His face clouded. "You holding out on me, Smithsonian!"

She shrugged. "I assumed you knew. We made a report. The cops weren't interested. Didn't think you'd be interested either. After all, nobody's dead. I'm sure you can find the traffic report. It was a big black limousine, on Eye Street."

"Black limousine, in the District? Oh, yeah, *that'll* narrow it down." Lamont lifted his mug meaningfully. "You know what I think?"

"What, Broadway?"

"I need another hit of this coffee." He drained his cup and handed it to her.

Lacey took off for the newsroom pantry again, leaving him sitting at her desk. He wouldn't learn much there, even if he went through her papers and her hard drive. Not unless he was deeply interested in what to wear to a wedding.

When she returned with his refill, Detective Lamont was on his cell phone, scowling. He uttered a few guttural noises and hung up.

"In front of the Arts Club, huh?" he asked her. "Limo took out an awning at the hotel next door. They got nothing from the car. Stolen yesterday, no forensics, no decent description of the driver, no trace of him. By the way, Smithsonian, what the hell were you doing there?"

"It was a walk-through for Stella's wedding reception. You remember Stella. It's going to be held there, this Saturday. Maybe."

"Maybe? Someone getting cold feet?"

Lacey sighed. "The bride." She sat down and told him about the black limo attack and the aftermath. "That's all I got, Broadway."

"Tell me this. Is your pal Stella Lake also convinced there's a damn haunted shawl at the root of all this?"

"Everybody is. I'm the only voice of reason."

"Damn! I hate all this hoodoo voodoo mumbo jumbo."

"I guess it's easier for her to believe the Curse of the Shawl is after us than to think someone is deliberately trying to kill her, or the groom, or the entire wedding party. Does any of this help?"

"Not a damn bit," he said with a laugh. "On the plus side, it'll make a heck of a story back at the station."

"You're a riot, Detective."

He leveled his gaze at her. "So what do you think, Smithsonian? Your limo attack connected to this Leonardo character being poisoned?" He rubbed his chin with his coffee cup.

"How could it be? Aren't poison and speeding cars two very different signatures?" Lacey asked. "What kind of criminal profile would that make?"

"Profiling." He snorted. "You been watching too much TV. Lots of folks who do violence to other folks use whatever comes to hand. Damn few killers fit that profile-and-signature stuff, like those criminal geniuses in the movies. But you profile me up a killer Russian shawl on the loose, roaming the city? All bets are off." He couldn't keep from smirking.

There was a rustling movement in the newsroom behind them. Lacey caught sight of Harlan Wiedemeyer lurking around Felicity's empty cubicle, no doubt trying to cadge some news bites for his death-and-dismemberment beat. Wiedemeyer hadn't had anything very interesting to dig into since his story on the mysterious exploding hog barns in Minnesota. He had tried, but failed, to tie it in with the mysterious phenomenon of the exploding toads in Germany. Broadway Lamont leapt out of his chair and towered over the shorter reporter.

"Winklemeyer, right?" Lamont bellowed. "What are you doing here?"

"Wiedemeyer. Harlan Wiedemeyer. And I work here." He pulled himself up to his full height, which wasn't very tall, especially in comparison to Lamont. "What are *you* doing here? Interrogating our Smithsonian? What's she done now?"

"What interrogation? We're having a private conversation and you are a fly in the ointment." He looked like a bull about to charge. Wiedemeyer took a step back into the cubicle across the aisle, bumped into the desk chair, and sat down.

Just then the aroma of something delectable perfumed the air. Lacey felt enormous relief, as if the bomb squad had arrived just as the bomb was about to go off like an exploding amphibian. Food editor Felicity Pickles appeared, food offering in hand, clad in a dreary slate blue frock that stretched tight across her chubby tummy. She'd paired it with a blazing pink sweater covered in red tulips. Even Felicity was ready for spring. She reminded Lacey of a kindergarten teacher. Nevertheless, Felicity's thick auburn locks were glossy and her china-doll face glowed with love for Harlan Wiedemeyer.

The reporters following in Felicity's aromatic wake weren't focused on her, but on what she was holding: a tray of artfully arranged biscotti—lemon, cranberry, and vanilla, all dipped in chocolate. For Felicity, presentation (in her cooking, not her clothes) was everything. Always aware of admiring and drooling male attention, Felicity stopped, posed with her tray, and smiled.

"Why, Miss Pickles, what do we have here?" Lamont inquired.

"Hello, Detective Broadway, just a little something I whipped up. A small assortment of chocolate-covered biscotti to go with your mid-morning coffee." Felicity glowed with pleasure. The big detective looked doubtful.

Biscotti? Can his sweet tooth really be assuaged by a mere biscotti, and not a gooey giant cinnamon roll dripping with icing?

"You could dunk it in your coffee," Felicity suggested. "Yummy with coffee. Even Lacey's coffee."

"I love biscotti, my sweet pickles," Wiedemeyer announced. "Your biscotti are the biscottiest."

Lamont followed suit, experimentally. He dunked and chewed. "Hmmm. Not bad." He finished one in three bites, then another in two. He reached for a third.

Police reporter Tony Trujillo, one of Felicity's biggest fans, arrived on the scene, drawn by the seductive scent.

"Ah, *dulce* Felicidad!" He reached for a vanilla biscotti and a chocolate without asking, and stayed to listen in without being invited. Felicity gazed at her audience of hungry, adoring men.

"What brings you here, detective? Not my little old biscotti."

"The usual. Death and Smithsonian. But your biscuits have surely brightened my day, Miss Pickles."

"Murder, my sweet," Harlan explained unnecessarily. "Some poor bastard bit the dust, and of course our favorite fashion reporter was there."

"I was not!" Lacey protested.

"A guest at a bachelorette party hosted by the most notorious fashion reporter in town dropped dead after the soiree." Broadway Lamont loved playing with Smithsonian. His pearly smile gleamed. *Like a wolf.* Everyone stared at Lacey.

"Hey, he didn't drop dead till much later. Nowhere near me, and not at my party. And he wasn't a guest, he was a party crasher. And I don't know if he dropped, or if he slowly sank."

"Oh, no. Did he eat something Lacey made for the party?" Felicity gasped. "Not from one of my recipes, I hope? It couldn't be! I test every recipe right here at *The Eye.* You're all my witnesses." She took great stock in not poisoning people with her food. Poisoning them with her attitude was quite another thing.

Everybody thinks everything is all about them, Lacey thought.

"Sweet Pickles, let us go make some decent coffee to go with your excellent biscotti," Wiedemeyer said. "We can discuss the poor deceased bastard in private."

"Language, Harlan," Felicity cautioned him. She had her own stash of superior coffee beans in her filing cabinet. All her files smelled like dark Colombian roast. Wiedemeyer grabbed the coffee stash, lifted one more biscotti from her tray, and steered Felicity toward the newsroom pantry. Trujillo followed the trail of the biscotti and the *good* coffee. Lamont watched them go. It seemed to sour his mood all over again.

"You come up with anything, Smithsonian, I want it," Lamont commanded. "Anything on Leonard Karpinski or Marie Largesse or Miguel Flores, or even that screwy shawl, you call me. Doesn't look good that the thing is missing, haunted or not. It turns up, I want to see it. Do not hesitate, call! You get me?"

"I get you perfectly, Broadway. If a Killer Shawl comes after me in a black limousine, I'll let you know." He grunted. "But I have a question. *How* was Leonardo poisoned? Food? Drink?"

He stood up to go. "One of the techs said it looked like he got it in the neck."

"The neck?" Lacey felt the blood drain from her face. She rubbed the back of her neck, the way Leonardo had. Lamont bore down on her. She understood how a real suspect must feel under interrogation by Broadway "the Bull" Lamont.

"What do you know?" It was a demand, not an inquiry.

"Nothing." She hesitated. She didn't want to tell him. And she rationalized that she really didn't *know* anything. "Except—"

"Except what?" The detective's eyes narrowed.

"At the party, Leonardo grabbed the shawl out of Marie's hands. He was being a jerk, pretending to dance with it. Sort of a tango. Then he complained that the shawl 'bit' him. On the neck. Right before he left the party. Actually, Miguel threw him out."

"It bit his neck? Like a vampire?" Lamont slapped his forehead again. "I know you're not messing with me here, 'cause you know better than that. Ain't that right, Smithsonian?"

"You are the last person I would mess with, Broadway. Just reporting the facts. It's what I do."

"Damn it all. I don't need no hauntings, no curses, no psychics, and no ghost-infused hanks of cloth." He echoed her sentiments exactly. "I want to see that shawl. Spread the word."

"You're going to take the haunted shawl into custody, Lamont? Go medieval on it? Rough it up till it squeals?"

"You smart-mouthing me?" Broadway Lamont treated her to one last wicked grin. "You just be glad we're friends, Smithsonian. I know cops who'd lock you up and throw away the key for less than that. You and your vampire wrap too."

chapter 15

KILLER SHAWL STALKS WASHINGTON

Lacey read the headline and seethed. It was exactly the kind of headline she'd dreaded. That headline didn't appear in *The Washington Post* or *The Washington Times*, or in the scrappy but semi-respectable *Eye Street Observer*. Even Harlan Wiedemeyer had agreed there wasn't enough of a news hook, yet. The shawl was a tease without a story. Tony's story had given it a few puzzled paragraphs, buried in the back of the paper.

But Damon Newhouse had struck again. The "Killer Shawl" and Leonardo's suspicious death led the hot news online at Conspiracy Clearinghouse, also known as DeadFed dot com:

> Whosoever mocketh the shawl shall surely die! Thus sayeth the legend of a haunted Russian shawl, possessed for generations by an infamous family linked to every major tragedy in Russian history. One hapless victim in Washington, D.C., has already paid the ultimate price for making sport of this ominous black cloth covered with secret symbols, which has suddenly vanished in the wake of his unexplained murder: Leonard Karpinski, known professionally as Leonardo, highly regarded Washington hairstylist to Capital City ce-

lebrities and a key figure in a notorious local murder last year, may be only the first identified American victim of the curse of the Killer Shawl . . .

Killer Shawl, my ass, Lacey thought. *If anybody should beware of the curse, it's Damon Newhouse. I wish the shawl would pay him a visit, shut down his Web site, and delete all his files.*

Lacey scanned the story. It was Damon's usual half-baked hodgepodge of paranormal fancy and conspiracy-obsessed conjecture. She didn't know what was more frightening, Damon continuing to get everything wrong, or someday possibly getting something right.

Leonardo's death was unfortunate and still technically "unexplained," but Lacey was certain there was nothing supernatural about it. He was poisoned, possibly with a homemade dose of nicotine. He complained about a bite and he scratched his neck. If there was poison in the shawl, someone put it there. And if it was deliberately put in the shawl, she reasoned, then it could not have been meant for Leonardo. Whom the poison was meant for, why and by whom, and where the shawl was now—those were the real mysteries that Damon couldn't be bothered to address, not the supposed supernatural powers of a haunted phantom shawl. It made her head hurt. And it was far too early for her first headache of the day.

She conjured an image of the shawl in her mind that reminded her of the elaborate embroidered Russian altar cloths she had seen on display at the Hillwood Museum above Rock Creek Park in the District, once the home of millionaire Washington socialite Marjorie Merriweather Post. The wealthy wife of the American ambassador to the Soviet Union in the late 1930s, Marjorie had purchased innumerable Russian artifacts and brought them home with her to Hillwood. The Soviet treasury at the time was empty of hard currency but full of Romanov booty, and it was eager to sell priceless trea-

sures to rich Western collectors. Marjorie took conspicu-
ous consumption to new heights, but she had the money
to do it and she did it with style.

Marie's shawl was not made of velvet, like the Hillwood Russian altar cloths. It wasn't woven with the same
amount of real gold thread either, but it was rich with
stories. In recording the history of the Kepelovs, it also
reflected nearly two centuries of tumultuous Russian history. Lacey prayed it would turn up soon. But if it did, it
would probably end up in the hands of Broadway Lamont
and the D.C. police. Lacey hated the thought of such a
priceless artifact hidden away in a police evidence locker,
possibly forever. It was a lovely garment with its own secrets, the multitude of stories it held in its fabric. If only
she had taken more time with it. If only she could touch
it and examine it more closely. *Without being bitten.*

Lacey didn't have time to dither over Damon that
morning, but she was still steaming when she dialed
Brooke, the source of Damon's leak.

"Hi, Lacey, what's up?" Brooke sounded cheerful.

"'Killer Shawl'?! Really? Are you kidding me?"
Lacey demanded.

"Great headline, isn't it?" Brooke said. "Leo mocks
the shawl, the shawl is cursed, Leo is found dead. Ipso
facto: Killer Shawl! Don't you love it? Murderous shawl,
fatal shawl, shawl suspected of foul play—those just
didn't have the same ring."

Lacey could hear the satisfaction in Brooke's voice.
She practically purred with reflected glory.

"And you fed this story to Damon without even a
shred of factual evidence?"

"We are soul mates, Lacey. Of course I had to tell him.
As for evidence, well, Leo's dead. That's a fact. That Russian shawl has unknown powers. That's sort of a fact. It's
missing, that's a fact too. Lacey, I thought you of all people would be all over this story."

"And where did he come up with that 'whosoever
mocketh' business? Nobody says *mocketh*! Or *sayeth*!"

Lacey complained. "Marie didn't say *mocketh*. And there are no secret symbols in the shawl. Marie explained all that."

"Damon has a creative way of telling a story. His readers like it. It's simply a different kind of journalism from the kind you do, Lacey."

"Yeah, his kind is the crazy kind. It's not creative, Brooke, it's not poetic license, it's just wrong. Where are the experts, where are the facts? I know Damon likes to call it 'gonzo journalism,' but this stuff is too far gone to be gonzo!"

"I suppose you wanted to keep this story all to yourself?" Brooke's voice turned frosty.

"If this *is* a story, which I doubt, I'd want it to be factual and accurate, not something out of a pathetic sci-fi movie." Lacey had to admit to herself that at another time and another place, she would want to write this story. *But only if it were true.*

"As a matter of fact, Lacey, I know Marie has already been questioned by the police, and I imagine they will be at our doors any moment. If Damon wants to write this story his way, he will. He is protected by the First Amendment to the Constitution."

"Protected, Brooke, but wrong. The shawl in itself might be a great story, but do you really think it's sentient? It has evil supernatural powers? It somehow walks the streets and murders people? It drives a speeding black limo?"

"Then you've considered all these possibilities too!"

Lacey growled into the phone. "Crimes of Fashion, that's my job."

"Of course it is. And Lacey," Brooke lectured, "you do believe in the power of clothes."

"The power we *give* them. The feelings we invest in them, the symbols we make of them. Not because they're possessed by demons or aliens or ghosts!"

"Oh, that's good. I'm taking notes." Brooke and Lacey could go round and round with this conversation for hours, and only Brooke would enjoy it. It was one of her talents as an attorney. Lacey didn't need to give her or Damon anything else. DeadFed had dragged her name into its loony stories often enough.

"That's not for publication, Brooke. I mean it. I'm not giving you quotes to hand to Damon," Lacey said. It was cold comfort that he never got anything she said completely right. His more credulous readers believed whatever he wrote anyway. "I have to go."

"Wait, don't you want to hear about my dress for the wedding?" Brooke asked.

Brooke could be planning on attending the wedding stark naked and painted in Burberry plaid, for all Lacey cared at the moment. "No, I don't. And for your information, the latest news hot off the press is that Stella is canceling the wedding. Good-bye."

Lacey had seldom been so irritated with Brooke. And Damon. And herself for rising to the bait. "Killer Shawl" sounded like a late-night television comedy skit, with the vampire-fanged shawl at the wheel of an out-of-control limo, cruising the streets for victims. This time it wasn't funny. It only made her think of yesterday's brush with death. And worse, if she didn't watch out, Mac would be wondering why Damon beat her to this story.

Her desk phone rang. "Lacey, cher, have you seen the story on DeadFed?" It was Marie.

"My blood pressure says I have."

"I don't want to make things worse, but I'm seeing a cloud rolling in, following you and Stella, and who knows who else, and it's about to burst."

"Is this one of your famous psychic weather reports, Marie?"

"No, the weather for Saturday is fabulous, a beautiful cherry-blossom-perfect day for a wedding."

"Stella's threatening to call off the wedding."

"I heard from her this morning." Marie clicked her tongue. "Targeted by a dressed-up taxicab. She's mighty shook up, and I don't blame her. I'm so sorry, cher."

"You were right about the traffic being bad." Lacey just remembered Marie's traffic prediction. "Turns out Gregor wasn't the one who wanted to run me down." *This time.*

"Of course he wasn't. Luckily you're all still alive."

"What about the wedding, Marie? Will it happen?"

"Stella, God love her, is just as changeable as the weather. When I think about her wedding, I see a roller-coaster. Up and down and up and down. I think whatever goes down, must come up, don't you? Truly I don't know. Stella has free will, she will decide."

Lacey chuckled. "Do you know anything more about Leonardo?"

"Not about who killed him, I'm afraid. Yet I know he's in a better place and he's holding no grudge, maybe for the first time. He was a tormented soul."

"I'm sorry you had to talk to the police again last night. Broadway Lamont told me."

"It wasn't so bad. They think I'm either crazy or I'm a crazy killer. They just can't make up their minds. It will all blow over in the end. Lamont is a sweetie under that big scary shell, and Detective Hopkins took turns telling me I was hiding something and asking me to tell his fortune." Marie managed a little of her trademark musical laugh.

"Did you?"

"I sure didn't want to! As a detective, he's been around so much death. I was terrified a faint would come over me."

"But it didn't?" Lacey asked. "His future looks good?"

"Oh, that. Not if he doesn't do something about his high blood pressure, and his arteries are cloudy, and he's feeling guilty about flirting with some female desk sergeant. I warned him not to eat that bag of greasy burgers and fries from Five Guys. That he needs to pay more attention to his wife—she is so much smarter than he is—because she is beginning to think there might be other men out there for her. He was startled, to be sure. I also told him he better not forget his anniversary is this weekend. Same day as Stella's wedding. Isn't that nice?"

"What was his reaction?" Lacey reached for her now-cold coffee.

"He said I was just guessing. People always say that. I warned him he better make a reservation for the Old Ebbitt Grill for their anniversary, and if he was lucky his wife might remember he was once a very romantic man. Why the Old Ebbitt, he asked. I said, That's where your first date was, wasn't it?"

"Is there any way to tell if that's true?"

"Not that I know of, cher, 'less his wife kept a souvenir of their first date, but I was getting all this very strong and clear. Anyway, he pulled his cell phone right out and called the restaurant. And then he let me go."

"Nicely done, Marie. You rock."

"Thank you, cher. Still, I'm worried about this cloud I'm feeling, Lacey. It has nothing to do with the rain. Something is clouding my vision, like I'm trying to peer through a veil."

"A wedding veil?"

"No, something else." Marie sounded worried. "More like a gray veil."

"Not a vale of tears?"

"No—a veil of revenge."

"Can you explain that?"

"Not really. Wish I could. This psychic thing is a charm and a curse, believe me."

Lacey slumped in her chair. *Why tell me these things, if you can't give me more?* "Will Stella marry Nigel?" Lacey wanted to know if she should pick up her pink dress. She was due for the final fitting.

"I can't see that far through this gray cloud, cher. Wait a minute, was it a gray car that jumped the curb and nearly hit y'all?"

"No. It was black. Doesn't help much, I know." As Broadway Lamont had said, black limos were practically the official D.C. vehicle.

"Stay safe, cher, till the sky clears, till I can cleanse my third eye."

Lacey checked her beautiful new watch from Vic. It was later than she'd thought. She also reached for the Saint Christopher medal from his mother and said a quick silent prayer for safe travel. She drank the last of the cold coffee in her cup.

"I'm worried about you, Marie."

"I'm safe. My sweet Gregor is watching over me."

"Yes, but what about his sister?" Lacey had unsettled feelings about her.

"Olga's an old soul and she is a bit scary, with a chilly personality, but that's probably because she's from a cold country."

Lacey cleared some of her desk. "Gregor is from that same country."

"Yes," Marie agreed. "But he's got a warm Southern soul. He's a big old Texas cowboy at heart."

"It's the love talking." In the background, Lacey heard the door chimes of The Little Shop of Horus. So Marie was at work. "Have you found the shawl?"

"I have searched and searched, high and low, up and down, and inside out, honey, but it seems to be on the move."

On the move? Lacey really wished Marie hadn't put it quite that way.

Harlan Wiedemeyer had the disquieting ability to pop up when he was least expected, like a chubby grinning jack-in-the-box. He stared at Lacey over her cubicle divider as she collected her purse and her own vintage (but not haunted) shawl. Behind him was Mac, wearing his grumpy editor's face. Lacey's spirits sank.

"DeadFed scooped us on the haunted shawl murdering Leonardo," Wiedemeyer accused her. "Poor bastard can't even get a decent story in this paper about his own death."

"How can DeadFed scoop us if its story isn't accurate,

Harlan? It isn't a real story!" Lacey had to get going or she'd be late to the restaurant. She leaned against her desk. "It's not true. We try to print things that are *true*."

"Haunted shawls and exploding toads, Lacey! This story was made for *The Eye*." Harlan practically did a jig. "We should have nailed this one! Your friend Damon scooped us big time."

Lacey looked at Mac. "Mac, referee this for me. If we'd run with 'Titanic Sunk by Sea Serpent,' one whole news cycle before the rest of the journalistic world ran 'Titanic Sunk by Iceberg,' would that be a scoop?"

Mac's expressive eyebrows danced their way across his forehead. "Smithsonian's right, Wiedemeyer. It's no scoop if you get it wrong. We only want the story if it's true and accurate. Go fight with Trujillo if you think there's more to it," Mac said.

"Thanks, Mac." *Maybe something will go right today after all*, Lacey thought.

"When you're right, you're right. And besides, you've got your hands full with that wacky wedding. And *Terror at Timberline*."

I take it all back. "About that title, Mac . . ."

chapter 16

"My surprise gift is a bodyguard?"

Lacey sat at the table waiting for the punch line. Instead, she spotted a large, handsome, heavily muscled man at the restaurant entryway, waiting for a sign from Vic. Lacey recognized him at once and her eyes went a little wide. "You hired Turtledove? I don't believe this, Vic."

"That's right, darling." Vic smiled. "But 'bodyguard' is so old school. These days we call them personal protection agents."

"Personal protection? Sounds like something you'd buy at the drugstore. And really, Vic, you shouldn't have. My new watch is quite enough of a birthday present. Not to mention the Saint Christopher medal. You can return the bodyguard for a refund."

"You're very cute for a smart-ass."

Lacey shut up and sipped her iced tea. She would rather enjoy lunch at Vidalia, the below-sidewalk-level restaurant on M Street, with its soothing cream and gold décor, than fight. She wondered if Vic had chosen it because it would be a nearly impossible setting for a drive-by shooting. She unfolded her napkin and picked up her menu to hide her disgust. *I don't want to live my life as if I were a target. Or actually* being *a target.*

"A bodyguard could seriously cramp my style, you know," she said, browsing the lunch specials.

"So can runaway limos."

The large man in the doorway smiled and waited for his cue. His real name was Forrest Thunderbird, but Turtle-dove was the nickname he let his friends use. He had an exotic, multiethnic look that the ladies loved, not to mention the allure of his well-disciplined and well-muscled physique. Turtledove was a bodyguard who occasionally freelanced for Vic and was also a jack-of-many-trades. One of them was playing a mean blues trumpet at little clubs in D.C. and Virginia.

"Forrest is going to be helping me watch over you for a few days," Vic said. "I don't know who's out there stalking you, or why, or exactly what the threat is—"

"Marie fainted," she filled in. Lacey might not have complete faith in all of Marie's predictions, but her fainting once again had proven a bellwether for disaster. "That's the threat."

"What I know is that Leonardo is dead and somebody tried to run you down in the street," Vic said.

"Actually on the sidewalk. Listen, I appreciate the gesture." Lacey tried to find the right words. "But—"

"No buts, Lacey. Not when your life is at stake."

She leaned back and stretched. Every muscle ached, no doubt from her tumble into the boxwood hedge yesterday, but also from sheer tension and anxiety. The scab on her knee itched and she just hoped the bruises would be gone by Saturday. "That car might not have been after me specifically. Could have been after Nigel. He has more enemies than I do."

"I can't tell you what a relief it is to know you might only have been collateral damage." Vic was cute when he was being droll, she decided.

"I love that you care." Lacey put her hand on his. Vic smiled and nearly won her over. "But I'm a reporter. It's part of the job. There are risks."

Vic gestured to the man who stood nearby to join them. "Nobody has risks like you do. D.C. is not a war zone."

"Not technically, no. And reporters do not get to have bodyguards. It's in the Newspaper Guild contract."

Besides, once the other female scribes see Turtledove, they'll all want one.

The hunky Turtledove took the chair next to Lacey. "Still in one piece, I see."

"Yes, thank you, Turtledove. Nothing personal, you know that. It just sets a bad precedent and—"

"Don't worry, Vic," Turtledove said, ignoring her protests. "I'll keep her out of traffic."

"Even on the sidewalk?" Lacey asked.

"Especially on the sidewalk." Turtledove appeared to be physically perfect. Bulging biceps stretched the short sleeves of his yellow polo shirt, the color vivid against his deep olive skin. He always seemed to be in a good mood too. Yet he had a few little flaws. One of them was that he was also a friend, and fan, of Damon Newhouse's whacked-out Conspiracy Clearinghouse. Turtledove was apt to believe Damon's shawl theory. "So are we dealing with a Killer Shawl or some other threat?"

"You already read DeadFed, I see," she commented.

"*The Eye* only had three paragraphs on the late Leonardo. Very dry reading. I checked all my usual sources. I keep an open mind." He grinned.

Lacey hid behind her menu. "Open mind, huh? You might try finding one of those for Damon."

He chuckled. "Don't want to taint the man's take on things. He has a unique viewpoint. Now, what's on the agenda for you and me this afternoon?"

Lacey sighed in surrender. "Back to the office, and then I have a full afternoon of errands. All sorts of girly things. You'll be bored."

"I doubt it." Nothing fazed Turtledove. "I'm going to enjoy this assignment, Lacey, especially if there are all sorts of girlies around."

"It's settled then," Vic said.

"No. No. No. I appreciate this, Vic. And you too, Turtledove. But I don't need a babysitter."

"Bodyguard, Lacey," Turtledove said. "Or personal protection agent, or hired gun, or ladies' home companion, whichever you like." He flashed his dazzling grin. "Vic and I both think you need safekeeping right now. He thinks you're worth keeping safe, and so do I."

"When I can't be there to make sure you're safe," Vic said, "I want you to be safe with the biggest, baddest, best bodyguard I know."

"That would be me." Turtledove turned on the high-wattage grin again.

Lacey shook her head. She certainly wasn't going to tell these guys she was giving in. The waitress arrived in the nick of time. Lacey ordered the crab cakes and the baked Vidalia onion. Vic asked for the Southern fried chicken, while Turtledove ordered the shrimp and grits. *Comfort food all around*, she thought, *what does that tell you?*

She whispered in Vic's ear. "Aren't you just a little bit afraid to leave me alone with such a good-looking bodyguard?"

He leaned over and put his arm around Lacey's shoulders, drawing her close to him. She could feel the heat of Vic's body and soul. "I would be, if I wasn't completely convinced of your utter devotion to me. And mine to you."

Her breath shortened, her heart raced. He still had that effect on her. "I guess you're safe then," she said. "For the moment."

"That's a relief." Vic kissed her on the forehead before letting her go. They were, after all, in a restaurant in Washington, D.C., and they didn't indulge in PDA the way Stella and Nigel did. And Turtledove was sitting there chuckling at them.

"Whew. Getting warm in here, or is it just me?" Turtledove said, fanning himself with the wine list while Vic laughed. "Listen, I only have one prior commitment. I'm sitting in with the band tonight at Velvet's Blues in Old Town. Lacey, you can be my date, or I can call someone else to take over."

"Are you kidding? Hearing you wail on that trumpet will be a treat," Lacey said.

"I'll meet you there later, sweetheart. After I finish with my client," Vic said.

"Any bad guys show up at the club, I jump off the stage and beat them down with my horn," Turtledove said with a smile. "No, not my trumpet—I hate to dent a good instrument. I got other weapons."

Lunch arrived and soon Vic and Turtledove fell into a deep analysis of the current state of the security business, what was wrong with the Redskins, and who might be after Lacey *this* time. Lacey finished her crab cakes and excused herself to visit the ladies' room. Turtledove leapt to his feet to escort her to the door. Vic had the nerve to chuckle as they left the table.

Lacey was finally alone in the ladies' room, refreshing her war paint—an essential weapon in her self-defense arsenal—when the sobering specter of Olga Kepelova appeared in the mirror behind her. Lacey dropped her blush in the sink and spun on her heel. It wasn't a specter; it was Olga herself. She looked half dead, a walking near-corpse with flat brown hair, wearing a gray sweater that drained all the color from her face. Only her somber brown eyes seemed alive.

"You startled me."

"It is a good place to meet, no? Quiet. No men to overhear." Olga moved closer.

Overhear *what*? Lacey's pulse was still racing. She picked up the pieces of her compact from the sink, keeping one eye on Olga and trying to control her breathing. Why did they need to have a private chat, without witnesses?

"What do you want, Olga?"

"Excellent. We get right to the point. I feel I must tell you, I fear Gregor's life is in danger. He could be next target of killer."

Olga was nothing if not direct. Lacey stared at the woman, wondering whether she could have been driving that black limo. But what motive could she have had?

"That's funny. *I* was nearly killed yesterday, along

with my friend Stella and her fiancé. If your brother is the target, why was someone after us?"

"Unknown. First there was Mr. Leonardo, and then you three from the wedding party. Danger is gathering. Often comes in threes."

"It's not gathering, it's already here. What's the connection? Gregor didn't know Leonardo."

"Human error, perhaps. Mistakes can be made."

"You think Leonardo was a mistake?"

"As you say, he was unwelcome guest. Bad luck."

"And the rest of us?" Did she know something more than she was telling? Lacey's thoughts threatened to explode into a full-blown migraine.

"Perhaps it was only a warning. You were not harmed."

Tell that to my throbbing knee. "Shaken but not stirred." Olga did not smile. "That was a little joke."

Olga still didn't smile. "When a guest dies after a bridal party, or what you call, bachelorette party, is no joke. Is very bad omen."

"As we've established, Leonardo wasn't exactly a guest."

"Still an ominous sign."

"Why are you telling me this?"

Olga was silent for a moment and pressed her fingers together. "Gregor does not listen to me. He is such a — what do you say — alpha dog. And Marie is too delicate. Too sensitive. I do not wish to upset fragile psychic equilibrium. Gregor's woman has a rare gift. Sadly untrained." Lacey had never thought of Marie as delicate, but she saw Olga's point. "Marie is very sweet girl. She is good for Gregor. Still time to give him babies. Never before has Gregor found a woman to love, to marry, to carry on the name Kepelov. Maybe they have beautiful psychic children. Think of the possibilities." Olga nodded to herself. "I approve of this match."

"I'm sure that's a relief to all of us."

Olga didn't detect the tinge of sarcasm in that comment. "Naturally. But to be most honest, Marie makes terrible coffee."

"The chicory. It's a New Orleans thing. Some people like it, some don't."

"Ah, the Louisiana connection. Thank you for explanation. I will bring my own coffee hereafter. Or tea. I prefer black tea, very strong."

Coffee. Tea. Psychics. Murder, Lacey mused. *Just another ladies' room conversation in Spy City.*

"You think Gregor will listen to me?" She reached for her makeup bag.

"More than you know, Lacey Smithsonian. He studies you."

That gave her a sudden chill. Lacey changed the subject. "Have you found the shawl?"

Olga turned the cold water on and washed her hands. "It is still missing. You know it is supposed to be haunted? Cursed?"

"Gregor was telling me something about that."

"Gregor. What does Gregor know of our family history?" Olga sniffed, a big sister's skeptical sniff. She leaned against the mirror, creating two Olga Kepelovas. Lacey was grateful that it wasn't a three-way mirror— there would be an infinity of Olgas surrounding her with their piercing stares. "He was never interested in the history. Until he had Marie to tell it to."

"Tell me what you know about the shawl. Please." Lacey dabbed some cover-up beneath her eyes, and on the fading scratch from the limo encounter on Eye Street. A good night's sleep was definitely in order.

Olga stalked the length of the ladies' room, checking the stalls for eavesdroppers.

"Very well. Early in the eighteen hundreds, the first Irina Katya Kepelova was very proud of her shawl. So different from factory-made. No one else ever stitched the way she did. The way she could embroider, they say her fingers were kissed by angels. Her needles made of gold."

"Fingers kissed by angels. I like that," Lacey said. *And needles made of gold? There's a story in this yet.*

"She has many offers to buy the shawl," Olga continued. "She refuses. It is meant for her daughter's wedding day. And her daughter's daughter. One day, emissary from court of the Tsar hears of the shawl, comes looking for crafts from the people, for the royal family. For some museum, not to wear. A tsarina would never wear the shawl of a peasant, but she might use it to exclaim, 'Look how talented are my devoted people!' The emissary does not even offer to pay Irina Katya. He says he will take the shawl for the glory of Mother Russia."

Lacey was taking copious mental notes. "What happened?"

"Fury! Irina Katya Kepelova was so angry! The Tsar wants to steal her daughter's wedding shawl? Oh, yes, such a great honor to be robbed this way. She poured her soul out into this shawl, but what can she do against the Tsar's man? Her husband holds her back from spitting and throwing rocks at the Tsar's emissary. To do that would mean prison or death."

Olga took a deep breath, relishing her tale. "But in the street before the whole village she curses him, this man who takes the shawl in the name of the Tsar. On the road back to Saint Petersburg, the carriage goes over a cliff, the emissary is killed, his soldiers are killed, all the treasures he has stolen are lost. All except one. One is saved. Those details I do not know, but the stolen shawl of the Kepelova soon returns to Irina Katya. And that is how the legend starts."

More chills. Maybe I'm catching the flu? Or is it just the Kepelovs? The fashion reporter in the ladies' room imagined that this was just the beginning of a very long family legend. "Gregor said there was a jealous niece?"

"That is true too." Olga dried her hands on a paper towel. "Many jealous nieces, jealous sisters, many other enemies as well. We have a long history. Big family. Very popular."

"Would someone kill for the shawl?"

"Why not? People kill for many reasons. Why not a valuable antique shawl?"

"True." A teenager in Washington had recently been

killed for a pair of shoes, such things as Air Jordan 11 Concords. And people were regularly mugged for leather and down jackets.

"Gregor also told me Russians love telling tales because the winters are so long. It keeps them occupied on long frozen nights."

"Also true." Olga laughed for the first time. She had large sharp teeth that made her look rather wolfish. "Lacey Smithsonian, Gregor is my brother. I do not want him to die."

"Who is after him? After us?"

"Sadly, I do not know, or I would not ask your help. In his life and work, Gregor has made enemies. We all have. Occupational hazard."

"Occupational hazard?"

"Is nothing." End of explanation.

"Why tell me?"

"Gregor says you are most resourceful in times of danger. And lucky. It is good to be around people with luck."

"You wouldn't say that if you'd seen me yesterday, about to be run down by that speeding car. Nigel Griffin threw me into a boxwood bush and saved my life."

"You see? You are lucky once again."

"My boyfriend just hired a bodyguard to follow me around!"

"Excellent luck," said Olga. "I saw the man. He is very big. You will be safe now. So talk to Gregor. I say, please. For his safety. For Marie and the future Kepelov babies."

"How? What should I tell him?" *I really just don't have enough to do this week.*

"I leave it up to you. May be difficult, more than just talk. May be dangerous. If necessary, I will help."

"What are you really asking me to do?" Lacey felt herself shiver in apprehension.

"You will know when time comes."

Olga marched away from the mirrors and out of the ladies' room, leaving Lacey all alone.

And this little chat was going so well.

chapter 17

A bodyguard: The perfect fashion accessory for spring!

Lacey's arrival at *The Eye* with Turtledove in tow caused a stir. She knew it would. It was hard to hide a man of his large size and alluring looks in the city, let alone in a newsroom filled with a hundred pairs of prying eyes—and questions.

Turtledove parked himself by her desk in the infamous Death Chair, so named because Lacey's predecessor, the previous fashion editor known as "Mariah the Pariah," had died there. By the time anyone in the newsroom had noticed, Mariah was in full rigor mortis and had to be wheeled out in a sitting position. In the old-fashioned wooden Death Chair. Some anonymous artist at *The Eye* later decorated it with a smiling death's head, partly in honor of Mariah's death in that very chair and partly, Lacey suspected, in honor of *her*—and the dead bodies she'd tripped over on the fashion beat.

Lacey refused to use it, but it was always floating around the newsroom, the Flying Dutchman of desk chairs. No matter how many times she tried to get rid of that ancient wooden contraption on wheels, it always reappeared, usually somewhere in the vicinity of her desk. She suspected the sportswriters were responsible.

No death's head could faze the unflappable Turtledove. He thumbed through a well-loved copy of *The Odyssey* while she tried to finish up some work. He told her

Homer's epic of resourceful Odysseus had inspired him as a child to fight monsters.

Lacey raised an eyebrow. She thought Odysseus was a dope, leaving his wife to go off to war, sleeping with Circe, recklessly taunting that Cyclops, and irritating every second or third Greek god on Mount Olympus. Just a few of his many other epically not-so-brilliant moves, but, she figured, to each his or her own.

Midway through the afternoon, Turtledove stretched and told Lacey, with a wink, that if she could stay out of trouble for five minutes he would take a break and go mix himself a protein drink in the pantry. He barely cleared the newsroom door before LaToya Crawford was looming over Lacey's desk.

"Lacey! My goodness, girl! I couldn't help but notice Mr. Tall, Dark, and Delicious hanging around your desk. Inquiring minds want to know: Who is that beautiful man?!" LaToya was *The Eye*'s head Metro reporter, African-American, tall, pretty, and polished in her severe black suit with hot-pink blouse and purple sky-high platform heels. She wore her hair today in a glossy black bulletproof pageboy. Bright pink lipstick matched the blouse and highlighted her generous mouth.

"Covering City Hall today?" Lacey asked.

"Evading my question, but how'd you guess?"

"Guess? You're wearing your City Hall suit," Lacey said. "Though for budget meetings, you usually choose the chocolate brown pantsuit with the turquoise shell."

"Huh? I do? I had no idea. Guess that city budget crap is so boring I need a big shot of chocolate. Anyway, enough about me. My question is, who is *he*? Tall, dark, and milk chocolate there is not your regular Joe, the divine Mr. Donovan. So what gives, girlfriend? New flame? And if he's not *your* new flame, can I have his number?" LaToya loved to ask questions and sometimes even left a little room for the answers. She was bubbly and curious, always on the lookout for Mr. Tantalizing. "How available is he?"

Before Lacey could fumble for a noncommittal answer, Turtledove returned with his protein. He nodded to LaToya.

"Ma'am."

"I am not a ma'am, I'm LaToya Crawford." She held out her hand. "And you are?"

"As of today, I'm Lacey's personal protection agent. Forrest Thunderbird. At your service." He took her hand, and LaToya held his for a few beats past necessary.

"Forrest Thunderbird! Handsome name. Very, um, ecological. And you're her bodyguard? Smithsonian, girl, what the heck you need a bodyguard for? Death threats on the dress beat? Never mind, I get it, if anybody hereabouts needs a bodyguard, girl, it's you. Or maybe me. Definitely me. I could use one." She turned back to Turtledove with her most dazzling smile. "Welcome to the neighborhood, Forrest. You need anything Lacey here can't provide, you just call on me." Turtledove nodded.

"Crawford, don't you have a city council story to pound out?" Mac Jones approached, bushy eyebrows on the warpath, in his best snarling-editor-on-deadline mode.

"I'm on it." LaToya winked at Turtledove. "Just waiting on a callback from the mayor's office."

"And you forwarded your calls to Smithsonian's desk?"

"I'm all over it, Mac." LaToya rolled her eyes at Lacey and silently mouthed, *Call me!* She put her thumb and little finger to her ear, mimicking the phone, winked at Turtledove again, spun on her purple high heels, and swiveled her hips provocatively as she strolled away.

"Smithsonian," Mac barked, "if you're finished doing whatever you're doing, why don't you go and do, uh, whatever you need to do. I got a paper to put out and you're disturbing the peace. No offense, Forrest."

"None taken." Turtledove grinned and stood up.

"Thanks, Mac." Lacey didn't need any more encouragement to turn off her computer and grab her purse.

"The sooner you clear your schedule of all this wedding business, the sooner you can get back to *Terror at Timberline.* Tony and I are calling it *TOT.* For short."

"Everyone loves a book with an acronym. We could do a sequel: *TOT2.*"

Mac clearly wasn't sure if she was kidding. "I sent you a file with a whole roster of questions. Maybe you can work on it tonight? Fill in the answers. Easy."

"Nothing here is ever easy, Mac."

"Ain't it the truth." He leaned over Felicity's desk and lifted the last biscotti before trudging away.

"Nice of him to let you leave early," Turtledove remarked.

"Nothing to do with me and nothing to do with nice," Lacey said. "You're what's known as an attractive nuisance."

Turtledove graced her with his broad smile. "No kidding. That's what Vic calls *you.*"

chapter 18

Lacey had never seen Stella looking quite so lost and forlorn. The bride-*not*-to-be answered her door with red eyes and no makeup. Even her pink-tipped hair seemed to droop in defeat, lank and sad. Lacey could have made a joke about hair product: After all, Stella would have, if she'd been in Lacey's shoes. But Lacey didn't have the heart.

"Oh, Stel. I'm so sorry."

"I'm not getting married." Stella threw her arms around her *un*–maid of honor and sobbed.

Miguel squeezed out of the apartment door past Stella and Lacey like a man escaping the flames of a fire. He shook his shoulders and straightened his black jacket. He looked up to see Turtledove standing impassively behind Lacey and he froze. Turtledove smiled.

"Miguel, what are you doing here?" Lacey said. "Oh. You remember our friend Turtledove?"

They shook hands politely, but Lacey thought she'd never seen Miguel so flustered. He smoothed his dark glossy hair back with both hands and fished his sunglasses out of his jacket pocket. He jerked his head urgently away from the door, signaling for Lacey to follow him out of earshot of Stella. He spoke under his breath.

"I've been consoling the bride! Who keeps insisting she can't get married or she will die, or Nigel will die, or they'll both die." Miguel had clearly had quite enough of

Stella's histrionics. "And possibly *you* will die too. Maybe *everyone* will die. It's the end of the world."

"Miguel's been an angel," Stella said morosely, shuffling back into the darkened apartment. Turtledove stood watching.

"Do something," Miguel whispered to Lacey. "I love her to death, but she's in such a state I am ready to jump off the roof of this building onto Connecticut Avenue into the traffic. Frankly, doll, we don't have time for this drama. In the event this wedding takes place as scheduled on Saturday—did I mention, in four days' time—there is a cake to be baked. And it is going to be baked, wedding or not, because my dear friend, Bruce the baker boy *extraordinaire,* has already started mixing pounds and pounds of flour and sugar. There is no going back now. And what about the wedding dress? Last I heard, the bride still hates it. Over and above how we will all *die* if she and Nigel get married Saturday."

Lacey looked back at Stella, who had gotten stuck in the doorway, leaning against the doorjamb, with neither the strength to go forward nor turn around. She wasn't listening.

"About the cake, Miguel—" Lacey began.

"Cake happens. What I need to know is whether to have it delivered to the Arts Club, or to a homeless shelter that needs a four-foot-high, utterly fabulous, pink-and-white castle cake."

"Maybe some kind of children's facility," Lacey suggested lamely.

"Whichever," Miguel said. "I am going to make sure it is the best damn castle cake there ever was. I don't know how to deal with Stella and the rest of the nightmare in there, but I do know how to ride herd on a baker."

"And the dress?" Lacey asked.

He made a face. "For once, the dress is not my responsibility, Maid of Honor."

"The dress doesn't matter," Stella yelled. "I'm not getting married. Besides, I hate the dress!"

A woman at the end of the hall poked her head out of her apartment and stared. Turtledove gently herded everyone into Stella's apartment. But Miguel took his stand in the foyer, like a prisoner caught at the gate, risking the firing squad.

"You're in charge now, Lacey. I'm cake-and-baker-bound."

"All right, Miguel, relax," Lacey said. "I'm your relief. Go play patty-cake, baker's man." Miguel kissed her cheek gratefully and bolted for the stairs, with one last admiring glance at Turtledove.

"Things will turn out. One way or another," Turtledove said to Lacey, like a Zen master. After checking the hallway, the perimeter, and the stairwell, Turtledove was the last one in. He turned the three bolts and put the chain on Stella's door.

Lacey groped her way through the gloom of Stella's living room and opened the dark brown drapes left over from Stella's Goth phase, letting the sunshine pour in through the tall windows facing Connecticut Avenue. The apartment was in an older building in the corridor of buildings that lined Connecticut above Dupont Circle, as it climbed the hill toward the National Zoo. Stella's place had good bones, Lacey thought, but it was buried under too many layers of paint. Most of the furniture was secondhand and well-worn, except for the bright red leather sofa Stella and Nigel had bought together. Lacey cranked the window open, letting the sweet-scented April air into the stuffy room. Below the window, on the avenue, a single late magnolia was hanging on to its waxy pink petals, the picture of optimism.

"Air! That's better."

"Much better," said Turtledove. Grabbing a chair, he posted himself by the window with a view of the door. "I'll stay out of your way. Anything you need me to do, Lacey, say the word."

Stella's wedding gown hung from the center of the curtain rod, looking fluffy and ethereal, rather like an exotic window treatment in a designer show home. The perfumed breeze through the windows made it rustle and dance. Lacey stared at it, hands on her hips. Behind her, Stella choked on a sob.

"Be honest, Stella. Is there even the slightest chance you'll be getting married to Nigel on Saturday?"

"Lacey, how can you even ask? How can I get married now?"

"Simple. One step after another, down the aisle, under the cherry blossoms," Lacey said. "Marie says it will be a perfect day for a wedding."

"I know. It's what I wanted all my life. But, Lacey. No. I can't."

"You're sure? Absolutely, positively sure?"

"Irretrievably sure!" Stella flung herself down on the red leather sofa in her best Camille pose, wrist pressed to her forehead, as if about to expire from sheer *malaise*. She moaned delicately. "Never say never, I guess. I mean, if there was even *remotely* the *slightest* chance that the Curse of the Killer Shawl might *possibly* pass us by . . ."

"There's no curse."

"I know what Marie said, but she didn't sound totally and completely sure. And sometimes, Lacey, you just can't outrun fate. The signs have been there all along." She rubbed her barely healed leg. "My love is doomed."

Stella's mother, Retta, emerged from the kitchen, carrying a pot of hot herbal tea. It smelled awful.

"I hope you're here to support my Stella in her hour of need," Retta said sourly.

"Of course I am." Lacey bristled. She told herself the edge in the woman's voice didn't *necessarily* mean she was perpetually angry at the world. Even if she sounded that way.

"She's not getting married. Stella's right—it's a bad idea. Bad, bad, bad idea."

Lacey wondered whose side Retta was on. "Where's Nigel? Surely he should be here right now."

"I told him not to come," Stella said. "If I see him, I

know he'd make me change my mind. I can't resist him, and I gotta be strong, for the both of us."

"It's for the best," Retta declared. She set a cup down and poured the foul brew into it.

"Nigel's not afraid," Lacey ventured. "Is he?"

"Are you kidding me? He'd brave bullets for me." Stella burst into fresh tears. "He keeps calling."

"I turned off her phone, it just upsets her." Retta set the wet teapot on a copy of *Modern Bride*, spoiling the cover with a wet ring. "Besides, how could this possibly work? He's English, from a totally different world. His father's an ambassador, for crying out loud."

"Retired ambassador," Stella corrected.

"And Bugsy's a Jersey girl. Like me. Salt of the earth. Oil and water. Blood is thicker than—"

Lacey didn't often feel like springing to Nigel's defense, but Retta's Earth Mother routine was getting under her skin.

"Shouldn't your fiancé be part of this conversation, Stella? Isn't it Nigel's life too that we're talking about?" There was more sobbing from the red sofa. "What would make you change your mind?"

"If we could find out! Find out who or what's trying to kill Nigel and me! And get him or it locked up, or something."

"Before the wedding?" *And hey, what about whoever tried to kill me?* "That's kind of a tall order, isn't it?"

"I didn't mean *you* should find out, Lace, but now that you mention it—"

Turtledove interrupted. "Lacey may have been a target too, Stella. That's why I'm here. My job is to keep her safe, not to throw her in harm's way."

"Is this your boyfriend?" Retta indicated Turtledove.

"No, ma'am," he said. "Personal protection agent for Ms. Smithsonian."

"What? You gotta have a bodyguard? Was this Vic's idea?" Stella propped herself up on one elbow. "Lacey, I'm so sorry! Jeez, I keep forgetting you were there too."

Maid of honor, Lacey thought. *All nursemaid, no honor.* "He's keeping me safe from oncoming cars," she said.

"Oh, I'm sure that's not necessary," Retta said. "Not now."

"Meaning what?" Turtledove stood up and towered over them, before Lacey could ask the same question.

Retta handed the mug of tea to Stella. "Meaning if my little Bugsy doesn't marry this silly Brit, her spell of bad luck is broken. Frankly, this frilly wedding has been nothing but trouble since day one. Drink this, Bugsy, it will give you strength."

"It tastes like moldy hay," Stella said. "And don't call me Bugsy."

"No, it doesn't. Add some honey."

As if on cue, Stella's cousin Rosalie emerged from the kitchen with a squeeze bear of honey and a plate of cookies. She'd obviously been listening to their conversation. And just as obviously, she had not gone to Stylettos to have her hair styled and straightened. It was as out of control as ever.

Passive aggression runs like a racehorse in this family, Lacey thought.

"I got your honey right here," Rosalie said, with the same cadence Lacey detected in Retta's voice. She turned the honey bear upside down and squeezed its plastic belly.

Lacey tried to figure out what these women had in common.

Retta wore a filing-cabinet-gray caftan blouse over gray leggings. The gray on gray brought out the steel gray in her frizzy hair and aged her twenty years. Rosalie had on a two-sizes-too-big mustard-colored sweatshirt over saggy, faded jeans, managing to look like a wayward orphan. Her pale skin was ruddy and broken out, her hair tangled. *Did they own a comb between them?* They were a sight. With Stella down in the dumps, the three looked like the Weird Sisters in a modern-dress Jersey Girl version of "The Scottish Play."

There was in fact a vague family resemblance among

the three women, which Lacey now glimpsed for the first time. Perhaps because Stella was looking her very worst. On her worst day, she slightly resembled her mother and her cousin on their best. And this was definitely Stella's worst. Some women could happily go all day without touching a comb or a mascara brush, but for Stella to face the world bed-headed and sans makeup? In a dingy brown T-shirt cut raggedly at the neckline and a pair of torn black leggings, an outfit that screamed I-don't-care-I'm-wallowing-in-depression-don't-bother-me? This indicated a mood so blue, so deep indigo, that Lacey knew she needed to take action.

"I thought you went back to New Jersey," Lacey said to Rosalie.

"This is a family emergency, so I'm helping out Cousin Stel and Aunt Retta," Rosalie said.

"And Mom just stopped by to give me a little gift." Stella reached for a big flat box on the coffee table. She lifted something out of it and handed it to Lacey. "Be careful. There's nails. Don't prick a finger on it. You might go to sleep for a hundred years."

Gingerly examining the thing, Lacey decided it *might* be a necklace, made out of rusted iron nails, fanning out in a prickly circle from a heavy iron chain. It looked like something the Inquisition might make a medieval witch wear to her execution. *Stylish.* Lacey tried to keep her eyebrows from hitting her hairline. This work of the jewelry-maker's art was awful even by Retta Lake Sloan's high standards of awfulness.

"Wow," she said.

"I knew you'd appreciate it," Retta said. "You being a writer and all. I collected these nails myself last year, just outside of Sedona, Arizona. Just for my little Bugsy. They got all that Sedona earth energy in them. And iron is like a major protection against bad luck, you know."

A mother's love is inscrutable. But does iron beat a Killer Shawl?

"What about tetanus?"

"No problem," said the proud artist. "They're treated. I cleaned them and polyurethaned them myself."

"And I've had all my shots," Stella said. "I knew Ma was coming."

"Ha. That's a joke," Retta said, but Lacey thought *some* kind of medication was certainly called for. Clearly Retta thought Stella was pleased with her gift. And just as clearly, Stella thought her mother was nuts.

"She says I'm making the right decision." Stella teared up again. "Not getting married, that is."

"But you love Nigel," Lacey said.

"Course I love him. I love him so much my guts hurt. That's why I can't marry him."

"He loves you too." Lacey surprised herself by standing up for Nigel Griffin, decidedly not her favorite person in the world. And yet he'd saved her life. It was confusing. *Something I'd rather not have hanging over my head the rest of my life.*

"I don't want him to die, Lace! You know better than anyone that bad luck's been dogging us ever since we met. We went over a cliff, we nearly got killed, I broke my leg."

"But that's all healed now."

"And then here comes the Limo of Death and some maniac tries to run us down. Before we even get married! You don't have to be psychic to see this is some bad juju. And then there's the shawl killing Leonardo."

"The shawl did not kill Leo and Marie sees a happy life for you. Not only that, you will have a mother-in-law who adores you," Lacey added. Retta made a sort of gurgling noise behind her, but said nothing.

"And I love Lady G too," Stella said.

"You're giving up on love? Just because of a little bad luck?" *Granted, not so little.*

"Don't make me the bad guy. I love him, but I have to let him go. I'm going to have to put all my memories of Nigel in a box and put that box on a shelf." Her voice choked up.

"Speaking of boxes—" Large brown packing boxes were lined up against one wall, all addressed to Stella Lake. "I hate to ask, but what's in all these boxes?"

"Boxes? Oh." Stella stared at the boxes. She wiped away a tear. "Our wedding favors and candy. For our guests. At the wedding I'll never have."

"They're still in the boxes? You haven't put them together yet? That's a lot of favors, Stella, for a lot of guests. It's going to take some time."

"It doesn't matter now. What's the point?"

Lacey knew Stella had agonized over selecting and ordering those favors. She'd chosen petite candy boxes in the shape of wedding dresses and tuxedos, each to be filled with delicious treats. Each guest would receive one of each, a matched set, like the bride and groom. The little tuxedo boxes represented the English groom and would be stuffed full of English toffee. The wedding dress boxes symbolized the Jersey girl bride, of course, who had planned to tie pink satin ribbons around the miniature bridal gowns and embellish them with pink rhinestones. The glue gun was at the ready. They would be filled with chocolate kisses and personalized miniature Hershey bars, on which flowery pink labels would read STELLA AND NIGEL FOREVER, followed by the date of the wedding. For the two hundred guests, four hundred favor boxes would have to be assembled. Plus an extra twenty or so, "for all the thieves in my family who are gonna steal more favors than they deserve," Stella had said.

I blame Modern Bride *magazine*, Lacey thought. *And the wedding-industrial complex.*

"Wedding favors are so froufrou," Retta said. "I mean, if you had to do favors, Bugsy, why didn't you think of something practical, like little shampoos or scrunchies? At least that would represent your trade."

"First of all, Ma, hairstyling is my art," Stella said, sitting up straight on the sofa. "It's an *art*. Not just a *trade*. Of course I expect people to buy *product* from

me, because my art is also my *business*. But *product*, for
something to give my friends? At something as important and romantic as my only wedding? Chocolate
kisses are the ultimate romantic symbol! Everyone
knows that!"

"I think kisses sound sweet and really cute," Cousin
Rosalie ventured hesitantly. "So maybe—"

Retta's raspy voice cut her off. "Rosalie, the world is
a nasty, cruel, hard place—it is neither sweet nor cute.
Nor should we encourage people who think it is."

"Oh. So as far as a symbol of romance goes—" Stella's
voice rose. "Maybe I should just give everyone a rusty
old nail! Like your necklace! So they could stab themselves through the heart with it at the reception! How's
that for representing love and romance, Ma?"

Retta scowled and took a step back. "I know you
don't mean that, Bugsy."

Lacey watched Retta disappear into the kitchen, dragging Rosalie with her. She knew Stella's mother would be
back in mere moments, with some fresh cause for gloom
and despair. Lacey saw her opening and she took it.

"Stella, if there is the *slightest* chance you're getting
married on Saturday, and if you want to do something
with the dress, it has to be now," Lacey said. "Miguel and
I will make it happen, I promise. You remember that
magical gown he whipped up for me for the Bentley's
ball."

"Yeah, Lacey, and I remember you in that gown. You
were amazing. Listen, I don't know what to do about my
wedding dress. It's really not me. I have no idea what
made me buy it. Except maybe it was the thrill of the
hunt." Stella slumped into the sofa and sighed as if she
were a deflating balloon.

"Is there anything we can do to make it better?"

"Well, if I *was* going to get married and if I *could* do
something with it . . ." Stella struggled back into a sitting
position. She squinted at the fluffy white gown floating
in the April breeze through the windows. "Maybe I

would add, like, some *pink* to it. Pink is really what's missing, I think. But there's no time! I mean, the wedding is Saturday! Not that there's gonna be any wedding."

"Pink what? Bows?" Lacey suggested.

"Nah, bows are too babyish."

"Some pink ribbon around the skirt?"

"Maybe." Stella thought hard. "No, no ribbon. Too Scarlett O'Hara. And Rhett Butler still left her in the end."

"Pink lace? Pink appliqués? Pink satin flowers maybe?" Lacey was reaching now. *How many pink things are there in the world?*

"It'll look like an afterthought. You don't want it to look like a bunch of stuff stuck on with a glue gun, like some crazed artsy-craftsy project of Mom's."

"Don't even think about wearing that dress!" Retta returned with a giant steaming mug of something that smelled like a swamp after a hard rain.

Lacey was nearly at the end of the universe of pink apparel. *What says Stella like nothing else could say Stella?*

"What about a pink corset?"

"A corset? Really? Maybe that could work. You mean like over the dress, around the waist? Like really cinching it in? And under the bust, so it would make the Girls look even bigger?" Stella finally seemed to come to life. She traced her hands around her waist, over her ratty brown T-shirt. "And all cinched up, it would make that skirt just explode, with all those ruffles!"

Lacey rolled all her pink marbles. "Stella, you've got a pink corset, don't you? Sort of cherry-blossom pink? One of the corsets Magda made for you? It could be cut to fit. Originally you were debating between the punky pink leather bustier or sexy corset look and the big traditional white gown look, right? Well, why not both?"

Let her look like Little Bo Freakin' Peep! Just let me get her to the cherry blossoms on time!

"Wow. Why not both! I never thought of that. And it

would be a tribute to Magda. So sorry she died before my wedding. She was the most incredible corsetiere. Yeah, that could be really cool." She was nodding, her eyes were starting to glow. Lacey felt she might finally be pulling Stella back from the brink of despair. "And maybe with some pink sparkles all over the lace of the skirt, like sequins, like the corset has just, like, showered cherry blossoms everywhere?"

"You know what I think? That dress has got bad karma written all over it." Retta sipped her hot swamp water and twisted a lock of gray hair around one finger. "But sure, you could change it. You could always just cut that Moby-Dick of a dress off at the knees and dye it a nice smoky taupe color. Earth tones, you need some earth tones for that earth energy—"

Stella leapt up off the red sofa. "Party dresses aren't smoky taupe! Who ever even heard of that? Maybe you'd like I should set it on fire and have a funeral for it? And bury it, wrapped around my heart."

"No need to be melodramatic, Bugsy." Retta started toward the dress. Turtledove stood up again, looking about twice her size. She froze. "But you know, a cere-monial burial and formal good-bye to that dress might be just the thing to start the healing process. We could maybe get a Native American healer to smudge it with burning sage, like I seen them do in Sedona, Arizona."

"Now that sounds perfect." Rosalie broke in. "Or maybe I could dye that dress for you, Stella, as a wedding gift. Like a tie-dye? I totally agree with Aunt Retta—the dress has got to go, or be totally changed. Should we do it right here, Aunt Retta, or take it home to Jersey?"

"Hold on. Nobody make a move." Lacey stood pro-tectively before the dress hanging in the window, her arms spread to defend it. She exchanged a look with Turtledove. He gave her the smallest possible nod. "You are not going to destroy this dress."

"Yeah, you got no reason to murder my gown," Stella

said, taking a stand next to Lacey. "It hasn't hurt anyone. That is a beautiful thing, even if it's not quite me!"

Lacey nodded to Turtledove, who carefully took the dress down from the curtain rod.

"I am the maid of honor," Lacey announced to the company at large, "and I am taking this wedding gown into my personal custody."

"And I am this dress's personal protection agent." Turtledove folded it over one of his rock-hard arms. He let the other arm fall casually to his side, but his hand curled not so subtly into a fist. Retta and Rosalie took a step back toward the kitchen.

"You heard him," Lacey said. "No one is cutting it, dyeing it, smudging it, burning it, or burying it in some screwy New Age ceremony. You got that?" Lacey unchained the chain, unlocked the locks, and opened the door, holding it wide for her, and the dress's, very impressive bodyguard. "Stella, I'm taking your dress to my seamstress, Alma Lopez. Right now. She made my dress. I'll talk to her about your pink corset and the pink sparkles, just like you said, so get me that corset too. I'll call you later."

Stella jumped up to pull the pink corset out of her closet.

Retta dropped her mug of aromatic swamp water. She looked like her world was ending. "Are you really going to let her do that?" Rosalie cowered behind her aunt. "Stella, just what does she think she's doing with that awful dress? The dress you said you hated? I'm your mother and I know what's right for you! She can't just take it away. She can't do that!"

Stella smiled for the first time since Lacey arrived.

"Sure she can. Lacey's my maid of honor. She's got certain rights. And she can do *anything*."

chapter 19

Turtledove pointed his enormous charcoal gray SUV down Connecticut Avenue onto Rock Creek Parkway, heading south. They were just in time, before the traffic flow made its daily rush-hour shift to one-way northbound. Lacey rode shotgun. Layers and layers of creamy white wedding dress filled the backseat. Somewhere beneath it lay a pale pink corset, made by the hands of the late lamented corsetiere, Magda Rousseau.

"I warned you there would be girly stuff," Lacey said.

"Duly noted." His mouth turned up at the corners in amusement. "It got pretty girly there for a minute, but we made it out alive. You, me, and the bridal getup."

Her cell phone jingled. It was Brooke. Lacey was feeling bad about the way her last conversation with Brooke ended. She reluctantly picked up, wondering if they were still friends.

"Lacey, I am so sorry! I had no idea someone tried to kill you! And with a black Lincoln Town Car, no less. And the chauffeur of the Lincoln is still on the run. It *was* a Lincoln, wasn't it?"

"I gather you talked with Stella."

"This morning. I've been in court all day. And I think it was Stella," Brooke said. "But the gloomy lady I spoke to sure didn't sound like our chirpy bride-to-be."

"Attempted vehicular homicide will do that to you," Lacey commented.

"Granted. This incident is obviously connected to Leonardo's death. And the shawl." Brooke sounded way too upbeat.

Lacey groaned audibly and Turtledove glanced over with concern. "Brooke, shawls don't drive cars," she said.

"Ah, but perhaps someone is doing its bidding."

"Shawls don't give orders. Neither do they practice mind control."

"Nevertheless, I believe his death and that limo are connected to this strange Russian artifact."

Lacey leaned her head against the headrest and closed her eyes. "If we were in an alternate universe where shawls were magical entities with minds of their own, I'd say *maybe*."

"Was that sarcasm?" Brooke asked. Lacey was aware that Turtledove was listening in, attuned to Brooke and Damon's particular wavelength of weirdness in the universe.

"No, that wasn't sarcasm. That was skepticism. Please remember, we did nothing to irritate the shawl, Marie's and Stella's superstitions notwithstanding. And don't forget, Marie predicts a long and happy life for these lovebirds."

"If they don't get killed." There was a pause. "Do I still need a pink dress?"

"I wouldn't bet against it. Especially now. I just took personal command of Stella's wedding dress and corset, and I'm going to try to save this mess." Lacey opened her eyes to make sure it was still there in the backseat. It was.

"You took the dress! Yay for you! What is going on?"

"Are you fishing for quotes for Damon's Web site?"

"No! He's promised to be a good boy and hold off till we get to the bottom of this. I'm not quoting you."

"All right. I have no idea who's behind this. I don't think I've incited my readers to homicide. Lately."

"Fashion can be murder. In the meantime, what can I do to help?"

A vision of Stella's cluttered apartment and those

packing boxes appeared to Lacey. "There is one thing. Favors," she said.

"A favor? Sure. Anything."

"No. Favors."

"Favors?" It was Brooke's turn to sound suspicious.

"Stella hasn't assembled her hundreds of wacky and wonderful wedding favors yet."

"And this concerns me how?"

"She's going to need help putting them all together and filling them with yummy treats."

"You think Stella's getting married after all?" Brooke considered. "Can't her family do that?"

"Um, no."

"Her hippie mom from Hell doesn't approve of wedding favors?"

"I'm not sure Retta approves of anything. Except misery. And Stella is in a state. I confiscated the wedding dress to keep her mom and cousin from mutilating it in the name of healing."

"Where is the dress now?"

Lacey stared at the Great White Whale Dress. It looked even larger and fluffier than it had before. "In a secret undisclosed location."

"I see." Brooke sounded impressed. She loved "undisclosed locations." There was a pregnant pause. "Exactly what is involved in making these favors?"

"A little assembly. It'll be fun. Be forewarned: There will be glue guns," Lacey said.

"No! You know I'm not qualified with glue guns. I'm much better with real guns. And not pink rhinestones again?"

"It's always pink rhinestone time at Stella's," Lacey said. "You know that. But on the plus side, there will also be chocolate. Tons of it."

"There had better be chocolate." Brooke clicked off, still groaning.

When Stella's leg was in a cast, she'd hosted a party for her friends to decorate it with pink and red rhine-

stones, stars and hearts. It was the most *fabulous* cast
ever, and Lacey had hoped Brooke had overcome her
fear of glue guns. But old fears die hard.

"You talking about the legendary Killer Shawl on
DeadFed?" Turtledove piloted the SUV down Route 50,
heading to Lacey's seamstress's house in Arlington, Virginia.

"Some people make up stories, Turtledove."

"It's old, it's Russian, it's mysterious, and it's missing?
And strange things have been happening around it
lately."

"Strange things are always happening," Lacey said.
"Maybe it's something about *me*."

The sign over the side door read: ALMA'S STITCH IN
TIME. CREATIVE TAILORING AND ALTERATIONS. Seamstress
Alma Lopez lived in an attractive little bungalow on a
side street in Arlington where the trees were leafing out
a light spring green and tulips were popping up in the
flower bed in front of the brick porch. Lacey and Turtledove stood at the door and rang the bell. It was loud
enough to wake the dead. No matter where she was in
the house, or even in her neat-as-a-pin garden, the seamstress wanted to know when her clients arrived.

Alma let them in and asked them to wait just a minute while she finished a phone call with a client. Her
dressmaking business filled a large converted family
room off the sunny kitchen. Alma's pale green and white
sewing studio was cheerful and filled with good light.
There was a long table along one wall, with three sewing
machines: her standard machine, one that quilted, and
one that handled specialized stitches.

Turtledove seemed outsized and a little uncomfortable in the studio. Lacey had warned him that things
were going to be getting girlier by the minute. He settled
onto a bench by the windows, where he could see both
the yard and the door. He pulled out his dog-eared *Odyssey*.

Lacey loved looking at Alma's domain, where elegant creations were crafted from cleverly cut bits and pieces of fabric. She loved being in the atmosphere of needle-and-thread alchemy that Alma had perfected. Lacey noticed something new every time she visited.

A round platform stood before a three-way mirror where Alma fitted her clients. The north wall was filled with shelves bearing bolts of fabric and white-paper-wrapped packages of finished projects, tagged with their owners' names. One rolling garment rack held clothing in various states of construction. Another held completed dresses and suits.

A tall and heavy Peg-Board leaned against one wall. Alma had decorated it with hundreds of spools of colored threads and dozens of sewing tools, including every size and description of sewing scissors and pinking shears, and a couple of large steel and wood T-square rulers. It wobbled a little as Lacey walked toward it. Alma always took pains to warn her that the Peg-Board was heavy and not very stable. Lacey was examining the collection of threads, admiring the vast array of colors, when Alma strode into the room.

"Don't even breathe wrong on that thing," she said with a grin. "It will fall over and kill you. Cut you to ribbons with all those scissors!" Alma had been issuing that warning for the past year and Lacey grinned in response. "I need to get my man to nail it to the wall."

Alma had sleek dark hair that she wore knotted at the back of her head. In her mid-forties, she had clear, unlined creamy skin and wore almost no makeup, except for the dark eyeliner and bright red lipstick that Lacey thought of as her visual signature. Alma was lovely when she smiled, which wasn't that often. Perhaps because when she was working she usually had a mouthful of straight pins for fitting and for pinning pattern pieces. In her studio, Alma liked to wear a pastel painter's smock over her clothes, with big pockets to hold the sewing tools she needed: scissors, marking pencils, tape measures, pincushions, and the inevitable straight pins and needles stuck to the outside of the pockets. She was the queen in her studio, and she could be abrupt.

Alma took one look at Turtledove and told him to sit still and not to touch anything. "You look like a bull in a china shop."

"Yes, ma'am," he said mildly. He was already sitting still. He winked at Lacey and returned to his book.

"And you, Miss Fashion Reporter—" Alma pulled a rose-colored dress off the in-progress rack and handed it to her. "Try this on to see if the hem is right."

Lacey slipped behind the changing curtains and poured herself into her maid-of-honor dress, slipped on the matching high-heeled sandals that went with it, then trotted over to the fitting platform and gazed at her reflection. *Pretty in pink.*

The dress might be new, but the style was old, and classic. Dating from the late 1930s, the pattern—one of Aunt Mimi's—featured a bias cut that skimmed the body, with a raised waist. The skirt floated below Lacey's knees. The shawl collar grazed her shoulders and revealed her collarbones. She had found the silk-blend fabric in Washington. The material was a delicate shade of pink that flattered her skin, neither too pale nor too shocking. The hemline and the fit were perfect.

As always, Alma was a wizard with a pair of scissors. She had stitched a small collection of pieces for Lacey, all of which had come from patterns or fabric, or both, excavated from Aunt Mimi's trunk.

"These old patterns. They're pretty, they fit, but they are a lot more complicated than they look." Alma said something like this every time. "And the old instructions—when they have them—they don't tell you exactly how to do everything. Way back when, they just expected a woman to know all these tricks, things most people who sew never learn anymore. So you are lucky to have me."

"You are a treasure, Alma. I know, and I'm so grateful."

"You didn't give me much time for this, you know," Alma complained.

"I'm sorry. Stella didn't give me much time," Lacey said.

"The bride? Is she pregnant?" Alma spoke with several straight pins stuck between her lips. Lacey was afraid she'd swallow one. "That doesn't faze people nowadays. Fact is, getting married before the baby? *That* would be downright old-fashioned."

"She's not pregnant. But she does plan to have blue-eyed babies someday."

"Hmph. When it comes time for babies, only thing she's going to care about is, are they healthy and do they have all their fingers and toes."

Lacey glanced over at Turtledove. He'd put down the *Odyssey* and was leafing through an issue of *Cosmopolitan*. He seemed to be enjoying himself. No doubt admiring the *girly* pictures, skipping the quizzes on how to tell if your guy is the perfect mate.

"Nice dress," Turtledove commented, with a thumbs-up.

She took another look. Her bridesmaid's dress was very simple, but very flattering, and yet in no danger of pulling anyone's attention away from the billowy white gown Stella planned to wear down the aisle. Particularly with the Bo Peep Special look that Lacey had just accidentally sold her on.

Now comes the tricky part.

"Alma—" Lacey began.

"No, no, no. I'm too busy."

"But you don't know what I was going to say."

"Do I have to know?" Alma said. "You use that tone and it always means more work for me. And I'm telling you, Lacey, I don't have time right now."

"Okay." Lacey turned slowly, checking her rear view in the mirror. "I know you're busy. Perhaps you could suggest another seamstress? Someone who could do a small job quickly? It's not for me, it's for the bride. Just a—you know, *a stitch in time*?"

Alma sighed at the mention of her shop's name. "This is the bride who decides everything at the last minute?"

"That's Stella. It's all because of the cherry blossoms."

Alma shook her head in exasperation. "Cherry blossoms! I got a bride who wants a wedding in the bluebells. Three blue dresses that must be the exact shade of blue of Virginia bluebells! Another has to have hers when the dogwoods bloom. They all have to be pink and white, dogwood colors. Don't even mention daffodils. I tell you what. Stella better already have a dress, because she's getting married on Saturday."

Lacey could almost hear the clock ticking over her head. "She has the dress. I have it with me. It just needs some, um, tweaking."

"Tweaking! Always brides need tweaking! What kind of tweaking? I'm only asking because I'm curious, not because I'm going to be able to do anything about it."

"A pink lace under-bust corset. It could be attached over the dress? She has a corset I think will work, I brought that along too. Maybe it just needs a little cutting, a little fitting, to pull it all together? Oh, yeah," she added in a rush, "and maybe some pink sequins on the skirt."

"A corset? Over the dress? Whose crazy idea was this?"

"Long story. Do you think it'll work?"

"Where's the dress?"

Lacey nodded to Turtledove, who slipped out the door to his vehicle and returned with Stella's wedding gown and the corset. Lacey prayed Stella would actually be cruising down the aisle Saturday, especially if Alma went to the trouble of trying to make this work. Alma had Turtledove hold the dress up and spin it around for her inspection.

"And it's already been fitted?" Lacey nodded, but Alma was not impressed. "Same old dress they all want this year. Typical. Not terrible, but not distinguished. It's not one of your special vintage patterns, Lacey. Not even special order."

"It's off the rack. She fought for it at a dress sale, mano a mano."

"That's the problem. Too off-the-rack for your crazy bride. Well—" Alma took the dress from Turtledove, shook it out, and peered in the mirror. Lacey knew Alma loved a challenge, and she was counting on this to be just enough of a challenge to be intriguing. "Let me see that corset too. Over the dress? Are you serious? It would look better if I cut the dress apart and set it in. And I'm not sure about under the bust. How about using the whole corset? I recognize this work. It would be a shame to cut Magda Rousseau's beautiful work. Well, I'll see what I can to do make this dress look a little less off the rack. You know what she's going to look like in all this, don't you?"

Lacey nodded. *Little Bo Freakin' Peep. With major cleavage.* "I know."

"So, maid of honor, you gonna give her a shepherd's crook to go with this crazy I-lost-my-sheep-and-all-my-marbles-too wedding dress? You going to carry the little lost lamb down the aisle for her?"

If that's what it takes to make this wedding happen.

chapter 20

The Little Shop of Horus sold nearly everything the state-of-the-art New Age hipster might be interested in: books on the occult, tarot cards, aromatic oils, candles, crystals, pyramids, star charts, astrology software. Anything labeled as self-help sold briskly. However, Marie Largesse had her limits. She refused to sell Ouija boards, which she said could too easily be used for evil—and were too dangerous in inexperienced hands.

For those who begged for a tantalizing hint into their future, Marie's consulting room was in the back, set off by purple curtains. In troubled times, troubled people sought reassurance from Marie and business was good. At present, though, the store was quiet.

The store walls were painted in soothing tones of blue and lavender, and atmospheric music played softly on the hidden speakers. As Lacey entered, Enya was singing "Exile."

Even before the door chimes announced Lacey and Turtledove's entrance, Marie lifted her head in anticipation. She was wrapped in swirls of gold and white gauze fabric, dramatic against her olive coloring.

"Lacey, you'll be wanting to see Gregor now," she said, then addressed Turtledove. "Hi, Forrest, nice to see you again!" He smiled and nodded in greeting.

"Did Olga tell you I was coming?" Lacey asked.

"No, cher. I just knew."

It was a last-minute decision on her part to stop there before Turtledove's jazz gig. Lacey wanted to get hold of Kepelov, and she didn't have to search very far: He was right there, chatting with his beloved zaftig psychic at the counter, in a gaudy black and red Texas-style cowboy shirt, faded jeans, and cowboy boots. He looked weird, as usual, but happy. Kepelov seemed like a different person now from the dark and dangerous ex-KGB agent she had first met in Paris.

"We've been expecting you, Lacey Smithsonian," Kepelov said.

"Really?" Lacey said. "You both must be psychic, Marie."

"Why don't y'all use my consulting room?" She retreated while Gregor led the way. Turtledove examined the astrology books and cast a watchful eye toward the street.

Marie's fortune-telling lair was so snug it might have been a storage closet at one time, but she had made it comfortable. A painted night sky tableau of golden comets and silver shooting stars decorated the dark blue walls and ceiling. The Eye of Horus anchored the wall behind where the resident psychic would sit. Lacey sat down in a black-and-gold wing chair and Kepelov took the one opposite.

"You want to see me?" he said. "Welcome change, Smithsonian."

"Olga says you're next. She thinks someone will try to kill you," Lacey said, without preamble. Kepelov simply stared at her. *He should be a poker player.*

"You must understand. That is Olga. Always the protective big sister. I am touched you would come to warn me. Admit it, Smithsonian, you are beginning to consider me a friend."

"You're a better friend than an enemy," she said, without quite admitting what her feelings were. Lacey leaned forward with her hands on the round table between them, a reporter's classic don't-even-think-you're-going-to-evade-my-question-this-time stance. "What is it with your sister, Gregor?"

"What do you mean?"

"I didn't expect to see Olga again. But she follows me, she appears out of the blue in the ladies' room at the restaurant where I'm having lunch, she has wild tales to tell me. Frankly, she's a little spooky." *More like a smoldering volcano.*

"Olga would be flattered by your description."

"Spooky? So she's a spook? You're telling me she's a spy?"

"Not at the moment. She will tell you she is simple suburban housewife."

"She's not married. Are you sure she's not spying for someone?"

He shrugged. "Not her forte. Olga is too obvious to be good spy. Even you see right through her."

"I don't see anything! What does she do for a living, where does she live, what's she after?"

"So many questions! Anyone would think you are a reporter." He leaned back in his chair, chuckling.

"I adore your sense of humor, Gregor."

"Florida, mostly. She has houses there. More than one. Olga likes the heat. Not fond of long cold winters." He rubbed his face. "Her job is weapons specialist. She strikes terror in my heart. Teaches police how to shoot and kill things. Well, mostly police."

"Where did she learn how to shoot?" In the front of the shop, Marie and Turtledove were laughing at something. Lacey cocked an ear to listen, then turned back to Kepelov.

"Here and there."

"Moscow? KGB?"

"Why do you need to ask, Smithsonian, when you are such good guesser?"

"Family business? Big sister spy, little brother spy?"

"Something like that." Kepelov reached for a coffee cup, but he had left his on the counter. He went to retrieve it, talking over his shoulder. "Perhaps that is good description. Certain talents can be inherited, from father to daughter and son."

"You're saying your father was a spy?" This conversation felt unreal to Lacey. *Is he having a joke at my expense?*

"In our family we say he was—diplomat." He returned with his steaming mug. "Until he was sent to the Gulag."

"Imprisoned by the Soviets?"

"Not just imprisoned. Disappeared. Dissolved, shall we say. A human life can be erased so easily. Makes you wonder. What would become of someone who is not nearly so good as he or so loyal? You begin to look for—a way out."

"You?" She waited, but Gregor said nothing. "Have you found the shawl?"

"No. It is gone. For the moment." He leaned forward, ignoring his fresh coffee. "Marie did not lose it. I can tell you that."

"It was stolen?" He pressed his fingers together and shrugged, just like Olga. "Why do you have to be so cagey, Kepelov? Do you really want me to just leap to my own conclusions?"

"You do it so well, Lacey Smithsonian."

"Only when I have no help. Is there a connection between Leo's death and the attempt on Stella and Nigel and me?"

"Very unfortunate. Troubling."

"Connected?"

"Perhaps."

Whose side is Kepelov on? "And Olga believes you're next."

He blinked. "Pay no attention. Since I was little boy, Olga always thinks I am in danger. Big-sister thing."

"There's a lot you're not telling me." Lacey hated having to drag every word out of a source. On the other hand, she'd learned something about his sister and his father. If he was telling the truth.

"Force of habit."

"Olga says you don't know the real story about the shawl's curse."

"The curse! Ha!" Kepelov slapped his head with both hands. For the first time Lacey had gotten a genuine reaction out of him. "Olga! That woman must have the last word if it kills her! I think maybe she makes up half the legend herself. All the old people in the family are dead or in Russia, no one here to say different. Maybe she made it *all* up."

Lacey laughed and Kepelov joined in. "It's still a good story," she said. "And if it's all family folklore, as you told me, there might be a dozen different versions, depending on who you talk to."

Still chuckling, he put his hands up—perhaps in surrender, perhaps not. "Someday, my intrepid Smithsonian—we must talk."

"We're talking *now,* Kepelov! Only you're not telling me anything important." He shrugged, still smiling. "So where will we have this big talk? On your ranch?" She knew owning a ranch was his fantasy of the American success story.

"That is right, on my big American cattle ranch. In Texas. We will ride the range, on my ranch. Perhaps we will write a book together."

"Sorry, I've got my hands full writing a book. *Terror at Timberline.*"

"And I cannot wait to read it."

Lacey pushed herself away from the little table and stood up. She seemed to see something in the distance, but not in the store, and not in the street beyond. She experienced the strangest vision, not just a picture floating in her mind, it was as clear as day. Gregor Kepelov and Marie Largesse, at home in a sprawling adobe-style ranch house set among cottonwoods and cactus under a big blue sky, with four children running around, two little cowgirls and two little cowboys.

"Lacey, cher," Marie said, stepping into the tiny consulting room. "What's going on? You just saw something, didn't you?"

Lacey blinked and shook herself. "Do you want children, Marie?"

"Why, of course I do. I'm hoping for a little boy or girl with my Gregor's blue eyes."

"You may get more than you bargained for."

*   *   *

"I have to change clothes, Turtledove. It's a moral imperative," Lacey said, as she unlocked her apartment door and ushered him in.

"Okay, but you look fine to me." He set about methodically inspecting the apartment for signs of a break-in or a security lapse.

"Fine is not good enough."

Lacey insisted on a short break before her evening's entertainment of watching Turtledove wail on his trumpet at Velvet's Blues in Old Town (and waiting for Vic to join them). Changing her clothes meant more than just a different outfit; it meant transitioning out of a stressful day into a fresh mind-set for the evening.

If she were alone, Lacey would have taken half an hour to let her hands, and mind, wander through Aunt Mimi's trunk. It was as relaxing for her as a martini and just as addictive. As it was, she only let her fingers dance over the lid of the trunk. She resisted the urge to unbuckle the lid and thumb through, say, a *LIFE Magazine* from the 1940s, which with any luck might give her a new perspective on the day's events.

"Your magic trunk, huh?" Turtledove said. "Where you get your secret powers."

"That's the one."

Turtledove knew about the trunk. He had even helped relocate it a couple of times. Once, when Lacey was afraid a designer might come looking for lost patterns from an old rival. And another time, when Lacey was staying with Vic for safety and she wanted the trunk with her, as a sort of security blanket. For other people, it was just an old trunk. For Lacey, it was her most precious possession.

"You want something to eat?" she asked him. She was hoping the answer was no because she didn't think he would enjoy a bowl of popcorn, which was pretty much all she had on hand.

"No, thanks. I'll get something later at the club, after

the set. I like to play on an empty stomach. Makes the blues sound a little hungrier."

"Well, if you want to stay hungry, you came to the right place. All I've got is popcorn, condiments, and eggs. Maybe some olives."

"That's an omelet that'll give you the blues. Anything to drink?"

"Beer, juice, or water. Or I could make you some coffee. Wait, there's a bottle of champagne."

"I'll take the juice, thanks." She poured a large glass of cranberry for him. "Lacey, you don't need to change clothes, you know. Anything goes at Velvet's. And you always look great."

"That's why you're changing into a shirt and tie?"

He was carrying a black shirt, white tie, and white jacket. "I'm in the spotlight. Clothes are part of the gig. I usually change at Velvet's, but I'm not leaving your side tonight. Not till Vic arrives."

"My clothes are part of my gig too. And I feel like dressing up." After all, it was her birthday, even though she had kept it very quiet. She was heading out for the evening, with not one but *two* gorgeous men. And with any luck, there might be a wedding this weekend after all, thanks to Lacey and Alma Lopez. She felt like celebrating.

"I'm down with that. Take your time. I'll be right out here," he said.

Turtledove took out his iPad, on which he would no doubt read the latest scandal on DeadFed dot com. Lacey retreated to the bathroom to wash her face, repaint her mouth and eyes, and figure out what to do with her hair. She heated up her curling iron and smoothed her highlighted honey brown locks into what she hoped was something reminiscent of film star Veronica Lake's glossy blond pageboy. Lacey wasn't quite as deft with her hair as Stella would be, but she'd picked up a few tricks along the way.

In her bedroom, she confronted her closet, with which

she had a serious love-hate relationship. She needed something sleek, sophisticated, and after-dark, like the bluesy jazz Turtledove would be playing at the little club in Old Town. But not *too* sexy. After all, she'd be starting the evening on the arm of one handsome man and ending it in the arms of another, and a woman needed all her wits about her to pull that off.

She chose a larkspur blue knit dress with three-quarter-length sleeves, a vintage-clothing-store prize from the late 1940s. It had an air of cocktails and witty banter in old movies. A draped V-neck was gathered into the bodice, which was attached to a smooth, wide waistband just under the bust. It was snugly fitted from the waist to the hips, where an accordion-pleated skirt fanned out to below the knees. The stiff stitched-in belt was bejeweled with sapphire-colored beads and white rhinestones. Lacey had to hold her breath for a second while closing the side zipper, but the effort was worth it. The dress fit like a glove. It would also keep her from eating too much. *From eating anything at all.*

She gazed at her reflection in the full-length mirror. It was turning out to be a blue day—color-wise, at any rate. This dress would be perfect for a visit to Velvet's Blues. Something a chanteuse might wear to belt out the blues in the night.

When she emerged ready for the evening, Turtledove looked sharp and handsome in his crisp black shirt and white tie. He slung his white jacket over one shoulder and slipped on the shades he liked to wear onstage.

"Well, aren't you are too cool for school," she commented.

"Yeah, that's what I was going for." Turtledove took a long look at her and whistled. "Why, Lacey S, you look like a femme fatale in an old Bogart flick."

"What I was going for too." Compliments came few and far between for reporters, and she'd take that one any day. She grinned back. "My work here is done."

chapter 21

Turtledove selected a small round table at Velvet's Blues that offered Lacey a great view of the stage. It also gave anyone onstage a great view of her. She sat with her back to the wall, far away from the front windows, feeling well protected. She sipped a club soda with a twist of lime and drank in the atmosphere, and the admiring glances. Her sharp-dressed bodyguard left her side only to move to the stage to begin the first set.

Velvet's Blues was a little jazz and blues club overlooking lower King Street, on the second floor of an eighteenth-century building in Old Town Alexandria, not far from Lacey's apartment, close enough that she and Turtledove had walked. Smoky blue velvet drapes framed the tall street-side windows and matched the velvet settees. The warm glow of little lamps illuminated every table, something like a nightclub out of the Forties, but without the noxious clouds of smoke. And the mobsters. She realized she didn't come here nearly often enough. *And never before in this perfect dress.*

Turtledove caressed his first set to a close with a soulful "Harlem Nocturne," and the musicians put down their instruments to appreciative applause. The room was about three-quarters full, but the night was young. Before it was over, Velvet's Blues would be packed and jumping.

As the applause died away, Turtledove moved with

grace through the room toward Lacey's table, but he picked up a friend before he reached her. He ushered the stranger to a seat next to Lacey and sat down on the other side.

"Lacey Smithsonian, this here is Rene Thibodeaux, one of my homeboys from New Orleans. Old friend of the family, good buddy of my cousin Timmy Tom."

"New Orleans?" Lacey repeated. "Pleased to meet you."

That sultry flower-filled city had been on her mind over the past few days, though she couldn't say exactly why, other than Marie's chicory coffee, which always made her think of Café du Monde in the French Quarter. The previous fall Lacey had visited New Orleans with Vic, chasing the legendary jewel-filled corset in which a Romanov princess had died. But those diamonds were covered in blood, forever staining the legend with tragedy.

Stella had gone too, in full-on party-girl mode, on the pretext of helping Lacey in the race for the jewels. It was in New Orleans that Stella met Nigel for the first time, and the rest was Stellarrific history. And Turtledove had been part of that adventure too, in a small but crucial way. *That must be why New Orleans is on my mind*, she thought.

"It's a pretty romantic city," she said, coming back to Velvet's Blues and the men at her table.

"Depends on what side of the romance you come out on," Rene said. His work-roughened hand shook hers.

Rene Thibodeaux was a thin, rawboned man who clearly made his living outdoors. His skin was dark and weathered. By contrast, his light blue eyes almost glittered. His jeans and clean blue work shirt were faded and well-worn. His attire was casual, but there was nothing casual about Rene Thibodeaux himself. An urgent energy about him made him appear tightly wired.

"Are you in town on business or pleasure, Mr. Thibodeaux?"

"Not exactly sure yet." He seemed nervous about

something. "And it's Rene, ma'am. Only bill collectors call me Mister."

"We can talk here," Turtledove said. "Lacey's a friend. But be on your guard, Rene," he said with a smile. "She's a reporter."

"Newshound, huh? No lie?" Rene looked ready to bolt out the door.

"I write about fashion," she said. "Crimes of fashion."

"Oh, girl stuff. Okay, in that case." He relaxed, dismissing "crimes of fashion" with a shrug.

That's okay—it's always better to be underestimated, Lacey thought.

"I can't let Lacey out of my sight tonight," Turtledove added.

"Until Vic comes," she said.

"She's a friend and she's my job too."

"A job?" Rene asked.

"He's my bodyguard," Lacey said. "Long story."

Rene cocked one eyebrow at his friend. "Forrest, man, how you going to be bodyguarding her from up on that stage?"

"If there's trouble," Lacey said, "Turtledove will jump down and whale on them with his trumpet."

"Only if my fists of fury fail me," Turtledove added. "I'm partial to my horn. And don't you be underestimating Lacey. She's been known to handle a little trouble herself."

"How's that?" Rene asked.

"She improvises. Like a jazz musician. But there will be no trouble tonight with Turtledove on the job— everybody got that?"

Lacey grinned. "Got it."

"So they still calling you Turtledove?"

"My friends do. What brings you to Washington, Rene?" Turtledove asked. "Been a long time."

"To run you down, man. Need a little help. I got trouble. Woman trouble." Rene stared at Turtledove as if he were wishing they could speak alone, without Lacey.

Turtledove caught his drift. "Like I said, Rene, Lacey's not going anywhere. Not without me. She even gets escorted to the ladies' room. So if you want to wait around and catch me later—"

"You might want a woman's perspective on your woman troubles," Lacey offered.

"She's got a point," Turtledove said.

"You gotta understand one thing, Miss Smithsonian. Lacey." Rene stared hard at her. "I'm a private man. I don't wash my dirty laundry in public. Especially not about women. When I got trouble I take care of it myself. Or I go to my friends, people I trust. I don't go to no *police*. I don't go to no shrink. I come up here to see my man Forrest, from the hood, 'cause we be like brothers, almost." Their waitress arrived with ice water and a wink for Turtledove and another club soda for Lacey, and she took Rene's order for a beer. He turned back to Lacey after the woman left. "You okay with that?"

"I understand," she said. "I'm off duty, and we're off the record." *For now.*

"What kind of trouble is this you're in?" Turtledove asked.

"The worst kind." Rene spread his empty hands on the table.

"She took your money?"

"Yeah, man. That ain't all. She gutted me like a dead fish. Might as well walk off with my heart on a hook, use it for bait, catch another sucker."

"That's cold, Rene," Turtledove said. He took out a notebook from his jacket pocket. "She got a name?"

"Leah." He spelled out the name. "It's biblical or something."

"Last name?" Rene shook his head. "What does she look like?"

"Medium tall, thin. Long dark brown hair, straight." Rene motioned to the midpoint of his arm. "Little longer than yours," he said to Lacey. "Big brown eyes. She's real nice-looking, and you can tell she was a real beauty once."

"Not now?" Lacey asked.

"Like all of us, time marches on."

Turtledove jotted down notes in a scrawl that only he could read. "How'd you meet this lady?"

"I— Just met her one day. That's all." His eyes were evasive. "See, how it was—she was sick, in a real bad way. I found her, took care of her till she got well."

"Found her? Did you take her to a hospital, or a doctor?" Lacey asked.

"Leah wasn't too keen on doctors. I figure maybe she had some trouble with the cops, no insurance, couldn't pay. Whatevah. Who am I to judge?"

"You fell for her," Turtledove said.

"Like a peach from a tree. Thought she fell too. Said she did." Rene thrummed his fingers on the table. "I ain't a pretty boy or a rich man. I know that, but Leah said she cared for me. Guess I'm a damn fool."

"We've all been there," Turtledove said, to Lacey's amazement. She found it hard to believe a woman could ever manipulate *him*. "What can I do to help you out?"

"Need to find her! Get my money back from her, if I can, maybe a little of my pride. And make sure she's all right."

"Why here?"

"She talked some about Washington. A lot. Said she had people here she wanted to see. She was talking about us doing our honeymoon thing up here. Not down the bayou like I wanted, far away from people. But she said you can get lost just as easy in a crowd. When she left, I kind of figured she was heading this way."

"You asked her to marry you?" Turtledove shifted in his seat with surprise. "Doesn't sound like you, Rene."

"I was a damn fool," Rene admitted. "Ain't gonna do that again."

"What did she do for work?" Lacey asked.

"Nothing, far as I could tell." He had a wistful look in his eye. "I didn't care. Like I say, she was sick. Needed a man to take care of her."

"How long were you with this woman?" Turtledove asked.

"Some months. Found her last fall."

"Pretty quick to be getting married. So, Rene, what about you, what are you doing these days, for work?"

Rene's beer arrived and he chugged it like a man dying of thirst. "You know me. Still working barges on the river. Mississippi. Boatman, like my daddy and his daddy, and your cousin Timmy Tom."

"What attracted you to Leah?" Lacey asked. "How'd she get under your skin so fast?" *Cut to the chase, guys!*

"Life roughed her up some."

"So you've got that in common," Turtledove said.

Rene shrugged and gazed out the window. "Her pretty face has a little wear, like mine does, but she's still pretty. I didn't think she'd turn up her nose at a man like me. I don't know. Leah just seemed like a sweet girl, had a hard life, and she needed me. Felt good to be needed, you know?"

Lacey wondered how life had roughed up Rene Thibodeaux, and how it had roughed up his Leah. At any rate, it didn't look like Rene had an easy life. His history was carved in his face by the sun, and by trouble. She guessed he and Turtledove might be about the same age, mid-thirties or so, but Thibodeaux had the look of a man at least ten or fifteen years older.

"It ain't what we had in common made me want her." Rene drained his beer. "Maybe it was what was different about her, you know? Some women, they give you a fever. She's one of 'em, and I ain't over that fever yet."

"Is that why you want to see her again?" Lacey asked. "You want her back?"

Rene looked up at the stage. Turtledove's band members were gathering, getting ready to play again. "Closure. That what they call it? I don't want to hurt her, I just want to know why. See she's all right. And maybe get my money back, of course. If any of it's left."

"How much did she take you for?" Turtledove asked.

"It wasn't every penny, but it was plenty. You know I live simple, 'cept every now and then, but I need what she took. Listen, Forrest, I got no one else I can ask, not anymore. Think you can help me?"

"Maybe." It was time for Turtledove to rejoin the band. "Stick around. We'll talk more later."

Lacey nursed her club soda and listened to Turtledove's music, letting it roll over her in deep blue waves. She had made a special request to hear "Summertime," and she hoped Vic would arrive before Turtledove got to that magical Gershwin song. It was one of Vic's favorites too.

Rene sat silently, seeming to have nothing left to say—at least not to Lacey.

"Excuse me, beautiful, is this seat taken?" Lacey felt her muscles relax when she heard Vic's deep voice. She hadn't realized how tense she had been until he arrived. She felt her mouth turn up at the corners in a big smile. She reached up for him and they kissed.

Then she remembered poor miserable Rene Thibodeaux, quietly watching all this romance. Vic took a chair and she made introductions.

"Now that Vic's here, Rene," she said, "Turtledove will be off duty for the night, so you two can discuss business without me."

Rene nodded and thanked Lacey for her kindness. *He might look rough*, Lacey thought, *but he's polite*.

He moved to the next table over to give them some privacy.

"You look especially beautiful tonight," Vic said.

"You look like a very smart man," Lacey said, congratulating herself on her vintage blue dress and its femme fatale vibe. And its effect on Sean Victor Donovan.

"Calls for champagne, don't you think?" He waved at the waitress.

"Why champagne?"

"Still your birthday, isn't it? And I'm glad you were born, Lacey Smithsonian."

"Me too! I'd love something festive to drink, thank you. And Turtledove promised to play a special request for me. For both of us."

They focused on the stage. Turtledove bowed with his trumpet, then nodded to Lacey and Vic. He hit the first notes of "Summertime." They settled back and let the music wash over them. She rested her head on Vic's shoulder and inhaled the spicy scent of him, content for the first time that day.

Champagne rested in a silver bucket on the table, and Lacey and Vic were lifting their glasses in another toast when a familiar, yet unwelcome, voice interrupted them.

"Bubbly! My God, my heart is fractured and you too are toasting—what? The New Year? What the hell is going on, I'd like to know?"

"Nigel," Lacey said, her spirits sinking. "What are you doing here, and why aren't you with Stella?" She had hoped all might be mended by now.

The Englishman was bleary-eyed and mournful. His hair was uncombed and in need of a cut, and his clothes appeared slept in. "One, I am looking for you. And two, Stella won't see me. I have tried. I have stormed the battlements and besieged the castle. To no avail."

"Why didn't you let yourself in?" Lacey asked.

"I don't have the bloody key! And she locked me out! We both have keys to our new condo, but Stella's holed up in her old apartment. I stupidly gave her my keys for her mother to use."

"So you retreated to the pub?" Vic asked. "You smell like a distillery."

Nigel was about to reply when his shadow, the purported best man, arrived at his elbow.

Culpeper was also bleary-eyed and staggering, and Lacey hoped they had cabbed it to the nightclub.

"Bryan Culpeper," he said, introducing himself to Vic. "Pleased to meet you. I am Nigel's best man."

"That's debatable," Lacey said. Bryan swiveled to face her and bowed. The bow nearly pitched him face-first onto the table. Vic choked back a laugh.

"And the delectable and dangerous Lacey Smithsonian. Howdy-do."

"Howdy-don't." Her champagne glass was at the ready. *This time I'm throwing, not spilling!*

"Keeping dear Nigel company." He backed up a step. "He's in a bad way, now that the wedding's off. Showing him that all is not so black as night. Silver lining, darkest before the dawn, and all that. Life goes on. Lucky break, I say. Let's drink to it. There are more women in the sea, or fish, or something like that. My sister, for one."

"Culpeper, you disgusting cad," the hapless groom said. "The wedding is not off! Just hit a small snag, that's all. Nerves, runaway car, horrible mother, put anyone off her game. Stella will buck up, you'll see. We'll be right as rain."

"You two are out of here." Vic stood up.

"To be fair, darling, Nigel did save my life yesterday. I should hear what he has to say." She touched Nigel's arm. "I forgot to thank you for shoving me out of the way and into the bushes. So thank you."

A bit of the old Nigel surfaced. "What? Smithsonian, thanking me? I must write this down! Date, time, notary seal, bronze plaque. Wait, I've got witnesses! Drunken witnesses, but no matter."

"I knew I'd regret saying that," Lacey said. She had thanked Nigel Griffin, and Gregor Kepelov thought they were friends. *What is the world coming to?*

Bryan burped. "I know you and I are no longer best man and maid of honor, Lacey, but— May I call you Lacey?" He blundered on. "If this silly wedding is not meant to be, well, what's that to us? We should make the best of it. You and I can still take beer showers and—"

Lacey tugged Vic's sleeve. "He, on the other hand, has

got to go!" She picked up her water glass and drew back her throwing arm. She was gratified to see Culpeper open his eyes wide and back up.

"No need for a bath right now, dear lady," he cried. "Must you douse me every time we meet?"

"Culpeper, you ignorant twit," Nigel stage-whispered. "She's with him! Him! That's the Donovan I was telling you about, Vic Donovan here is her—whatever he is!"

"That's right, I am," Vic said, "and Lacey and I were enjoying a glass of champagne together." He grabbed hold of Culpeper by one arm and averted his face to avoid the boozy fumes rolling off the man. "You weren't invited."

Turtledove materialized at his side. "Need a hand, Vic?"

"Thanks. I could throw him out myself, but I'd like to spend some time with Lacey. However, for some unaccountable reason, she wants to listen to what this other drunk has to say."

"I'm not nearly drunk," Nigel said. "I can get much drunker. I'm English, it's my birthright."

"Not a problem. I'll just take this one off your hands." Turtledove picked Culpeper up as if he were a loaf of squishy white bread and propelled him to the front door.

"It's my birthday, Nigel," Lacey said. "So if we could move this along?"

"Birthday? Happy birthday and all that," Nigel said. "I had no idea. I mean, I knew you must have birthdays, many of them, well, not *that* many, just never knew when." He sat down at their table, oblivious to Lacey's tête-à-tête with Vic. "Many happy returns. Oh, God, life is awful."

"Do you want something, Griffin?" Vic asked. "Spit it out and then get out. Please."

"I want to marry Stella," he said sadly. "What can I do, Smithsonian? To convince Stella of my undying devotion? You do believe we belong together, don't you? Admit it."

From the next table, Rene Thibodeaux leaned in to listen.

"Nigel, I didn't trust you when you first met Stella. I thought you'd just take advantage of her."

"Smithsonian here thought I was a man-slut," Nigel announced to Rene, and several other uninterested club patrons nearby. "Man-slut, she called me. Man-slut, man-slut, man-slut."

"Yes, I called you that, but it was before you went over the cliff for her," Lacey said.

"Are we talking for *real* you went over a cliff?" Rene asked. "Or some kind of, what do they call it, metaphor or something?"

"No metaphor, mate. Stella was pushed off a cliff and I flew right over after her. Well, Smithsonian?"

"You two love each other. Yes, I believe it. Besides, Marie thinks you guys will make it. Not that I always believe in Marie's predictions, but this one I might. Love does amazing things," she said.

To her amazement, Nigel reached over, hugged Lacey hard, and kissed her on the cheek. "Capital! Thank you!" Lacey wiped her face with a napkin.

Vic chuckled at her discomfort. "You let him stay."

"That was not very English of you," she commented.

"Being too English ne'er won fair maid. Tell me, Smithsonian. How can I win her back?"

Lacey had been thinking about that very question. "Three things. First, you have to get her away from her mother, Retta."

"Horrible woman. Harridan. Harpie. Battle-ax hates me, doesn't she?"

"Yes. Her mom says you and Stella are from two very different worlds and your marriage could never work." *Or maybe she's just jealous that openhearted Stella found her prince and Retta was on Husband Number Four.*

"Like Romeo and Juliet, hey? That's pretty romantic."

"Until they die in a tomb," Vic reminded him.

"Okay, so I get Stella away from Mama Battle-ax. Then what?"

"Two. Flowers never hurt. Lots of flowers," Lacey said. "And not just any old bunch of daisies. Stella's wedding bouquet is pink peonies, pink and white roses, and lily of the valley, so if you bring her something just like that—"

"Brilliant! It will remind her of our vows. Our vows to be. Yet to be. Genius. Done, Smithsonian. Just give me the name of the florist. What else?"

"Three. Take her out someplace extra-special. She's been talking about a restaurant called Co Co. Sala. Stella and Brooke and I thought it might be nice for girls' night out."

"Instead of the gun range?" Nigel said. "How traditional of you. I don't approve of you three running around shooting guns, and for the love of heaven, never tell my dear mother! The Gorgon would strap on a six-gun at the very first chance and wreak havoc in every direction."

"What's so special about this restaurant?" Vic asked. "And why haven't I heard of it?"

"Because it's all about chocolate, expensive chocolate, decadent chocolate," Lacey murmured in his ear. "You can get a five-course chocolate dessert menu at Co Co. Sala. Yum." Vic shook his head in disbelief. "It's on F Street near Gallery Place."

"Special dinner, lots of chocolate. Got it," Nigel said, looking more hopeful. "Anything else, Smithsonian?"

"Yes. Nigel, sober up, clean up, straighten up. And buy a new shirt that is not blue. Stella's favorite color is pink. Have you noticed?"

"I'll look like a bloody flamingo wearing pink," he said. Lacey glared at him and he withered. "Very well, pink flamingo it is."

"And lose the albatross."

"Albatross?"

"Bryan Culpeper."

"What, dump Bryan? He's my oldest mate! He's my best man!"

"He's nobody's best anything. He doesn't want you to marry Stella, and he'll be an obstacle every step of the way."

"Culpeper is a swine, Nigel," Vic added. "He's your past. Stella is your future. If you know what's good for you."

Rene Thibodeaux leaned over again and nudged Nigel. "Dump him if you want to get married to your girl. That fool's cramping your style."

"But—but—" Nigel started to protest. "And excuse me, just who are you?"

"Put it this way, Jack," Thibodeaux said. "I don't know you and you don't know me, but I know you got a choice to make. You want to spend your life with your drinking buddy? Or with your lady?"

chapter 22

"I thought he would never leave," Lacey said.

"One more minute and I'd have made that decision for him." Vic held her hand as they descended the stairs at Velvet's Blues.

"At least you got rid of Culpeper right off the bat. And I'm glad Turtledove shoveled them both into taxis."

"As long as there are no more interruptions tonight."

Lacey opened the club door to King Street. The air was clear and cool, with a hint of the coming rainstorm. "We're alone now, alone in the crowd." Her ears were adjusting to the street noise, which was many decibels lower than the music in Velvet's Blues. "I'll take it."

"And who is that Thibodeaux character?" Vic inquired.

"Friend of Turtledove's family, from New Orleans," she said. "His fair-weather girlfriend up and left suddenly."

"With all his money?"

"You already know the plotline."

"I've heard this song before," Vic said. "Hear it a lot in the P.I. business."

"Rene came here to see if Turtledove can help him. He's wary of police."

"Probably has a record. He looks a little rough."

"He said he wants to keep his trouble in the family, and apparently Turtledove is practically family. A friend of his cousin or something." It was not a cold night, but Lacey shivered. Vic wrapped his arms around her and she felt herself warming up. "Just talking about New Orleans takes me back there. It was wonderful, and not so wonderful. I just wish nobody had had to die there. That day on the river."

"It wasn't your fault, sweetheart."

"Feels like it."

Lacey tried to block out the memory of the woman who had been killed in her search for the lost corset of the Romanovs. Lacey had fought her hand to hand on the upper deck of a riverboat.

The woman's name was Natalija Krumina. Overtaken by greed and rage, Natalija ran at Lacey, intent on throwing her off the top deck. Lacey ducked at the last minute and Natalija went flying over the rail of the riverboat, hitting the wooden paddles of the big wheel. She tumbled into the muddy waters of the Mississippi and was gone.

"All you did was duck. Lacey, she was crazy, and she was trying to kill you." He guided her to a navy blue van his company used for surveillance. "Over here."

"Where's the Jeep?" Lacey asked.

"In the shop."

"You just had it tuned up."

"Brakes went out."

"What?" Lacey stopped short. "Vic Donovan is all about car maintenance."

In the days before her old Datsun 280ZX was stolen, she resented Vic's Jeep, which always seemed to run flawlessly, while her car far too often did not. Her sporty Z thrived on drama. Every day was a potential vehicular adventure: Would it start, would it run, how *long* would it run, would it get her to work and if it did, would it get her home, would the radiator blow on I-95, and would her regular mechanic have the parts, or would someone have to swim to Japan for them? Even so, Lacey had loved her sleek vintage sports car, the way it cruised the highway, the way it hugged the curves, until the entire matter was taken out of her hands by someone who stole her car and used it for—something else she didn't want to think about.

She looked to Vic for an answer, but he was talking to two guys in a plain gray Honda Accord parked across the street. Lacey recognized them as one of Vic's crack surveillance teams. The guys were laughing and giving him a thumbs-up. Vic walked back across King Street and waved to them. "Everything's okay."

"And by that you mean—what?" Lacey's alarms were going off. "And why were you having your guys watch this van?"

"Get in and I'll tell you." He opened the passenger door and waited for her to buckle up. "Someone messed with the Jeep's brakes. Deliberately, I assume. I was on Lee Highway and hit the pedal, and my foot hit the floor. I downshifted and got off the road and called a tow truck." He laughed at her expression. "Everything's fine, I didn't hit anyone, no one hit me."

"You could have been killed!"

"But I wasn't."

"Not reassuring. Any idea who messed with them?"

"Not yet. Nothing to worry about."

"Are you crazy, Vic? Of course there's something to worry about. Someone messed with your brakes, and someone tried to run me over yesterday. It's not a coincidence. You always tell me there aren't any coincidences. And what about *this* thing? How do you know it's not sabotaged too?"

"Just got it back from a job in Lynchburg, checked it out myself, and my guys kept an eye on it. I'll have them watching your building tonight too. But, darling, I don't think you should drive your car until I check it out."

"You won't get any argument from me."

"This must be my lucky day." He turned the key in the ignition. Lacey held her breath. Nothing blew up. Vic drove down Union Street toward her apartment building. She didn't see the gray Honda following them, but she knew it was back there somewhere.

"Go ahead. Everyone is mocking me today. First Nigel, now you." She gazed down the Potomac River rippling beneath the moonlight, where a ferry was taking the last load of tourists to National Harbor on the Maryland side. She realized she hadn't updated Vic on all the day's events, not thoroughly anyway. There had been champagne to drink, and drunken louts to deal with. "Leonardo's death was a mistake," she began.

"Go on."

"Broadway Lamont said Leonardo was probably poisoned, and it looks like he 'got it in the neck.'"

"When did you discuss this with Detective Lamont?"

"At the paper today. He showed up to have a little chat with me."

Vic cocked his head and raised an eyebrow. "He had to see you in person?"

"Me? No. He came to see what Felicity was baking. He has a crush on her, or at least on her food. And of course he came to shake me up. To tell me Marie is crazy, as well as a suspect. And he blames me for everything, because I hosted the bachelorette party. He wanted to let me know he's irritated to have to work on another murder case with a possible fashion angle."

"Broadway's crazy about you. He knows he'll always get something to talk about with the guys," Vic said. "And he gets to visit Felicity and gobble her baked goods."

"I only wish she'd made something sweeter than biscotti."

"Back to Leonardo and this supposed poison. Do they have toxicology already? Any guess as to type?"

"No to the toxicology, but apparently they found a bartender who saw him in distress late that night and his symptoms fit nicotine poisoning. I suppose it could be something else, but they suspect nicotine. The poison may have entered through a wound in the neck. Leonardo complained that's where the shawl bit him," Lacey said.

"Bit him?"

"I thought maybe a metallic thread scratched him. He was such a big crybaby. But the point is Leonardo crashed the party. No one knew he was coming. He wasn't meant to have anything to do with the shawl. He wasn't the intended victim. He was just an accident."

"You're not saying the poison was in the shawl?" His skeptical expression was back.

"I was hoping you'd ask." She took a deep breath. "Now this might be a stretch."

"No, not from you, not Lacey Smithsonian! Not another extravagant fashion-clue theory!"

"Who's the smart-aleck now? Well, I don't have to tell you."

"Yes, you do." He reached out and touched her knee. "Darling, you know I'd love to know your theory. Please."

"Right. Do you remember reading about a Russian defector who was poisoned with a pellet shot from the end of an umbrella? Happened way back in the Seventies."

"Right—the Bulgarian umbrella business. Spy stuff? Leonardo was no spy."

"He wasn't supposed to die either."

"And who was?" Vic pulled into the apartment building lot.

"Maybe Marie or Stella. No one else would be touching the shawl. Or that's what someone assumed, because of the curse," Lacey said.

"So-called curse. Lamont's going to love this."

"Maybe the poisoner loves weird spy stuff. And believes in curses."

"So it's a Three Stooges type of spy. Like your friend Brooke."

And Kepelov, who was some sort of spy. "Anybody could have seen this at the Spy Museum. They have the umbrella on display there. A poisoned needle or a barbed pellet of some kind could have been inserted into the shawl. You wouldn't see it because of all the raised embroidery." Lacey was getting warmed up. "When Leo rubbed the shawl across his neck, the pellet or the needle stuck him, and the poison—went in. Hey, it's a theory."

"You tell that theory to Lamont?"

"Ha. Do I look like a forensic crime scene investigator?"

"No, but that's never stopped you before, darlin'. And spies with poison pellets? You're awfully close to Dead-Fed territory."

"Then we have to be very careful that Damon doesn't hear a word of it. Or Brooke, for that matter. As for Lamont, I'm sure the crack D.C. crime lab will figure out how Leonardo died. Eventually. Then we'll see how close my theory is."

"Why would Marie be a target?"

"Not a clue."

"This theory of yours is crazy, you know."

"Better than a haunted Killer Shawl stalking the District of Columbia." The wind picked up, shaking the trees in her parking lot, making them look like black shawls waving in the night. They sat for a moment in the van. "There are all kinds of crazy theories in this spy-ridden town. Some of them are even true. Mine is as good as any."

"Please tell me you haven't shared this theory with anyone."

"You're the first, you lucky boy."

"Before you go public with this, let's see what we can figure out."

"You're going to feel pretty silly if I turn out to be right. Besides, if this pet theory of mine, though weird and twisted and dangerous, is *newsworthy*, I am Bogarting this baby till after Saturday."

"Stella's wedding day."

"That's right. At least theoretically her wedding day."

* * *

Although it was late when she and Vic got to her apartment, Lacey felt obligated to open birthday packages from her family. They were waiting right where she left them, on her cherrywood dining room table, which was also a gift, from her Aunt Mimi. Lacey sank into Mimi's lovely velvet sofa with the sparkling glass of champagne Vic had poured for her, grateful that she could be surrounded by such lovely things, even on a reporter's salary.

"Here." Vic dropped a present in her lap, as curious as she was. More, in fact. Lacey knew the kind of things her family liked to buy her.

"It's a shame to open them. The wrappings are so pretty and no doubt ecological. Probably nicer than what's inside."

"Don't they buy you nice things?"

"You don't understand, Vic, honey. I'm sure these are great, whatever they are, but my family just doesn't *get* me. Any presents they might ever buy me will be perfect—for someone who is not me."

He sat down next to her. "Now I really want to see what's in there."

She unwrapped the first one. Her mother, Rose Smithsonian, had sent her a gluten-free and sugar-free gift basket of tasteless organic snack bars. Lacey was certain they'd have the palate-pleasing flavor of twigs and tree bark. Along with a fresh supply of vitamin D, of course, because she was sure her daughter wasn't getting enough fresh air and sunshine, there in the foggy humidity of the East Coast.

"Do you like these things?" Vic asked with a frown, picking up a snack bar.

"No, but squirrels do." Vic handed her the other wrapped gift box from Rose. Lacey shook it. "It's pajamas."

"You don't know that."

"Oh, yes I do."

Lacey attacked the wrapping with grim determination. Rose had outdone herself. These pajamas were made of her mother's favorite earth-friendly fabric, a scratchy blend of recycled cotton and hemp. At least they weren't in the usual earth-tone palette of hemp: They were a neon orange that would wake the dead. They would also alert hunters to her presence in the woods at bedtime, if she wore them on a camping trip, which was another thing Lacey wouldn't do.

"Those are bright," Vic said, trying not to laugh too hard. "Sexy too, what with all those buttons. Where on earth did she find blaze orange pajamas?"

"The color is the least of it, Vic. I never wear pajamas! I haven't worn pajamas since I was ten years old. I wear nightgowns. And not neon orange nightgowns. T-shirts only when I'm sick. If she knew anything about her own daughter, she'd know that." Lacey closed her eyes and leaned her head against the back of the sofa. "My mother has given me a pair of pajamas every birthday and Christmas since I was a little girl."

"Maybe she really doesn't understand."

"She understands. I've told her not to waste her money. Somehow she thinks if she sends me sex-defying PJs every year in increasingly garish colors, one day, magically, I will look at them and fall in love with them."

"Can't you return them?"

"Too much trouble, and it would hurt her feelings. I'll put them in my special pajama box for the poor. Vic, I love my mother. We just don't live on the same planet."

Her sister, Cherise, sent her another winner, a shiny, reflective lime green windbreaker, in a breathable but waterproof high-tech fabric that the tags promised would wick away perspiration and defy the elements—not to mention Lacey's fashion sensibility. Not only that—it could be seen from at least a mile away. It apparently came highly recommended for nighttime bike riding.

"Talk about a crime of fashion," she remarked.

"You could wear them together," Vic said.

"My God. You could see this thing from *space*."

"Wear it with your blaze orange jammies. Give the astronauts a thrill."

"It doesn't matter, darling. You've already given me the nicest birthday. I love my new watch, and the champagne." She threw her arms around him and kissed him. "And you."

"And the bodyguard?"

"Not exactly the perfect accessory. However, he is something I never would have bought myself."

"Hey, there's one more thing under the wrapping, from your dad."

She picked up the package, puzzled. "That's odd. He never sends me anything. He lets my mother take care of everything. Who knows what horrors lurk beneath this wrapping paper?" She tore it open. "Oh, my. This is gorgeous."

Lacey was happily shocked. Steven Smithsonian had given her at least five yards of beautiful patterned red silk that he'd purchased on a recent business trip in Thailand.

She had mentioned silk to her father, and he actually listened. *Amazing.* The material was an unusual red, with notes of rose and coral, which shifted depending on the light. She stroked the lovely fabric and wondered if there was a dress pattern in Mimi's trunk that would be perfect for it.

Gazing dreamily at Vic, she wondered whether she might even find a pattern that would work for a wedding gown. Aunt Mimi had never been married. Lacey wondered if she'd ever seriously considered it.

Mimi had a long string of boyfriends, many of them serious suitors, and she'd had many chances to get married. But she also loved her work in Washington and would not easily have given up her independence and freedom. A formal hand-tinted photograph of Mimi, taken during the 1940s, showed an attractive young

woman who looked directly into the camera with determination and good humor. She had blue eyes and dark
auburn hair and she wore a navy suit that meant business. But marriage? Maybe Mimi could simply never
decide.

Lacey had decided. She'd decided on Vic. However,
after witnessing all the cumbersome logistics and super-
charged emotions involved in putting together a wedding, she was hesitating, even more than before. The
details were daunting and intimidating. She unbuckled
Mimi's trunk and opened the lid.

"You're not going through that thing now, are you,
sweetheart?" Vic asked. He understood that Lacey and
the old trunk had a special relationship. But it was late.

"No, I just want to put this beautiful silk away, where
I'll know where to find it."

"And how about that snazzy glow-in-the-dark bike-
racing jacket your sister gave you? Where does that go?"
He put his arm around her and she slumped against him.

"The poor box. Along with the pajamas." Lacey
started to laugh.

"What's so funny?"

"Wondering what to get Cherise for *her* birthday. Payback is a bitch."

Lacey Smithsonian's

FASHION BITES

The Wedding Guest's Nuptial
Non-Compete Clause,
Or: Remember, the Bride Always Rules!

What to wear to a wedding? If you're a guest, resist the temptation to use your outfit to make a political statement, show your disdain for tradition, or rebel against your parents.

Remember: That's the bride's job.

You've responded to the wedding invitation, you've bought a nice present, and you want to look your best. Yay for you! But here's a word of warning: This is the bride's day. She rules this day. Do not try to compete with her or overshadow her. First of all, any such attempt is doomed. She's wearing a big old wedding dress, and you're not. Second, don't even try. The laws of karma will find you and punish you. And third, if karma doesn't, the bride will. Above all, you will suffer the pangs of the stylistically and socially inappropriate.

Yes, there are all kinds of wacky weddings and all kinds of weird wedding attire that might be acceptable, depending on the location, theme, and type of service.

Brides have parachuted, skied, and scuba dived their way to their vows. They have wed on sandy beaches, in grassy meadows, and on snowy mountaintops, in valleys and on riverbanks, in airplanes and submarines, in subways, hotels, synagogues, mosques, temples, cathedrals, and humble drive-in wedding chapels.

Brides and grooms have dressed as everything from clowns to zombies, from medieval lords and ladies to pirates and their wenches (and parrots). Sadly, many of us will never have the fun of witnessing such a celebration, or debacle. We may never enjoy a courtly jousting tournament or a sumo wrestling match at a wedding. Most of us have to settle for variations on the classic theme of white gown and black tuxedo. But classics become classics for a reason. And every bride believes that her dress and veil are unique in all the universe.

But you're not the bride. What is *your* appropriate attire then, O worried wedding guest? It depends on the type of wedding, whether casual or formal or somewhere in between. Dressing in all white is considered an unpardonable affront to the bride, whether the bride is wearing white or not. Wearing white on her wedding day is her special privilege. If she makes another color choice that's her privilege too, but that doesn't leave that choice open to the rest of us. She's in psychedelic purple and you're wearing white? Someone will mistake you for the bride, and the bride will make you pay for that mistake, now or later. As she should.

Traditionally, wearing black to a wedding was considered equally inappropriate, as if the guests had mistaken the happy occasion for a funeral and arrived in mourning garb, ready to grieve. Nobody wants mourners at their wedding. But then came the vogue for elegant black-and-white weddings. In general, refrain from wearing black unless it's a very formal evening wedding, where black-tie dress would be acceptable. The invitation should give you a clue. If it doesn't, ask someone who should have a clue, like the maid of honor. The maid of honor is expected to know *everything*.

In any case, do arrive looking clean, bright, and well groomed. The groom might be hungover and look like something the cat dragged in; that's his affair (and the bride's, and the best man's, if he's up to his job), not yours.

It is most appropriate for women to wear a dress; however, if you feel compelled to wear pants, they should be well tailored and dressy, and up to the level of formality set by the bride. Even if you and all the other guests plan to ride your bicycles to the nuptials in an earth-friendly and ecologically correct manner, bike messenger outfits and their ilk are ill-advised wedding attire. Weddings are a ceremonial occasion! Simply being there makes you part of a life-changing moment. Rise to the occasion.

But don't rise above the bride. Beach weddings where the bride wears flip-flops and the groom wears a Hawaiian shirt allow for some informality. Sundresses and sandals for women and light resort shirts and pants for the men might be perfectly acceptable, even flip-flops—if and only if the wedding party wears them. (Your best flip-flops, please.)

A midday wedding in the big city, on the other hand, calls for nice dresses and heels, high-heeled sandals, or attractive flats for the women. Maybe even a big gaudy hat, depending on the local culture and the season. Men should wear suits or reasonably professional office attire, slacks, dress shirts, jackets and ties, dress shoes, and socks. Go easy on the black. (Do not wear flip-flops.)

A formal evening wedding demands the most of the wedding guest, and there is less room for error or improvisation. Cocktail dresses are generally acceptable for the women, and dark suits or tuxedos for the men. It will be stated on the invitation, unless the bride and groom are clueless. If they are clueless, ask the maid of honor. A note about flip-flops should not be necessary.

General Reminders for
Proper Wedding Guest Deportment

- Compliment the bride and the families, and thank the waitstaff. Smile. If you cannot in good conscience say the wedding was *lovely* or *wonderful* or *moving* or that it touched you *deeply* or what a *perfect* day it was for a wedding, practice saying phrases that can (and will) be interpreted as approval. Such as: Breathtaking! Amazing! It's *unique!* It's so *you!* I've never seen anything like it! That was really *you* up there! I couldn't take my eyes off the two of you! If all other words fail you: WOW!

- Watch where you stand, walk, and sit, and do not drink too much. Try not to stumble over the photographer and her assistant, who are focused on the bride and groom, not on you. Avoid contact with burning candles, and do not step on flower girls, trailing tablecloths, or long skirts. Above all: Do not step on the bride!

- A wedding is not the place to wear your tightest, sexiest, skimpiest attire, unless you are a bridesmaid at a wedding at a strip club and *stripper wear* is how the stripper bride has decided to humiliate her non-stripper bridesmaids. You are not there to snag one of the hot groomsmen and drag him under the wedding cake table. If that happens, it's a bonus.

- The reception is not the place to pass judgment on the bride's alien lizard-queen gown and Star Trekkie headpiece, the bridesmaids' lime green Southern belle dresses, the flower girl's inability to scatter the rose petals, the ring bearer's violent meltdown, the best man's drunken revelations about the groom, or the frothy pastel concoctions the mothers of the bride and groom have decided to wear. Wait until you get home to dish (or post the video online for the world to enjoy). Taking mental notes (and photographs) is perfectly acceptable. And if you end up with really juicy wedding gossip or fashion blunders to share, *call me.*

Finally, enjoy yourself! If you're lucky, this might be a perfect day for a beautiful wedding. If you're really lucky, it just might be that legendary debacle of a wedding that will provide endless cocktail chatter for every wedding guest for years to come.

But remember: *Someday it might be you up there.*

chapter 23

"They think I killed Leonardo. Me!" Miguel was in the highest of high dudgeons as he handed Lacey a cup of coffee from a white paper bag. They were in Farragut Square, across from Lacey's newsroom. The spring morning air was delicious.

"Are you sure they aren't just trying to rattle you?"

"Sweetie, that's just a bonus for these guys. I don't know why he didn't just read me my rights."

"Because you're not under arrest. And *who* didn't read you your rights?"

"That big Broadway Lamont character who has a crush on you. As if I would *bother* killing Leonardo," he continued without taking a breath. "Honestly, Leo's so not worth it. And as if I'd kill anybody at a party, I mean *really*. Give me some credit. And certainly not at Stella's party! I'd wait till after the wedding." He sipped some espresso. Miguel didn't need any more caffeine—he was already at an adrenaline-induced fever pitch of wakefulness. He simply needed to talk.

"Speaking of the wedding, Miguel, have you heard from Stella?"

"This morning. She still hasn't washed her face or changed her clothes. Obviously, she's in some kind of ritualistic mourning, or fugue state, or psychotic breakdown, or something."

"You saw her this morning?" Lacey squinted. Her

head hurt. It wasn't the champagne, but the lack of sleep.

"I dropped by on my way to chat with the police. It set the tone, I'll tell you."

Wednesday morning was too pretty to stay inside. Lacey and Miguel were lounging on the giant stone steps at the base of the statue of Admiral David Farragut, which stood guard over Farragut Square. It was just before the noontime crowds would start streaming into the streets for lunch, and office workers would gather at the statue, sunning themselves like cats. Even though rain was predicted for the rest of the day, the girls in their summer dresses were out in full force. It would have been perfect—except for the semi-hysterical state Miguel was in.

"I am never leaving Manhattan again! Shut the door, lock the gate, roll up the bridges."

"Don't roll up the bridges. I wouldn't be able to visit you," Lacey said.

"Bad things happen to me here," Miguel went on. "Armed robbery. Heartbreak. Leonardo. Weddings." He paused in mid-rant, noticing what Lacey was wearing, and perked up. "Fabulous dress, by the way."

"Thanks. Fabulous is my middle name." She smoothed her skirt, admiring its cream-colored linen and lace appliqués. The lace reminded her that she had to call Alma Lopez and inquire as to how Stella's dress was coming along. If the wedding really stayed canceled, Lacey would be in possession of a wacky wedding gown that Stella would never want back. She wondered idly where she could find another Bo Peep in need of bridal attire.

Lacey was dressed to ward off a cloudy day. She had chosen a simple sleeveless dress with a square neck, natural waist, and flared skirt, which she'd found at Bygones, a great little vintage clothing store in Richmond. It was the kind of pretty-for-its-own-sake dress that could only be found in a Southern city that still believed in *prettiness* as its own reward. It was dressy for day, but Lacey didn't care. She toned it down with a wide black belt and a long-sleeved black bolero jacket. Today she needed the extra boost a great dress could give her.

"What did Broadway ask you?" she asked.

"Ask? He practically threw me against the wall. Ask indeed."

"Miguel, really?"

"Very well. He looked like he *wanted* to toss me through the wall. Seriously, do I look like I'm capable of gay-on-gay violence? I'm not even a gym rat. Absolutely not," he said, answering his own question. "Just because I loathed Leonardo, why would I kill him when I could simply cut him dead for life? But murder him? Who does that? Tacky, tacky, tacky. And I wouldn't look good in those baggy prison togs." Lacey's eyebrows lifted.

"Please, Lacey, you could line up the people who hated Leonard Karpinski and they'd wrap all the way around Farragut Square here. Twice. Not even counting all the people whose innocent heads of hair he butchered. I hated him in a mere vanilla kind of way."

"There's vanilla-flavored hate?"

"Ordinary everyday hate." He picked an imaginary speck of dust off his shirt. "It wasn't deep dark boiling rage or anything like that. I don't have the dark energy." He leaned against the stone step and closed his eyes.

Lacey thought about the theory she'd shared with Vic the previous night. The poison needle in the shawl, meant for someone else. Mysterious spies plotting murders, motive and target unknown. It sounded much crazier by daylight.

Vic is right about one thing, I'm trampling on DeadFed territory.

Leonardo's murderer probably was much more prosaic than a spy. If someone simply wanted to ruin the wedding and split up Nigel and Stella, it could be Bryan Culpeper. For that matter, some of Stella's nearest and dearest were opposed to the wedding, including her bitter mother and her jealous cousin Rosalie.

Lacey gave Miguel a hug. He rested his head on her shoulder for a moment. "Better now? Broadway didn't arrest you, after all."

"Because I know my rights." Miguel straightened up. "Hey, your big beautiful bodyguard is missing! Where is he?"

"I convinced Vic I couldn't get any work done with Turtledove following me everywhere. And nobody else could either, what with all the staring and sighing."

"We're only human." He sighed. "Your bodyguard, on the other hand, is some kind of a dusky Greek god."

"He'll be on duty after work."

Vic had finally agreed that Turtledove didn't need to be glued to her side at the office. And Vic would make sure some of his guys were nearby, unobtrusively. Lacey had hesitated momentarily about meeting Miguel in the open, forcing Vic's invisible guys to cover two potential targets instead of one, but she decided she was being as paranoid as Olga Kepelova. If someone wanted to break up Stella's wedding, *mission accomplished.* What more could they be after? *What about Vic's brakes? And who's next?* She pushed the thought out of her head.

"How did Broadway know you hated Leonardo, anyway?" she asked.

"That would certainly be from Kevin, Leo's roommate," Miguel said. "He despised me, or anyone who had ever been with Leonardo. The two of them! Such drama queens! Frankly, my dear, I think Kevin fingered me because he's afraid the cops would focus on him."

"Kevin who?"

"Kevin Early. Yeah, it's really his name. And he never is—early."

"So he's taking the offensive? Did Kevin Early have a motive for killing Leo?"

"I suppose." He threw his hands up in the air. "All they did was fight and scream. And scratch. *Meow.* The way they carried on, you'd have thought they were married. But they never even did the deed, as far as I know. Kevin always had a serious thing for Leonardo, but that wasn't going to happen. Between you and me, he's much too frumpy-dumpy for the great Leonardo. A little cute though."

"Did you tell that to the detective?"

"Did I tell him! Oh, honey, I sang like the proverbial canary. If the canary was an opera singer named Maria Callas. Kevin is terribly upset though. He called me, crying. He's putting together a memorial."

"When?"

"Not sure, I expect it will take a week or two. Kevin's no ball of fire. I'm sure you'll be invited."

As long as Lady G is safely back in England, Lacey thought.

Miguel studied his cold coffee. "Leonardo was poisoned, did you know? Nicotine, of all the crazy things, so says the big detective. And Leo had quit smoking. Talk about irony."

"The final toxicology results aren't in yet."

"So he told me. But he sounded pretty convinced, for some reason. Large Lamont said the entry wound was in the neck. Remember, Leo and his ridiculous tango with the shawl? And how he went on and on about how it *bit* him on the neck?"

"What did you tell Broadway Lamont?"

Miguel shrugged and sipped his cold espresso. "What everyone else says: The shawl did it."

A pair of sturdy, well-tied brown oxfords planted themselves in the aisle next to Lacey's desk. She noticed them as she reached down into her drawer for a fresh notebook. Shoes that brown and that sturdy and that polished could belong to only one person Lacey knew. She thought about staying down there until the shoes departed. But they were positioned there with a purpose. They weren't going anywhere.

The guards let just anyone in these days. If this keeps up, my reading public will never know what's in and out for spring.

She straightened up slowly, noting the rest of the tweed outfit that accompanied the sturdy brown oxfords. *How could one person own so much tweed, in so many shades of heather brown and blue and beige?*

"Good morning, Gwendolyn. What brings you here on this beautiful day?"

"A mission of mercy. Well, perhaps not mercy. You are well aware of the situation, Lacey. We must stop this catastrophe from happening."

Stopping a catastrophe? And I thought this might be difficult.

"What catastrophe? I can think of several."

Lacey pulled over the Death Chair and offered it to Gwendolyn, who stared at the death's head. Was it simply the type of droll décor American journalists found amusing? Lady Gwendolyn Griffin wasn't afraid of death's heads, but Lacey hadn't told her the chair's peculiar history. Gwendolyn might want to take it home with her.

"The wedding. Rather, the imminent threat that there might be *no* wedding. Nigel and Stella are indubitably meant to be together. Why, who can say? But we can't let them be torn apart by some silly superstition."

"There is silly superstition, and then there are speeding limos out of nowhere trying to run them over. And me."

Lacey bitterly wondered for the smallest moment why no one, except her, seemed to care that *she* might have been run over, along with Nigel and Stella. Lacey craved the chance to do a little therapeutic whining, but this was no time for self-indulgence.

"Granted, that sort of unpleasantness would throw a normal person off their stride. But Stella, I believe, is made of sturdier stuff."

"She thinks she's protecting Nigel by *not* marrying him. Stella is sure she's saving his life."

"She really is a dear, brave girl. I should have stayed

there after our little tour of the Arts Club, instead of running off to frolic with the ambassador." It was charming how Lady G referred to her husband as "the ambassador." But her, frolicking? Difficult to imagine. Gwendolyn stood there like an implacable force of nature. "Now, how do you propose that we prevent this disaster? You are, I scarcely need point out, her maid of honor."

"Averting disaster is part of my job too?"

"Most assuredly! As you well know, Lacey. Besides, someone's got to do it and Stella will listen to you. I have complete faith in you."

Lacey hunted for her FASHION *BITES* coffee cup. "Just because Stella listens, it doesn't mean she'll do what I say. Would you like some coffee?"

"No, thank you. Do you have any good English tea?"

"Good? I seriously doubt it. There may be some old tea bags in the kitchen. Stale, dreadful."

"It will have to do. Milk and sugar, please. Thank you, Lacey. I'll just make myself comfortable here in this most picturesque chair. American Gothic, what?"

"The most Gothic thing we have around here. Someday I'll tell you all about it." Lacey picked up another FASHION *BITES* mug and trotted off to do Gwendolyn's bidding. She returned shortly with a cup of tea that she hoped wouldn't damage the woman's kidneys.

"Lovely. Thank you, my dear." She took a sip while Lacey held her breath. "Not half bad."

"What about the curse of the shawl?" Lacey asked.

"Curse, my right eye. Someone is trying to harm them and keep them apart."

"Who, do you think?"

"Some strange and twisted miscreant. Perhaps jealous of their happiness. His dark motives we can't really know. Yet." Gwendolyn relished the mystery. "This is all very troubling, of course, but it is these kinds of trials that can bind a couple together forever."

Perhaps Gwendolyn reads romances as well. "You think so?"

"Why, of course I do. If those two lovebirds succeed in making it down that aisle under those cherry blossoms despite all this trouble and strife, they'll have a very strong marriage." Gwendolyn Griffin had a strange look on her face, determined yet wistful.

Lacey wasn't so sure. Stella was unable to commit to a hairstyle for more than a couple of months. How could she commit to a man forever? Nigel was trying to be a reformed "man-slut," but once a slut, Lacey worried, always a slut? Her thoughts must have shown on her face.

"Oh, I know my Nigel can be a very naughty and flighty boy. A man as attractive as he is often leaves a trail of broken hearts. That man-eating Adele, for instance. But little Stella Lake has stopped him in his tracks. Nigel is a changed man. He cares for her above himself. That has never happened before. And miracles like that do not happen every day, believe you me."

"You really like Stella, don't you?"

"Stella is the rebellious daughter I never had." Gwendolyn chuckled. "Well, perhaps not. But she's very sweet and I adore her. And she never bores me."

"And you have a hat for the wedding. I have a dress. We wouldn't want them to go to waste."

"Precisely. Oh, dear, my tea is gone." She handed her cup to Lacey with an implied order. Lacey trotted off to make another cup of stale Lipton tea for Gwendolyn and poured herself a stiff cup of java.

"Stella's crazy about Nigel, and he can turn her around if anyone can," Gwendolyn insisted. "If Stella decides she's getting married after all, nothing will stop her."

"I talked to Nigel last night. I tried to set him on the right course, or something like it. I don't know if he remembers it."

"Too much to drink, I take it. This time at least he had an excuse. What did you tell him, my dear, if it's not too private?"

"Nothing between me and your son ever seems to be

private," Lacey said. "I simply suggested how he could win Stella back. Get her away from her mother. Sweep her off her feet with the flowers she loves and a big date, at a restaurant she's been dying to try. A lot of chocolate. And buy a new shirt that isn't blue. Preferably pink."

"Sounds rather simple. Is it enough?"

"Sometimes it's the simplest things that work. Stella loves romance, and time is short. But Gwendolyn, you've got to keep Nigel away from that nasty Bryan Culpeper!"

"Bryan? He and Nigel were school chums, at one of the many schools my dear boy was thrown out of. Come to think of it, Bryan was thrown out too. You don't like him?"

"I don't like him and he doesn't like Stella. Doesn't think she's good enough for Nigel, thinks they are better off without each other. He's happy the wedding is off."

Lacey remembered something she'd overheard Bryan say. He'd complained about Marie's shawl, how it almost smothered him. He'd been close enough to stick a pin in it, so to speak. She shook her head. It was a ridiculous thought—or was it?

"But why?"

"Something about his sister being a better match for Nigel."

"Aha! Adele! That conniving barracuda of a girl! He's pushing her on my Nigel? You think he's trying to interfere, with a hidden agenda? Oh, dear, a mother is the last to know." Gwendolyn sipped her tea and examined her cup, as if she were reading tea leaves. "I shall call Nigel and remind him about what you told him. Then I shall ring up Bryan and invite him to tea, where he will be under my thumb for the rest of the day."

"What if Bryan says no?"

"He wouldn't dare say no to me. I know his mother." It was as good as saying she knew where the bodies were buried. "That should leave Nigel free to mount his white horse and woo fair Stella. All the way down the aisle."

"You're very optimistic," Lacey said.

"Merely determined. Now you call Stella and see which way the wind blows. If she wavers, you must convince her to give him one more chance."

And to get out of her old sweats and into the shower. "I'll do what I can," Lacey promised.

"Now about that young man who died? Such a puzzle." Her eyes glowed with interest. "When is the funeral?"

"There's talk of a memorial service. But not until next week or later."

"Very well. Do keep me informed, if you would be so kind. Any word on what happened to him? How exactly did he die?"

"As far as I know, Leonardo's body hasn't been released. And there's no official cause of death yet. The police are still questioning people. More than that, I can't say," Lacey said.

I could say, but I won't. She wanted to turn Gwendolyn's energy to the problem of Nigel and Stella. If Nigel's mother heard a word about spies and poisoned needles, it wouldn't come from Lacey.

"I read that lunatic Web site today. DeadFed, or whatever it's called," Gwendolyn said, rising to take her leave. "Lovely stuff. Delightfully deranged. 'Killer Shawl' has a certain ring, don't you think? But believe you me, Lacey Smithsonian, there is a human being behind this mysterious death, not a Killer Shawl on the loose."

Lacey didn't believe in curses or haunted clothes either, but she did believe in signs from the universe, and in staying alive.

And in the maid of honor's work never being done.

Before calling Stella, Lacey checked in with Brooke. She texted her fellow bridesmaid. "Did you finish the favors?"

"Boxes and chocolates and rhinestones, oh, my," Brooke texted back. "Favors and glue guns nearly finished me, but they are done. And so am I. Talk later."

Lacey didn't know why that message made her feel better. But she was convinced that if there was hope enough left within Stella to assemble hundreds of bride and groom boxes and glue on all those rhinestones, there was enough hope for her to waltz down the aisle. Lacey ignored the press release on her desk about what fashions were hot for spring and called Stella.

"Yeah?" Stella yawned.

"It's me. How are you?"

"Napping."

"Brooke told me you finished the favors."

"Yeah, I couldn't believe she showed up out of the blue to help. She's so goosey about glue guns and crafts and stuff. But we rocked and rolled, Lace. It was fun. And even though Brookie acts all phobic about rhinestones, I think secretly she likes them."

"So she really was helpful?"

"Oh, yeah, by the time she left, we were like an assembly line. And she kept me from eating all the chocolate kisses." Stella paused and giggled. "It got a little intense during the rhinestone fight."

"Rhinestone fight?"

"Brooke totally fights dirty. Pink sparkles everywhere. I still got glue and rhinestones in my hair." Lacey was trying to visualize this rhinestone fight. "It's kind of awesome here with all the boxes everywhere, all the little bride and groom boxes? It's so pretty, Lacey. As a bonus, Brooke and me and rhinestones totally drove my mother back to New Jersey. I think I should keep some pink rhinestones around always, like garlic against vampires. But what am I going to do with all the favors?"

"Get married on Saturday." *Do not turn into Miss Havisham with a glue gun.*

"Ah, Lacey . . ."

"How are you feeling?"

"I'm kind of sad." Stella's voice dropped low and Lacey felt bad for her.

"You can still marry him."

"If I want us to *die*!" Stella moaned. "I gotta tell you, Lacey. It's getting harder and harder to stick to my guns here. But I don't want to be responsible for killing the man I love."

Lacey stretched back in her office chair. She moved the Death Chair out of her cubicle. The painted skull seemed to wink at her.

"You've spoken with Nigel?"

"No. He called, but I was sleeping. Brooke was here till, like, forever."

"Miguel said he dropped by."

"I guess so."

"He said you were wearing the same thing you wore yesterday."

"I guess. Like I had a naughty sleepover? Oh, God!" Stella gasped loudly. She must have looked in the mirror. "What happened to me? I look scary, Lacey. Poor Miguel, I didn't want him to see me this way. I should get dressed. But who has the energy? I'm going back to bed."

"Stella! Listen to me! No bed! Get in the shower. You'll feel better if you get the glue out of your hair."

"Oh, my God, Lacey, pink rhinestones are stuck to my pink highlights. It's all Brooke's fault."

"I'm sure it is." Lacey suppressed a laugh.

"Ow. I am going to have to use clarifying shampoo to get this stuff out."

Lacey wished there was a clarifying shampoo for the *brain*. It would be a bestseller. "Don't forget conditioner. Use some product."

"Ha. Like I could forget conditioner. Some product, and some finger curls, and hey, look at that, I've got like twenty-seven calls on my phone from Nigel!"

"He's trying to make things right. Talk to him, Stella."

"I can't talk to him."

"You have to. You owe it to him. You owe it to me." Lacey was fed up. "I thought I would never say this, but he loves you."

"Oh, Lacey . . . I'm terrified. I'm not ready to meet my maker."

"I saw him last night. Nigel, not your maker."

"What! You never told me."

"I'm telling you now. Nigel was drunk and frantic. You know he had to be desperate to come to *me*."

"Oh, my God. Nigel is brokenhearted."

"Buck up, Stella. What if he came over right now and saw you looking defeated like this? With strawberry sparkle hair?"

There was a gasp on the phone. "I would totally kill myself. Okay! Jeez! I'm getting cleaned up. You really think he might show up here?"

"Of course he will. You're not answering his calls! What would *you* do?"

Stella squealed and hung up. Lacey mentally marked that chore off her maid-of-honor to-do list. Now it was up to Nigel to convince Stella to marry him. Or not.

Just when Lacey thought she could forget about wedding chatter for a few moments, Felicity, food editor and yet another bride-to-be, strutted over to her desk with a platter of frosted mini cupcakes.

Lacey was more fascinated by Felicity's outfit than the cupcakes. She had broken out one of her spring sweaters, worn over a shapeless daffodil yellow print dress. The sweater was lilac, embroidered with purple and yellow pansies. Lacey had no idea where Felicity shopped. She had never seen sweaters like Felicity's in department stores. Was there some catalogue or Web site specializing in shapeless sack dresses and festive seasonal sweaters for gardeners? And cupcake-baking, information-seeking missiles, like Felicity?

"I'm trying out a new caramel praline cake with dulce de leche icing," Felicity said, wielding her platter of cupcakes like a weapon. "These are tiny, Lacey, just a bite. Hardly any calories at all. Go ahead."

"Thanks, Felicity. They look fabulous. But I really want to fit into my dress on Saturday."

"I can't believe your bride is actually letting brides-maids choose their own dresses?"

"Less bloodshed that way," Lacey said.

"Seems way too casual to me." Felicity shook her head disapprovingly. "Brides shouldn't leave the dresses to chance. What if she hates what you pick?"

"What if she picks what we hate?"

"That's the bride's prerogative."

"We're all wearing the same color." *That's the least of Stella's problems*, Lacey thought.

"Everything is on the bride's shoulders. It's so not fair. My maid of honor is hopeless," Felicity set the platter on her desk and picked up a cupcake. She took a bite. "Is everything set for your friend's wedding? She really hasn't had much time. My wedding is in September and I am spending every single minute to make sure it's perfect."

"She finished the favors." Lacey thought that was a neutral enough statement.

"Good grief! The wedding is this weekend!"

"I wasn't actually on the favors committee."

"Have you seen them? How do they look?" Felicity clicked a key on her keyboard and a wedding site popped up. "She's using the bride and groom boxes, right? They're so *adorable*." She turned her screen so Lacey could see. Lacey didn't recall telling Felicity about the favors, but she'd no doubt overheard. There were few secrets in a newsroom. "And her personalized miniature Hershey's chocolate bars must have come in by now, haven't they?"

How does Felicity know about the personalized chocolates? "Yes, they came in, no problem. Boxes of them."

"And the English toffee for Nigel?"

The Eye's food editor certainly had news-gathering skills when it came to food and weddings. "That's right."

While Felicity worried over the details of someone

else's wedding, Lacey dug through her in-box to make sure she'd taken care of any pressing news before she left for the next couple of days. Felicity, she knew, would happily babble on about weddings and food. It didn't really matter if anyone answered.

"Lacey"—Felicity leaned in conspiratorially—"do you think you could bring me a set of her favors—the bride and groom boxes? I know it's a lot to ask. But I'm working on what to give my guests. I've been looking at all kinds of wedding favors. It's *research*."

"Top secret, no doubt."

"Classified, on a need-to-know basis. I need to make a final decision soon about favor boxes. There are so many choices. And I want to make sure they're perfect. Not cheap, not flimsy. Not tacky. So I'd really appreciate seeing what Stella's look like."

"With or without the pink rhinestones?"

"Rhinestones?" Felicity flinched. "Well. I'd like to see the total effect, of course. It's not like I'd be copying her. And I'd never glue rhinestones on mine. I mean, my wedding is out of town, none of our guests will overlap. Except you and your boyfriend. And you are in the wedding party, of course, because you introduced us, and there was that incident at Christmas with the police where you helped out. Harlan insisted you should come. And—and—I do too."

"Understood. We wouldn't miss it." *But I'll try.* "Tell me, Felicity, are you getting your personalized chocolates from Hershey's, like Stella? Or are you going with M&M's?"

"I was born in Hershey, Pennsylvania. So of course I'm getting Hershey's, I grew up with Hershey's, but I'm not copying Stella. My favors will be *unique*."

Sure they will. "I'm sure she'll have a few extras, one way or another." *Maybe hundreds.* "I'll bring you a set."

The color rushed back into Felicity's face. "Thank you!" Felicity picked up a pen and pad and marked through a line on her list of things to do.

*   *   *

Brooke was unavailable for lunch, so Lacey hailed a cab, to head to Stella's. She didn't want any more surprise visitors, but she ran into Turtledove in the lobby. He and his old friend from last night were coming in as she was going out.

"Hey, Turtledove. I thought you were off duty," she said.

"Thought I'd check in. And here I find you on the run."

"Very funny," Lacey said. "I'm checking on Stella. See if she's okay."

"She the one that sloppy drunk last night is crazy 'bout?" Rene asked.

"That's the one," Turtledove said. "I'll drive. You mind Rene hanging with us?"

"Not at all. How's the search for your lady going?" Lacey asked Rene as they headed for Turtledove's SUV.

"I don't hold out much hope. She is a needle and D.C. is a mighty big haystack."

chapter 24

Lacey had her hand poised to knock on Stella's apartment door when it opened and Detective Broadway Lamont emerged. Lamont was snorting and practically pawing the ground like the thick-necked bull he always made her think of. He took one look at Lacey and bellowed.

"One more person tells me that damn shawl killed Leonard Karpinski, aka Leonardo, I'm arresting them."

"For what?" Lacey ventured to ask.

"Obstruction of justice. And irritating an officer of the law beyond human endurance. I want answers, not some haunted-Killer-Shawl load of crap. You hear that, Smithsonian?"

"Loud and clear, Broadway."

Turtledove stood still and smiled. "How do, Detective."

Lamont grumbled, "I've been better." He was a big man and muscular, but Turtledove was bigger and in better shape. "What are you doing here, Forrest?"

"Working." Turtledove inclined his head toward Lacey.

"Hot on a fashion story, Smithsonian? That why you need a bodyguard?"

"I want to see how Stella is doing," Lacey explained.

"The wedding is still off, if that's what you mean," Lamont said. "Ms. Lake is afraid of the shawl, which I gather is missing. Pretty damn convenient."

"How'd you hear that?" Lacey asked.

"I sure as hell didn't hear it from you, did I? And I thought we were friends. I'm curious to see this Killer Shawl everybody's talking about, so I contacted the psychic woman, who tells me it's gone. If she's so psychic, why can't she peer into her crystal ball and find the damn thing?"

"Apparently being psychic doesn't work that way," Lacey said.

"Oh, you think?" Lamont was a master of heavy sarcasm.

Stella stood in the doorway, warily watching the others. She had cleaned up and pulled on some black leggings and a man's blue oxford cloth shirt, probably one of Nigel's. Lacey figured the shirt was a positive sign: a metaphorical hug, or at least a sartorial one.

"Lacey, I only told him—" Stella began, but a glare from Lamont silenced her.

Rene seemed to melt against the wall. He obviously had no wish to tangle with a cop, any cop, anywhere. Detective Lamont picked up on that.

"Who are you and why are you joining this little tea party?"

"I'm with Forrest." Rene barely looked up.

"This here is Rene Thibodeaux, friend of mine from down New Orleans way."

"How long you been in town?" Lamont asked.

"Drove up yesterday."

"He wasn't anywhere near the party, or Leonardo," Lacey said. Even as she said it, Leonardo's death seemed very far away, as if it had happened ages ago.

"Says you." Lamont switched his attention back to Rene. "What do you think of haunted shawls killing folks? Crazy-ass story or what?"

Rene stared at Lamont and spread his hands wide. "Being as how I'm from the neighborhood of New Orleans I wouldn't discount a thing like that."

Lamont lowered his head. His body language said he was surrounded by idiots.

"Have you spoken with Brooke Barton yet?" Lacey hazarded to ask him.

Lamont leaned against the wall and crossed his arms. "That would be the other bridesmaid who hosted this deadly little shindig with you?"

"Leonardo did not die at the party, and you can't say for sure he was poisoned there."

"Not yet, I can't. But if he did get the fatal dose from your party, I will prove it. And I will come looking for everyone who was at that party. And speaking of that lunatic lawyer, I don't care to hear that the shawl is conspiring with a purse or a pair of shoes or something, unless it kills off all the idiots in this town. You better be glad I'm not questioning her. That particular pleasure belongs to Detective Hopkins. He's got more stomach than me for dealing with lawyers."

"Things happen that we can't explain, you know," Turtledove said calmly.

"You're right about that, Forrest. Nothing can explain why I'm standing here talking to a bunch of know-it-alls who know nothing and tell me less. Stay available. All of you."

"Good seeing you, Broadway," Turtledove said with a grin. Lamont took the stairs without another word. The trio walked through Stella's door and stared.

Inside Stella's apartment every surface seemed to be covered with miniature boxes. A veritable army of brides and grooms marched across her dining table, coffee table, end tables, bookcases, and windowsills. More were lined up along the floor.

Rene picked up a small tuxedo box and shook it in wonder. "What on earth is all this?"

"They're what the wedding guests will take home as a party favor," Lacey said.

"Party favors? For a wedding?" The thought had clearly never occurred to him. "You getting married?" he asked Stella, still fascinated with the box. He opened it and stared at the pieces of toffee as if they were pieces of eight.

"I don't know." Stella wrung her hands. "Maybe. Maybe not."

Rene put two and two together and turned to his friend Turtledove. "She's the little bitty pretty thing that Nigel dude was talking 'bout last night?"

"That's her," Turtledove said.

Stella stood still in the middle of the hundreds of boxes. She looked almost herself again.

"Stella? What did you say to Broadway Lamont?" Lacey asked.

"I don't remember. I should have had a lawyer here. Or you, Lace. I mean, you know how I am with cops. I can't take them. They make me just— I don't know. Crazy."

Stella's father had been a cop who had abused his family and abandoned them long ago. She hadn't seen him in years, and she hadn't bothered to try to find him to invite him to the wedding. She wasn't interested in seeing him on her wedding day or any other day. "It's not like he's giving me away," she had told Lacey. "He did that long ago." Stella was determined to walk down the aisle by herself.

"I'm sorry you had to go through the interview, Stel. But what did you tell Lamont?"

Stella blinked a couple of times. "Rosalie is totally going to be pissed at me."

"Why, Stella, and what does this have to do with Lamont?"

"It's the cop thing. I don't know what to say when they get in my face and he was *totally* in my face, like *this* close to my face." Stella held her thumb and her index finger an inch apart. "This close, I tell you. So I said I thought the shawl was haunted or possessed and like, hunting people down, and he kind of went berserk. When he calmed down he asked me if I knew anything about poisons, because of Leonardo being poisoned and all. And it didn't occur to me to mention how permanent wave solution and hair dyes at the salon are poisons, so

I blurted out the only thing I could think of. About Rosalie. About how she was, like, a chemistry major in school before she switched to accounting. A total chem nerd. And she's a fanatic gardener and she's totally into pesticides. Poison, pure and simple."

"What did Lamont say?"

"He just listened. Think I should call her and warn her?"

If Rosalie had something to do with the poison that killed Leonardo, best not to warn her, Lacey decided. But could Rosalie really be a suspect? Would she have gone to such extremes to ruin Stella's wedding? And how exactly was the poison administered, and who was it meant for? Had she been in contact with the shawl before Leonardo arrived? If she was a chem nerd, whipping up a little homemade nicotine dose would be a snap. *Wouldn't it?*

Rosalie knew about cars too. She'd disabled Stella's car in retaliation for a bad haircut. She worked at an auto supply shop. Maybe she knew how to hot-wire a car as well? Lacey wondered whether Rosalie could have been behind the wheel of the limousine. But why? Jealousy? Family squabbles? Revenge for a bad haircut years ago? It didn't seem to add up. But didn't Vic always warn her about trying to hunt for motives? Everybody has a motive for something, and yet they never quite add up.

Lacey stared at a framed photograph of Stella and Nigel, cavorting on one of the huge stone griffins outside the old Art Deco Acacia Life Insurance building, just a few blocks from Union Station. After Stella discovered the griffins, she insisted on having her engagement photo with Nigel Griffin taken there. The two of them looked daffy and thoroughly in love. Stella was sitting on top of the griffin's wings while Nigel knelt on the griffin's paws and handed a red rose up to her.

These two goofballs deserved each other.

"Did Nigel call?"

"Yeah. I miss him so much, Lacey."

"Just imagine, it's been two whole days and he still wants to marry you."

"I know. He asked me to go out with him tonight. He wants to take me to Co Co. Sala, can you believe it? I mean, how did he know I've been dying to go there?"

"Soul mates have a psychic connection." Lacey gagged mentally. It sounded stupid to her even as she said it, but Stella nodded. Rene and Turtledove shared a look.

"If there was any way I thought we'd have a chance, I'd marry him in a heartbeat. But with Leo dead and now with the shawl missing, I don't know what to think." Stella ran her hands through her hair. "I feel like a target. Like I got a bull's-eye painted on me. And Lace—"

"You love him," Rene broke in. "This man loves you. He wants to marry you. What's the problem?"

"People are dying," Stella said. "And wait, who are you again?"

"I tagged along with Forrest, my buddy, we go way back. I don't mean to butt in, I got my own troubles, but you say people are dying because of a haunted shawl? Could be. I don't disbelieve in weird things happening in this world. Where I'm from, folks leave bottles of bourbon at the tomb of a voodoo queen who died a hundred years ago, just to keep her happy, and her body's probably not even in there no more. People believe all kind of strange things and maybe I do too. But love should be stronger than any crazy thing people say, stronger than any ghost, stronger than any evil spirit." Rene picked up one of the wedding dress favors to go with the matching tuxedo box. He clicked them together, like they were dancing. "I mean, love can move mountains, ain't that what it says in the Bible?"

It was faith that moved mountains, but Lacey wasn't going to correct him. She liked Rene's version just fine. And Stella was listening to him, really listening. *Sometimes it takes hearing it from a stranger.*

"Yeah, I guess," Stella said. "I'm Stella." She wiped her eyes and put out her small hand for him to shake.

"I'm sorry," Lacey said. "I should have made introductions. This is Rene Thibodeaux."

"He's an old friend of mine from New Orleans," Turtledove said. "Rene, this is Stella Lake."

"Up here on some personal business with Forrest. But we were talking about you and what you gonna do. Your man is in pain," Rene said to her, "and so are you. You're the cure for him. And he's yours. You gotta cure each other."

Stella looked around at her visitors. "I don't want anyone else to die."

"Try wrestling gators sometime," Rene said. "Me, I'm scared to death every day in this city, with all the crazy cars and crazy drivers and crazy politicians. Druther wrestle gators than be here. But I'm here to find someone I lost. You already found your someone."

Stella took his hands in hers. "She really hurt you, whoever she is?"

"Do me a favor, cher," Rene said. "Go out with your man tonight. Get real pretty for him. He's trying his best. Give him another chance."

Stella's eyes filled with tears. "Yeah. You're right. How can I say no to him? Oh, my God! Wouldja look at the time! I gotta get going if I'm gonna pull off a major va-va-va-voom by seven."

Lacey herded Turtledove and Rene out of the apartment and issued a last-minute order at the door. "Call me, Stella. After your date. I want a full report."

"Okay, Lace, but it could be late." Stella started to giggle. "Really, really late."

"Girl, you are twitching like a bug on a hot sidewalk," Rene complained as they reentered *The Eye*'s lobby.

Lacey couldn't shake the feeling she was being watched. Even though she was with the very capable Turtledove and the rough but ready Rene Thibodeaux, she was wary of every face and shadow on the street behind her. She jumped at the sound of every horn and

every siren, of which Washington, D.C., was full to over-
flowing.

"At least I'm alive and twitching," she said. "Thank
you for escorting me, Rene, Turtledove. I'll be fine."
Lacey nodded toward the guard's desk, which theoretically provided a barrier to unwelcome guests, but never
really did. "I'm safe here from everything but my editor."

It struck her funny that in a town like Washington,
where cameras were watching all over the city, she almost always felt anonymous and invisible. As a reporter,
she witnessed up close and personal how hard it was for
someone to stand out in the flood of information pouring forth from other journalists on papers, on radio, on
television, and on the Web. Her articles and columns
were just a drop in the media ocean. The ever-present
crowds were a form of protective camouflage.

Not today. She was glad Vic had arranged to have
Turtledove bodyguarding her. She couldn't wait for
Broadway Lamont to figure out who killed Leonardo
and who was behind the car attacks. She couldn't live in
this limbo much longer.

Her lunch hour had been spent in a good cause, but
now Lacey's stomach growled and reminded her she was
starving. On her way to the newsroom she detoured to
the small takeout deli on the first floor of the building.
She picked up a container of Greek yogurt and a ba-
nana. It would have to do.

She sat at her desk and stared at her notes and her
computer screen. The deadline for her Fashion Bites column was looming. *Come on, Smithsonian. Snap out of it,*
she told herself. *Wrap this up and you're free for the
week. Free to be . . . Supermaid of Honor!* There were
times when she had no energy left for the last story of
the day or the week, and this was one of them. Even a
story as silly as "What's Hot for Spring." She called a
couple of her favorite boutiques for quotes on this vital
question of the day and powered through it.

What's in this spring? Easygoing pieces in breezy colors that evoke the season without being garish. Brighten up your wardrobe and your outlook with crisp tailored separates, as well as versatile spring dresses that take you from day to evening . . .

Even though Lacey's workdays were spent parsing the meaning of hemlines and necklines and sleeve lengths, and debating the optimism and pessimism of colors and how it affected women in positions of power, she believed the real secrets to dressing well were simply *confidence* and *planning*.

Think about what your clothes are really saying. Make sure they say what you *want* them to say for any given occasion, don't let your clothes talk you into something you'll regret, and spend time in advance planning what to wear, instead of wasting time panicking at the last minute. Then you can forget about your clothes for the rest of the day or evening, and just let them do their job. If you started the day off in your well-planned, perfect-for-you outfit, you won't have to worry four hours later about the fit and style, about unexpected creasing and wrinkling, about whether your skirt is riding up or whether the fabric adds ten pounds to your frame. . . .

Today, Lacey wished the life-and-death issues of fit and fabric were all she had to worry about. She finished the article and sent it to Mac's queue.

It'll have to do. So says the maid of honor.

chapter 25

Something landed with a soft thud on Lacey's desk.

"You're welcome," Trujillo said. "This was waiting for you at the guard's desk downstairs. I thought I'd bring it up."

"That's funny — they didn't say anything to me."

"Maybe it just came. And I'm just a pal doing a favor."

She handled the large padded envelope. It was thick, but there was nothing hard inside. Papers? Brochures? Press releases? Some designer's sketches for a spring line? She wasn't expecting anything, but it probably was not a bomb that would blow them all up, she thought, and certainly not body parts. Lacey's name was printed in block letters. There was no return address or name of the sender.

"Did you see who left this?"

"No, it was just sitting there for you. You gonna open it or what?" Trujillo leaned against the corner of her desk and propped one cowboy-booted foot on the Death Chair.

"Why are you so curious?" She leaned back in her chair, holding the package to her chest.

"I'm always available to watch you open your mystery mail, if you'll remember. I hate to point out the obvious, Lois Lane, but trouble follows you around like a lost puppy. I don't see Clark Kent or Superman around here to help you out in a tight spot."

"So, I can depend on Tony Trujillo, Intrepid Police Beat Reporter?"

"Especially if there's story value. It's a slow news day."

"A slow news day and you haven't managed to snag a sugar bomb off your sweet Felicidad? She had mini cupcakes this morning. Yum." Lacey said this just to torment him. "Caramel cake with, what was it—oh, yeah, dulce de leche frosting."

"Dulce de leche? Madre de Dios! Do not mock my love for Felicity's cooking. I get through many a long day here because of Felicidad. Did I miss them? Are they all gone?" He leaned over Felicity's cubicle divider to see if any tempting treats remained on her desk. Empty. Not a crumb. He sat down in the Death Chair, forlorn, leaning his head against its tall back.

Lacey wrinkled her nose. Tony wasn't going to budge, so she picked up her letter opener and slowly and delicately pried loose the sealed end of the package. She peeked inside. There was no note, letter, or papers that she could see. She opened the envelope carefully, just far enough to see a mass of black fabric covered with colorful embroidery. The missing shawl had come to roost. In her cubicle.

Oh. My. God.

She squinted at Tony. "Go away."

"Not on your life."

"This could be delicate."

"And newsworthy?" He leaned forward, trying to see inside the envelope.

Leonardo merely rubbed the thing across his neck and died. Her throat went dry and her heart danced the rumba in her chest.

"Sorry, Tony, I can't open this here." Her face flushed with fear, and she hoped Tony would take it for blushing. "This is for Vic's eyes only, if you know what I mean." She batted her eyelashes, hoping for coquettish.

"Dang, you're blushing? Now I really want to see."

"But you'll be a gentleman and back off. Right?"

He reluctantly took a step backward. "This isn't fair, Brenda Starr. I delivered it to you, I ought to get a peek. What is it, a new silk nightie? Velvet panties? Tell me."

"No! This is not a sexy surprise for Brenda Starr from the island of the black orchids, Tony. This is just—for my eyes only, and Vic's. You're just going to have to use your imagination."

He grinned at her wolfishly, and Lacey wasn't sure she liked it. "All I gotta say, Miss Starr, is that Donovan is a lucky guy."

"Everyone knows that. Wipe that smirk off your face, Tony."

"Can't make me." But he shrugged in surrender and walked away. No cupcakes from Felicity, no peeks from Lacey. *No fair.*

She watched him until he reached the middle of the hall and turned toward the cluster of cubicles where the police beat lived. Finally, she allowed herself to take a deep breath. She picked up the phone and called the guard desk in the front lobby.

"Hi, Lacey Smithsonian up in the newsroom. Did you happen to see who dropped off this package for me? Trujillo brought it up. Plain padded envelope, kind of thick, but soft?"

"Let me think," the guard said. "You know, you're not the only one in this building getting packages." That was true. Even with computers and the Internet, D.C. was still awash in messengered packages of great import. "I gotta look at the log." There was a pause. Lacey tapped her foot on the plastic floor protector covering the sad beige carpeting. A different guard came back on the line.

"Miss Smithsonian? I remember. Some kind of bike messenger dropped it off."

"You get a name of the sender, or a signature?"

"They signed the log. Can't read it. Just a squiggle."

"Description? Male, female, young, old?"

"Hey, bike messenger, you know what they look like. Skinny, youngish, fit-looking, funny helmet, mirrored shades, those funky skintight bike pants and bike gloves, some kind of loud sponsor-logo bike shirt. You know, Coors or Snapple or something. Brought the bike in the lobby, which we don't appreciate, by the way."

"Man or woman?"

A pause. "No idea."

"Thanks." Lacey hung up. *Not exactly a trained observer.* But he was right—the messengers were often pretty sexless in their riding garb.

The glare from the mid-afternoon sun over her desk was blinding. She lowered the shades, and for just a moment she wondered if someone was watching her from the building across the street. The paranoia was taking over, like Kepelov had said.

Who took the shawl, and why? And why send it to me? What's the point?

Lacey still believed that something deadly was attached to the shawl. After all, she'd been to the Spy Museum. It was one of Brooke's favorite places, and she and Lacey had admired the lipstick gun, the Aston Martin from the old James Bond movies, and all manner of spy gear that tickled the imagination. It was the story of the spy who died after being shot with a poison pellet of ricin fired from the tip of an umbrella that Lacey now pondered. She peeked at the shawl inside the manila envelope.

Did someone want her to prick her finger on it and die, or fall into a hundred-year swoon like Sleeping Beauty? Lacey slipped the padded package into a large Tyvek shipping envelope from the supply room and tucked that package into an even larger one. She stuffed it all into the bottom of her tote bag.

It crossed her mind that Olga Kepelova herself might have taken the shawl for safekeeping and told no one, allowing everyone to think it was stolen. Why? So no one would suspect its whereabouts? That sounded a little improbable, but everything about Olga seemed improbable. Was it possible that she'd now sent it to Lacey?

Why, again? She retrieved the card Olga had given her and dialed the number.

"Yes?" the woman said, not hello.

"This is Lacey Smithsonian."

"You have found something out?"

"Not yet," Lacey said carefully. "Did you find the shawl?"

"No. Gregor and Marie have turned the house upside down. The restaurant found nothing. The thief might demand a ransom for it, but nothing. So far."

"Why would someone take it, Olga?"

"Why does anyone take anything? Greed, jealousy, fear, anger."

"Maybe." Lacey had no reason to either trust or distrust Olga Kepelova.

"What do you think happened to it, Lacey Smithsonian?"

"Perhaps someone took the shawl to protect it."

"Protect it?"

"To keep it out of the wrong hands."

"That is very optimistic of you," Olga said.

"That's me, Miss Optimism."

"If someone was protecting it, why have they not returned it?"

"Maybe they will." Lacey touched her tote to make sure it was still there.

"Perhaps. You talked to Gregor?"

"He thinks you're being—overprotective."

"No matter. He will be more cautious now. In any case, the shawl always returns. Eventually." Olga hung up.

What can I make of all that? If she was the one who sent the shawl to Lacey, she didn't tip her hand. Maybe the shawl had nothing to do with Leo's death. For all Lacey knew, someone had scratched his neck with poison *before* the party. His complaint about the shawl biting him might have nothing to do with the garment. Maybe the fabric or the embroidery had irritated the wound. The way a splinter might be irritated. Leonardo had been acting bizarrely from the moment he crashed the party—perhaps the poison was already in his system, and the shawl simply took the fall.

Lacey's phone rang. "Oh, hi, Brooke."

"You didn't forget we're having drinks after work, did you?"

"Completely. It fell out of the black hole I call my brain." Lacey turned her wrist to admire the lovely watch Vic gave her. *The gift of time. Unfortunately, it seemed to be running out.*

"Not surprising, Lacey. Weddings cause stress, and stress does terrible things. Come on, we both need a drink."

"I shouldn't." She needed a break, not a drink. And she had a hot shawl burning a hole in her tote bag. She needed to discuss it with Vic, and possibly Gregor Kepelov. And soon enough, Detective Broadway Lamont. She dreaded the thought of that little interview. *Vic first.* But Vic would be busy until seven.

"Really, one drink? I'm right around the corner," Brooke said, adding a tantalizing bit of information. "I had an interview with Detective Hopkins. And I won't divulge a single detail unless you come meet me."

"You are heartless. I'll be right there."

Her tote tucked carefully under her arm, Lacey checked in with her editor. "I'm leaving, Mac. I've done all the harm I can do for one day. See you at the wedding, with my favorite junior bridesmaids?"

"It's back on now? I can't keep track." Mac's bushy eyebrows were knit closely together. "I haven't said anything to the girls yet. I assumed you'd fix things. No need to get the household in an uproar. They are looking forward to this wedding, cowboy boots and all."

"You assumed I'd be able to fix everything?" She groaned as dramatically as she could.

"Maid of honor, right? Keep me in the loop. You got that, Smithsonian?"

"You bet, Mac."

"I mean everything, Smithsonian. The wedding, the Leonardo murder story, the missing shawl, everything. Especially if it's newsworthy. Say, for instance, that shawl has something to do with the murder? Some kind of fashion crime? I want it. And yes, I am referring to the Killer Shawl story crawling all over the Web."

"I haven't proven anything one way or the other yet, Mac."

"So you have been thinking about it?"

"If there is a story, Mac, a real story, nobody will write it except me. Nobody gets it but *The Eye Street Observer*."

"Fair enough. You're off tomorrow and Friday?"

If I live through it. "Yes." She exhaled loudly and her shoulders drooped.

"You don't have to look so happy about it."

"There's a lot of ground to cover between now and then."

He leaned back in his chair and folded his arms behind his head. "Okay. I'll be herding my little cowgirls to the wedding."

"I forgot to ask, did they get their pink dresses?"

"Did they get pink dresses! They'll be wearing them to church for the rest of the spring and summer. Kim said they have very good taste. All I can tell you is they're very pink."

Lacey beamed. "I bet they're adorable."

"Yeah, apparently good taste plus pink costs a lot of money."

"You're learning, Mac. Well done, Dad."

"Get out of here."

chapter 26

Free at last! Well, not really.

Turtledove sat between Lacey and Brooke at a small table at Teatro Goldoni, an Italian restaurant on K Street, where the gaudy harlequin décor promised a colorful drinking and dining experience, for those lucky people who weren't preoccupied with things, such as sudden random death.

The large bodyguard would have scared any random guys from flirting with the ladies. If random guys in Washington had the inclination to flirt. So many men along the K Street corridor were afraid of sexual harassment accusations, they were physically unable to flirt until they'd had at least two martinis. Lacey was as safe there as she was ever going to be. Her tote bag was securely tucked next to her feet under the table. Still, a quiver of anxiety ran up and down her spine.

Brooke sipped wine while Lacey and Turtledove worked on their (virgin) Bloody Marys. Looking overly serious, Brooke wore one of her tailored and expensive attorney pantsuits. This one was charcoal gray, which she paired with a lighter gray shell and a charcoal scarf.

Rene Thibodeaux had taken a pass on joining them. He'd had enough girl time, according to Turtledove.

"Just pretend I'm one of the gang tonight," Turtledove said to Lacey. "Tell me anything, all your secrets. It's been an illuminating week for me, with all the girly stuff."

"Don't mock the girly stuff," she replied.

"I'm not mocking it, I've had fun. Really." Turtledove was practically irresistible when he smiled. Washington men might not know how to flirt, but that didn't stop Washington women. Every woman in the bar was looking his way.

"In that case . . ." Brooke leaned down and retrieved a large sack. "I need your opinion."

"On what?" Lacey asked.

"I ordered this thing from J. Crew. I didn't want to be spotted pink-dress shopping at Neiman Marcus. Did you know J. Crew has a whole wedding line for brides and bridesmaids? I figured I'd better buy something fast, with Bridezilla on the warpath. It just came today."

She scanned the restaurant as if afraid she'd be recognized, and possibly disbarred. It was not often that Lacey saw Brooke so nervous. She was always in command of the situation, whether it was presenting a contract to a client or combating an adversary in court. She pulled out a rose-colored dress for their inspection.

Lacey told herself to relish the moment. It was rare when she held the apparel approval card over her friend. But Brooke had chosen well, a simple sleeveless dress with a natural waist and a V-neckline trimmed in a wide ruffle. The pink confection was pretty and eminently suitable for a springtime wedding beneath the cherry blossoms.

"It's pretty, Brooke. Perfect."

"It's called azalea." It was a full-bodied pink, close to the color of Lacey's dress.

"It's great," Turtledove said. "I like it."

"You're sure?" Brooke looked doubtful. "It's pinker in person than I expected. Much pinker. Much, much pinker."

"This shade suits your coloring," Lacey said. "Azalea. It would be a nice color to cheer up your suit."

"It is rather pretty," Brooke admitted. "But don't quote me. Do you think Damon will like it?"

"Ask him yourself. He's coming through the door right now," Turtledove said.

"Oh, no," Lacey said. "Speak of the devil."

"Don't worry," Brooke said. "He's here to see me, not you."

"Good, because I don't know anything else about the shawl, or its murderous intentions," Lacey said, loud enough for Damon to hear. It was a fib, but one she felt she was committing for the greater good.

"Then it's still missing in action, I guess." Damon pulled up a chair next to Brooke and kissed her cheek. "Hey, T-Dove." He punched Turtledove playfully on the arm.

"Could be anywhere," Lacey said. "Even right under our noses. You heard anything?"

"'Fraid not. But if I do, you'll read it on Conspiracy Clearinghouse first."

"Second," Lacey said. "Right after you read it in *The Eye Street Observer*."

"Any more deaths? Attempts on the lives of the wedding party?" he asked cheerily.

"At the moment, Damon, we're more concerned with what the wedding party is wearing. What do you think of my dress?" Brooke asked, holding it up again.

Damon leaned back to get the full effect, peering over his tiny black-framed glasses. "Wow! It's so—pink! And luscious. Oh, and the dress is nice too."

"Silly boy." Brooke leaned in for a quick kiss.

"You have a bodyguard on board, Lacey?" Damon noted. "What's up? You're in danger? Again? What's the story?"

"None of your business, newsboy. And you are under a gag order not to disclose any information about me," Lacey said. Damon looked at Turtledove.

"I gotta say no comment," Turtledove said. Damon looked pleadingly to Brooke.

"So sorry, Damon, I promised Lacey no news until after the wedding."

"Besides, it's in bad taste to be overly interested in my possible demise," Lacey said, sipping her non-Bloody Mary.

"There'd better be a wedding," Brooke said. "I broke down and went against all my principles of proper attorney apparel and bought a pink dress. If there is no wedding, it will hang in my closet forever. A big pink indictment of my folly."

"May I quote you now?" Lacey asked.

"No."

"You are going to look adorable, Counselor," Damon declared to Brooke. He was in his usual full cyber-beatnik mode, black pants, black shirt, black jacket, black high-top sneakers, shaggy dark hair, and carefully clipped short black beard. His square black-rimmed glasses made him look like the hippest dude in the record store, but Lacey thought he still looked like a college kid with a fake ID, trying to hang with the grown-ups. Together, as a couple, Damon and Brooke looked like somber emissaries from the Dark Side.

"What do you think, Lacey? Will this wedding happen or not?" Brooke asked.

"Who knows?" Lacey said. "Stella's got a date with Nigel tonight."

"Thank God. I'd hate to think I glued all those rhinestones in vain."

"Not to mention the epic battle," Lacey said.

"What battle?" Damon asked.

"Sources say it was a pink rhinestone fight. Would you care to elaborate, Brooke?" Lacey teased. "Inquiring minds want to know."

Brooke gave Lacey a look of exasperation. "Things got a little crazy, as you might expect when you send someone like me to help with a"—she shuddered delicately—"*crafts* project with a deranged bride-to-be." Brooke studied her menu casually. "That's all."

"Stella said there were rhinestones everywhere and she had glue in her hair," Lacey told Damon.

"*Her* hair?! She dumped an entire box of pink rhine-stones in *my* hair!" Brooke squealed. "I was still comb-ing them out this morning. I found rhinestones in my ears. Hot-glue guns are a double-edged sword, you know. You have to expect retaliation when you attack someone with rhinestones and glue."

"I'm sure it's a sparkling new look for you, Brooke," Lacey said. Turtledove and Damon snickered behind their drinks.

"Move along, people," Brooke said huffily. "Nothing more to see here."

Lacey remembered why she agreed to meet for drinks in the first place. "Brooke, you met with Detective Hop-kins today."

Brooke smiled, back on her own turf. "Why, yes, I did. Homicide Detective Donald Hopkins, known as Don. We had quite a chat. Nice guy, for a cop. Could be smarter, but then he might not be a cop."

"What does he think?" Damon pulled out his iPad to take notes.

"He doesn't think the shawl killed Leonardo," Brooke said.

"Does he have a theory?" Lacey asked.

"First he had to do the big-tough-detective routine and impress me with his hard-ass attitude. Been there, seen that. He's got his own theory and it's not the shawl. He's looking at Leonardo's housemate, one Kevin Early, and also your pal Miguel Flores."

"Romantic entanglement?" Damon asked.

"He's calling it a domestic situation. He said it's al-most always the spouse. Or pseudo spouse. Or ex-boyfriend."

"But there was no romantic relationship with Kevin, according to Miguel," Lacey said. "Although Kevin wanted one. But Leonardo spurned him. The relation-ship, I'm afraid, was with Miguel. And it ended badly."

"Spurned and scorned, always a motive," Turtledove said.

"But it doesn't explain how the shawl fits in," Brooke said. "How could the shawl come in contact with this Kevin Early person?"

"It didn't. The shawl is not alive," Lacey pointed out. "It doesn't roam the streets seeking prey. And, according to my sources, clothes don't appear to make good vectors for spirits or hauntings. No matter what *you* say, Damon."

Lacey was uneasy talking about the thing while it was lying concealed in her tote bag at her feet. *Good shawl. Go to sleep. Just be quiet down there.*

"So say you," Damon said.

"New subject," Lacey announced. "What's Detective Hopkins like?"

"He's a little bantam rooster to Broadway Lamont's big bull in a china shop." Brooke ran her fingers through her hair, untangling a knot. Perhaps a stray rhinestone. "Short, wiry. Balding. Standard-issue khakis, green shirt, blue tie, Brooks Brothers navy blazer. You do want to know what he wore, right?"

"So he blends in with your average Hill worker, or at least the average EPA staffer," Lacey said.

"You got it. He looked like a greenie." Brooke liked to call employees of the Environmental Protection Agency "the greenies," because so many of them wore green shirts or ties, as if visually embodying the agency's green mission.

Lacey was better at decoding women's clothes than men's. Men so often dressed exactly the same, whether they were pen pushers, bill collectors, cops, or congressmen. And very often, women were involved, for good or ill, in a man's choice of pants, shirts, ties, suits, even his casual wear. Take Mac. Lacey often wondered why Kim allowed him to go to work in his shabby corduroy pants and frayed plaid shirts, when she clearly had such good taste in her own wardrobe. Was she irritated with him, had she given up on changing him, or did he simply insist on comfort over style? Or did she think he was cute that way? It was a mystery.

"His wife probably bought him the jacket," Lacey said. "What did you tell him? That the infamous Killer Shawl was responsible for Leonardo's death?"

"Give me some credit. Hopkins cleverly made a pre-emptive strike. Warned me not to mention the shawl, because he read all about it on Damon's site." Brooke smiled at Damon and patted his knee. "He said he wasn't in the mood for comedy when he was investigating a murder. Well, when someone rolls out his idiot game plan for you like that, you have to respect his limited horizons. So I didn't mention the fact that we don't know who or what might be out there, shawls included, and that murder doesn't necessarily follow a detective's neat little script."

"My favorite kind of bureaucrat," Damon said. He was no doubt contemplating how to make Hopkins look like a fool, at least to his readers on Conspiracy Clearinghouse. "What about the poison? Have they identified it yet?"

Lacey didn't mention the nicotine. She'd given that tidbit to Tony for *The Eye*'s news story.

"No, but Hopkins said poison is personal and intimate, typically a woman's method," Brooke said. Turtledove and Damon nodded in agreement. "But that doesn't explain the speeding limo that tried to run you over, does it? That was pretty personal, but not intimate or typically female."

"No," Lacey agreed. "It doesn't explain anything."

Or why someone tampered with Vic's brakes. How many killers do we have out there? Lacey tapped her tote bag with one foot, to reassure herself that the shawl was still under her control.

For the moment.

"Lacey. Lacey Smithsonian!" A man on the sidewalk yelled at her as she and Turtledove exited the restaurant. "I have to talk to you!"

She spun around. As she turned, Turtledove grabbed

hold of the man before he could reach her. He was dwarfed by the big bodyguard.

"Do you know this gentleman?" Turtledove asked, lifting and shaking the man gently, like a cheap suit on a rack.

She stared at the stranger. He seemed disheveled and his clothes—standard D.C. fare of khaki slacks, white shirt, blue blazer—looked slept-in. His pale blue eyes were red rimmed.

"I'm Kevin!" he yelled. "Kevin Early."

Realization dawned on her. "Wait a minute. Leonardo's roommate Kevin?"

"That's me." He nodded furiously.

"That explains your haircut," she said. It was similar to Leonardo's blond Caesar cut. Kevin was a little pudgy, but not quite the hot mess that Miguel had described. People were starting to stare. "Let him go, Turtledove. Gently, please."

Turtledove glowered at Kevin and set him on his feet, gently. The smaller man took a step backward.

"I like this haircut," Kevin said, smoothing it down. "Leonardo cut it for me."

"Are you stalking me?" she inquired.

"No! I just wanted to talk with you. You weren't at your office."

"Why?"

"Because I want—well—you have to find out who killed Leonardo."

Lacey stood still. "I do?"

Kevin rubbed his hands as if he were freezing. Or pleading. "You proved Leonardo was innocent of murder last year."

"I didn't do it for him." Last year! It seemed so long ago now. Just the year before, in April, Lacey had been dragged into her involvement with murder and its aftermath. It was never intentional. But Lacey was tired of being involved with death. She simply wanted to get through the wedding alive.

"That doesn't matter," Kevin said. "You saved Leonardo and his reputation."

"You told the police Miguel did it? You know Miguel's not a killer."

They were discussing murder a little too loudly on the crowded sidewalk. Lacey ducked into a quiet entryway to dodge the crush of workers leaving their jobs in the afternoon exodus. Kevin and Turtledove followed.

"I never did that!" Kevin ran his hands through his hair, mussing up his Caesar cut à la Leonardo. "Don't you know that whenever there's an unsolved crime involving gays, the cops automatically suspect the rainbow community first? We're all guilty until proven innocent."

"Man's right about that," Turtledove said. "Cops always look close to home first. Usually the right place to look."

"Leonardo hated Miguel. And me," Lacey said.

"But in a good way!" Kevin said. Lacey snorted. "Listen, Leonardo hated everybody. He hated me too, but he was grateful to you. He told me, but he didn't want you to know it. You found the killer of that Angie Woods girl and cleared his name. He was terrified of going to jail. I mean, notwithstanding all the shower jokes, prison was Leonardo's worst fear. You saved his ass."

"I'm sorry he's dead," Lacey said. She was sorry about the whole damn mess. She was sorry for everyone's faith in her.

"Then you'll do something?"

Lacey planned to deal with the shawl, somehow, and very soon, but she hadn't considered the ripple of after-effects on Leonardo's entire circle. "What do you want me to do?"

"Whatever it is you do, that voodoo you do, that's what Leonardo always called it. He may have called you a bitch because you wouldn't let him touch your precious locks, but I know he also thought you were really clever."

"Gee, thanks." *I love backhanded compliments.*

"You know what I mean," Kevin said.

"Why did he crash Stella's party? To make a scene? To embarrass everyone?"

Kevin looked around nervously. "The thing about Leonardo is he kind of hated the world, and envied everyone for everything, but he really believed everyone liked him. He wanted to believe that, anyway. And it hurt him to be disliked, even though he could be such a jerk. Yeah, I know, crazy, makes no sense. It was like he was eight years old sometimes. Stella was sort of his mentor early on, and he was so hurt that he wasn't included in her party. I guess he wanted to surprise her, and probably he wanted to see Miguel again. I knew that would go nowhere. They were so over."

"You're a suspect," Lacey reminded him.

"Yes, I'm a suspect, like Leonardo was and Miguel is, an *innocent* suspect. That's why you have to find out who really did it."

"All I can do is ask questions and see where they lead. And I can't do a lot of that until Stella's wedding is over. I'll do what I can." She nodded to Turtledove and they pushed on, leaving Kevin behind on the bustling sidewalk.

"Okay, Lacey," he called after her plaintively. "I'm counting on you."

Walking swiftly to Turtledove's car, she asked, "What do you think, Turtledove? Is he the type to kill Leonardo?"

"There's no type for murder, Lacey. Anyone can do it. Even him."

Lacey Smithsonian's

Fashion Bites

The Bride's White Satin Rule: Dress Your Attendants As You Would Have Them Dress You!

A wedding is more than the organdy, chiffon, satin, silk, and lace worn by the bride.

Yes, she will always be the center of attention, however, she should give a thought to those standing up with her. Bridesmaids are not mere clowns and puppets (even when they act that way), and they do not deserve public humiliation through their bridal attire. Unfortunately, for some brides that's a tempting bonus. That's why there are rules.

Therefore, let us establish a rule, not unlike the Golden Rule. We'll call it the White Satin Rule for Brides: *Dress Others as You Would Have Them Dress You.*

Bridesmaids *may* not want to don that hoop skirt and those Scarlett O'Hara curtains. They *might* not desire to be on display in skintight sheaths or fluffy gowns that point out their particular figure flaws. Put yourself in their place. Would you wear that dress? Without irony? Without blaming the bride forever after?

If the bridesmaids' dresses are too hideous, they will become the focus of attention, not you. They'll be all the guests will talk about. Behind your back, of course. Instant karma, as they say.

You can wield your power as a bride with grace, not greed. Your wedding is not a race to force your friends to spend as much money as possible. Bankrupting your BFFs in pursuit of your perfect day, adding up the dress, the shoes, the shower and wedding presents, and the tickets to an exotic location, will simply breed resentment. Unless you're all millionaires or TFBs (Trust Fund Babies). If you make her wear a potato sack, a dress with flying buttresses, a bustle in a hue that turns her skin green, or a garish flower-patterned, puff-sleeved monstrosity, can you imagine what she'll make *you* wear someday? Not a pretty picture, is it?

News Flash: Bridesmaids' dresses do not have to be hideous and eye-poppingly hilarious. If your maid of honor is your friend, must you abuse her in puce? A considerate bride will often let her bridesmaids select their own dresses in an approved color palette and length—for instance, all tea-length gowns in pale yellow, or all cocktail-length in peacock blue. Your bridesmaid can choose the style and cut most flattering to her and still fit into your visual theme. She will be thankful and praise you, O Happy Bride, not curse your memory.

Brides, be kind, even to your third step-cousin twice removed who was foisted on you as a sop to fractured family relationships. You might have to be her bridesmaid one day. Remember, she who marries last has the last laugh, as well as the most time to plot revenge.

If you ignore your bridesmaids' wishes, there will a come a day when your unhappy friend is the bride and the omnipotent ruler of her own wedding day, and you will surely suffer retribution.

Turnabout is fair play in the world of the Bride's White Satin Rule.

chapter 27

Gregor Kepelov once told Lacey that a mystery was like a set of *matryoshkas*, the famous Russian nesting dolls. Open one up and inside you'll find another, smaller doll. Open that one and you discover yet another doll, and so on, until finally you reach the tiniest doll of all. It might resemble the original elaborately decorated doll, but it would not be an exact duplicate. It might be very different from what you expected. But it was the kernel, the beginning and end point of the set. You never knew how many dolls you might have to open to solve the mystery.

How many dolls to go?

Several dolls had been opened, but no one was any closer to an answer. Was Leonardo the target of a killer, or an unfortunate bystander? Who wanted to kill the bride and groom and maid of honor, and why? What happened to Vic's brakes? The Russian shawl might have been a witness or an accessory to these crimes, but Lacey wondered whether it could tell her anything at all.

Turtledove, staunch and silent, drove her to Vic's office after their drinks with Damon and Brooke and their encounter with Kevin. She pushed everyone out of her thoughts and concentrated on the "material witness" in this crime.

Lacey didn't believe in clothing that was haunted, but there was an order and synchronicity to the universe, and she was beginning to wonder what New Orleans and

Rene Thibodeaux had to do with the things that were
happening. Why was he in D.C. right now? No such thing
as a coincidence, Vic often said, and Brooke too. Lacey
just didn't know how Rene fit in. Turtledove might know.

"Who is Rene Thibodeaux? Is he really here to look
for a woman?" she asked, breaking the companionable
silence. "Or something else?"

"Rene is a simple man, Lacey," Turtledove said.
"Keeps to himself. Works hard. Tight with his money. He
doesn't always make a dollar the usual way. Not that it's
illegal, necessarily, but maybe a little under-the-table."

Living on the edges of society? What did he find there?

Turtledove turned onto the Key Bridge linking
Georgetown with Arlington, Virginia. Gray clouds over
the Potomac held rain and the trees on Roosevelt Island
were getting fuller and greener every day. Rowers on the
river were making their way back to the boathouse.

"He trusts you," she said.

"We're old friends. Went to the same schools. I'll say
one thing—Rene doesn't have the mind-set for subter-
fuge," Turtledove said. "It took a lot of courage for him
to come up here. I don't doubt there's a woman who took
him for a ride, but I don't know if we'll ever find her."

"Rene's not telling you everything, is he?"

"Not yet. And maybe he never will," Turtledove said.
"Too proud to tell it all, every last humiliation. Not even
to me. And I don't want to take what's left of his money
if I can't help find this Leah for him."

"I know." A few drops of rain hit the windshield. "By
the way, thank you for protecting me. I know Vic hired
you to, and I was snarky about it, but I feel safer with you
around."

"It's a privilege. Besides, I want to know about the
shawl too. I believe in mystery. I believe you have a gift.
Way more fun than my usual clients."

Lightning strikes appeared in the sky to the west and
the clouds spilled the rain that had been threatening all
day. It gushed down, releasing the pent-up pressure in

the air, and Lacey wished it would release the tension she felt.

"If I find out anything you'll know as soon as I can tell you, Turtledove. Promise."

"Hi, Lacey, want to marry me?"

Vic greeted her at the lobby door of the steel-and-glass office building in Rosslyn where Vic and his dad, Sean Daniel Donovan, ran their security company. His low, soothing voice did something lovely to her spine. Lacey turned and waved to Turtledove that he was off duty. He waved back and pulled out of the lot.

"Yes, Vic, I want to marry you, but not right this minute." She held on to him and kissed him. Her heart beat faster because of him, and it felt good. In his arms, she realized how fatigued she was and how much she wanted to let him take over the mystery for a while.

"My evening is yours. What do you want to do?"

"Play detective." She nuzzled his ear.

"Not again!" He groaned, but it was a happy groan. "It's not as much fun as playing doctor."

"Later, darling. Let's go upstairs. I have a surprise. Unfortunately, we have to ask Kepelov to join us."

"Gregor Kepelov? That doesn't sound like fun at all."

"I know he's not your very favorite person. Nor mine. And you should meet his sister, Olga. However, this is important." She handed him the tote as they headed toward the elevator. "Top secret."

Lacey pulled out her phone and called Marie at The Little Shop of Horus. Kepelov answered. "Gregor, where is Marie?"

"Not feeling good. Tired out by police," he answered. "I am closing up the shop."

Lacey hoped there hadn't been another fainting spell. "I wouldn't ask this of you if it weren't important, Gregor, but can you come to Vic's office right now?"

"How important?"

"I have the—the thing that was missing."

"What?" Kepelov and Vic both exclaimed at the same time.

"I don't want to say much on the phone. It was delivered to my office."

"I will bring Marie."

"Of course."

"Ten minutes."

"It takes at least twenty minutes," Lacey corrected. He clicked off.

Vic stood waiting, quizzical eyebrows in place. "Lacey, I hate to be Desi Arnaz, but you've got some 'splaining to do."

"Can we do it over a fresh pot of coffee? Suddenly I'm not wired enough."

The elevator took them high into the sky and Vic led the way to the office's small kitchen, which gave Lacey a chance to look around. Although she had met him there a couple of times, she'd never had an official tour of the premises. Vic's suite of offices in one of the Rosslyn high-rises had fabulous views to the north and east. She could see the Washington Monument looming over the Mall through the rain. The rest of the suite looked suitably neutral and corporate, but this window on the Capital City across the river made up for the bland décor.

With their coffee, Vic guided her to the conference room, where she could see the rooftops of Georgetown and the spires of Georgetown University. The lights of Key Bridge were lovely, especially because she wasn't caught up in the traffic jam. The wind had picked up, and the trees far below looked like they were dancing. The storm had waited till most of the rush-hour traffic was over, but cars were still bumper to bumper, their headlights glittering in the beating rain. It felt good to be inside where she could see the amazing light show of lightning strikes on the river, and not out in the deluge. Lacey sat down in one of the oversized leather chairs and spun it until she was looking out the windows. Vic placed her tote bag on the long conference table.

"I hope this downpour leaves some cherry blossoms," she said. "For the wedding."

"At any rate, it's out of your hands. And the wedding too." He put his hands on her shoulders. "Lacey Smithsonian is not personally responsible for Mother Nature. Or for Stella, who is just as much a force of nature."

"Thank you, dear," she said. "I seem to be responsible for everything else. This maid-of-honor business is a tough gig."

"Stop worrying. By now, Nigel should have given Stella her flowers and whisked her off to the chocolate orgy of her dreams. The rest is up to them. And hormones." He turned away from the storm and hefted the tote bag. "Now, about the shawl? This is really Marie's famous Russian shawl? The haunted Killer Shawl?"

"Not you too! Reading my competition, Vic? Wait, Damon's not my competition. Let's postpone the interrogation until Kepelov gets here."

He crouched down next to her and whispered in her ear. "Okay, but I reserve the right to put you in the interrogation room with a bare lightbulb if I don't get everything I want."

She kissed him. "Yes, dear. And how was your day?"

"Ran a background check on Bryan Culpeper," Vic said. "I didn't care for the way he was talking last night."

"Good. Me neither."

"Something's not right with him, darlin'. It figures Culpeper's a friend of Nigel's." He stood up and stretched, gazing out the window. It was growing dark, and the rain created halos around the lights below.

"But you were at prep school with Nigel. You didn't know Bryan?"

Vic grimaced. He hated to be reminded of sharing a past with Nigel Griffin.

"Sweetheart, Nigel took a world tour of prep schools. Some here, some in England. St. Albans, my old school, was just one of them. And I was only there for a year. I was on my own tour. You know I'm not a fan of Griffin's.

But a man should be able to get married without dead bodies blocking his way. And with a best man who's not a saboteur."

"He did spy with Nigel on the bachelorette party, but do you think Bryan is capable of more?"

"Murdering a random gate-crasher is pretty extreme, and he wasn't at the party," Vic said, "but you never know."

"What did you find out?"

"Culpeper works at some lobbying outfit on K Street where he's a flack. His hobby seems to be flouting traffic laws. He's got a boatload of parking violations, he's been booted twice, DUIs, speeding tickets. And he was arrested for vehicle theft. No charges filed."

"He stole a car? Wouldn't be a black limousine, would it?"

"No details, and it was a few years ago. At the very least, he doesn't think the rules apply to him."

"Anything else?"

"Nothing violent, outside of drunk and disorderly."

Vic was interrupted by a call from the downstairs desk announcing the arrival of Gregor Kepelov and Marie Largesse. He escorted them up to the conference room. The visitors shook off their wet raincoats, and they seemed excited and happy. Marie looked anything but ill. Her eyes were shining. Kepelov obviously had told her the shawl had been recovered.

"I do love a thunderstorm," she said.

"Gregor said you were ill." Lacey took her coat.

"Oh, yes, I always get a little queasy before a big storm. The air pressure gives me a terrible headache, but once the rains pour down, I feel so relieved." She sighed with pleasure. "I smell something delicious."

"Care for coffee?" Lacey headed toward the aroma and Marie followed. "I was worried that you might have fainted."

"No, no, cher, nothing like that, but thank you for your concern. I am trying to learn to let the visions come and just wash over me without giving in to the panic. Olga is teaching me some breathing exercises and focusing through the darkness," Marie confided. She sat down, breathed deeply, and closed her eyes, gesturing with her arms.

"Does it work?"

"Can't hurt. I'm hopeful. And thank you, Lacey, for shaking Stella out of the glooms."

"You heard from her?" She handed one of the cups to Marie and poured.

"Did I ever! She seemed practically her old self. Bubbly and bouncy and looking forward to seeing Nigel." Marie dumped in sugar and creamer.

"Do you have any predictions for her?"

"Just the one I've always made. A beautiful wedding."

Lighting struck and thunder cracked, as if to defy Marie's prediction. They both turned toward the light show outside.

"What about the pink petals? This storm is going to wash most of them right off the cherry trees." Lacey strolled back to the conference room and gazed out the window.

"Don't you worry about that. There'll be enough left for a wedding."

"Yes, enough for a wedding." Kepelov was behind them. "Enough coffee talk. You have the shawl?"

From his jacket pocket Kepelov pulled heavy leather gloves and a magnifying glass. Lacey carefully extracted the big envelope from her tote. Vic noted the white Tyvek wrapping with a raised eyebrow.

"Taking precautions, I see."

"Precautions are good," Kepelov said. "Be bold always, but careful."

"You have a plan, Kepelov?" Vic asked.

"To conduct a very careful examination. Bold, and careful." He sliced open the end of the Tyvek envelope and smiled when he found the second Tyvek envelope covering the original padded envelope. "How did the shawl come to you?"

"It was dropped off by a bike messenger at my office today. Typical messenger outfit, according to the not-very-observant guard who accepted the package. He couldn't even tell me if it was a man or a woman. I'm guessing it was an actual messenger, but there's no way to tell who it was or who sent it. No name, of course, and no return address."

"I can't believe we'll have our beautiful shawl back," Marie said.

"We make sure it is safe, my love," Kepelov said. "And we must know how the young gate-crasher was killed."

"What if it was sent by someone who accidentally took it from the party?" Lacey looked at Vic. She knew she was grasping at straws, trying to make the shawl's arrival seem less ominous. "Maybe it fell in someone's bag in all the confusion after Leonardo left? She found it later, embarrassed, and sent it to me anonymously? Although why to me and not to Marie, I have no idea." She thought about Rosalie with her degree in chemistry and her dislike of Stella. Could this be her doing?

"A little complicated, Smithsonian," Kepelov said. "The accidental taking, the embarrassment, the anonymous return? Occam's razor says more likely a thief. But why the return?" He shook his head, puzzled.

Vic, who pulled on thick rubber gloves of his own, carefully withdrew the beautiful shawl and spread it out on the conference table, after covering the table with a large sheet of white paper. He brought bright work lights to illuminate it. The shawl was even larger than Lacey remembered, jet-black with an explosion of embroidered colors, pictures and symbols and ornaments that somehow fit together beautifully. Gold metallic and multicolored silk threads created raised patterns in the wool. It took her breath away.

"I suppose it's crazy to think that something like a poison pellet or needle could have been inserted in it somehow," Lacey said. "Like in an umbrella."

"Ah, yes, old KGB umbrella trick," Kepelov said.

"You do your homework, Lacey Smithsonian. That was a good piece of tradecraft with the ricin. And a poison needle is not so crazy. Now we look for needle in haystack. In this case, shawl is haystack."

Kepelov bent over the table and examined both sides of the cloth closely under his glass, as Marie and Lacey and Vic watched. After the first pass he pulled an ultraviolet forensic flashlight from his jacket pocket and asked Vic to turn off the lights. He repeated his examination with the black light, turning the fabric in every direction to inspect every thread. Finally Kepelov straightened up.

"Someone is having their little joke with us," he said. "Nothing here. No pellet, no needle, no poison, no nothing. Wait, I see a slight tear, couple of pulled threads, maybe recent, so perhaps something was hooked there. Gone now, whatever it was. The shawl is safe to handle. This is good, but now we know nothing."

"Where would the rip be if it were folded, the way it was when Leonardo grabbed it and danced with it?" Lacey asked. Marie took it and folded it the way she was wearing it that night.

"Right there," Kepelov said, pointing to the tiny flaw in the fabric where it would have rubbed Leonardo's neck.

"Then it's possible that something in the shawl scratched him," Lacey said. "Just the way he said it did."

"But why all this?" Vic said. "Why steal it and then return it to Lacey? Kepelov, any theories?" The Russian shook his head. "Lacey. You have any clue, darling?"

Lacey spread the shawl out on the table again and leaned down to stare at it. "Could you all give me a moment alone with the shawl? Don't go far away, just a little space, please."

Marie put her hands up like a referee. "If Lacey thinks there is some message for her to read, let us give her some *space*. Back off, boys."

"There. The boss has spoken," Kepelov said with a wink. "Take all the moments you want, Smithsonian."

Vic kissed her forehead. "Take your time. Call when you need us. Do do that voodoo that you do so well." She stared at it. "Darlin', is it hypnotizing you?"

"I'm still thinking," Lacey said. "Go away. Please."

"You think. I need more coffee." Kepelov looked around the conference room.

"Through there. We can put on a fresh pot." Vic motioned to the kitchen, reluctant to stray too far from Lacey's side. "Make it two."

"Make it three." Lacey touched the shawl with her fingertips. It was mysterious. A little intimidating.

"Four's a party," Marie said.

Gregor returned presently with a tray and a glass pot of fresh coffee, sugar, creamer, and nondairy sweetener. He refilled all their cups at a credenza well away from the shawl. "She is still communing with the shawl, our genius with the EFP?"

"When was the last time someone added to the embroidery, Gregor?" Everyone stared at Lacey. "I'm talking about the pictures, not the flowers and so on. I mean the illustrated history of the Kepelovs."

Gregor scratched his bald head. "I could ask Olga. Though she has never sewn a stitch herself, she might know. Perhaps my mother, adding a symbol for each child born. You will find our initials, somewhere, if you hunt for them. In Cyrillic, of course."

"What's tickling your brain, Lacey?" Marie asked.

"This." She pointed to a small group of threads, part of what looked like an unfinished drawing of—something. It was hard for Lacey to say of what. "This gold thread looks recent. It's brighter and shinier. And this red thread over here. Other colors too. All these bits are brighter, newer-looking, maybe even some kind of polyester. They have that look of polyester thread. Not the old silk thread used almost everywhere else in this thing. But these bits don't make a picture, not to me. Does this mean anything to you, Gregor?"

Lacey pointed and Kepelov followed her finger.

"Nothing to me. Perhaps someone started a little picture, didn't finish it."

"Maybe it's a mistake," Vic offered.

"This shawl doesn't have mistakes, honey," Lacey said. "It's a family artifact. Every stitch means something. Right, Gregor? And there's only so much room left. You wouldn't start a new story and then stop. You'd have it all worked out, every stitch, probably on pattern paper, before you put needle and thread to the shawl. And the more I look at it, I can tell that even the more primitive stitches, from long ago, from the women in the family whose fingers *weren't* kissed by angels—they all have meaning. They all tell a story, even if we don't know all the connections. But these—" She pointed out more disconnected stitch lines of newer-looking thread, in several more places. "What if—" She didn't finish the thought.

"What?" Kepelov said.

"Don't stop her," Marie cautioned the others. "She's listening to the shawl."

Lacey took one corner of the shawl and folded it. "Could the lines of new thread match up somehow?"

Marie and Vic were watching quietly, but Kepelov jumped to his feet. "Smithsonian, this is good! Good stuff. You think there is a new meaning in the new lines?"

Lacey shrugged. She took the opposite corner of the garment and pulled it in, made another experimental fold. "Not yet."

"You think there's some weird message in it?" Vic asked.

"A cryptogram in cloth." Kepelov clapped his hands together.

"We just don't know what the message is," Lacey said.

Not yet, she thought. *But any message someone can write—or stitch—someone else can learn to read.*

chapter 28

Puzzles.

Lacey didn't know what made her think of those old-fashioned paper finger puzzles children played with, but it was an image that wouldn't let go of her. *Fold it this way, open it that way, and inside . . .* She folded the shawl looking for a way to connect the disconnected lines of new stitches. *What are those things called?*

"I never was any good at puzzles," she said, baffled.

"Not true, Smithsonian," Kepelov said. "You are doing good."

"Darling, you may have exhausted the possibilities of the shawl," Vic said.

"Do not interrupt our Smithsonian," Kepelov scolded. "Something is telling her to look again, look a different way. ExtraFashionary Perception."

"Do you see what she's talking about?" Vic asked him.

"No, but I do not have the EFP," the ex-KGB spy said.

"Please stop with the EFP nonsense," Lacey said.

"That means quiet," Marie said.

"Marie, do you know how to fold one of those children's finger puzzles? The ones that open and close when you put them on your fingertips, like this? They have colors and numbers, and then you open up little squares, like so?" Lacey made the motions with her fingers, as best she remembered them. The men stared, obviously not understanding a word she was saying.

Marie's eyes lit up. "I believe I do, cher. And here's something you'll like. Do you know what that little paper puzzle is called?"

"No. I was never any good at that paper-folding stuff. I never made one, but I remember seeing them. How do you fold one, and how does it work?"

"It's called a *fortune-teller*," the fortune-teller said. Lacey's mouth fell open. "Some folks back home in New Orleans, they call it a *cootie catcher*, but we called it a fortune-teller. It's a children's game. I bet they have them in Russia too. Sort of an origami thing, but they're easy to make. Is that what you meant, cher?"

"Yes! An origami fortune-teller! Can you show me how to fold one? Vic, can we use some paper, please?"

Vic pulled some letter-sized sheets from the copier. Marie took one, deftly folded it into a square, and cut off the excess with Vic's scissors. She folded and creased the square again and again until it opened up into a palm-sized object, rather like a little four-cornered crown, which she slipped over her two thumbs and fingertips.

"Like this. See? You either color these little squares or draw symbols on them, like, say, crystal balls and tarot cards or eyes of Horus, or whatever you like, and you write numbers or letters on the other squares."

"Show us, please." Kepelov crowded in to see.

Marie gave him the puzzle, which he turned over and over. "When you open the inside triangles, you have little fortune-telling sayings written on them. Like *yes*, *no*, *maybe*, *the future looks bright*, *the future is cloudy*. Or *You will meet a beautiful stranger*, or *You have a secret admirer*, *You will be rich and famous*, *You will marry a handsome fool*. Silly things, just for fun. The other child chooses a symbol and a number, which you unfold to find their fortune. And you charge them a nickel." She laughed. "Not real fortunes, you know, just pretend fortunes." She handed it to Lacey.

"Thank you, Marie. Shall we try it with the shawl?"

Marie nodded. Vic took the paper puzzle from Kepelov. "Lacey, I haven't got a clue in the world how this works."

"I know this looks crazy, but it's my last idea. Then I'll stop and you can try something else. Ready, Marie? Show me where to make the folds."

"Ready, cher." Marie stood on one side of the table and Lacey on the other, hovering over the magnificent garment.

Lacey carefully refolded the shawl, with Marie directing. First the corners, in and out and over and under, the way Marie had just done with the sheet of paper. The shawl wasn't as stiff as the paper, so it wouldn't stand up, but it was nearly square, so Lacey was able to re-create roughly the same set of squares and triangles as in Marie's folded paper fortune-teller.

There were a couple dozen of the broken, abstract-looking stitch lines of bright gold and red thread. With the shawl spread out flat, they formed no discernible pattern and were barely noticeable. But with the shawl folded, they joined together to reveal—shapes?

Pictures, or diagrams?

Lacey grabbed the magnifying glass and leaned in close. It took her a moment to put the lines together. Both men crowded in, fascinated.

"It can't be that." She put her hand over her mouth. "Not that."

"Can't be what?" Vic was at Lacey's side, his hand on her shoulder.

"Talk, Smithsonian," Kepelov said, staring at the shawl.

Lacey barely whispered. "The riverboat." She didn't look up.

Marie touched her fingers to the edge of the fabric and closed her eyes. "New Orleans. Yes." She started to sway, as if she were about to faint.

Kepelov helped Marie into a chair. "Just breathe, my darling. What is going on?" Marie was glassy-eyed, but awake. He held her hand and crouched down next to her. Lacey and Vic went to her other side.

"Marie, are you all right?" Lacey hovered over her.

"She is seeing something, somewhere else," Kepelov said. "Don't be afraid, Marie. I am here with you." He held her close, but spoke to Lacey. "You saw something in the shawl, Smithsonian. Tell me." His blue-eyed stare seemed to pierce her.

"New Orleans," Lacey repeated. "Marie is right. But I'm not sure what it has to do with anything. How could it?"

"You're the only one who can be sure, sweetheart," Vic said. "Show us."

"Whoever stitched this is no expert with a needle and thread. So you have to use a little imagination." She handed him the magnifying glass and pointed to the way the stitching joined together at the puzzle folds. "This seems to be a riverboat. See it? See the paddles? And the water? Blue thread for water, see the waves? And there's a stick figure falling from the boat into the water. It's a little abstract. Like that universal symbol for women on ladies' room doors."

"Okay, wait, I see the riverboat," Vic said. "And the figure. Weird."

Lacey traced the thread to the next picture, across another fold. "But here's another boat, next to the stick figure in the water. Might be pulling her aboard? Another touch of blue for water. And that bit of red thread might mean blood, indicating the figure was injured." She felt shaken and faced Vic. "You don't think she's alive, do you?"

"Lacey. If you're talking about Natalija Krumina, she's dead," Vic said. "We saw her go under the water. In the Mississippi. She never came up again."

"Natalija Krumina, that crazy woman?" Kepelov said. "She died in the water. A just end for her."

"But what if? Natalija tried to kill me. And remember, she used poison to kill my friend Magda, but Natalija didn't just use poison. She also used a gun and a knife." Lacey rubbed her eyes and blinked. "Now, there's more tiny needle-and-thread work over here." She stooped over the shawl again. "Maybe I'm crazy, but does this look like a death's head and five strokes? As if someone's counting by fives: four vertical strokes and one stroke diagonally across. Wait, plus one more line, to make six."

Vic studied the shawl intently. "I'll be darned."

"There were five of us in New Orleans," Kepelov said.

"There are six lines, if you count Marie," Lacey said. "You gave Marie the shawl and someone used the shawl to kill." She exhaled. "Natalija."

"Hunting the lost Romanov diamonds," Kepelov said. "What a chase that was! Are you saying that Natalija is alive? She cannot be. Not after what happened."

"Kepelov—you and Nigel and Stella," Vic said, counting on his fingers. "Lacey and me. Five."

"The sixth line is for me." Marie suddenly returned to the here and now. She was back from wherever she'd gone in her mind. She staggered to her feet, with Kepelov's help. She leaned over the shawl, placing her fingers on it. "I got news for y'all. The one you been suffering so much remorse over, Lacey, cher, and you too, Vic. You didn't kill her. She has a terrible thirst for revenge."

"How do you know that?" Vic asked.

"It's what I do, cher, I know things, I just don't know *how*," Marie said with a sad chuckle. She grabbed hold of Kepelov's hand. "Only the thing is, this time, I didn't faint. It all washed over me and through me and I remember it all and I didn't faint."

"Natalija Krumina is alive?" Gregor thumped his chest. His face was contorted in something between bafflement and rage.

"Or someone wants us to think so." Lacey and Vic locked glances. Attempts had been made on four of them. "Leonardo was a mistake. Natalija never knew Leonardo."

Marie nodded to Kepelov. "Go ahead, take a peek at the shawl, Gregor. I'm fine."

"But, Marie, my love, you had a vision, and you did not faint," he said. "This is wonderful. Momentous."

"I'm powerful dizzy, I have a headache! Could someone be a dear and fetch me some aspirin?" Lacey dug a bottle of Advil out of her tote bag. "I'm just so pleased with myself for not fainting," Marie added. "I will have to humble myself and thank Olga for helping me with her breathing exercises."

"She will be most happy to claim all credit for it." Gregor reached for the magnifying glass and Vic handed it over. "So only when the shawl is folded this way, your pictures appear?"

"As far as I can tell," Lacey said. "No other way seemed to work."

He was silent for a few moments, breathing heavily. "My God, I see it now."

"I'm getting a camera," Vic announced. "We need to document this."

"Sean Victor, dear, would you be sure to note the date and time?" Lacey asked sweetly. "And just caption the pics, 'Lacey was right.' It's for the bronze historical marker I want to put right *here*."

He kissed her on the cheek. "Smart-ass."

Kepelov was grinning. "I am proud of you, Lacey Smithsonian. Of your gift."

"But I'm still confused," Lacey said. "How could Natalija put something in the shawl?"

"The woman who fell into the water. She wants revenge, she wants blood," Marie said. "Returning the shawl, I think, was to send you a message, Lacey, to see if you could decipher it, and see how clever she is. So you'd feel her power. That's what she wants now, power and revenge."

Vic returned with a big Nikon DSLR camera and a tripod and set it up. "If what you're saying is true, Marie, then Natalija is here in town. Or someone wants us to think she is. As far as I know, her body was never found, but other people probably know that too. If we go with

Lacey's theory that the poison was inserted somehow into the shawl, how did Natalija find out about it and get to it? Any of us who were there in New Orleans would know Natalija on sight, but nobody has seen her."

Lacey felt the blood drain from her face. "Yes, I might have. The waitress who admired the shawl at the party. Tilda was on her nametag. She said her grandmother had a Russian shawl. Dirty blond hair, and a prominent nose."

"Oh, yes. That plain little thing?" Marie remembered. "I told her to be careful, but she handled the shawl anyway."

"Her voice," Lacey said. "It had a lyrical quality about it. It was so at odds with her appearance."

"Let me think—she touched it while she talked to me."

"But you didn't feel anything psychic from her?" Kepelov asked.

"Sugar, I was concentrating so hard on the bachelorettes, I just thought she seemed respectful. I was concerned for the shawl."

"That was her chance to slip a needle into the shawl," Vic said, thinking out loud. "Lacey has been saying that Leonardo's murder was just a crime of opportunity. And a mistake, if Marie was her real target."

"She had to assume Marie would be the only one to wear the shawl, and she hoped—" Lacey began.

Marie took Kepelov's hand. "That's why I couldn't see her intent. I can't read my own fortune. I'm blind in that direction. Natalija Krumina hoped to kill me."

"And to make me suffer," Kepelov said. "To take you from me. She must have followed us."

"But Tilda didn't look anything like Natalija," Lacey protested.

"Blond wig," Kepelov said. "Simple."

"And the distinctive nose?"

"False. Easy enough to do theatrical effects. Art of disguise is practically first thing you learn in spy school. They give you fun part of curriculum first. People say disguise doesn't work? Ha. Works all the time. Nobody sees it working."

"If phony noses are part of the first lesson, where does mixing poison come in?"

"That we save for more advanced classes."

"The waitress we saw had a scar down the side of her face." Lacey drew an invisible line on her cheek with her index finger. "It looked real, not like makeup."

"If she survived hitting those riverboat paddles," Vic put in, "she has real scars. The rest could be spycraft."

Spycraft! Brooke would just love to be a fly on the wall here, Lacey thought. "You're saying Natalija was trained as a spy? You knew her best, Kepelov. And you were involved with her once, romantically."

"No romance. Only sex. Nothing more." Kepelov sat on the end of the table and gazed at his family treasure. He pointed out his initials in Cyrillic, stitched in the shawl, and smiled sadly. "As for being professionally trained? I don't know. Maybe a little. She wanted me to think so. Natalija is such a bad girl. That part I liked. Mix of Latvian and Russian, been around the world, speaks many languages, smart, fearless, no scruples. Maybe she looked valuable to Russian government. Or somebody's government." Kepelov rubbed his shiny head. "But if Natalija is a spy, she is spy like that Anna Chapman, famous so-called Russian Mata Hari. Party girl, nightclubbing, sleeping around, posing, looking mysterious for the camera, no real spying. Chapman was in it for glory and money. To go to America, get on Russian television, to get rich and famous. Reminds me of Natalija. What you call a gold digger. And all this complicated stitching and folding, stealing and returning? All to send a crazy message? Amateur showoff wannabe spy stuff. Amateurs always doing things the hard way. Showing off how professional they are."

"This is all healthy speculation, people," Vic cut in, "but if this is true, we have a crazy woman out for blood. Blood times six. She's killed one person already, and he doesn't even count to her. We need a plan."

"Lacey, you must talk to the boatman," Marie said.

"What boatman?" Lacey said.

"The man who fished her out of the water and saved her life. You've already met him, the man from New Orleans." Marie smiled patiently, waiting for Lacey to catch on.

"From New Orleans? Rene Thibodeaux? He's here looking for some woman named Leah—oh, my God. Is that Natalija?"

He'd said life had roughed her up and you could see it in her face. Was he talking about the scar?

"He doesn't know who she really is," Marie said. "His vision is clouded by love. My vision hit me like a tidal wave, and I'm still amazed I didn't faint. I may be growing. As a psychic, I mean."

"He's following her, and she's following us," Vic said. "But if she has been trained as an agent or a spy, even a bad spy, why has she missed so often? Why did she kill a man she apparently didn't plan to kill?"

Kepelov settled his chin on his fingertips. "Three thoughts. One: Natalija is bad spy. Still dangerous, maybe more so. Two: Her goal is to stretch out suspense, make anticipation worse. Torture makes revenge sweeter. Three: After her fall into Mississippi in the water, she has gotten sloppy. Out of shape, out of practice, or maybe her head is damaged. Maybe crazy. Crazier than before, I mean. She was always crazy."

"She can't be as skilled as she thinks she is," Lacey said.

"Good point," Kepelov said. "She tried to kill me in Paris and I am still here."

Natalija had known about the legendary diamond-filled corset because her great-grandfather and Magda Rousseau's grandfather had stolen it together after the Romanovs were executed, and then hidden it away for almost a century out of remorse. People believed he was out of his mind, but Natalija listened to his ravings. She had been a bewitching woman. Apparently she still was, despite her scars, physical and mental. When she started her affair with Kepelov, he believed he was hunting a lost Fabergé egg. She knew better. Natalija followed Kepelov to Paris and tried to take him out of the competition, with a nine-millimeter pistol. But the old spy proved tougher than she thought.

At that time, Lacey didn't know who to trust, except Vic and Brooke and Stella. Since then, time had tested how she felt about Nigel Griffin and Gregor Kepelov. Lacey had warmed to them, though she'd never allowed herself to trust them one hundred percent. Yet one mystery remained for Lacey: why women were so attracted to Kepelov. She certainly wasn't attracted to the cool-eyed spy. Natalija Krumina was once his type—beautiful, tough, and heartless—but he'd fallen hard for Marie, the gentle zaftig psychic with the big heart. Marie's many charms, Lacey reflected, included *not* wanting to kill him.

Kepelov lifted his eyes to her. "Anger and pain make Natalija careless. Lucky for me. Lucky for all of us. But still very dangerous."

Silence fell over the group. Lacey was the first to speak.

"We have to call Turtledove. He knows where to find Rene Thibodeaux, and we have to let Rene know what he's dealing with," Lacey said. "I don't get it—she used him and ripped him off, why didn't she kill him?"

"Maybe he's part of her plan," Vic suggested.

"If he is, he doesn't know it."

Marie was holding up well, but the strain was beginning to show. Her eyes were at half-mast, but she managed a sleepy smile for Kepelov, along with a wink.

"I must get Marie home," Kepelov said.

"One question, Gregor," Lacey said. "Is she going to keep trying to kill us? All of us?"

"Of course," he said. "Definition of crazy: Keep doing the same thing, no matter what the result."

Vic retrieved a black Glock pistol from a lockbox in his office. He checked the clip and chamber and secured

it in a shoulder holster. "I'll ask our friend Forrest to arrange a chat with Mr. Thibodeaux at his earliest conve-
nience. Tonight," he said. "What are you going to do with
that shawl, Gregor?"

Kepelov carefully folded the shawl, smiling broadly.
"I will see that it goes to proper authorities in investigation," he said. Lacey suspected he lied.

No doubt he thinks he is the proper authority, Lacey
thought. *But it's not my problem tonight. Let Kepelov
deal with Broadway Lamont.*

They said good-bye in the lobby. The rain had stopped,
but the sidewalks and streets were still wet. The earlier
storm had chased everyone home, leaving the downtown
Rosslyn neighborhood quiet.

The building had a secure parking garage for employees, but Kepelov had parked hastily on the street by the
front doors. Vic and Lacey waited to watch Marie and
Gregor cross the street safely to their purple Gremlin.
He was walking slightly behind Marie at the streetlight
when two shots rang out, echoing in the empty street.

Kepelov clutched his chest and staggered. As he fell
he pushed Marie to the ground. He lay still, his body
partly covering hers.

chapter 29

A dark-colored car was speeding away. Its lights were out and the evening's post-rainstorm gloom made it impossible to read the plates or see the driver. But everyone knew this wasn't a random drive-by shooting.

Natalija Krumina was at the wheel.

Lacey and Vic sprinted across the street to where Kepelov lay sprawled on the pavement. She pulled out her phone as they ran and dialed 911. At the operator's request Lacey kept the line open as she scanned the street. Kepelov was moving, trying to get up. Marie had struggled out from beneath him and she was sitting beside him, cradling his head. Her hair was a dark veil that reached for him. Vic raced to Kepelov's side and tore the Russian's shirt open, looking for bleeding bullet wounds to compress.

"Talk to me, my sweet Gregor." Marie's eyes filled with tears that splashed on his jacket. Lacey didn't see any blood yet, but Vic was blocking her way.

"Don't cry, Marie." Kepelov opened his eyes and took her hand in his. "I am hard to kill. I am tough old dog." He grimaced and tried to sit up. "Catching bullets is what bulletproof vests are for." He coughed and his face contorted in pain. "Kevlar catches the slugs, but the impact—whew! Like a giant punches your gut."

Lacey felt so much relief she nearly fell down herself. "But we saw you fall," she said. "Vic, is he really—"

Vic got to his feet, smiling. He held Lacey steady. "He's wearing a good vest, no penetration. He had to fall to make her believe she put him down. So she wouldn't keep shooting. Like he said, a gunshot is a great big punch in the gut, and he took a couple of them. How are you doing down there, Kepelov? Don't move. Paramedics will be here soon, we already called."

"Not moving, thank you. Could be worse. Unfortunately, I think maybe broken ribs." Kepelov coughed again and gulped for air. "People expect you to fall down when they shoot you. Because of TV and movies. Bullets don't always make you fall, sometimes you have to help them a little. How did I do, Marie? Convincing death scene, yes? You all right?"

"Convincing? I nearly died of shock!" Marie kissed his face. "We really have to chat about your ex-girlfriends, Gregor."

"What if she comes back?" Lacey asked.

"She might," Vic said, his gun drawn and ready. "But she knows we've called 911. Hopefully she'll keep her distance and watch out for cops and paramedics. I'd better check to see if she put a GPS bug on their car. Purple Gremlin, right?"

Kepelov was still trying to sit up, but Marie gently restrained him. "Don't you dare move, Gregor, cher. Not until you're checked out and those ribs are tended to. Because I love each and every one of them."

"No worries. I am not dead. Good thing I wear the vest. Because Smithsonian warned me. And Olga nagged me," Kepelov said. He sounded strong, but he didn't look good.

"When the cops get here, give them the basic description of what happened, no extras," Vic told them all. "They don't need the backstory right now, and they won't appreciate what they'll consider a loony conspiracy fantasy."

"Got it." Lacey wasn't interested in amusing the Arlington cops until the wee hours of the morning. "I wish

I didn't have a creepy feeling that we'll find Natalija in the rearview mirror going home."

Sirens screamed. The police and the ambulance arrived and blocked the street.

Marie was strong and stoic throughout the ordeal. Her tears dried, and she watched over her man like a protective bulldog as the EMTs lifted him onto the gurney and into the ambulance. Once she was sure Kepelov was taken care of and in capable hands, Marie promptly fainted.

Vic caught her before she hit the pavement. The EMTs bundled the unconscious psychic into the ambulance beside her fiancé.

It was almost eleven p.m. by the time Lacey and Vic finished their interviews with the Arlington police. The responding officer said it was very unusual to see a drive-by shooting in "their neck of the woods." After all, he said, this wasn't the District of Columbia.

"You're telling me that my sweet girl, my Leah, is a killer? She maybe never cared about me at all?" Rene Thibodeaux said. "I can't picture it. Maybe she had to clear out of New Orleans in a hurry for some damn reason, but there was a time she cared about me. And she shot at some kind of a Russian spy? Good God Almighty! That's gotta be just pure fantasy."

"Didn't you notice how she talked?" Lacey asked.

"Sure, she had a little accent. I thought the way she talked was so pretty, like music. She told me she grew up overseas, her hippie parents dragged her all over Europe when she was growing up. So, she spoke a bunch of different languages—like French and Russian and—" He buried his face in his hands for a few moments. They gave him time to let the story sink in.

Turtledove sat by silently. They hadn't had any success so far in locating the lost "Leah," and both men were very interested in what Vic and Lacey had to tell them.

The four of them met just before midnight at the all-night diner on Route 50, where the customers at that hour were few but the coffee was hot.

The diner, straight out of the 1940s, was the kind of place that served breakfast all day and all night. The décor of polished chrome and Formica and fluorescent lighting, a combination that flattered no one, cast its greenish light upon all. But the old blue tiles and cramped booths were pleasantly kitschy.

Rene contemplated his beer, holding it up to the light. "It's like we're talking about two completely different women." It was harder than Lacey thought it would be, telling Rene that the woman he adored was trying to murder everyone who stood in her way. "Besides, her name is Leah."

"Her real name is Natalija," Vic said. "Most people who choose false names pick something similar to their real names. Makes it easier to remember."

"Natalija Krumina fell off a riverboat on the Mississippi, the steamship *Natchez*, in November of last year," Lacey said. "After she tried to kill me, and several other people. What happened after that, Rene?"

"I don't know nothing about no Natalija, whatever her name was. I fished a drowning woman out of the water. It was November. I'm not saying she was this Natalija you're talking about. It was my Leah." He paused a moment. "But I found her some ways from where the riverboat *Natchez* was running. She wasn't breathing. I gave her mouth-to-mouth, slapped the water out of her, got some air into her lungs, and she started living again. She was cut bad on the face, so I taped it up. Got her cleaned up and took care of her. She was bruised bad too, bruised all over, but still I could see she was such a pretty girl once."

"What happened after that?" Lacey said.

"She woke up real confused. Didn't know where she was, what happened to her. I was taking care of her, so I guess she trusted me. Eventually she told me her boyfriend tried to kill her, hit her, threw her off his boat. Now I don't like the idea of cops, but I told her to go make a report, told her I'd go with her, tell them how I found her, help her get the man locked up. She said no. Leah and I feel the same way about *po*-lice. No offense to present company. We just don't need them, we do just fine for ourselves without 'em."

"Why didn't you take her to a hospital?" Vic asked. He squeezed Lacey's hand under the table.

"People go to hospitals to die, man. I never had nobody in my family go into a hospital and come out alive. Besides, I got a friend, used to be a medic in the service. Forrest knows him too. Does a little first aid, sells a few, um, pharmaceuticals on the side. He stitched her up, used real tiny stitches so the scar wouldn't be so bad. He did a right nice job. Guess she cut her face on the side of the boat when she went over. Leah's still pretty upset about that cut. Said it ruined her life, but I don't agree with that. She's still a beautiful woman, if only she'd just see that. See, how I feel about her—"

Apparently Natalija was still attractive enough to use her looks to her advantage. And she had an impressive talent for deception. *Maybe she really was trained as a spy. Or she's simply a natural-born sociopath.*

"You said Leah stayed with you for about four months," Lacey said. "Why didn't she try to find anyone else she knew?"

"Said she didn't know anyone in Louisiana, except the guy who tried to kill her. I kind of figured she was on the run, either from him or her family or the law. Didn't matter which one to me." Rough in appearance in his worn jeans and plaid flannel shirt, Rene Thibodeaux seemed a little too trusting, as long as he wasn't dealing with police, doctors, or other authority figures. Staying under the radar seemed to be his main goal in life.

"You didn't care about her past?" Turtledove asked.

"Why should I? That was all over and done. I took her for face value, like she took me. She didn't ask me no questions about *my* past. She cooked for me, she took care of me, she kept me company. She even cleaned my damn house," Rene said.

Cleaned it out, you mean. Lacey understood Natalija's reasons for staying. Rene was a safe haven, no questions asked. He cared for her like she was a bird with a broken wing. In her few months with him, Natalija recovered from her injuries, safely tucked out of sight in Louisiana. Everyone believed she was dead. No one was looking for her.

She had plenty of time to plan her next move. Perhaps she'd read news stories about the trove of Romanov diamonds that had been found in the French Quarter—the treasure she felt should have been hers. *The Eye Street Observer* certainly played it big, and named all the players. The story had made national news and it was all over the Web for weeks. Mac had even gotten copies for the newsroom of Russian newspapers that ran *The Eye*'s coverage word for word, or so he was told. In Russian, of course. The Russian ambassador even visited *The Eye* to meet Lacey, after which a security team swept the office for bugs.

It was easy for Natalija to choose her targets for revenge. And make her plans. Perhaps Kepelov had mentioned the shawl to her sometime in the past. But there was no way Natalija could have known the shawl would be at the bachelorette party. She seized the moment and spiked it with its poisoned needle—and then later stole it, after its barb pricked the wrong target.

Embroidering the shawl with the puzzle message? That was probably an improvisation too, Lacey decided. *Something to do in those long hours late at night, with no one handy to kill.*

"Leave her past crimes out of it for the moment," Vic said. "She tried to kill Lacey and two of our friends the other day, and she tried to kill another friend of ours tonight."

"You sure of that?" Rene looked up from his beer.

"We think you're in danger too. Especially if she sees you with any of us, and she probably already has. We're why she was in New Orleans and why she ended up in the Mississippi. She's proven she'd mow down anyone in her way."

"She'd want to kill me? Me? Just because I know she's alive and I came looking for her?" Rene sat up straight. "Let me get this straight, y'all. What you're saying is I don't have to find her? She's going to find me?"

"Maybe with a bullet. Thought you should know," Vic said. He fished a business card out of his jacket pocket. "And call me if you see her, anytime, day or night, or if you think of anything else we should know."

"Even if she did all these other things, Leah wouldn't want to kill me. I saved her life. But listen, I appreciate your concern." He snorted a short laugh. "Leah took my money and my heart. Sounds like a damn country song. I'm just lucky she left me with my old truck. Couldn't get along without that truck. Even slept in it on the way up here. Forrest here was kind enough to let me stay with him. I'm grateful, man."

"No problem, Rene," Turtledove said. "It's not safe sleeping out in the open like that. Especially with her out there."

"Mind if we swing past the liquor store if one's open? I got a feeling I need to get drunk tonight. Real drunk."

Turtledove smiled. "You sure you want to do that?"

Rene stood up to pay his bill. "Oh, yeah. I've got some forgetting to do. A lot of forgetting."

"Calm down, Lacey—even killers need their sleep," Vic said. "And she's been hard at work. Been a big day for her. She probably thinks she killed Kepelov."

"That is so reassuring, darling." She was craning her neck to watch the road and every inch of the landscape all the way to Alexandria. They were back in Vic's Jeep, which Vic now deemed safe, with new brakes and a thorough checkup by his mechanic.

Lacey's nerves were on edge all the way home. Every car on the road made her flinch. She tried to chill out and calm her fears, but when she managed to forget that Natalija might be lurking behind every bush, she realized she had other things to worry about. Like Stella's wedding.

"Should we tell Stella and Nigel?" she asked. "About Natalija?"

Vic shook his head. "Hold off. Things are already in such an uproar with them. First, Turtledove and I will try to track Natalija down tomorrow. I'll put as many of my guys on it as I can. I'm guessing she'll be watching Thibodeaux as well as the rest of us, so she won't be too far away. Lacey, I'm curious—what would you do if you were her?"

"Not sure. Making a big splashy entrance at the wedding might be tempting. Say, with a bomb, or a missile launcher. Bow and arrow maybe, just to mix it up. And she's already used nicotine, stolen cars, damaged your brakes, and shot Kepelov. Natalija's ruined everything."

"The bachelorette party wasn't ruined, exactly, was it?"

Lacey eyed him. "I don't know. One dead uninvited guest, a killer disguised as a waitress, a stolen shawl, a fainting fortune-teller. *Ruined* is a pretty good description."

"Cheer up, sweetheart. We'll stop her. I promise."

"No more bodyguard for me?" Lacey asked.

"Depends on what happens tomorrow. I still have my guys watching your apartment building tonight, anyway." He glanced at her and squeezed her leg. "You're off work tomorrow, right?"

"Yes."

"Think you could stay home and stay put?"

"I could sleep all day if I put my mind to it." That was part of Lacey's plan, to take some time for herself before the wedding, after her maid-of-honor chores were done. She mentally ticked off the list. The reception was booked, the menu was settled, the flowers were confirmed, the cake was being baked, the bridesmaids had their pink dresses, Alma Lopez was hard at work on the dress, and God bless Brooke, the favors were all assembled. The only thing in doubt was the bride.

Lacey looked at her nails. They were a mess, as usual. *Real reporters don't have great nails.* "I need to call Alma and check on Stella's dress, but with any luck Stella can pick it up. And I suppose I could put off my mani-pedi until Friday."

"You do that. And I'll be your bodyguard tonight." Vic grinned at her. She smiled back and squeezed his hand.

It's like he can read my mind.

"Lacey, the dress is finished," Alma was saying on Lacey's answering machine. "I only did it for the challenge, you know, and because it's for you. It looks like — well, it doesn't look off-the-rack anymore."

"That's good," Lacey said aloud over Alma's message as Vic checked under her bed, in the closet, and on the balcony for monsters named Natalija.

"This dress is like something out of a fairy tale. Pink and white and fluffy," Alma's phone message continued with a chuckle. "And I'm not sure that's a good thing. But you or Stella or someone can pick it up here tomorrow. I'll be home all day." Alma hung up.

"What's good?" Vic asked, as Lacey clicked off the answering machine.

"Stella's dress is done. At least one thing today is going right." *Bo Peep will be ready to find her sheep after all.*

chapter 30

Lacey brought her morning coffee out to her balcony, overlooking the Potomac River. Her old and shabby-though-built-to-be-bombproof building had a million-dollar view of the river. The view from her balcony would be her attempt to start Thursday on a serene note.

After last night's rain, the morning was crisp and the trees fresh and spring green. The pavement far beneath her seventh-floor balcony was drying out and the pink and white azaleas around the building were blooming early. Lacey spotted an osprey swooping down through the air and then flapping its way back up, with a big fish in its mouth. It landed on its nest, built on pilings in the river.

Her south-facing balcony would be lovely until about noon, when the sun would heat the bricks like an oven and force her back inside. It would be livable again in the late afternoon, when the sun dipped behind the south wing of the building.

Lacey loved mornings like this, when she didn't have to be at the office, when she could take a moment to breathe. When she forgot about the potential menace of Natalija Krumina, life was good. She watched sailboats launch from Belle Haven Park.

And then she saw the pink car pull into the parking lot.

There could be only one bright pink 1957 Cadillac El-dorado Biarritz like this one. It was a classic land yacht with fins and it belonged to Vic's mother, Nadine Donovan. The vintage pink Caddy was Nadine's pride and joy and only eighteen hundred of them had been made, she'd told Lacey. Today the top was down, the better for the world to admire her big bold car.

Nadine grew up a cowgirl in Nevada. She rode horses and roped calves before meeting Sean Daniel Donovan, Vic's dad, and following him around the country, throughout his military and Pentagon career, before eventually becoming a McLean, Virginia, matron. Nadine was equal to any situation: Piloting a giant pink Caddy was no challenge for her. Lacey watched her get out of the car, which she patted lovingly on one fin. Nadine's favorite toy emerged from its climate-controlled garage only on lovely days like today. For more mundane purposes she drove a big Mercedes sedan.

She must be in a fine mood, Lacey thought. *This can only mean trouble*.

In her early sixties, Nadine wore the glossy patina of the well-bred, well-groomed Washington woman. Her soft brown short pageboy veered awfully close to the classic Washington Helmet-Head, but Lacey would never have breathed that sentiment aloud. Vic's slim and fit mother could still wrangle a horse, as well as her husband and son. Not to mention the way she wrangled Lacey, who at Nadine's command had dutifully concocted ridiculously labor-intensive homemade desserts for family holiday dinners.

Today, Nadine wore bright green slacks with a green and white cardigan set and designer sunglasses. Stepping out of her vintage Caddy, she belonged in a retro car ad. She took that moment to look up, and spotted Lacey on her balcony. She smiled and waved, and pulled her phone out of her purse. Lacey's phone rang.

"Hey, girl, you got some coffee up there?"

It was the first time Nadine had seen Lacey's apartment, and Lacey could only hope it, and she, would pass muster. Nadine had missed seeing her son. He had just left only an hour before.

Lacey peered in the mirror to smooth her hair and inspect her casual vintage dress. She could have thrown on jeans, but the day was too pretty and fresh for that. The violet polished-cotton dress with the wide belt and purple detailing around the neck was softer and cooler to wear, particularly with the flared skirt and short cuffed and buttoned sleeves. Her vintage mood from the previous evening had extended to the morning and she wanted to wear something with style.

"Isn't this cozy," Nadine remarked, moving past the trunk and the blue velvet sofa Aunt Mimi had bequeathed to Lacey. She walked straight through the living room and out to the balcony. "What a view! I can see why you wanted to be out here this morning."

Lacey brought a tray with coffee, cream, and sugar. "I'm sorry I don't have anything special to offer you." It was the kind of moment that called for coffee cake or a slice of homemade nut bread.

"Nonsense, you've got other things on your mind. I know you only whip up one of those fabulous desserts at my request." Nadine's eyes were twinkling. "They're not for every day."

"Having you visit is an unexpected surprise."

Nadine found that amusing. "I imagine so. I wanted to make sure you're doing all right. I understand there's trouble brewing over this wedding of your friend's."

"You've been talking to Vic." Lacey topped off her coffee.

"Interrogating him, you mean? As his mother, it's only natural to take advantage of the privilege now and then."

It was Lacey's turn to be amused. "Only natural."

"God knows I try not to pry, but I do get curious. And concerned."

"I understand."

Lacey was glad her own mother was back in Denver.

Rose Smithsonian had a certain something in common with Nadine Donovan and Lady Gwendolyn Griffin. It wasn't merely that these women wanted to protect their children. They wanted to be *front and center* protecting their cubs.

"I cannot tolerate people who use cars as weapons. First trying to run you down, and then messing with Vic's brakes! Shocking."

"No one would dare touch your Eldorado," Lacey said.

"If anyone lays a hand on my pink baby, I'll run them down myself. Justifiable homicide." Nadine smiled and sipped. "Where do you think all this is heading?"

"I'm not sure, but we finally think we know who's behind it." Lacey briefly described their theory about the return of Natalija Krumina, hell-bent on revenge.

"Quite a story! The more you know about this woman, the safer everyone will be. Knowledge is power. And Lacey, that brings me to what I wanted to talk to you about." Nadine narrowed her eyes. "What's up with you and my Sean Victor Donovan?" she said, using Vic's full name. "He's been—*twitchy* ever since you two came back from Colorado."

"Twitchy? Are we in trouble?"

"You will be if you up and elope on me," Nadine said. "Like he did with his practice wife, Montana. *Hussy* is an old-fashioned word, but in this case it fits. And in Las Vegas, of all places. Of course, I am thankful they didn't do it in a church, so he's free to marry in the church *this* time. Now, I can understand, under the circumstances, what with your friend's wedding gone wild, why an elopement might suddenly look rather alluring."

Uh oh. "What has Vic told you?"

"Not a thing." Nadine laughed at Lacey's discomfort. "That man is a stone wall. Why would he tell his mother anything? I came here to tell you that there are a number of—well, it sounds silly to call them family jewels. But there are a few old rings with some lovely biggish diamonds that would be nice to keep in the family. That is, *if* you were actually engaged, and *if* you were planning an actual wedding, as opposed to an elopement, and *if* you thought you might like a wedding ring with a Donovan family diamond. The settings aren't much, they're rather gaudy old-fashioned things, but the stones are quite nice, and you could always have them reset. Just something to think about."

"I don't know what to say." Lacey's face registered shock.

"Don't say anything for now. I wanted you to know that option is available."

Lacey's cell phone rang in the nick of time. "Excuse me, Nadine. I really have to take this."

"Hey, Lacey!" It was Stella. "Look in your parking lot." Lacey stood up, scanned the back parking lot, and spotted Stella's red Mini Cooper, the one with the American flag on the roof.

"What do you know? There you are." She turned and whispered to Nadine. "It's the bride-maybe-to-be." Nadine peered down over the balcony.

"Is someone else up there, Lace?"

"Vic's mom, Nadine. You sound happy, Stel. Anything I should know?"

"I am happy!" Stella popped out of the Mini and Lady Gwendolyn Griffin extracted herself from the passenger side. They both waved at Lacey from below.

"Would you like to come up for some coffee?" She didn't know what else to say.

"I thought you would never ask!"

Stella and Lady Gwendolyn were soon at her door. Stella came with a small bag of chocolate caramels from Co Co. Sala, the restaurant where Nigel had taken her the night before. *Must have been a successful evening,* Lacey concluded, overseeing a fresh pot of coffee in her vintage electric percolator. She didn't need any more coffee.

"Wow, that thing is old," Stella said, barely through the door. "Same one you've always had?"

"Sue me, it makes great coffee," Lacey said.

"I totally love it, it so goes with the décor. And your dress."

Lacey led them out onto the sunny balcony. "Let me introduce Nadine Donovan, Vic's mother. And Nadine, my friend Stella and Lady Gwendolyn Griffin, Stella's mother-in-law-to-be."

Lacey busied herself pouring coffee while eyeing her friend's look and demeanor. Stella had changed out of the ugly T-shirt and old leggings and into a navy mini-skirt and red and white striped knit top. Topping her pink-tipped curls, she wore a navy beret with a red heart pin. She looked fresh and adorable and rather French. *Alternate universe French, but French.*

Clad in yet another tweed combo was Lady Gwendolyn, who today wore a gloomy moss green with flecks of mud brown. Lacey wondered if perhaps she secretly had her own designer line of tweeds: *Tweeds R Us! If we don't carry it, IT'S NOT TWEED!*

"We came to inform you that your, let us say, *timely* suggestions to my Nigel are greatly appreciated," Gwendolyn said.

"Do you have news?" Lacey asked.

"Yes!" Stella hugged her and squealed. "I'm getting married on Saturday!"

"Hurray!" Lacey hugged her back.

"It was touch and go for a while," Gwendolyn said. "I wanted to thank you for your part in bringing our two lovebirds back together."

"Oh, yeah," Stella continued. "Nigel fessed up about your suggestions over dinner, which was fabulous by the way. Nothing like chocolate endorphin overload. But when he showed up in a brand-new pink shirt and tie, with that exact copy of my bridal bouquet—oh, my God. I burst into tears, Lace. How could I say no? Have one of these chocolate thingies, they're great."

"That's wonderful, Stella." Lacey sighed with relief and helped herself to a chocolate caramel.

"I mean, I love him to death! What kind of coward would I be if I was afraid of killers with random limos?"

Nadine smiled, and Gwendolyn said, "Yes, my daughter-in-law-to-be is an exuberant girl. So refreshing, isn't she?"

"Very," Nadine agreed with a grin. "And you'll always know what she's *really* thinking."

"Wait a minute!" Stella said. "Vic's mom! You're the one!"

"The one?" Nadine asked. "Which one?"

"The one with the pink Valentine's Day party that Lacey made the pink cake for," Stella said.

"*That* cake?" Gwendolyn said. "Oh, my. I remember when you made the practice cake and we all ate it."

It wasn't supposed to be practice, Lacey thought. *And I had to make it twice.*

"It was delicious," Nadine said. "Lacey, I had no idea you made a practice cake too."

"Practice makes perfect, they say. You don't want to let your boyfriend's mother down."

"And Nadine, you're also the one with that fabulous pink Caddy, right?" Stella squeaked. "O.M.G., Lady G! That's the Caddy I pointed out in the parking lot."

"Spectacular," Gwendolyn said. "Nothing quite like that in the UK. Wouldn't fit down half the streets."

Stella leaned over the balcony wall to admire it again. "Wow! Look at those fins! What a car! We have a white stretch limousine booked for the wedding. Had to go with white. I just couldn't find anything big and beautiful and *pink*—" Stella was struck with a brainstorm, but didn't know exactly how to finesse what she wanted to say.

It didn't matter—Nadine was already there. Nevertheless, she wanted to hear the audiobook version. "Nothing in pink? What a shame."

"Well, there was one, but it was already reserved. I mean, I'm having a *pink* wedding. Under pink cherry blossoms. And a pink reception, and a pink cake."

"Not to mention the pink tent," Gwendolyn offered. "And pink balloons."

"How great would it be to have a fabulous pink wedding car too." Stella sighed meaningfully.

Nadine put her cup down on Lacey's wicker table. "Stella. I know this has never crossed your mind, but would you and your groom like to be chauffeured in my pink Cadillac Eldorado Biarritz? And did I mention it's pink?"

Stella lit up. "I know it would be too much to ask, but Vic's coming to the wedding and maybe he could drive —"

"Not Vic. He'll have his hands full with the maid of honor, I expect," Nadine replied. "But if, say, *I* were a guest, and my husband, we would be happy to drive you and the groom around the Tidal Basin. It would make quite a show."

Stella jumped up and hugged Nadine. "You're invited! Thank you, thank you, thank you!"

"It's a deal." Nadine beamed. "One way to see my son, after all. He seems so preoccupied these days." She sent a knowing look Lacey's way.

"Wedding photos of Nigel and me in a vintage pink Cadillac! I can't believe it. Yesterday was all gloomy and gray, and today it's all *La Vie en Rose*."

What a difference a day makes. Nadine winked at Lacey and smiled.

"Stella, before I forget," Lacey said, "your dress is ready to be picked up."

"Everything is coming together. Just like a miracle," Stella said.

"Do you want Alma's address? She's my seamstress," Lacey explained to the others. "She's up in Arlington. It's a little tricky to find."

"Gee, Lacey, we're kind of on our way somewhere. Could you pick it up for me? Pretty please? Lady G and I are heading down to Mount Vernon."

"A little together time," Gwendolyn said. "You understand."

"She said I should get away from my troubles for a little while. And you know what? How long have I lived in Washington and I've never been to Mount Vernon? And then I have a massage scheduled for later, and tomorrow it's mani-pedi time. Please, Lacey? You are the best maid of honor *ever*!"

"I'll pick up the dress. That's all? Need a pint of my blood too?" She stuck out her arm for emphasis.

"You've been so great, Lacey. I totally appreciate this, believe me."

"No problem. Everything else okay?" Lacey asked.

"To be honest I'm still a little worried that someone's after us. I mean, sure, it could be a fluke, that limo crash. I still feel a teensy bit uneasy, you know? Like when the DC sniper was out there and you just didn't know who was going to be shot next."

"All I can tell you is that Vic and Turtledove are working on it."

"And another thing, I haven't heard from Marie today. Have you?"

"I'll give her a call," Lacey said.

"And Brooke, I love her to death, but she drives me crazy," Stella said. "I couldn't get a straight answer out of her. Is she going to have a pink bridesmaid's dress or not?"

"Chill, Stella. I saw it yesterday. It's so pink she'll never live it down."

"We'll make sure she doesn't." Stella giggled a little too gleefully and gave Lacey a big hug.

"We've heard there will be a memorial service of some kind next week," Gwendolyn said. "And a cocktail reception. For Mr. Leonardo," she added, for Nadine's benefit. "The poor unfortunate man who died the day after the bachelorette party."

"I'll be on my honeymoon," Stella said. Lacey knew she wasn't eager to be anywhere near Leonardo, living or dead.

"I've offered to represent Stella at the sad event," Gwendolyn said. "Happy to be of service."

Of course you are, Lacey thought. A wedding and a funeral? Perfect bookends for Lady Gwendolyn's big Washington weekend.

"Perhaps you could accompany me, Lacey," Gwendolyn said.

Lacey could feel her smile start to wobble. And Nadine burst out laughing.

After everyone left, Lacey collapsed on the sofa, put her feet up, and called Vic. "Any word?" she asked.

"Game on. Natalija's just made contact with Thibodeaux." He sounded edgy. Lacey sat straight up.

"She called him? What are you going to do?"

"Let them arrange to meet. This afternoon. The cops will take her down the moment she shows. And Forrest and I will be there to make sure it happens."

"Oh, Vic, that will be a huge relief! I'm supposed to pick up Stella's dress from Alma Lopez, but I could do it tomorrow. Where do you want me?"

"Out of harm's way. Doing your dress thing with Lopez sounds all right. She's way out in Arlington, right? But no other errands today, please, and stay in touch. Stella should give you a medal of honor after all this is over. For being maid of honor above and beyond the call of duty."

"I'll settle for a few weeks of peace while she's on her honeymoon. They're going to the British Virgin Islands, and I wish the Virgins luck. So you really think it's okay for me to go to Alma's? Without either Turtledove or you?"

He paused. "Natalija sounded intent on seeing Thibodeaux, so he's our bait. Miles away with Alma might be the best place for you to be. Check in with me, watch the traffic, have your cell phone handy. Text me—I'll see your message even if I can't answer. I checked out your car before I left this morning. It's okay. And my guys have been watching your building, but I'll have to pull them off today. By the way, I understand it's been coffee club time out on the balcony. What did my mom have to say?"

"She's bursting with curiosity."

"As usual."

"It's nothing compared to the dress. What if it turns out to be as awful as I think it's going to be?"

"Stella will love it, no matter how awful it is. Take a picture. After we take down Natalija, we'll have a good laugh. And we'll celebrate."

chapter 31

Alma Lopez had come through for Lacey once again, even though she'd been pressed into service at the last minute. Again.

Lacey was more than aware that Alma's eleventh-hour rescue of Stella's wedding dress was a personal favor she'd better not ask for very often. She pulled her little green vintage BMW out of the apartment's parking garage to run up to Alma's bungalow. Stella's emotional turnaround and having the gown finished with *one whole day* to spare before the wedding made it seem like Lady Luck had finally made her entrance.

Though she couldn't imagine why Rene Thibodeau was going along with this, she had faith in Vic's plan. Maybe Rene hoped Natalija could prove her innocence somehow? Or maybe he would do anything to see her again.

It was a beautiful day to drive the George Washington Memorial Parkway. Lacey opened the windows and turned the music up. She sang along to a CD of Josephine Baker songs from the 1930s. Seeing the light at the end of the tunnel of her endless maid of honor duties, Lacey felt better than she had in days.

When Lacey arrived at her seamstress's house the side door was slightly ajar. The house was quiet. She didn't hear the radio tuned to the classical PBS station Alma loved and always kept playing as she worked.

Lacey rang the bell and knocked on the open door, but there was no answer. Had Alma stepped out for a few moments to a neighbor's?

Arlington wasn't a small town; people didn't leave their doors unlocked. Lacey wondered what was wrong. She couldn't leave without checking. At the very least, she could pick up the dress.

There was a bad feeling in the pit of her stomach, though. She tried to shake it off, but it wouldn't go away. She pulled out her cell phone and texted Vic that she was at Alma's, asking him to send Turtledove. She pushed the door open with her foot, phone in hand.

"Alma, it's Lacey. I'm here to pick up Stella's dress." Lacey peeked through the doorway to the living room, to the left of her sewing studio, but she didn't see anything. "Alma, are you there? Anybody home?"

There was no answer.

She took another step inside and scanned the sewing studio. A vision of white caught Lacey's eyes, like a blizzard had struck inside the room. White strips, white shreds, and fragments of white silk and organza and pink satin hung over lampshades, decorated the tables, and covered the floor. Lacey gazed at the garment rack where Stella's dress should be hanging. The white satin hanger was empty.

Stella wouldn't be wearing the gown now.

Someone had shredded the wedding dress, as if all the rage in her body and soul had found its object in that dress. Natalija Krumina must have made her way to Alma's studio, somehow, and brought her fury with her. *How did she know? And where's Alma?*

Lacey held her breath. She stood still, tensed for something to happen. She called Vic: no answer. He must be on the road. Or perhaps on the stakeout, where he couldn't afford to have a phone jangling. She texted him again, a single word: NATALIJA.

It was eerily quiet. Lacey could feel a thumping in her chest, a surging fear, or maybe it was Natalija's rage, hanging in the air like a dark fog. The woman's attacks were increasingly messy and brutal: poisoning the wrong person, missing three targets at the Arts Club, sabotaging Vic's brakes, and shooting Kepelov in the street like a dog.

But going after Stella's wedding dress? That's really low.

Natalija didn't want to merely kill—she wanted to inflict pain, physical and psychic. Lacey inched slowly toward the wall behind the sewing table, so no one could surprise her in the open doorway. It was the wall that held the huge Peg-Board with all of Alma's sewing tools. There were many pairs of scissors, something Lacey had used before in self-defense, but she didn't want to get anywhere within scissor distance of Natalija. She looked at a heavy steel T-square, the one Alma used to measure fabric on her sewing table, to make sure her cuts were straight. Over three feet long, it vaguely reminded Lacey of a pickaxe.

"Alma?" Still no answer. Lacey prayed the seamstress was alive. Was she tied up somewhere, or had she fled the scene and run to the police? The woman who had been stalking the wedding party was still there—Lacey could feel it. Her knees were shaking. She gulped down a deep breath of air, then another. Her voice was steady when she called out.

"Natalija!"

The double doors of Alma's clothes closet burst open and Natalija Krumina emerged, grinning, blocking Lacey's way to the side door and wielding a long chef's knife in her hand. The blade gleamed in the light, the way the madness gleamed in her eyes. Gone were the frowzy wig and fake nose she had worn as the waitress Tilda, and her heavy eye makeup enhanced her best feature and made her look even more exotic. But as she turned toward the light, Lacey recognized the scar that marred one side of her face.

"Lacey Smithsonian. I'm so glad it's you who came for the gown. I thought it would be the bride. Sadly, you will not bring back a wedding dress for your friend Stella." She kicked the snowstorm of white silk and shreds of the lost dress floated in the air.

"Where is Alma? Is she safe? What did you do to her?"

Natalija dismissed Alma with a flick of her hand, the hand that held the knife. "She is boring. But you are interesting."

Back off, try a different tack. "How did you know about the dress?"

"So easy. A little surveillance, a little spycraft, a little bug in your phone. Workers in your apartment building were stupidly happy to let me in your apartment. Your cousin, I told them."

"Did you have to destroy the dress?" Lacey edged to her right.

Inching closer, Natalija grinned again, one side of her mouth lifted up into the scar. "No—and yes. I didn't plan on it. When I saw it, I went maybe a little—crazy."

Evidently.

"You survived the fall from the riverboat," Lacey said. "You hit the paddle. Not many people could survive that." She sidestepped again. And Natalija stepped toward her.

"You ruined my face." Lacey slowly moved toward the large T-square on the wall. "But I am from tough Latvian and Russian stock." Natalija pulled her hair away from her face. "You see this scar? This is your fault. Everything is your fault. You ruined my face, my plan, you ruined my life."

I'm always doing that. "You did try to kill me, you know," Lacey said, in what she hoped was a neutral tone of voice. *I'd say we're about even.*

"You deserve to die. You stole my fortune."

"It wasn't yours. And I only found the diamonds, I didn't take them. Now it's a fight between governments."

"You think governments care? They do not. They play games with our lives. Why should I care what they do? The diamonds were meant for me!" Natalija shouted. "I lost everything that day, even my beauty. Today you will lose something more."

The scar was still slightly purple, beneath her makeup, and Natalija's face was less symmetrical than Lacey remembered it. A broken cheekbone, a broken nose, healed a little off center? Natalija's once perfectly proportioned face had an asymmetry it hadn't had before, but it was still compelling. "You're alive," Lacey pointed out, but she knew that wouldn't help.

"Who would want me now?" Natalija danced forward and back, teasing Lacey with the flashing blade, leaving her not knowing which way to turn.

"Rene Thibodeaux."

She paused and her voice softened. "Rene. He is different."

"You called him, you set up a meeting."

"Fools. To get your big bodyguard and your big boyfriend far away from you and your silly bride. Such an obvious trick! I didn't think you would fall for it. Lucky me. Lucky you. Now we have time to reacquaint ourselves."

"Rene must have been in your way too. He wasn't useful to you anymore. After he saved your life. Why didn't you get rid of him? You had every chance."

"That is true," Natalija said. "It would have been easy, he is so trusting. But I think it is bad manners to kill someone who has saved your life. And Rene is a sweet man. He doesn't even mind the scar on my face. Says it is not so bad."

"He loves you."

"I know. I am quite fond of him. Poor man." If Natalija ended up in prison, where she really deserved to be, Rene Thibodeaux would surely be her constant visitor. "I would never kill him. It would be much simpler for everyone if I had died. That's what you're thinking now, isn't it?"

"You're a mind reader too," Lacey said.

"Yes, I am. Better than Gregor's fat fortune-teller. How could he prefer her to me?"

An age-old question. "Marie is not a killer."

Natalija ignored that. "You like my scar? You will have more scars than I do. Of course you will be dead, but not a pretty corpse."

Lacey fought the impulse to touch her face. *Show her how frightened I am? No way.* "Why not just stay with Rene?" Lacey took another step toward Alma's big board.

"And live in the swamp? Be a boatman's pet bird forever? I don't think so. The diamonds were all I lived for."

"But you didn't know where the diamonds were! And I didn't either, until the pieces fell into place. If you'd killed me then, no one would have found them."

"No matter. Now I live for revenge. And for the surgery I will have to fix my face. With Rene's money. Maybe someday I will repay him."

A truck of some kind screeched to a stop outside and Natalija turned toward the sound. Lacey managed one step to her right before Natalija whipped her head back toward her. Her knife was pointing right at Lacey's midsection.

"Don't move!" she barked.

There were two thumps from inside the deep closet in answer. Lacey realized the seamstress was alive. Lacey's relief was palpable, but there still was a madwoman in the room.

"Alma, are you all right?" There were more kicks.

"No tricks, Lacey Smithsonian." Natalija stepped forward again, waving the knife.

Keep talking. "Why did you send me the shawl?"

"A little test, to see how smart you could be. You were lucky with the diamonds." Natalija shrugged. "I have to admit, you are clever. I didn't think you would figure out the puzzle in the shawl. Well done. It is good to have a worthy adversary."

"Were you a spy? Like Kepelov?" No matter how often Lacey heard there were more spies in Washington, D.C., than any other place on earth, it was still hard to believe. She wondered where Natalija learned so many ways to kill. *Was she born that way? As long as I keep her talking, at least we're not fighting hand to hand. And where's Vic?!*

Her phone was buzzing in her jacket pocket, but this wasn't a good time to take a call.

"I was not like Kepelov! He was old-school KGB. He has gone soft, predictable, while I have special skills and talents. When I make people die, I make it look random." The corners of Natalija's smiling mouth reminded Lacey of a jolly death's head. "Poison, cars, guns, knives, different method every time. All part of my catalogue."

Natalija charged forward and Lacey jumped back, bumping into the board full of tools. She pulled down the big steel T-square and swung it at Natalija like a double-bladed ax. The T-shaped bar at the business end wasn't sharp, but Lacey hoped it could do some damage, if she found room to take a real swing with it. The only thing she was sure of was that it was longer than the deadly blade Natalija brandished at her. But Natalija dodged, laughing.

"What are you going to do, measure me?"

"Maybe," Lacey said. *And keep you talking until someone gets here!* "What happened with Leonardo? The man who got the nicotine in the neck."

"That idiot! The poison kiss was meant for the woman Gregor loves. Not my fault that stupid man grabbed the shawl after I so carefully inserted the capsule. Dancing with the shawl like a lunatic." She sliced the air in front of Lacey's face with her blade. "He got what he deserved. He was too stupid to live."

"I don't know, Natalija. That kind of mistake is messy. Your skills must be rusty. See how many of us you missed. Kepelov is alive."

"Shut up!" Natalija lunged suddenly.

Lacey swung her weapon in front of her. It was heavier and more unwieldy than she expected, but it made a very impressive *swish*.

Natalija dodged to the right. She was lithe and agile with her long blade, like a cat with sharp claws, playing with a mouse. Lacey flashed back to that final fight aboard the riverboat, and her stomach knotted. Natalija had moved then with the same catlike grace.

Lacey swung the T-square again and nailed Natalija on her knife arm. Natalija leapt, the knife still moving, narrowly missing Lacey's face. She rocked back on her heels, the steel edges of the ruler cutting into her hands.

"You'll pay," Natalija said. "Your face first. Your man won't even know your corpse."

"You're weary, Natalija." Lacey hoped it was true. "You can't keep this up."

Sweat glistened on Natalija's forehead. Both were breathing hard and Lacey gasped for air. She fell back, closer to Alma's leaning Peg-Board, heavy with the tools of the seamstress's trade.

"After you, your unfortunate seamstress will go next," Natalija said. From the closet there came a furious thumping on the wall from the imprisoned Alma. Natalija laughed. "Perhaps with her long knitting needles. I have never used those, but I think they will be most exciting."

"You enjoy this, don't you?" Lacey asked, disgusted.

"I don't hate it, you know? I have a certain talent."

Natalija cut a figure eight in the air with her knife, and then with a lightning-quick lunge drew the blade across Lacey's arm. It stung and instantly drew a line of blood. Natalija's face was hot with joy. "The next slice will be on your face," she announced. "Shall we be twins?"

The sound of Natalija's laugh made Lacey cringe, and she almost dropped the T-square in pain and surprise. She wanted to let go, but she held tight. She thought distractedly of the gold Saint Christopher medal around her neck, ironically the patron saint of safe travel. *Safe travel out the door is all I ask.* She had only time enough to murmur *please.*

Another vehicle pulled up outside. *Is that Vic? Or Turtledove? Or just a neighbor?* She heard a car door slam, and Natalija heard it too. Her head twitched toward it ever so slightly.

With a huge effort, Lacey swung the T-square like a baseball bat, making sure she followed through. One point of the heavy steel head hit Natalija square in the throat and her knife clattered to the floor. She staggered back from the blow, choking and gasping for air. She bent down to retrieve her blade, reached too far, and staggered.

Lacey scrambled around behind the wall-sized Peg-Board and pushed hard. The whole thing toppled, tumbled, and crashed, as Alma often threatened it would. Threads, scissors, ribbons, and more fell in a terrible clatter on top of Natalija, pinning her facedown beneath it. Lacey landed on top of it. Natalija screamed in fury. She struggled to get to her knees and buck the board off her, but Lacey rode the board, holding it down. She had trapped Natalija.

Her heart beating furiously, sweat streaming down her face, Lacey sat on the tilting and wiggling Peg-Board and tried to gather her wits. Everything was still for a moment. Then Natalija let loose a bloodthirsty scream.

"OFF! You are crushing me! Get off!"

"No."

"I'll die! You're killing me."

"Die then!" Lacey sat still, panting. Then slowly, unbelievably, the board beneath her began to move, like a snake trying to slither across the ground under a newspaper, carrying it along on its back. Natalija pushed up with all her might. The board bounced and threatened to throw Lacey off, but she held on tight. "You're not dying. Now how can I ever trust you, Natalija? You always lie to me."

"It's what I do," Natalija responded in grunts. She panted heavily and Lacey prayed the woman really was worn out this time. The board stilled, the panting and grunting continued, and Lacey held on. Natalija kicked the board with her heels in frustration. "How long are you going to crush me?"

"You'll be the first to know."

Footsteps outside the door gave Lacey hope that this wild ride might soon be over.

"Lacey? Where are you?" It was Vic.

"In here." The door opened and she lifted her head.

She realized she wasn't in the most flattering of positions,
spread-eagled on the back of the big Peg-Board. "I can't
get up. I'm riding a tiger."

Vic entered, pistol drawn. He was followed by Turtledove and two other guys, all with pistols drawn. They
stared at the sight of Lacey on the bouncing board, like
Aladdin sprawled on a bucking magic carpet.

"What the hell?"

"It's a new carnival ride I invented. I call it Spy Surfing."

"What's under there?"

"*Who.* It's who's under there. And the answer is—"

"Get me out of here, she is killing me, she is a murderer!" Natalija screamed.

Vic signaled Turtledove to cover him as he reached
for Lacey's hand. "Natalija Krumina. We missed you at
the rendezvous," Vic said.

"She misdirected you," Lacey said.

"We gathered that when she didn't show up to meet
Rene. And then I got your messages."

"Point one way, go the other. Oldest trick in the world,"
Natalija spat, her voice muffled by the Peg-Board and
scraps of wedding dress. "Fools! Fools, fools, fools!"

"My God, Lacey, you're bleeding," Vic said.

She hadn't realized how bad the knife slash on her
arm looked. Blood was dripping from her arm. She had
left a scarlet trail on the floor and the board on top of
Natalija. Lacey was shaking as Vic pulled her up off the
board. Her arms ached with tension and fatigue. She
wanted to cry, but that wasn't behavior befitting a mem-
ber of the Fourth Estate. Vic picked up a scrap of the
wedding dress to wrap around her arm.

"Oh, don't use that, Vic. That was part of Stella's wedding gown," Lacey said.

The woman under the board started to laugh. "Not
now. She'll never wear that dress."

With a final burst of strength, Natalija bucked the
board off her back and staggered up, scrambling for the
fallen knife, but Lacey kicked it out of her reach. Natalija

grabbed one of the many pairs of scissors that lay scattered on the floor. She twisted around and was met with the business end of Turtledove's Glock. Three more pistols were pointed in the same direction. She arched her upper body as if to lunge with her scissors, then she thought again and exhaled. Four men with guns against one exhausted woman with a pair of pinking shears. Her head rolled to one side. The fight went out of her.

"Why don't you kill me?" she asked, her voice flat.

"That's not how we roll," Turtledove said. "But don't expect any special treatment. Now shut up."

Turtledove pulled the scissors from her limp hand. With the other guys covering him, Turtledove holstered his gun, effortlessly lifted Natalija off the floor, pulled her arms behind her gracefully and cuffed her. He shoved her face-first against the wall.

Lacey surveyed her own damage. She saw scrapes and cuts on her arms where the scissors and sewing tools had landed on her, and blood was seeping through the improvised wedding-dress bandage.

Natalija smiled and looked over her shoulder at Turtledove seductively. Her lips parted, her tongue flicked over her lips—she was about to say something.

Lacey watched, amazed. *Is she really going to try to sweet-talk Turtledove? This woman is relentless!* Then Natalija looked around at her captors and decided it wasn't worth the effort. The fire went out of her eyes and she shut her mouth. Her head dropped in defeat.

Turtledove kept watch over Natalija while Vic called the police. Vic's two security guys surveyed the studio and shook their heads in disbelief at the mess. Lacey looked around too and thought, *Something's missing. What is it?* Her eyes opened wide.

"Alma! Oh, my God!" She'd almost forgotten. She waded through the remains of Stella's wedding gown and the wreckage of Alma's sewing studio and threw open the double closet doors, to find one furious and frightened seamstress on the floor, bound and gagged.

Lacey loosened the gag while Vic cut the fabric ties that held her.

"Just what kind of maniacs do you people hang around with?!" Alma shouted.

Olga Kepelova arrived at the emergency room waiting area, grim-faced and dressed in black. Lacey decided she resembled an undertaker, or possibly a Russian angel of death.

"This is becoming bad habit," Olga told Lacey calmly. "First, Gregor. Now you."

"Sorry to trouble you." Lacey wondered what on earth Kepelov's sister was doing here. Her arm throbbed while she waited for a doctor to stitch it up. Apparently bleeding wasn't the most impressive injury in the ER that day. Vic held her arm gently and kept pressure on her wound. She didn't think it was that bad, but Vic had insisted on taking her to the hospital anyway.

Olga briefly inspected the arm. "I have seen worse," she informed everyone within hearing distance.

"Is that why you are here?" Lacey inquired. "To inspect the injury?" *And add a little insult while you're at it?*

"I understand you captured Natalija Krumina, who tried to kill my brother Gregor on several occasions, including last night."

"Don't forget Lacey," Vic said. "She tried to kill Lacey too."

"I wish I could have seen it," Olga replied.

"Luckily, there are no photos." Lacey was grateful for that at least. She could imagine how ridiculous a photo of her wild ride on top of Alma's giant Peg-Board would look. These nonexistent photos would fortunately *not* be making the front page of *The Eye Street Observer*.

"A pity."

"How did you know I was here?" Lacey asked.

"Marie said cloud of revenge had reached you, and you were in mortal danger." Olga seemed quite cheerful. "She is getting more comfortable with her gifts. She did not faint. I am very proud. I am to be congratulated, of course. For teaching her how to breathe, how to focus, how to fight the fear."

"She told you where I was?"

"No, I called around. Checked police radio. Gregor suggested I come here. So here I am."

Olga took something out of her pocket and placed it in Lacey's hand. It was a small oval-shaped box, lacquered in black with brilliantly colored figures and flowers. Lacey inspected the petite piece. The pattern was inlaid in mother-of-pearl and gold leaf.

"It's lovely."

"Is Russian. Is token of my gratitude for watching out for little brother Gregor and catching crazy Natalija Krumina, madwoman who kills for revenge and pleasure. So wasteful. You are to be congratulated too."

The box might have great sentimental value for Olga, despite her unsentimental manner. Another thought struck Lacey. "It's not haunted, is it, Olga?"

"Haunted?" Olga laughed. "No, it's not big enough to hold a human soul. In that case, I would sell it to a Russian collector."

"But it must be valuable. A lacquered box with inlays like this one." Lacey showed it to Vic. "Some can take up to a year to make. This is too much, Olga."

"What is too much for a life? It is a simple thank-you. Of course, it is Russian, so there is also a legend that comes with it. It is said that if a woman knows her true love, when she opens the little box, she will smell roses."

"This has a legend of its very own? Like the shawl?"

"What can I say? Russian people are hopeless romantics. And Russian nights are so long."

Lacey turned it over and over, admiring it, and then she opened it—and sniffed. Vic was watching her, smiling a little. She detected a faint aroma of roses. *The legend? Or just an antique box made of rosewood?*

"Thank you, Olga. I will treasure it always. And the legend too."

chapter 32

The dress was in tatters and Stella was in tears.

On Friday morning, Lacey Smithsonian did her best to explain to the bride-to-be how her wedding gown wound up shredded like a classified document. She was between a rock and a hard place. She'd gotten the wedding back on track—and lost the dress. She was trying to accentuate the positive, as the old song says, but nothing seemed to help.

"We caught the woman who was trying to kill all of us." Lacey gazed at the bandage on her arm. Fifteen stitches, not quite as fine as Alma's, but they would do. "It started in New Orleans and it ended here. Natalija Krumina will never hurt us now."

"But why did she have to murder my dress? I'm not *blaming* you, exactly," Stella said. "I'm not blaming you at all, Lace. I mean no one's going to die now. What am I going to do? I should just cancel the wedding. Again." She choked on a sob. Her mascara was running.

As tempting as that sounded, Lacey hadn't risked her life for Stella to back out now. "Something can be done. It was only a dress."

"Only a dress?! That was my wedding dress! And my corset! Magda's corset! And Magda was the one who sent us off on that wild chase for the lost corset that took us all to New Orleans, wasn't she? Maybe it's all Magda's fault!"

Lacey threw up her hands. It was Miguel's turn. He made another stab at making things better. "Stella, sweetie, it's not like it was the dress of your dreams. You hated that thing. Remember? Loathed it, despised it—"

That might have been the truth, but dissing the dead dress was the wrong thing to do. Stella cried even harder.

"I know!" she wailed. "But it was still my wedding gown! And now it's just rags! And besides that, it was getting fixed! With my favorite pink corset. Which is now rags!"

Like Cinderella in reverse, Lacey thought. *We need a fairy godmother.*

"I know it's late," Miguel said. "But we can find a dress. I can call around. Remember, Stella, I am the Wizard of Oohs and Aahs and I will mobilize all my loyal Munchkins—"

"Dress or Munchkins or not, I'm not getting married to Nigel. That's final."

"What?" Lacey and Miguel said at the same time.

Stella sniffed and wiped the tears from her eyes. "The signs are clear. It's been a disaster from start to finish." She started a fresh round of wailing. "If I walk down that aisle, we're all doomed!"

"Not going to happen, Stel." Lacey couldn't take much more of Stella's misery, it was too raw. "Marie didn't see any bad signs for you either. She says it'll be happily-ever-after."

"Hon, it's only a dress," Miguel said. "You just need a new dress."

"The wedding is tomorrow! Except it isn't anymore. It's never. And I spent almost a thousand dollars on that dress. Sure, it was a super sale, seventy-five percent off, and I had to go mano a mano with another bride over it, but it was *my wedding dress*." Stella gulped back a sob. "And Lacey almost got killed for that stupid dress! Where am I supposed to get another one?"

She sat on the red leather sofa and sobbed. Miguel fetched a cold wet towel to soothe her eyes. Stella took it and wept into it. Miguel, on the verge of throwing in the towel, took the other end of the sofa and waved at Lacey.

"Maid of Honor? Wake me up when the Titanic hits the iceberg."

As God is my witness, I will never be a maid of honor again.

Lacey was on the verge of offering Stella her own Morning Glory Blue Gloria Adams original that Miguel had created for her. Miguel could fit it for Stella. But a blue gown wouldn't work with Stella's cherry blossom theme. A tiny pink lightbulb flickered on in Lacey's brain.

"Stella. Listen to me. You might have something else you could wear," Lacey said. "In your closet."

"What?" Stella lifted her head. "This is my wedding we're talking about."

"You want a pink wedding, right, Stella?"

"Since I was like, eleven, or something."

"Then think pink."

"What are you getting at, Lacey? I mean, you are getting at something, right?" She sniffled.

Miguel opened his eyes and sat up straight. "Enlighten us, please, Smithsonian. I can't take any more tears. The Tin Man will rust."

"Remember New Orleans, Stella? The good parts, I mean."

Stella used the cloth to wipe her eyes and squinted at Lacey. "I fell in love with Nigel in New Orleans." Her lips quivered.

"And you bought a dress there. Remember?"

Lacey was referring to the preposterously un-Stella-like dress the stylist had fallen in love with at first sight at a little boutique in the French Quarter. It was a rose-colored confection of organdy and lace with a romantic late-Twenties vibe, a dropped waist and a full skirt that fell almost to the ankles. The three-quarter sleeves were transparent and floated dreamily around the arms. Stella had told everyone there that day that she imagined herself wearing it to a fantasy wedding in Great Gatsby Land. It was wildly different from anything Stella had ever owned, but somehow it had wrapped itself around her heartstrings. How could it have been forgotten?

Easy, it's not a wedding dress. But it's pink and it's lovely and it would do beautifully.

"That dress? I never wore it. I don't even know if it fits anymore. I've never had an occasion worthy of that dress," Stella said, sounding mournful. "It's too special."

"Too special for your wedding? Now you have the occasion," Lacey said.

"Where is this dress?" Miguel asked. "What does it look like? Does it even look remotely like a wedding dress? And who cares anyway, where is it?"

"It's pink. It could easily be a wedding dress. In fact, it's beautiful and different and appropriate for a wedding under cherry blossoms," Lacey said. "What more does it need to be?"

"O.M.G.!" Stella's eyes lit up. "It *could* be a pink wedding dress! I love that dress. I never thought I'd actually wear it. Where the heck did I put it?"

Miguel was on his feet. "Stella, there is a dress in your life that I haven't personally seen and approved?"

"Only one!" Stella ran for her bedroom closet and emerged a few moments later with a dusty garment bag.

"Oh, Stel. You know you shouldn't ever leave clothes hanging in plastic. They can't breathe, and they—" Miguel stopped talking when the layers of rose organdy emerged.

"I fell for Nigel and this dress in New Orleans. Almost the same day, I think." Stella was in a dream. "You think I should get married in this?" She held it up and stared in the mirror at her reflection in pink.

"Do *you* think you should get married in this?" Lacey asked. "Oh, but wait. Then it would be a completely pink wedding. Pink bride. Pink bridesmaids too. Too much pink. And I know how *iffy* you are about pink."

Miguel took the dress and examined it. "It could work, Stella. It's really something. Try it on, let us see you in it."

"Okay." Stella smiled again and Lacey felt a ray of

hope. "It would be a perfectly pink wedding, perfectly romantic, perfectly me." But then her face fell.

"What's wrong?" Lacey asked.

"But the veil and my shoes! They're white!"

"The tiara is pink," Lacey said, hoping against hope.

"Good. We can salvage this thing yet," Miguel said. "We've got a park permit, a reception site, flowers, and a pink castle cake. And a pink Caddy. And me, you have *me*. The Wizard. Just ignore the little man behind the curtain. Now Stella, honey, try on the dress. Lacey, dear, find me the veil and the shoes."

Stella retreated to her bedroom while Lacey flew into action. She presented the veil to Miguel, along with the Victorian high-heeled lace-up shoes that Stella had special-ordered to support the ankle she'd broken.

"What are you thinking, Miguel?" Lacey said. "Is it possible?"

"I know a guy. Well, I know lots of guys."

"Of course you do." Miguel seemed to have a boyfriend or an ex-boyfriend or a future boyfriend in any number of fashion and clothing-related fields.

"This particular guy is great with dyes."

"He can match them?"

"Please. With my guidance? I am the master magician."

Stella emerged from her bedroom, a vision in pink. The dress fit her body like it was custom made. It floated delicately around her, and the color made her skin glow and echo the pink highlights. She looked like a delicate pink china doll (with swollen red eyes). This pink frock was much more suited to her than the white puffball of a dress that had been the victim of Natalija's revenge.

"It's beautiful," Lacey said. "Even prettier than I remember."

"It's genius," Miguel said. "I couldn't have done better myself. And that's saying something."

"I love it. This is it!" Stella was back. "This is the dress I'm getting married in."

FASHION BITES

When Fashion Disaster Strikes, Strike Back!

A fashion disaster can strike at any time. It is the stuff of which nightmares are made. But you don't have time to worry about that. When a clothing catastrophe leaves you wailing, don't wallow in your misery! Dry your tears and take action.

An outfit kerfuffle can range from the minor—say, spilling coffee on your snow-white blouse on your way to an important job interview—to the apocalyptic—say, the destruction of the perfect gown you planned to wear to that very formal ball at the embassy. Some women can overcome these upsetting events. They are survivors in style, and you can draw on them for inspiration.

The ever-resourceful former U.S. Secretary of State Madeline Albright once spilled salad dressing on her skirt at an event with other world dignitaries. Commence a sensitive summit conference wearing a skirt full of blue cheese? Unthinkable! With no time for a wardrobe change, she turned the skirt around so her jacket hid the stain, and she carried on. Diplomacy and style savvy won the day.

Actress Sharon Stone once wore to the Oscars her husband's crisp white dress shirt tucked into a long satin skirt, reportedly after something went disastrously wrong with the big-name designer dress she'd planned to wear. And hers was one of the most photographed and talked-about outfits of the evening. What the husband wore is not re-membered, because after all, a guy wearing his spare dress shirt to the Oscars is hardly newswor-

thy. But a famous woman making a clever save out
of a fashion disaster? Pictures at eleven.

And let us not forget everybody's heroine Scarlett O'Hara, in the midst of poverty and scarcity,
tearing down the velvet drapes to make herself a
stunning new dress to impress Rhett Butler. Another
fashion disaster averted (and movie history made)
by a quick-thinking woman.

What can you do when fashion disaster strikes?

- Girl Scouts come prepared to deal with minor
  problems before they become major disasters.
  For an important event, carry a purse-able little
  sewing kit with needle and thread, safety pins,
  some sticky tape, and an extra button or two.
  Also, a small stain-removing stick comes in
  handy to attack sudden enemy spots.
- If your hem falls out, masking tape is a good
  temporary fix. A desk stapler can be used in an
  emergency to staple a hem, or even a burst
  seam. But remember, staples are not a permanent repair! People will talk if you routinely walk
  around wearing visible staples; you'll look like
  a Raggedy Ann doll come to life.
- A lost button on a jacket or blouse can be secured with a decorative pin if a safety pin isn't
  handy. Pretend you *always* wear it that way.

However, when the very worst happens and
your ball gown is shredded by vengeful stepsisters
on the eve of Prince Charming's ball, you might
not have a fairy godmother of your own to fall
back on. But you've got ingenuity that won't turn
into a pumpkin at midnight. Necessity is the fairy
godmother of invention.

- *Go to your closet.* That's right, venture all the way
  into the deep, dark, hidden recesses of your closet.

If your closet is anything like most women's closets, there are things in there you have long since forgotten. One of them might just be perfect for the event at hand. As well as a complete surprise.

- *Call your best fashionable friend.* She'll understand your dilemma and she might have the perfect dress to borrow. If you don't wear the same size, she at least can offer you an unemotional, or less emotional, response to the crisis at hand, and she can probably point out a stylish solution to your woes. If she can't, keep calling friends till you find one who can.
- *Go shopping!* I know, it's a crisis, you need it *now*, there's no time to shop. But there's always time to shop, if you have an hour or two and a store with an open door. Not much money in the budget? Try consignment stores, often heavy on evening wear, lightly used formal dresses that have only been worn once, by someone you don't know, to an event full of strangers who will not recognize that gown on *you*. And don't forget vintage stores, costume shops, and thrift shops. Even Goodwill has been known to have a few wedding gowns and other formal attire on hand.

This is no time to wallow in your misery. A crisis can unlock your creativity, and what better time to get creative? People love moxie. When you come up with the right solution to your fashion dilemma, they will applaud your grace under pressure. *If* you tell them. (If you want to keep it a secret, my lips are sealed.)

And remember, just like Scarlett tearing down the velvet drapes, overcoming your fashion disaster will make a great story—a much better story than simply wearing what you'd planned and having everything go like clockwork.

So turn that fashion disaster into a well-tailored tale—and a triumph of *style*.

chapter 33

"This is worse than a monkey suit," Vic complained, tugging at the pink-and-silver-gray ascot Lacey was tying around his neck. "This has to be the most ridiculous piece of apparel ever created."

"Not true, Vic," Lacey pointed out. "Bustles, leg warmers, and platform sneakers, just to name three. Your ascot isn't even in the running."

Vic snorted. "All right, the most ridiculous piece of apparel *I've* ever had on."

"You look adorable," Lacey protested. "And very distinguished."

Vic wore a classic English morning suit with striped charcoal gray pants, a pale gray waistcoat, and dark gray cutaway coat. "I never planned to be in this damned wedding in the first place. I have no business in it. And I will never forgive Nigel and Stella for this hat!"

It was a tall top hat, in a soft dove gray. He held it in his hands, refusing to put it on until absolutely necessary.

"Brits love their hats, sweetheart. The hat is to die for. You look like Mr. Darcy, straight out of *Pride and Prejudice*. If you get any sexier, I will die right here on this spot."

She took a picture of him with her little digital camera. Lacey's dislike for gray dissolved utterly when a man was wearing it like *this*. And the snowy white shirt against Vic's tanned olive skin with the ridiculous ascot heightened the green of his eyes. They almost glowed when he looked at her. *Swoon.*

"I look like an extra in a road show of *My Fair Lady*."

"Vic, dear, you'll always be the leading man for *this* fair lady."

He relented and smiled at her. "You look gorgeous, Lacey. You know that?"

"Thank you. Sadly, this is the last thing Alma will ever make for me."

"She'll change her mind," Vic said. "You saved her life."

"And ruined her shop. She won't forgive me anytime soon."

"See how much trouble this wedding business has caused everyone?" Vic said. "I can't imagine *anyone* could ever *possibly* want to get *married* after all *this*—"

"Me neither."

"Wait, I do want to marry you! But not like this."

"Me too. How about we elope and I make all this up to you later?" Lacey winked at him and he laughed. He mock-glowered at his handsome visage staring back at him in the mirror.

"Stupid English wedding traditions. Why couldn't *they* just elope and leave us out of it? And Nigel! I don't even like Nigel! It figures that thoroughbred twit would make us all wear something so wussy on his wedding day."

"Wussy? Vic, you look like a Bengal Lancer on holiday. All you need is a lance. And I think the morning suits were more Lady Gwendolyn's idea."

They strolled toward the wedding party waiting on the west lawn of the Jefferson Memorial. It was a perfect spring day, in spite of Vic's grumbling. The Tidal Basin was a pool of blue beneath the April sky, ringed by Washington's famous cherry trees, still miraculously in bloom. The cherry blossoms and the bridesmaids' dresses were a blizzard of pink on the green lawn. Lacey thanked God that it was a beautiful day, as Marie had predicted.

And that she had picked up her own dress before Natalija performed her Jack the Ripper act on Stella's wedding dress.

"Lacey, this whole thing is ridiculous, you know. Why me?"

"You know why," she said, straightening his ascot. "You're the best man."

Best man. Vic had been pressed into service at the last minute when Bryan Culpeper suddenly backed out. In fact, Culpeper had left town, on something described vaguely as "urgent family business." Lacey didn't know whether Lady Gwendolyn was to be congratulated for this, or perhaps Stella had a hand in it, or if Nigel had finally taken the rest of Lacey's advice. His so-called best man had been his worst asset in his wedding portfolio, and whoever it was who sent Bryan Culpeper packing had her heartfelt thanks. No one needed a poisonous best man. This wedding had already had too many brushes with poison.

However, when Nigel begged Vic to stand up with him as his best man, Lacey was more than a little surprised. So was Vic. He was still trying to find a replacement, even as they strolled toward the wedding party.

"What about Kepelov?" Vic complained. "They're buddies. Partners. Sort of. Even though Kepelov was going to kill him at one point. But then, I've threatened to do that too."

"Gregor is out," Lacey replied. "He's already one of the groomsmen, his broken ribs are still taped up, and besides, Nigel says he's too scary."

Vic growled. "I'll show him scary. It's a fine cosmic irony when I wind up as Nigel Griffin's best man."

Lacey stopped and made him face her. "You are the best possible man. Nigel is lucky to have you, and you saying *yes*, and saying *yes* to the morning suit, made everyone very happy. It makes *me* happy. And remember, this is a corporal work of mercy. Major celestial brownie points." She stretched up on the tiptoes of her pink high-heeled sandals and kissed him. She started to giggle and he finally gave in and laughed.

I wonder if I can convince him to wear something like this at our wedding?

They were nearly at the knot of pink-clad ladies and elegant gray-morning-suited men, when Nigel, taking very long strides, caught up with them and pumped Vic's hand. Nigel looked nervous but happy, in his own gray morning suit and top hat. His ascot, unlike the best man's and the groomsmen's, was not striped, but a solid pale cherry blossom pink.

"Hello, Vic. Well done! Can't thank you enough for stepping in. Last minute and all that. Old school ties. Saved the day. Cavalry to the rescue. And so on."

"Yes, well . . ." Vic straightened his silver-gray ascot and donned his top hat. He seemed to make a small but momentous decision. "My pleasure, Griffin. Glad to do it. All my best wishes for you and Stella. And so on."

"Here." Nigel handed him the rings. "These will be safer with you than with me, old man, believe me. And Smithsonian, smashing dress. Simply smashing. Wouldn't be here at all without your usual gung ho, savoir faire, derring-do, bashing, slashing, and thrashing about with nefarious Natalija. Jolly impressive. As usual. And so on."

"I'll take that as a compliment," Lacey said.

"You saved the day with the wedding dress too. I mean the *real* dress, the pink New Orleans dress, well, you know what I mean. I'm perfectly thrilled we're all here in one piece. Well, not *all* of us, but the ones who count, the wedding party, well, you and Vic most of all, well, no, I don't mean *most* of all, that would be my Stella of course, but—"

"Shut up, Nigel. We're glad too." Nigel's nervous stammering was interrupted by the junior bridesmaids, who came running to hug Lacey in their rose-colored finery and pink and blue cowboy boots. Lacey smoothed the pink ribbon covering her left forearm to hide the stitches, where she had been slashed by Natalija's knife.

"Miss Lacey, you look so pretty," Jasmine said.

"Jasmine and Lily Rose! So do you two. You look fabulous!"

"Do you like our dresses?" Lily Rose asked, jumping up and down as if her boots had springs in them. "I can't wait to see Miss Stella's wedding dress."

"You're as pretty as a picture, both of you. Prettier." Lacey admired their pink polished cotton dresses and took a photograph of the grinning girls. Kim and Mac arrived to round up their children. "Your parents look pretty nice too."

"I picked out our dad's tie," Jasmine said proudly.

"And I picked out his shirt," Lily Rose added, not to be outdone by her big sister.

Lacey was startled to see her editor looking positively spiffy, in a Brooks Brothers navy blazer, gray slacks, a pale pink shirt, and a pink-and-white-striped silk tie. And his cowboy boots.

"Mac, is that you? Or an alternate universe you?"

Kim beamed and looked very proud of him too, in her smart raspberry-colored sheath. Mac looked abashed. "It's me, Smithsonian. In the pink. Gotta keep up with my ladies. I seem to be outnumbered these days." But he was clearly pleased and proud, in spite of his unfamiliar new outfit.

Kim took her daughters' hands. "It's time we took our places, girls."

Across the lawn, Nadine Donovan waved at Lacey and winked broadly, holding hands with Vic's dad.

Nigel and Vic stood side by side beneath an arbor of cherry blossoms, as a chamber trio played Pachelbel's *Canon* and the crowd grew still in anticipation. The mothers-in-law nearly stole the show. Lady Gwendolyn Griffin, in her glory and on the arm of her husband, the former British ambassador, smiled broadly in her violet dress, proudly piloting a hat so large it might have been the prow of a sailing ship.

And Retta Lake Sloan was looking at least fifteen

years younger, in a pale blue knee-length dress. Her frizzy gray hair finally had been tamed and dyed (by Stella) into a halo of sparkling nut brown locks that curled softly around her shoulders. She looked resigned. She actually smiled.

Wonders never cease, Lacey thought. *The salon must have been a madhouse this morning.*

She almost failed to recognize Stella's cousin Rosalie, whose makeup had been expertly applied and whose free-range frizz had, at last, been wrangled into shape by Michelle at Stylettos. Rosalie looked quite pretty and didn't seem to hold a grudge against Stella for giving her name to the police as a possible murder suspect. Saving the wedding seemed to have healed all wounds.

Brooke was lovely in her azalea pink frock, with her beautiful blond hair worn down in Pre-Raphaelite ringlets. Michelle, Stella's right-hand woman at Stylettos, was elegant in her pale pink dress. And Marie, even in her abundant bridesmaid's dress, had the air of a Gypsy fortune-teller. She carried her storied Russian shawl draped over one arm, in the event the bride might require its warmth and protection.

And those must be Nigel's female cousins, all in pink and all wearing their "fascinators." *Fascinating doesn't begin to describe them*, Lacey thought.

Miguel, most dashing in his morning suit, directed traffic and took his place with the other gray-clad, morning-suited groomsmen, standing next to Gregor Kepelov and Damon Newhouse. Lacey thought she had never seen such a mismatched trio, all dressed so splendidly alike.

And then came Stella. The bride was a vision of rosy glory, from her pink crystal tiara and pink-tipped hair, to the top of her (freshly dyed) pink high-heeled Victorian boots. The delicate pink New Orleans gown was far better suited to her than a big fluffy white wedding dress could ever have been. Stella never cried, she glowed.

Nigel, however, wept like a baby.

From her position next to the bride, Lacey surveyed the crowd. She spotted Turtledove standing by his friend Rene Thibodeaux. Turtledove smiled and gave Lacey a nod, but Rene's rugged features betrayed nothing but grief. He hung back at the edge of the crowd and slipped away right after the vows. Off to the side of the Jefferson Memorial, Lacey caught a glimpse of the bright pink fins of a vintage Cadillac Eldorado Biarritz, just waiting to carry the happy couple in style to the Arts Club for the reception. From afar, Olga Kepelova was keeping a cool eye on the nuptials—and the shawl.

Vic caught Lacey's eye and inclined his head toward a couple standing outside the circle of invited guests, in a knot of curious tourists wearing cameras, who had lingered to watch.

Lacey couldn't be sure, but she thought she saw a chubby little cupid of a man and his china-doll lady love. Was it Harlan Wiedemeyer and Felicity Pickles, conducting a little pre-wedding reconnaissance of their own? Or a mysterious pair of Washington's famous spies? Whoever they were, as the services began she saw the little man take the woman's hand and gaze into her eyes.

Love in all its many guises had saved the day. And then a breeze caught the cherry blossoms, and the musicians began to play the Wedding March.